For Brenda

Thanks for all

John Moon

THE

ALERI ENCOUNTER

THE

ALERI ENCOUNTER

TOBY MASON

For information contact; masont2nd (at) gmail (dot) com

Book and Cover design by Toby Mason

Cover Photos used in the composite: Foreground; Mathew Smith at Unsplash, Barn; DonnasDesigns, Sky; Bigsky

ISBN: 978-1-7923-0393-7

Copyright Registration # TXu002132580

First Edition: April, 2019

For Chris, Thomas and Robin
and all those I hold close.

Preface

This story was born on the wings of an auto accident. I walked away when I probably shouldn't have and it instantly changed my priorities. Got slapped by the cosmos, message clear as a bell. Stop everything else and write down what's important for the grandchildren to know. Put it all down in one place, in one story they might have a good time reading. Because... you never know.

Through months of recovery, I two-fingered it in, a line at a time. The characters spoke. I wrote it down. They said things I wouldn't have dreamed of saying, so I just followed along and listened. Tied up the loose bits when they were done. You will know by the end how much this surprised me and how grateful I am to be walking, still on the right side of the grass.

Acknowledgments

These are the people who helped, though not all of them. There would never be room for all of them.

To my wife Chris, without her none of this would be possible.

To my sons Thomas and Robin for listening.

To my mother Lucia who insisted language be well spoken and that one have something to say and my father Tom who insisted I learn to think.

To my brothers and my cousins and the rest of my family here and not who shared my world.

To my early readers: Chris first, then John Morton, Mark Richter and Gail Morton who all gave their good advice.

To my English teachers: Jesse Snowden who taught me I could write 250 words on the topic of her choosing every night and Bill McGert (Will Inman) who encouraged me.

To Kathryn Johnson who edited me into better shape.

To Alan Orloff and Gus Russo for their publishing insights.

***

To Jerry Bechtle, first to the rescue who stayed and helped.

To Officer Dean Bailey and all the other first responders, doctors and ER nurses.

To Dr. Linda Mosely who fixed my hand, Dr. Daniel Thompson for my shoulder care and Dr. Bijal Katarki for the rest of me and the wonderful physical therapists: Therese Garstka, Tom Cox, Dakota Ferrell, Yvonne Umayam, Tommy Meeusom and all the other unsung assistants who helped me heal.

To Dr. Danny Hockstra who knows how to ease what hurts.

To Meyer Friedman and Eunice who helped me grow up making pizzas and subs.

To Randy Sewell, John Mogayzel, John Landi, Bruce Middle, Phil McCreedy, Barbara Parry and Rusty Hassan for the music.

To Gary Pierson, Jamie Toole, John Turner and the boys in the band, who eased me into Venice Beach.

To Tom Sennett and Andy Desantis for teaching me stills and video, Betty Endicott, Joe Rizzo, Diana Pumphrey and all the good people at WTTG who helped me survive television.

To Scott Siedman for the art.

To Garrett Parkers and the many other fine souls with whom I hung out.

To Sheena Moore who introduced me to J. Krishnamurti's *Freedom From the Known* and Dr. Russel Targ who taught me a way to see into the unknown, and all those with whom I share a connection.

To everyone who ever gave me a lift or a place to crash, especially when I was going coast to coast.

And for all the good people who loved me when I needed it and will read this and think "Hey, where the hell's my name?" My hope is this leaves you a little better than it finds you.

Toby

Contents

1. A Box of Parts 1
2. Changing of the Guard 12
3. Corn Off the Cob 15
4. Dust Piles 22
5. Not Exactly Lakefront 32
6. Families 40
7. Out in the Barn 45
8. Graduation Day 50
9. The Top 55
10. Marathon 65
11. Fresh Eyes 72
12. The Wedge 78
13. Here We Go 89
14. Ladder Me Not 93
15. Who Dunnit 101
16. Pickup Lines 110
17. Bugs 119
18. The Hookup 130
19. Copper 136
20. Little Green Men 144
21. Whatcha Got 151
22. A Night Out 159
23. Tergana Slips the Gap 173
24. Lunch 185

25. Deep Shit City 195

26. Back to Class 201

27. Mind is Faster Than Light 208

28. Mean and Stupid 221

29. Smelt Me 225

30. Pole Position 229

31. Dinner at Arney's 242

32. It's Catching 253

33. Pissed Off 262

34. No Time 268

35. Message of the Gathering 274

36. Ohmera 286

37. The Trip Back 289

38. The Past 302

39. The Future 306

1

A Box of Parts

The external anti-gravity alarm erupted just beyond the orbit of the fourth planet. Captain Andin Ducar of the Aleri starship Xelanar had only encountered its warbling klaxon in training, a rarity that was in no way a measure of its importance.

Gravity had been tamed and with that came imperatives and protocols. Anti-gravity motors, ultimately powerful and dangerous, were the key to the stars and required shielding to avoid disrupting time and navigation. Sentrybots posted along the main trade routes between the water planets warned of shield leaks. But out here, an on-board alarm meant local trouble.

"Turn that damned thing off," Ducar barked. "Test the hull and main stack motor sensors now."

Jasca Sitor, second in command, touched the panel flasher and the sound died. "They check out sir."

"Well, if it's not us, it's external. Why aren't there any anti-grav sensors around our water child?"

"Too soon sir. The Culsci report estimates a minimum of two hundred fifty years before First Discovery, and even then they won't be ready for it. I'd say more like four hundred before they have any anti-grav at all, at least a hundred before we start to track them."

"We haven't relieved the Carei yet. They should handle this. Didn't Admiral Tergana get an alarm?"

"They got a blip but nothing strong enough to trigger an alert. They say it's quantum resonance or a solar flare, just an anomaly."

Ducar shook his head in frustration. "I don't think they take their mission seriously. They're still on station. They should handle it."

"I know sir. But they've asked to be relieved early, some issues at home. They want to start retrieving their bots." Jasca could tell Ducar wasn't happy. The captain's mind was easy to read.

"Swell," said Ducar, letting the sound draw out with a hint of sarcasm. After three tours it was still his favorite Earth word, spoken with a touch of irony that made the language bearable. "Tell them we'll handle it. Then set a rendezvous in moonshadow. I don't want that short-tempered fool to waste one moment of my life. This is supposed to be an easy deployment."

The hand-off was usually routine, a perfunctory ceremony and records exchange, shake some hands and be done. The crew being relieved couldn't wait to depart, so things were brief.

Ducar knew why Tergana wanted out. After three years making sure the population of planet S3alpha didn't blow themselves up while they continued their march out of the mud, it all got boring. Sentrybots did the work. Except for an occasional stroll among the natives, waiting for alarms to go off was life aboard a patrol vessel assigned to the watch. They were interstellar volunteers on the front-lines of prevention.

Emerging civilizations could not join the galactic community until they discovered the secrets of anti-gravity and the stardrive that followed. Of course, there were social and evolutionary milestones to be met. Telepathy came first.

2

Without it, a communal world-mind could not evolve. Without fundamental empathy, cohesive purpose could not develop. Without enlightenment, war remained the primary solution to cultural and political differences.

If an immature world invented the stardrive before they learned peace, local systems had to defend themselves until the upstarts could be contained. It was all so wasteful that the galactic community had long ago set up the Shepherds' Watch to nudge emerging sentient societies toward useful choices.

In this quadrant that job belonged to the five nearest water worlds. It was Aleria's turn to man the normally quiet watch. Easy duty if you could get it, because the inhabitants of this planet, beautiful as it was, had barely begun to empathize with each other, much less use their emerging telepathic skills to think to each other.

Nevertheless, according to the alarm someone on this water-covered world, toward the end of a long arm of galactic spiral, had discovered anti-gravity far too soon.

"Scan the sensor, the switch and the light path between them. And somebody turn down the alarm. It's loud enough to wake the dead. If it goes off again I want to be able hear myself think. *Stack my ass*, Ducar thought. *This world's not close to ready. Just a busted sensor. I'd bet my rank on it.*

━━◆━━

"Harry what's all that noise? Are you alright? I heard wood breaking." Donna Miller stood in the barn's side doorway, staring at a foot-wide hole in the far wall with a toolbox stuck in it. "What in God's name are you doing out here anyway?"

"Nothin' hon, just throwin' some electrical parts and old stuff from my experiments that didn't work into that toolbox over there. Only a minute ago it was over here. I can't figure it."

"What do you mean over here?" Donna's brow wrinkled as

she looked at the toolbox wedged into the hole.

"I mean right here, by my feet. Must have somethin' to do with the last bits I threw in. I shook 'em to get 'em to settle and the whole thing just took off, ripped right out of my hands. Slid across the floor and cracked that 4x4 clean in two."

"Harry, now quit it. You know I don't like jokes at my expense. Things don't just move by themselves."

"Seriously. That toolbox moved from right here where I'm standin' to all the way over there. I wouldn't bust a hole in the barn for a joke."

"This isn't funny, Harry."

Harry sighed. The truth was, he didn't really know what had happened. It had torn from his hands with enough force to move across the floor and break boards in a solid wall. "Don't worry, I'll fix the hole and clean this up in the morning."

Donna shot him a look of concern, then retreated up the porch steps to her kitchen, informed but not consoled. He watched her go as his head swam with ideas. The sliding toolbox excited him, but he couldn't share it with her.

Instead he whispered, "What are you? Where are you? Why have you eluded me for so long?"

There were many 'conversations' with the force he sought, as he talked to himself to encourage discovery. Throughout the testing process he had watched meters and dials for a flicker of movement, anything that might indicate he had found a new force, but three months had passed and he had nothing to show for it. Finally, he'd promised Donna he would stop experimenting and clean up the barn.

Pure irony, he thought, glaring at the now motionless toolbox. *Just when I might have a result. How am I going to tell her I'm not going to stop?*

The old barn had good bones – 8x8 white oak beams trucked down from the sawmill eleven miles north, held up the pine siding, now gray with time and lack of paint. The steel box had split a 4x4, shattering the siding. Harry wondered if the force could have split one of the 8x8's. He looked through the hole. "Three new boards at least," he murmured.

His family farm held the view on this rise for a hundred and forty years, a quarter section purchased by his great grandfather. Water was good, and the land had seen corn and wheat and soy. Gently rolling terrain meant a tractor could disappear in a valley only to reemerge moments later, going up the far rise and trailing dust that left a promising taste on the wind. Beyond the vegetable garden was the apple orchard and five acres of maple and pine that followed the slope down to the stream with old oaks near the house for shade in summer heat.

I'm riskin' all this. Ain't fair not to tell her, he thought and walked into the kitchen a few minutes later.

"What are you going to do about that hole in the wall?" Donna asked with both hands on her hips.

"Don't worry, Arney can help me fix it in the morning. In the meantime, I want to find out what happened. A toolbox doesn't just move by itself. It's like something kicked it or dragged it across the floor, and it sure wasn't me."

Donna turned away, then looked back. "Harry, are you sure you're okay?"

"Sure I am." He forced a chuckle. "Why wouldn't I be?"

"We've been married forty-two years and you always knew what-was-what. But lately you've been—"

"Been what?" He frowned.

"Sort of flighty, I guess." She let out a weary breath. "Harry, can't you let this go?"

He hugged her as if she was still eighteen, without the aches and pounds that time had added. "I need to find this force. I wouldn't be working out there at 65 with my bum hip if it wasn't important to me."

She returned to the dinner preparations in spite of her apprehension. "Go on then. I'll call you when it's ready."

5

He went out to the front porch to mull things over. She was practical to the bone out of necessity. Funny when she wanted to be and not without her beauty when she smiled. They were childhood sweethearts who had grown up together, familiar in their ways. Still, he knew his recent need for so much science was beyond her.

Farming was straight forward, graspable, ancient, rewarding and, with the exception of weather and insects, predictable. But three months ago Harry had leased most of their 160 acres to his son and began experimenting with 'a force of nature' as he called it. It had come to him in a dream—the idea that coils controlled a new force. For a while they were all he talked about. For Donna, his obsession had been life changing, their contented farm life forever altered. He knew she loved him and she rarely protested but today had been different, her concerns more urgent. Had he pushed her too far?

He sat staring at the barn as the smell of hot dinner rolls wafted out onto the porch. The creak of the oven door and the clink of a baking pan announced the end of preparation.

"Harry dinner's ready. Go wash up," she called out.

"Be there soon, hon." He eased himself out of his chair. "I should get that toolbox back inside."

Five minutes later, Harry was still tugging at the box wedged between the 4x4 and the splintered wood planks. It hadn't budged. He tried to make the opening larger by moving it from side to side, then up and down. Then he braced himself, grabbed the end handle and pulled as hard as he could. The steel box flew from his hands, splintering more planking. And vanished.

❦

On the bridge of the Xelanar, the klaxon erupted again. This time Jasca shut it off without being asked.

"What the hell is going on?" Ducar asked no one in particular.

"Did anyone test the array? And did we get a fix on the source?"

"Forward sensors put it on the surface of number three in the midwest of the United States, but the signal was too weak to identify the exact position. The rear sensors got no reading at all, so I'm not sure." Jasca tried not to sound apologetic for the condition of the sensor arrays.

Ducar disliked those who complained about their disk, an older, flatter bell built for shorter missions but easy to hide. "That's two hits on the same sensor in a couple of hours," he grumbled.

"More like ninety minutes Captain. That's got to be a quantum fluctuation or a flare."

"I doubt it from that location. My money's on a black hole collapse or a broken sensor"

———

At seven in the morning Arney Miller, who got the best of his parents' genes, climbed off his 67 Harley XLCH and walked around the side of the barn following the sound of the shovel.

"It's a little early to be digging, Pop. You said you had some trouble yesterday. What's up?"

Harry pointed to the broken wall.

Arney started grinning, which annoyed the hell out of Harry. "Would ya' look at that. How'd you manage to make a hole like that? What a mess. This is gonna take some time. I'll get my tools and the boys are bringing the lumber over in the truck. And Pop, what are you digging for anyway?"

"Looking for my toolbox. It's down here somewhere. Just not sure how deep."

"You mean the steel one with all the junk in it? Are you telling me that's what made the hole?"

"That's the one, except I emptied most of it out so I could put my leftover parts in. It's a long story. Well actually, maybe

7

not. I know what I did, and I know what I saw. But I've got no idea why this happened."

Arney stared at him somewhat perplexed.

Harry decided his son might need more of an explanation. "You see, I was throwing in some wire spirals and rods from my experiments, but when I shook the box to settle them, the dang thing took off like a rocket. Busted that hole in the 4x4 and got stuck. When I tried to pull it out, it just took off again. Wound up out here, buried."

"Damn Pop, it pushed your beam out six inches, and this trench. That's a lot of force.

"I know." Harry went back to digging, a little frustrated. "I didn't want to make a big deal out of it in front of Donna. You know how she gets. She'll try to make me stop again. There's something to these rods and coils, even if I don't know what it is."

The ping of metal on metal stopped his shovel. "Ah, there you are," and he leaned down to dig by hand.

"Some of the parts in this box must have amplified my force, but in the opposite direction. I was trying to pull it back, wiggling from side to side. Nothing. But when I pushed and pulled, it took off and wound up out here. I don't know how, and there's a part of me don't want to. Help me dig this out, will you?"

Together they dug with their hands and cleared the top of the box.

Arney expected to see more damage. "Hey Pop, look at the lid. It's like nothin' touched it."

"That ain't right."

It was then that Donna stepped onto the front porch and called out "Arney! It's your oldest. He says he'll be over here in fifteen minutes. You want to talk to him?"

"No. Thanks, Mom. That's fine."

Harry beckoned Arney closer with one finger. "Listen,

somethin's goin' on here. I don't know what it is, but I'd like to keep this quiet for a while and not tell the boys. Might be better if folks didn't get nervous and nosy. Always want to mistrust what they don't understand, better they don't know at all."

"What are you gonna tell 'em?"

"Don't know."

"Okay, how 'bout we say you lost control of your riding mower? Tell you what, we'll push the mower up to the hole from the inside the barn and use a tarp and the tractor to cover this. Start that green puppy up and park it right over the hole. Folks won't think twice about it or the barn, but you'll be their fool for a couple of weeks 'til they find a better story."

"Suits me. Good idea."

Luke, Arney's oldest boy, pulled their Ford pickup close to the damaged wall and began unloading a 4x4, pine planks and power tools. He was diligent and bright and taller and darker but never as fast as his younger brother Mark, who was already out the other door helping with the lumber.

Harry had watched his two grandsons grow up on Arney's nearby farm, the 80 acres that he had helped him buy. It hadn't been easy on any of them.

The boy's mother Louise died when they were young, leaving Arney to raise the kids, with his daughter Jennifer's help. They had enough of everything, except the caring tenderness that mothers bring. Luke, in particular, always seemed to walk in a shadow of melancholy that left him cautious about life.

"Looks like you had a little tussle with the wall, Grampa," Luke commented. "How'd you make that hole, anyway?"

"Oh, just movin' my mower. Foot slipped off the brake. Not payin' attention like I shoulda."

Luke inspected the damage from the inside and called out through the hole. "Dad woulda killed me if I had done this."

Harry smiled. "Everyone makes mistakes. He'd have just asked you to fix it." Minutes later, the boys were yanking at the wall. Splintered planking broke away with a crack as Mark cleared debris. Demolition had begun.

By noon, a new 4x4 and some 2x4 cross bracing allowed Luke to nail new siding in place. Finally the hammering stopped. The wall looked none the worse for wear except for the brand new boards. That lighter patch would give the neighbors a good laugh for years to come.

It was time to settle. "I brought $40 in lumber and we spent four hours at $10 an hour, Grampa. I make that $80 for the two of us," Luke said.

"That's not enough, Luke. I appreciate you boy's help today. How about $80 for you and $80 for Mark and $40 for the lumber? I know you're both saving for school."

"Thanks Grampa, this is great." After a round of beer and sodas and short goodbyes Luke and Mark were rattling back down the driveway, raising clouds of dust. Arney took a short-cut home between two fields, just to give his Harley some real dirt.

"How much was it?" Donna called from the bedroom window.

Harry filled her in. "Seems like a lot," she said.

"You know I like to spoil my grands." He laughed. "Anyway, it's good insurance. They'll brag about the money as much as how stupid they think I was for driving into the wall."

"Is that what you told them?"

"Yup, it was Arney's idea. *Better to let this die down*, he thought, *until I know what I'm dealing with.*

Harry started the old John Deere and moved it from above the toolbox, then dug around the box until it was perched on a mound of dirt. He wanted to take pictures but when he went back into the house, his camera wasn't where he remembered leaving it. At the bottom of the stairs he called up. "Hey honey, you know where my little camera is?"

"On your dresser where you left it. You want me to bring it

down?"

"Please."

He needed pictures, in case the box disappeared again. He thought to document it layer by layer, not that this would reveal its mysteries—but it seemed the sort of thing an archeologist or crime scene investigator might do.

Leaning over the hole, he snapped a half dozen shots from different angles, pulled out some parts and did it again. Then he put the camera down and dug some more.

By supper the contents of the old toolbox lined the top of the long work bench near the barn's side door—electrical parts, metal coils, rods and flat metal plates of various sizes. The empty box sat on the floor beneath. He would have to test all the parts to determine a cause for the movement. He wasn't sure whether the toolbox itself had contributed anything. But since he couldn't rule it out, it too was a part.

2

Changing of the Guard

The five nearby civilizations that watched over Earth had patrol craft of different shapes, so the locals were never sure what they were seeing. The Shepherds accepted that accidental sightings of interstellar vessels were inevitable, but every effort was made to avoid contact. What governments knew about aliens they held secret, preferring to sow their own confusion.

It worked. Planetary Watches were rarely discovered. They intervened only when disaster was imminent and then only to nudge. Cultural manipulation was rarely tolerated. Avoid contact and above all resist the urge to interfere, that was the mantra. UFO sightings near military bases and missile sites seemed a small price to pay.

"Tell Admiral Tergana we will rendezvous in two hours to transfer the watch," Ducar ordered. "That should give them plenty of time to retrieve their peripherals."

Gratto Tergana was just the sort the Carei liked to promote—a fat, well-heeled bully whose voice rang with the sound of entitlement. The less Ducar suffered it, the happier he was. Relieving the Carei early would be a gift to himself. He reigned in his thoughts and returned to empathy. Polite telepathic transfers were expected, secondary emotional judgments were not.

The Carei cruiser Morowa rose from the bottom of Lake Baikal in southern Siberia before moonrise, its resonance dampers eliminating splash as it broke the surface. An immense cigar-shaped frontline vessel as ready for war as for peace, it cloaked and slipped silently toward the moon's far side. The cover of night gave planetary telescopes and cameras less chance at a picture.

Admiral Tergana knew Captain Ducar. They had relieved each other before. Their ships would as usual meet precisely on time, moving to rest side by side, cruiser dwarfing disk. Thought greetings and hard data exchanges were perfunctory. As they and their first officers stood together on the cruiser's bridge, only one question broke the telepathic silence.

"Gratto, did you get a fix on the source of that anti-gravity signature?"

"Somewhere south of the Great Lakes of the United States, but it was too weak and brief to be anything but a quantum anomaly. Nothing of consequence."

"What about the second pulse?"

"What second pulse? No, we were packing up. Our sentrybots were already stowed. Whatever our outer hull array recorded is in the data we gave you. If the sensors picked it up, it's part of the log. Relax Ducar, this is easy duty. I've seen this before. It's a solar flare, or a quantum pulse."

"You make it sound too normal." God, how he hated being dismissed.

"Look, this world is a long way from the rod and coil, much less the stack. Just look how violent these people are. It's too soon. Maybe in another thousand of their years you'll see that sort of advance, if they can keep from exterminating themselves. That's our biggest problem anyway, isn't it? Keep them from blowing themselves up. Relax. We'll be doing this for some time to come. Anyway, my best to you and your crew. Good luck, Ducar."

Ducar and Jasca transported back to their bell, a domed curve that flattened toward the sensors in its circular rim.

13

Gratto's still a fatuous ass, thought Ducar as the larger Carei cruiser eased off and then abruptly vanished. He had hoped to command a craft of that size with all its capabilities. It carried scout craft of different sizes, which meant less exposure. Settle in moonshadow or somewhere in the sea and let the scouts and the bots do the patrol work. That was the life.

Most of the worlds assigned to monitoring duty did it. The smaller Aleri vessel was no less sensor capable, just a little cramped on a long watch. And because it carried only two-man and six-man scouts, sometimes it was necessary to patrol using the Xelanar itself.

Ducar glanced at Jasca who was floating three small crystal spheres above his head to exercise his mind. He seemed too handsome with his chiseled features and dark hair to be so capable. "Take us to station, Jasca. We are losing our window." The hollow spheres spun down to rest in a small bowl.

"Shall we use the Carei shelter in their absence?"

"No. I want to be nearer the source of that signal. The Great Lakes are more exposed, but we'll be closer if the indicator proves genuine. Take us to control point twenty-one in Lake Michigan. "

They were on a fishing expedition, tracking an errant sensor reading. And it didn't seem like the easy duty Admiral Tergana had spoken about. He watched Jasca touch a panel then received his crewman's thought instruction: *Please take your seat Captain, I'm cloaking now.*

After a last look at the sky there was no more need to be airborne. In a flicker of visibility, Jasca took Aleri Disk 4IX, the U.A.S. Xelanar with a crew of twenty-one aboard and slipped beneath the waves of Lake Michigan, there to begin their 36-month tour of duty monitoring water planet S3alpha for signs of a more intelligent life.

3

Corn Off the Cob

M ost of the houses out Harry's way were built hard by two-lane blacktop roads that connected the farming towns together. Just rolling by you could see they were in need of more money and attention than they were getting. Tucked between the fields and timber breaks of southern Indiana, their peeling paint spoke of better times. But somebody warmed them up at night and called them home, hardworking folks who had more energy than luck, not living thin by choice.

Every now and then, a little farther off the road, one passed a well kept farmhouse, where good fortune had favored hard work or chance. But sometimes a faded mailbox was all that marked a road to another farm out of sight beyond the trees, a mystery that tugged at those passing by. Harry got lucky.

Aunt Julia Anne's Road was a stripe of crushed limestone, veering off between the oaks lining the patchwork quilt of asphalt that was Priors Lane, not exactly a main road itself. The thin poles that carried power and telephone wires away over the hill alongside its gravel track spoke to the investment Harry's grandfather Edward made when he paid to have the services put in.

You wouldn't have thought that building a farm house that

far off the main road was wise. But there are views, and then there are views. Once you were over the rise, it all made sense, one of those tucked-away places that takes your breath. Out of sight from all but a few, sky touching hills of field and forest, ice-carved from sea bottom.

Harry always thought Julia Anne must have been the one who found it and got herself a road named after her, even if it was just a single lane of gravel. Rain puddled in deep ruts along the lower parts, but it served the Herberts, his and Arney's farms and two more at the bottom of the road, before feeding back into Prior's Lane a mile down. It had signs at either end and the mail got delivered. Out Harry's way, you couldn't ask for more.

His driveway started at the road, wound down past the house, cut slightly into the slope of the front lawn near the big oaks to make a turn by the front door and then down to the lower level of the barn. Great grandfather George had laid it all out to please his eye. Then each generation added their own touches to the house, pushing it just short of lace curtains, while the barn remained mostly unchanged.

Big Red, a gable-roofed behemoth, was just beyond the herb garden by the kitchen door. Large enough to house a regulation-sized basketball court, with faded lines on the floor and hoops that hung at either end attesting to its versatility. Tucked into the hill, the stone foundation had once framed horse stalls below the main floor. Now it was filled with cars and a tractor, four bays in all.

The shed-roofed addition housed Harry's workshop. He would have preferred a little more space between the house and the barn. Extra distance might have offered peace on several fronts, as the barn's side door and the kitchen door were within shouting distance.

Donna used its proximity to her advantage, always taking his temperature, nudging and nagging. Keeping tabs on his eccentricities and a fence up around his impulses. It was one of the ways she loved him best. She had an affection for his easy humor and the disheveled silver hair that fell over his still handsome face. He wore his sixty-five years well in spite of his aches.

He loved her too, and couldn't live without her, even if her fuse was a little shorter than his.

"Harry, what in God's name is all that racket? Did you break something else? You'll wake the dead."

He was cleaning up his workspace, a rare moment of desperation. "I dropped some clamps. Nothing to worry about." They had anchored his homemade coil winder to the bench when his fascination with electromagnetism pushed him to build an electric motor.

Harry knew magnets and copper coils and iron cores could make electricity if you moved them. They could also be a motor, if you applied electricity as a force. The beauty of a machine that could generate electricity or use the same force to become a motor was etched in him as a boy, so what followed seemed natural.

Electromagnetism was not the only interactive force affected by matter, it was just one he knew about. But what if there were other materials that produced a different kind of energy? He couldn't shake the idea. And as he grew older, he dabbled and toyed with it. Then he had a dream.

He saw a coil of wire spinning around a rod and a grid of red light that flexed and folded. It felt important. At breakfast that morning, it struck him how vivid the memory was. And somehow, the dream made sense, even if he had no place to fit the knowledge.

Three nights later he dreamed about three flat rings, stacked one upon the other, largest on the bottom, spinning on an axis and emitting a shimmering purple glow. The next day he could hardly finish breakfast because he felt so pushed by the need to draw them. In that moment, Harry's farm life came to a screeching halt.

How the idea arose made no difference. He was bound to it. Without knowing exactly what the force might do, he began his work. He knew he was smart, but could he realize his vision? Could he make one?

He drew what he could remember, the rod standing in the center of a flat plate and a coil of metal floating around it. *Make 'em small,* he thought, *No need to make things difficult. Five inches should do.* He could see how to machine the rods, and so he started sawing and grinding and turning rods and coiling springs from all the different metals he could find. A scrap box yielded iron, copper and lead. The bottoms of various drawers held tin, aluminum and nickel. It was a start.

He made the rods on his old Southbend lathe. As they stacked up, he muttered, "Damn, what if it isn't metal at all?" The possibility rattled him. There might be a lot more to do than he thought. He ran down a list of elements; carbon, gold, copper and silicon and rare gases in glass tubes—and felt stretched by the sheer number of possibilities.

How to get the coils to move was quite another problem. Harry set about making a mechanism that could test them without interference. He made wooden brackets and gears of oak without metal fittings, so as not to add influence. Crank handles, axles and bearings controlled the rate at which materials were brought together. First back and forth. Then spinning over the rod. The motions had a lazy grace about them. It was a work of art.

A week later he was ready for the first test. With meters on and gauges zeroed, he passed metal coils over rods of every material he had managed to shape.

Except for the magnets, nothing else had an internal power potential, but some samples might need some excitement as he called it. So he hooked up a power supply to provide direct current, scraped radium from the face of the pocket watch Donna gave him, and found heaters and a small refrigerator. He set up his array of sensors and meters at the far end of the long work bench and began to test various combinations by applying different energy sources, first to the rod, then to the coil. He knew he had to measure everything he could, because he was stepping into a scientific abyss.

Weeks went by. Move the rod, watch the meters. Spin the coil, watch the meters. Crank the fixture closer to the sensors. Do it all over again. Swap DC current for AC. Then try light, magnets, heat, cold, radiation—over and over and over—until Donna's voice calling him to dinner put an end to it for another day.

One night Donna wasted no time getting to it. "You alright? You look pissed."

"Buried's more like it. The monotony of repetition."

The mechanism he built was quiet and efficient, but after observing its motion, day after day, without result, he had checked off what seemed an endless list of possibilities. The weeks became months. Still no meters moved, not a flicker, and frustration set in. The sheer number of possible combinations and the fact that his best guess about size and spacing might be completely wrong did nothing to improve his humor. After what seemed like weeks of pressure from Donna to stop for his own sake, he decided to pack it in. That is, until the toolbox moved.

Spontaneous movement has no place in physics. There is always cause for effect. He had the effect. It was the what, and how, and why of the cause that eluded him. He was searching for something subtle. Something he had missed.

He trained himself to notice the smallest flicker of movement on the gauges. Whatever he hoped to discover would not reveal itself until a meter jumped or a thermometer varied. When he decided he needed more sophisticated equipment, he bought a

Geiger counter.

After that purchase Donna started leaning into his obsession.

"Harry what do you hope to find out here?"

"A new kind of energy, I guess. I don't know exactly."

"If you're not sure, why waste your time?"

"'Cause I can feel it an' smell it."

"Oh Harry, please."

"You know if my toolbox hadn't moved, I'd say you're right. But it did. Honey, I'm serious. This is some new kind of energy. Not electricity, something else. I know I ain't got the science for it, or the words. Sometimes there ain't no words, just a push of thought, ideas that ain't mine."

Donna knew about the voices. Harry had tried to explain how they came into his head. Thoughts that couldn't be his, because they were about things of which he had no knowledge. He called it telepathy. She called it crazy.

Still, the idea of voices was easier to understand than feelings. Men weren't supposed to be intuitive. Harry didn't like to call it intuition either, because it didn't have the same quality the women spoke of. He had let the voices guide his work, marrying them with as much science as he could bring to bear. From one combination of materials to the next, he chose by instinct not result. There were no results. No meters moved. No bells rang.

So much for intuition. The telepathic push and his dogged determination were not enough. Reason and order were required. To that end now he began to organize his possibilities. Everything that had been in the toolbox was now lined up like soldiers on the workbench. He spaced them out, fearing an interaction. Each had an identification number and a note indicating its relationship to other parts. Taped to the wall near the side door were pictures of the parts inside the toolbox with corresponding numbers written over them.

It was all neatly arranged except for a shattered bottle of

mercury. He had no choice but to pour the silver liquid at the bottom of the box into a new bottle and save the glass shards in a jar. A thin film still clung tenaciously to peeling paint on the left side and back wall of the toolbox, but he resisted the urge to remove it.

Harry looked at the clutter under the bench. "I should've taken pictures of all this." Anything on the top now might contribute to his ephemeral force. What was nearby might contribute or interfere—so it stayed put until he took more pictures.

In one box, a pine dowel wrapped in copper mesh caught his eye. He remembered thinking about corn when he had first teased the metal lace over one end. Now it was time to save the copper, and add the pine to the kindling. The answer, if there was one, beckoned from the table top, troops at his command. His excitement grew.

4

Dust Piles

Harry picked up his point and shoot and took as wide a shot as he could from each corner of the barn, then climbed to the loft and took more pictures from above. There was good reason to think that the layout of things on the floor had contributed to the toolbox effect, so he documented the position of everything. The thought of how the toolbox had ripped from his grasp made him smile. "It's to be reckoned with," he murmured, "this primal thing. I need to build some containment before I do anything else or I'll be the fool for not." There would be no explaining another hole.

At his feet lay the answer. Corn husks. Those that didn't go back in the ground blew into the corners and up against the sheds and outbuildings or stuck in low points until they rotted. Harry would not want for padding. He set about collecting what he could, making so many trips to the edges of the fields and scouring the perimeters of the outbuildings that he could feel Donna watching him, wondering what he was up to and decided not to look toward the house.

Soon the sound of hammer and nails echoed as he built six thin wooden frames covered with chicken wire to keep the husks in place. They would be light enough to move around as necessary and strong enough to prevent another hole. Not works of art, but they would do. When he was finished, the 4x6 foot frames were clamped together, two deep in a triangle. He knew he could stop his toolbox, but he needed more room.

He cleared the center of the floor stacking tools and bags of fertilizer and seed against the walls. The more room he made for the padding, the more obvious it became that he needed a cover story. *What the hell do I tell 'em?* He mulled over possibilities, rolling a small workbench to the center of the now empty basketball court. *Hoops, that's it!* he thought. *This doesn't have to stay here. Roll it out when I need it, back when I don't. I'll tell 'em I'm playin' some ball.*

The sun was going down, but he decided against turning on the lights to continue and closed the door behind him.

That night Harry had his dream again. Usually he saw the rod and coils, then the spinning discs. This time the spinning discs bathed in the purple light were all he saw, and he took it as a sign. *Those coils might have made my toolbox move, but these discs have to be the motor. I can feel it.* It woke him and left him staring out the bedroom window into the summer night.

"What's the matter? You have a bad dream?" Donna was barely awake.

"A good dream actually, at least I think so. Go back to sleep honey. I'm fine."

The morning saw him up at dawn sorting parts and tools. The oscilloscope, rf meter and Geiger counter were of no use now. A simple dial indicator would do. Any pressure on the plunger would move the needle. And movement, any movement, would be his proof.

Harry's mind spun, trying wrestle his prize from the mystic. His previous experiments were for naught, except that they narrowed his possibilities down to the contents of the toolbox. Copper wire and plates, tool steel, wrought iron, various alloys, magnets, some plastics, motor oil, dirt, charcoal, glass from the small broken bottle that held liquid mercury, brass, tin, lead, aluminum, nickel, old carbon resistors, capacitors, and rubber were some of his choices. Even the paint on the toolbox had to be considered. *I'm not making a disc out of paint*, he thought.

With springs and rods he could test pairs of materials, but flat discs could be drilled out, stacked and spun. That meant more combinations were possible. If a needle moved at all, he could further test those that showed promise. He smiled. "This is beginning to make sense."

What did not work could not be allowed to become the enemy of what might. It was time to clear the decks. Harry carted the last remaining boxes of his early failures to a rickety corn crib, but took care to save the rod and coil adjustment mechanism. It was clear evidence of his best mind at work. He carefully placed the components into a steel box. "Rats won't get in here," he chuckled under his breath. "Put your teeth on this, suckers."

They didn't like him either.

A cleaner barn freed his mind, as if the extra space allowed more room for thought. He searched through his stock and scrap piles to find pieces of plastic, stone and metals like what had been in his toolbox, until he realized only the metals made sense. There were too many elements in the plastic and stone. And he had plenty of metal stock, at least enough to get started. Harry wondered just how close to true he needed to machine each disc. His precise self said be as accurate as possible, while his cagey old man self declared that nothing was precise about the toolbox shake, so maybe a little wobble was okay.

He used his lathe to turn the flat round discs. It went on so long that what had been a clean floor became covered in piles of metal curlings and chips and little spears that demanded the blood of the unfortunate. No matter, there would soon be a few combinations to try. He wanted to see them spin, put them to the test and resume his journey into the unknown.

The sound of Arney's Harley ended with a couple of soft puffs from the exhaust. Bored out, it made more noise than most of the bikes in the area, but Harry knew his son liked it that way.

"Hey Pop, how are you?"

"I'm fine Big A. How 'bout you?"

"I'm good, I'm good." Arney walked through the barn, sending small piles of metal shavings and swarf swirling away from underfoot. "Whoa, I see you've been busy. What's Mom say about all this? Does she know you're pushing this hard?"

"She's your mother, of course she knows."

"Well, any little breeze that blows in here will kick up a cloud. If you're done machining, how 'bout letting me help you clean up these piles? You don't want to be tracking this stuff into the house."

"Thanks. I'll take some help, and I appreciate I don't have to ask. Somebody must'a raised you right."

"Whoever it was, it's the least I can do. You and Mom sure helped with the kids, after Louise died. Besides you know me, I wouldn't be here at all if I wasn't interested. I've seen beautiful things come out of that head of yours, so I'm flat out curious."

"Quit blowin' smoke."

"Got a feelin' about you Pop. Whatcha makin' those discs for?"

"Tell ya' when we're done cleaning."

Arney connected the long hose to the shop vac and went to work. A half hour later the two men were face to face on old oak chairs, swapping stories and sucking suds.

"Nothing like a cold beer on a hot day, a just reward I think." Harry put down his bottle. "Listen, I've been meaning to talk to you about the toolbox. First of all, thanks for your good idea about the mower the other day."

"You're welcome."

"There's more. Just you, me and your mom know what happened, and I'd like to keep it that way. You can understand why, can't you?"

"Mum's the word."

"Especially the boys."

"Especially the boys. I haven't told a soul. Kinda figured you'd be back experimenting sooner rather than later. So, you want to tell me what you're thinking and how I can help?"

Harry shifted to scan the door and the window. He could see Donna in the kitchen, but still paused and quieted as he began. "I've found a force. Maybe not exactly what I was looking for, but a force nonetheless."

"Is this something Mom's not supposed to hear?"

"I'm trying to make it easy on her. This force comes from some combination of the stuff on that workbench. They must have rubbed against or moved past each other, or been in just the right place for an instant and caused the motion."

"Pop you know I love you, but you've got nothin' but a hole in the ground."

"And the wall, too."

"Okay, the wall, too. How? Why? Got any idea at all?"

"Zip, nada, but it was a strong pull, a lot of energy to move that much weight."

"So why the discs then? Why not stick with coils?"

"Cause those rods and coils are just one part of my dreams. I want to build the stack of spinning discs I keep seein'. Feels more like a motor to me."

"So what now?"

"I need rotors that I can stack on top of each other, different combinations at different speeds. But unless I get lucky, this will take some time. If you can help me around the farm, that would be great."

His boy looked around slowly. "You know Pop, I'm doin' most of it now as it is."

"I know. I just need a second pair of eyes and hands, and another mind I can trust. Oh, and this might get dangerous.

What do you say?"

"How long's this gonna take?"

"As long as it takes."

"It ain't much of a bargain, but I'm game. When do you want to start?"

"Now would be good. I need you to get some things for me. It's all the metals I don't have enough of and some dial indicators. The list is behind you on the workbench next to my notebook."

Arney stretched out, turned and managed to just tease the piece of paper onto his fingertips. When he turned back he asked, "Beryllium? You want me to get Beryllium?"

"It's the help I need right now. Anything you can do will be appreciated."

Arney shrugged, as if he knew further protest served nothing. He began to sort out the things he might have in his shop, versus the things he would need to order. "Okay, I'm in. I'll start the search and order as much as I can when I get home. I'll call you tonight and let you know where we stand." Then he waved his father goodbye.

Harry heard the Harley's growl fade as he looked at the dwindling pile of metal stock. There wasn't much left for the lathe to chew on. He decided to call Arney before anything got shipped and tell him to put a rush on it.

Hang the cost, he thought. *I need to know. I want this stuff now.*

The Harley's motor had barely died when the phone on Arney's kitchen wall started ringing.

"I'll get it," Jennifer called out. "Hello. Oh, hi Grampa," Arney heard her say. "You okay? Dad just drove up."

Arney reached for the phone wondering what was rankling his father now, besides the general slow pace of the universe's unfolding. "Hi, Pop. What's up?"

"Listen, when you put in those orders will you put a rush on

27

them please? Don't worry about the cost. I'll cover it."

"Sure, I can do that. You alright Pop?"

"Yeah, I'm sorry if I got a little pushy. It's just, I'm so close I can taste it."

"You? Pushy? Never happen. I'll be over after I finish the orders tomorrow and help you knock those discs out."

Donna could see Harry wasn't waiting for Arney to show up in the morning. The need to find answers was burning again, her old friend deep in thought. He had that here-but-not-here look as he scribbled his designs on scraps of paper, wrestling with how to make it all work. It was an easy decision. She gave him the gift of dinner delayed and time to think.

He smiled from the den, detached by visions and then mumbled something.

"What did you say Harry?"

"It's nothing honey. I'm just trying to work this all out in my head."

"I know that's the truth. I can hear you thinking from here."

Harry finally fell asleep in his easy chair, snoring loudly until Donna coaxed him up to bed at two a.m. She imagined him still working on his experiments from the depths of his sleep.

"Well, you look better," she said the next morning when he appeared in the kitchen. She offered him a cup of dark coffee, and he took a sip.

"I am better, thank you. 'Cause I see the next thing to try."

"I knew you'd get it. You always do."

"Trying to use my head as much as I can. No fun if it's not difficult."

"I swear you're going to underplay this the rest of your life, aren't you, how smart you are?"

"It's easier this way. Safer, too."

Arney arrived after breakfast, hopping off his hog with an easy grace. "Mornin' Pop. You look a little intense. You okay?"

"You are gazing upon a lack of sleep and a bad case of the itchy-twitchies, 'cause I've got a design for a mechanism that will spin the discs and I want to get started."

"We waitin' on makin' more discs?"

"Yeah, til we get more stock."

They finished the first spinner, as Harry called it, late Wednesday afternoon. Flat plywood circles rested on soft rubber wheels, while other wheels kept the outer edge aligned. When the rotors were stacked, each could be adjusted for height, lateral position and speed. Everything was made of pine and oak. Neither had been in the toolbox when it moved. That made wood, some glue, and nylon screws the basis for most of the construction.

Each layer needed to spin its metal disc smoothly at high speed. It took Harry a while to get the wobbles out, but once the bottom layer was smooth, he worked on the next. When all three discs were running true by themselves, it was time to spin them up together, a moment Harry had struggled toward for days.

He switched on the bottom disc and increased its speed until it hummed. Then he started the middle one. As the speed increased, an interference began. He could hear the problem before he could see it, a quavering oscillation that tore at the edges of a purer tone.

"What the hell!" Harry slowed the middle disc down until the sound was gone, then gradually increased the speed again. He put one finger on the frame near the edge to see if he could feel anything. But as before, he could hear the quaver before he felt it. "Give me a break. By themselves these are as smooth as silk. I don't get it," he said to no one in particular.

He turned off the middle layer and turned on the uppermost. As he increased the speed of the smallest disc a higher pitched oscillation crept in. He turned them all off and sat in silence staring.

"It's almost as if they don't like each other," he groused. "I need to be careful."

It was one of those moments when Harry took his own advice seriously and ran the control wiring under the baffles. He felt safer behind them and acknowledged the tingle of fear that drove him to it. He could see the spinner through the gaps, enough to keep an eye on it, and began to search for his whining demon.

Maybe I can tune 'em to notes, he thought.

Harry headed into the house to scrounge up a guitar tuner, thinking as he walked. *I might be able to tune for harmonics, if I can't hit the fundamentals.* Once back in the barn, he placed the tuner near the discs and retreated behind his protection.

He slowly spun up the bottom layer, searching for a note as the tuner bounced from red to green, never quite settling.

"There's got to be one note that's pure." He had only one option and kept increasing the speed until the tuner locked on a steady red. "I'm flat. That's fantastic. Easy baby. Walk, don't run." The LED flickered green, then settled. "Low G, very cool." He made note of the position of the dial and the types of metal— aluminum on the bottom, copper next and tin on top. He was about to restart the copper disc when Arney poked his head through the door.

"You want some lunch Pop? Mom's giving us a choice, BLT's or ham and cheese."

"Tell her BLT's please and that I love her."

Fifteen minutes later Arney was back with a large plate of bacon, lettuce, red onion and tomato sandwiches. Blots, Donna called them. "She says she loves you too."

Harry deftly grabbed bites of sandwich while dialing up the speed on the middle rotor. It didn't take long before the copper disc was singing a B. When both layers were on, the harmony lasted only a moment before the dissonance returned. He shut off the current and adjusted the layers until they were as close as possible.

"That should cut down on some of the vibration, don't you think?"

"I don't know Pop. It's your show. Go for it."

Harry switched the current back on and found the dissonance reduced. "That's more like it," he said grinning. "Now we're getting somewhere. Hand me the tin disc will you?"

After carefully tuning it to an F#, Harry decided it was time to test all the layers at once. As they reached their notes the machine shuddered slightly and twisted on its axis. Harry killed the power.

"Something's not right here. This is basically a top. The whole machine shouldn't twist."

"Begging your pardon Pop, but why not? When you spin a toy gyroscope that's what happens to the gimbal. It starts to spin right along with the rotor. How about running one of the layers in the opposite direction to compensate?"

"Now that is a good idea, son. Swap the wires on that middle rheostat and let's see what happens."

Arney swapped the wires to reverse the motor's direction, then joined his father behind the baffles. A wise move. When Harry applied current to all three motors, the dissonance grew shrill and the wooden frame suddenly cracked under the load.

"Kill the power! Kill the power!"

Arney yanked the cable from the wall. "What the hell was that? What happened?"

"I don't know. I'm gonna to have to think on it awhile. Right now all we know is that closer is better, and reversing direction is disruptive. Coulda failed for a bunch of reasons."

5

Not Exactly Lakefront

Ducar was never happy when water filled the viewports. He preferred to see green growing things or the vastness of the cosmos. Still, the submersion into Lake Michigan had gone smoothly and the voyage was over. They were on station and that meant they could gather for a ship-wide feast. The whole crew including the kids looked forward to a family dinner. It took their minds off the odd fish swimming by. The lake bottom was no aquarium.

Before the festivities Ducar ordered the deployment of sentrybots with anti-gravity detection arrays, placed a thousand miles east and west of the last signal. It seemed so unnecessary to Jasca. "We wouldn't be doing this if we had just cloaked and been orbital," he mumbled under his breath, then regretted having spoken, even quietly.

"What did you say sir?" Shereen Delare, the Xelanar's empath and third ranking officer asked, as if asking was enough to deter further disparagement. She read him well enough and he knew it.

"Forget I said anything. I'm tired." Telepathy offered access to a mind's inner workings, but speaking out loud risked being overheard. So much for musings. He gathered his mind and headed for the bridge to inform Ducar that perimeter protocols were nearly complete.

"Why so much focus on these weak signals, sir?" Jasca asked, trying to mask his feelings.

"Because they're too brief to be black hole or neutron star collisions. They rise too fast and decay too quickly. I can see they're mostly hash like a wave, but they could also be the signature of a shielding malfunction."

"Out here in the middle of nowhere?"

"Precisely my point. Since the Shepherds sealed this system off right after receiving the first signals of animal thought, either we have a sensor problem or somebody is..." Ducar trailed off. "Listen, those four will be fine. Give them a general scan protocol in addition to the anti-grav and cover the surface. I want all their media and data streams collected, every scrap. And increase their sensitivity. Pick up every flicker you can. Anything out of the ordinary, let me know."

"Yes sir. I'll reprogram them now."

"See you below then."

Ella Bartole was a great cook. She grew what she could in the onboard greenhouse and was not above knocking off a cow for the freezer. Her mantra was 'fresh whenever possible' and she was always teaching, so she had no trouble recruiting help.

Her son Warehan had been roped in long ago. Tall and handsome and deft with a knife, he liked showing off in the kitchen as he watched Shereen's younger sisters Niriar and Filaire moving to music while they rearranged the communal living space to form two long tables with chairs. Ella was pleased to see that when laid out with some grace, even the shipboard utensils and green plants from the air purifier banks made the common area festive.

The families gathered around the tables and when everyone was settled, became silent and lowered their heads at the same time. A quiet, low-pitched humming began in the room. One pure note rose in volume, then split smoothly into a 5-part harmony, only to fall gently back to silence. Then after some time, all heads rose as one and animated conversation began.

Ella watched Niriar, the brightest of the Xelanar's teenagers, who was tall and fair with fine bones that would age well. As a mother she knew her son Warehan would not be the one to win her because she was too complicated and hard to know. And the beauty that she carried without pretense made her brighter still.

Niriar hid her wit to spare herself and spent her time studying the gathered minds. To her, Unomeri seemed more than just the telepathic communal mind her people took for granted, it was her focus, her obsession. She had told Ella that she wanted to know how a species first discovered they could think to each other, and then overcame the inevitable fear that followed. Ella thought she would probably write a book about it.

Almost every person had at least one experience of mind sharing that could not be attributed to coincidence or advanced knowledge or an educated guess. A mother might feel her child in trouble, then talk to him or her only to discover the feeling had been right. But in the absence of any measurable means of transmission, centuries of anecdotal evidence were required before scientists took it seriously.

It wasn't a particle or a radio wave or other electromagnetic radiation, but without an instrument to measure it, the skeptics prevailed. Slowly however, the best stories of such communication began to win out. That was Niriar's thesis topic. How did the sharing evolve and grow if one couldn't measure it to prove it?

Her studies showed that it wasn't so much a process of putting out feelers as it was letting walls come down. An experiment that gave each person a unique fact to share with the group proved to be the breakthrough. There were multiple links among the participants.

Some worlds would never master the sharing. They were the warring worlds, most of whom would self-destruct because they could not agree on an inclusive social structure. It happened all too often.

The reason Planet Watch was formed was to help sentient societies achieve mental harmony and avoid that destruction. It was efficient as well as charitable. Less cosmic rancor meant a greater chance for any given world to not only communicate with itself but to communicate with other worlds as well. The sharing opened up the possibility that thought was ubiquitous, that the sum total of everything one could see or know was alive and thinking. That fact was hardest for the fearful to gather in. How small would they be then?

Ella looked up from her thoughts. The usual noise of dinner utensils tapping on plates abated as everyone finished their dessert. Then with no outward sign, the younger crew members rose to begin clearing the tables. When they sat back down, conversation died and heads bowed. Two brief musical notes, a perfect third of harmony, rose then fell to silence. The gathering pushed back their chairs and got up from the table as if they were one being, then spun off to their individual duties.

Ducar left the meal and walked toward the viewport where Jasca was whispering to Shereen. As he approached, they pulled apart slightly, which spoke to the nature of their conversation.

"Captain, did you enjoy your dinner?" Shereen asked.

"A fine meal, thanks. Ella and the girls did a nice job getting it together. You and Warehan, too. Good work." He gave a quick nod to the viewport and its murky view. "Not much to see is there?"

"It's like living in a bowl of soup," Jasca said. "Sir, Shereen and I would like to take a two-man scout and see the surface, with your permission. It's hard on the mind to be so close to such a beautiful place and be stuck in a mud puddle. We will remain cloaked."

"Alright, report in regularly. And please, don't wake the natives. I'm no fan of the murk either, but it's better than quelling a disturbance."

Jasca and Shereen fit on paper. Most of the crew were selected for compatibility as well as their skills. Psychological profiles were cross-referenced to encourage close relationships, because isolation on long patrols was most easily countered by affection, but there were no guarantees.

They needed time to adjust to their earthly bodies. The physical change was easy. The Aleri had long ago evolved the ability to alter themselves down to the cellular level, becoming just like those they wished to watch, not so hard if you select for it. But emotions were a different story. Knitting thought into a new body so that it functioned seamlessly took time and an awareness of self.

Shereen liked Jasca, even if she found him somewhat stiff. She knew they were supposed to be with each other, because they were close in age and temperament. Jasca was handsome, popular and on the fast track to become a commander, a prized catch. It was his push for promotion that gave her pause, something about the way he gave orders that betrayed an imperious nature running deeper than profiles could discern.

Still, she found his chiseled features and strong physique attractive. And loneliness had a way of clouding perception. When he asked, she had gladly accepted his invitation to go exploring in the two-man scout that night.

They loaded the synthesizers with Syngel and waited until dark, then departed. The trip up from the lake bottom was brief and kept them busy preparing to cloak and break the surface without disturbance. As they slipped into the night sky she whispered, "Can we go somewhere green? I want to see the sun and flowers and smell the air. Please Jasca, somewhere warm."

"The captain told us to stay dark and remote."

"What's the harm?" she begged. "In this form even if they see us, we won't be noticed. Especially if the scout stays cloaked." Her pleading was having its effect and she was drawn to the excitement of the form he had chosen.

Jasca read her desires and felt his loins begin to churn low and deep. He had been longing for such a night as well. "Alright," he said, "if we go west we can just catch the sun before it sets. Will that do?"

"That would be wonderful." She smiled as she met his eyes.

He accelerated and guided the craft to a bluff at the edge of the western sea, then landed quietly. The sun over the ocean was breathtaking.

"Will this do?"

"Yes, thank you. This is a gift" She took his hand and guided him to the edge of the bluff. "Let's put the cushions here."

He arranged them into an inviting curve and sat.

She stood for moment, looking at the water. "It's different when you are near it, so beautiful."

"So are you." He gently pulled her down to the cushion beside him. "It's a joy to be in this body. The neural pathways are so different from ours." He spread his fingers as he stroked her skin.

She shivered, let out a little sigh and rested her head on his shoulder. A moment later she sat up, turned and kissed him.

"That was a gift, I wasn't expecting."

"Don't expect anything, just be," she whispered, leaning back and drawing him closer in a warm embrace.

They journeyed through new sensations, their bodies and nerves not always corresponding with anything they knew. It was discovery as much as pleasure. They traced their forms with their fingertips, exploring erogenous zones that were unfamiliar yet utterly tempting.

Jasca's fingers moved deep into wet places that made

Shereen shiver with joy. She loved the body she was in. Of all the forms she had assumed, this one was by far the best. She wanted everything Jasca could give her and she wanted it now. She let him know by warmth and musk and moisture and her soft whispers of desire.

He groaned. "I want you and I need this place in you to be mine, now." He rode her soft mound of fur for the pleasure it gave them both.

"Deeper, push deeper. Oh yes! Deeper, faster." She begged out the fluid seed she desired. But as Jasca neared climax, Shereen felt his mind turn from sharing to exploitation. He began to hurt her with too much pressure, unable to fully control his new body. Joy turned to pain until he exploded in her, draining himself before she was ready.

"You hurt me," she whimpered, pushing him away. "What happened? Don't you like me?"

"I like you a lot, more than a lot. I'm just not used to ladies taking the lead." He stood up and began putting on his clothes. "Look, I'm sorry. I lost control of this new body, but it's dark and we've been gone for hours. We need to get back."

She remained on the cushion slowly getting herself dressed as she stared at the wave tops that moonlight touched in endless procession. A sadness crept over her as she retrieved the cushions and food Jasca had left behind. He had become her superior officer again.

A hiss of escaping air announced the opening of the airlock as Jasca and Shereen stepped out of the two-man scout back onto the Xelanar's hanger deck. Filaire watched her sister with a skeptical eye. Something had changed. *That didn't go well,* she thought, sensing a touch of sadness in mind and in carriage. Jasca however seemed pleased with himself, so she wasn't sure if she was reading the situation correctly. She went off to tell Niriar. She would know.

Filaire found her a few minutes later. "Hey sis, have you seen Sher since she got back?"

"No, why?"

"I don't know, she felt a little off to me. "

When the three sisters finally had a chance to be alone, Filaire couldn't resist ribbing her sister. "Have a good time?"

Shereen hesitated, looking cornered. "You know me, I love oceans. We had a fine time watching the sun set. It was beautiful on the coast. And getting out of here is always a gift." Filaire nodded and silently accepted the answer, but knew better.

6

Families

The Planet Watch was manned by volunteers comprised mostly of families with children over the age of sixteen. The most serious problems on long patrols were social, not technical. Whole families could age together and avoid the time shift that occurred when only one volunteered, but they had to be compatible. They had to respect one another. Telepathic profiles were cross referenced to ensure harmony. One did not go interstellar without impeccable credentials. Still, there were plenty of volunteers. Intense curiosity about other sentient worlds drove the desire, yielding mountains of applications that required lengthy processing. Wait times were long and chances were slim.

Shereen Delare had an edge. She was an empath. She could read minds light-years away as easily as reading a book. It was the sort of gift that got a family noticed. So after meeting entrance requirements and passing the exams, she, her sisters and their parents were selected to undergo the rigorous training. The coursework was difficult. Subjects ranged from the latest technical upgrades to protocols for alien species interaction and assuming an empathetic form.

All Shepherds were required to absorb and speak the

local dialects and eat the local cuisine, but the choice of what appearance to assume was a personal matter. The inhabitants of most interstellar capable worlds could morph their appearance to some degree. But the Aleri could assume the shapes of other beings, medically indistinguishable in form and function. They looked and spoke exactly as the inhabitants of the world they were watching did. This reduced the risk of exposure. The families did not want a confrontation with the beings they watched. They just wanted to see the sights.

Family members filled the technical positions, but the captain and the first officer were almost always unaccompanied to avoid the natural tendency to shield one's own family from danger. They were socially isolated to allow the detachment command required. And while this did not entirely preclude relationships, it did nothing to encourage them.

The next afternoon Shereen was tucked into a soft chair watching PJ Joney pull a cup of coffee from a bank of food synthesizers affectionately known as indigestion row. Angular and fair with a handsome face, dressed in a green flannel shirt and jeans held up by an oval brass buckle, he was a cowboy, gunslinger to the core, as close to the edge as you could get among a peaceful people. He manned and maintained the disruptor, which was mostly used to eliminate meteors by time shifting them out of the way and then bringing them back after passing. But in times of trouble, it could be used as a weapon and that badge was pinned right to PJ's cockiness.

"Whatcha up to?" he asked with a smile. He liked being near her for all the obvious reasons and held her in high regard. "Mind if I sit?"

"Hi PJ, I'm just looking at the new schedule to see how much my life's about to be disrupted."

"You know, now that we've begun the watch, everyone's schedule will shift. Anyway it's going to mean time off, and that'll be nice, won't it?"

"Yeah, I could use a break."

"Hey I know this is a little forward, but what made you volunteer?"

"Well, nothing made me. I just wanted something more out of life. An adventure, I guess. It wasn't going to happen back home. But out here I get to test myself. You know, follow the road where it leads."

"Me too, especially after a world goes atomic and you get long postings instead of just a quick look." PJ liked the increased responsibility that came with the possibility of intervention, but it was not what was most on his mind. "You thinkin' about takin' any time off?" he asked with hint of expectation. "Maybe we could take a scout and see the sights. Whadaya say?"

Shereen liked PJ but not in the same way he liked her. She didn't encourage his advances even though she felt an urge to be kind. Her brief hesitation told him it was "no" again this time.

"Sorry PJ, I promised Jasca I'd—" She shrugged, regretting she'd said even this much, then looked away as if her mind was elsewhere.

Shereen thought of her last encounter with Jasca and realized she preferred her own company. *No big deal. Mom doesn't like him anyway.*

Rabel Delare was not a fan of the swaggering Jasca, not for Shereen or anyone else. He wasn't nice to women, not down deep. She suspected he secretly feared them, his charm just a mask, so she threw up a shield of discouragement around her daughters.

Shereen's sister Niriar was nine years younger, a fine junior navigator who could be counted on to program the navigational computers while she studied. Filaire, the youngest, liked to stir the pot with questions that probed just a little deeper than was polite. Their father Okuh ran robotic maintenance and Rabel was a culture specialist. All the Delares studied navigation and empathy as their primary specialties and took the obligatory social science courses as well. But it was Rabel who stressed the need to thoroughly study the cultures of those they might shepherd. It was part of the art of empathy that allowed them to appear so genuine among the beings in their care.

The evening found Shereen and Niriar silent and gesturing to each other from adjacent seats on the bridge deck in a syncopated dance. It was Shereen's watch, even if there wasn't much to do because automation monitored traditional functions. She preferred the command chair for its ability to instantly conform to her shape and took her turn with every other adult, making sure things ran smoothly aboard the starcraft. Interstellar was a distinction every member of the crew wore with pride, although displaying pride was discouraged. Their congenial personalities, so useful on long deployments, made command somewhat of a pain and an honor at the same time.

Niriar knew her older sister as kind and generous, and they had become fast friends of the heart. They often thought of their paths and what lay ahead. And because they thought rather than spoke their conversation, the casual observer would have seen them gesturing, silent but for the rustle of their clothes.

I like this body, thought Niriar. *Do you think it looks like the me you know?*

I could pick you out a mile away. You can only alter so much. Why would you want to change?

To cut down on the attention. This world is obsessed with how they look. They covet a perfect form, but few are so lucky. We evolved to this over time. We look this way because we chose to. They have no idea what it will take to reach uniformity.

Frankly I find their differences fascinating, don't you? The different colors and shapes. Just think of how long it's going to be before they blend.

And still just the beginnings of telepathic awareness. There will be Shepherds looking after them long after we've been reabsorbed.

Next to Shereen, steadily blinking status lights flashed for every sentrybot currently deployed. They monitored the relevant indicators of planetary and societal wellbeing from weather to war, from food surplus to famine, gathering as much information as possible about a world while the ship's onboard computers processed the flow in real time. They were central to Planet Watch's purpose. All crew members over the age of 21 were required to be familiar with their function and maintenance.

A flicker from an indicator caught Niriar's attention. "Hey Sher, did you see that on the anti-gravity panel? A little flash of purple?" The sound of her voice broke the silence and the mood.

Shereen turned to look. "There's nothing now and it didn't trip the alarm. Are you sure?"

"It lit up, I swear."

"Alright, I'll let the captain know."

"Before you do, there's something I need to say."

"About what you just saw?"

"About Jasca. You need to stay away from him."

"I know."

"Do you? I think loneliness has clouded your vision Sher. You need to be careful."

"I will. I promise."

7

Out in the Barn

Harry unpinned the clearest picture of the toolbox from the wall above the workbench and put on his magnifiers. His instinct to take lots of pictures before pulling the box from the ground had been right.

Up close, he could see a splash of something reflective peeking out from behind the jumbled contents. It was an oddly symmetrical wave and appeared to originate from more than one point.

"I can't imagine what made this, except some long equation. Damn, I might have scrubbed it off," he said, and pulled the empty toolbox from beneath the bench. He turned on a flashlight and opened the lid, but there was nothing obvious. Just a few shiny beads of mercury that refused to be wiped out of the corners.

He moved his light closer to the edge.

A shimmer came from a high angle that wasn't visible straight on. There it was, part of the wave trapped in the edges where rust met paint. It was time for more pictures.

He hurried from barn to kitchen. "Hi baby, you good?" He used to call her 'baby' back in high school and it always made her smile.

"Hi handsome, we're having chicken for dinner. Is that okay?" She turned to study him, as if his good mood made her suspicious. "What did you come in for anyway?"

"You." He found her waist and pulled his first love and best friend a little closer until they became one being again.

Sometimes they would hold on to each other for what seemed like a minute, just swaying slowly side to side, wrapped around each other smiling, two batteries charging each other. Arney used to tell the boys to just be quiet and not interrupt.

"I came in to see how you were doing and get my point and shoot." He released her and walked into the den, opened the top drawer of the desk and grabbed his camera. "You know I love ya'. See you later hon. Have fun." The spring squeaked and jangled until the screen door closed with its usual bang. "Sorry 'bout the door."

Harry adjusted the empty toolbox for the best light and got some closeup shots. The images were distorted by the rough surface, but he could see the rhythmic pattern in the spray. He took pictures from several angles. A shadow outline of some items inside the toolbox defined where the spray stopped.

It must have hit other surfaces, he thought to himself and carefully inspected each object on the workbench for signs of the toxic metal. Seven had traces, and some showed more of the curiously wavy spray pattern. They too were photographed. He returned the original print to its position on the wall and made room for more. For now, the wavy pattern would be relegated to a pigeon hole marked 'curious.' He slid the empty toolbox back under the bench.

What nagged at Harry didn't have words at first. The toolbox had been a diversion to avoid facing the real mystery. He knew his answer lay in the broken spinner at his feet. He would have to dissect it to learn the cause of its demise, but his flashlight and finger were the only scalpels required. The discs still spun freely but when he looked down from the top he could see the wooden frame was bent as well as cracked. And the electric motors that drove the belts had skewed.

He moved closer. The twist in the spinner had Harry's full attention. *Somethin' bent this bigtime.* But the harder he thought on it, the farther away the answer seemed. Nothing fit. He would have to call for it, something he thought he was good at. At least it had worked before.

He found his beat-up green-and-brown easy chair, leaned back, settled in and closed his eyes. They were old friends.

After a while a low 'om' sound began to rise up out of him, so quiet you had to be close to hear it. Slowly the sound rose in volume. Harry could feel the hum deep in his head as he vibrated himself into a peaceful trance. He had been wrestling with the details all morning. Now it was time to let go and give the idea room.

The words that came between stretches of silence led him on. The next spinner would have to be stronger, better engineered to tighter tolerances and tunable. Then it hit him. *It wasn't badly built, it's the movement.* "That's what I've been looking for!"

His eyes popped open. "You're in there, I know it." He was wide awake and bolt upright, standing with a grin. "I'm gonna find you if it's the last thing I do."

It was an epiphany of sorts, but it didn't answer the engineering questions. He thought about sitting back down to continue, but decided to leave it for deeper sleep. He was looking for something to do with his hands when Arney pulled up.

"Hi Pop. You gonna wipe that shit-eatin' grin off your face and tell me what you've been up to?"

"That ain't polite."

"You oughta' see yourself. I ain't seen you lookin' this happy since you got the old Ford runnin'. Come on, spill it."

"We got some movement."

"What movement? You mean your force?"

"I think that's what broke the spinner. Something powerful.

See? It's twisted."

"Come on Pop. The nuts came loose, or maybe the glue failed. You're gonna hafta' prove it to me."

"Think what you want, jus' sayin' it's in there. You watch."

It took no time to confirm. As soon as Arney looked from above he knew a different force was at work. "Okay Pop. I see what you mean. Some of these pieces of wood are bent when they should've broken."

"Told ya."

It was the impetus they needed. Arney helped his father machine three-eighths-inch thick discs from the scrap metal left over from the first run. The plan was to make as many as they could out of what was on hand.

While Arney cut the mostly round blanks on the bandsaw, Harry roughed and trued and then finished them on the lathe. Metal chips and filings piled up around the chuck end of the table. Truing them to the correct thickness and turning the edges of the circular flats became more time consuming as Harry sought the tighter clearances. What had been haphazard became precise. When there was enough material, they made smaller circles of several different sizes.

By 4:30 in the afternoon the heavy machine noise had stopped and the sweeping, dusting and occasional vacuuming sounds began. Just as the cleanup finished Donna appeared at the barn's side door. "Harry, there are three small boxes and one big one sitting on the porch by the front door. UPS came while you were working, so I told him just to leave them. They're too heavy for me."

"Thanks honey, we'll get them."

The two men brushed the last metal filings from their clothes and walked around the house to retrieve the cartons. "It's too late to start turning more. We'll deal with them in the morning."

"Pop, how are we gonna to test all these discs once we're done machining them?"

"Spin 'em, just like before. I'm going to stack 'em and spin 'em and see what I get. Only they're going to be closer together and faster."

"I don't see how you're gonna to do that."

"Neither do I. I'm workin' on it."

"You don't even know what you're looking for."

"Son, if I knew why I feel compelled, I'd tell you. It's a problem I have to solve. Besides, what am I going to do, farm 'til I'm too old?"

"You're already too old Pop, and you won't stop diggin' into the unknown."

"Call this my retirement. The fields are yours to manage as you see fit. They'll be yours soon enough anyway. You wanna to stay for dinner?"

"No thanks. I gotta' get back, tomorrow's the last day of school. I gotta make sure Jen and the boys are organized. Remember, she graduates Saturday at eleven."

"It's only Wednesday."

"Yeah, but there are clothes to wash, books to return. I don't know if Mark turned in his last assignment. You forget you didn't do this alone. You had Mom."

"Jen helps," Harry reminded his son. "She's great with her brothers."

"I can't lay all this off on Jennifer, even if she does want to be superwoman. I'll be back to help Sunday when they're on vacation."

8

Graduation Day

There's a moment in June when pencils hit desks for the last time. No school tomorrow or the next day, or the next. All the kids wait for the bell. They twist in their chairs and whisper plans behind the doors that won't open as long as they watch the little hands on the clock. They must wait for the chime, the moment of pure joy, easier now that things are about to get a lot better. Then "Brrrrnng" and the stampede begins.

Everyone in the room can feel those bursts of joy, but they dare not name them. That would imply something bigger, a wider sharing. Do their minds connect? Of course they do. Thoughts have force. The children know. Walking home, getting on the bus, climbing into a car with friends, the feeling is the same all over the county. The joy meter just goes way up. The hugs and hoots and yearbook signings, all their happiness flows out to the benefit of all.

You know this because you have done it. You've shared your thoughts with others—mind to mind—when it felt safe, like in that moment of pure ecstasy.

Donna was up early Saturday morning pressing Harry's blue wool suit. When he saw it on the ironing board, he protested immediately. "I don't have to wear that, do I?"

"You do. It's your granddaughter's graduation, and you will honor her by looking your best."

"Honey please, it's June. There's no decent AC in that old gym. I'll roast. I want the sports coat I like, the silk one and my parrot tie. You know that bird makes her smile."

"She laughs at your smart ass. She knows you're a rebel. So's she. Just not today, my love. Today you'll love her best by honoring her struggle to be excellent. Be excellent yourself and dress up, mon cher. If not now, when?

"I'll get a white shirt, button down, and a purple-and-blue pinstripe tie. Will that do ya?"

"It'll do her. She'll know and she'll tell you so."

Harry walked back down the stairs in his underwear. It wouldn't be the first time he'd started cup number three in his boxers. He gazed at the barn through the screen door and resigned himself to waiting. *Back at it tomorrow*, he thought. The coffee maker beeped three times and turned itself off, which prompted Harry to call up the stairs, "Honey, you want more coffee before it gets cold? Donna?"

"Yes?"

"You want more coffee?"

"Yes please."

The wooden stairs creaked as they do when a house is over one hundred years old. His bare feet knew every board.

"Here you go baby. I hope it's the way you like it."

She took a sip, "Thanks my love, you're the best." She paused, as if to savor the taste of warm, dark coffee. "You know, I've been thinking about Luke and Mark, now that Jen's graduating. I think they're going to need some lookin' after when she starts college. She can't drive all that way to school and back, do her homework and then be expected to take care of them too."

"Time they started lookin' after themselves," Harry said. "She's too good to 'em."

"Nonsense Harry. She took over after Louise died when

those boys needed her. Cooked for all of them, kept the house straight. She didn't spoil 'em, just loved them. And I agree with you. They should be doing more, but that's not it. It's the Harlin twins. Jen's been the one keeping their panties on. If the boys are allowed to spend time alone with those two, we'll be great grandparents and their lives will be a mess."

"So what are you thinkin'?"

"I want to bring them over here and keep an eye on 'em. Besides Arney could use a break. He picked up Louise's end the best he could after she died, but he has to work. He can't keep an eye on them all the time."

"Neither can you." Harry wasn't prepared for an invasion of grandchildren. "You look nice in that dress. Let's talk about it when we get back."

The school was twelve miles away, serving students from nearby towns dotting the valley. That meant a long ride for Jen and her brothers as the bus wound its way down dusty roads that tied the farming communities together. He remembered his own journeys. It took a little longer than usual to make the trip but they arrived in time for him to tie his tie, with a little straightening from Donna, put on his coat, and walk in.

Neither of them had still been in school when this building was erected. What remained of theirs lay somewhere beneath their feet, and in pictures on the wall near the trophy case that showed the old building before new construction began. That was thirty-five years ago. New was not what they saw now. Age gave the building some character and dignity. The cement columns and brickwork that had replaced wood and stone were worn down by the abrasion of youthful spin that whittled and polished. They liked it for the children but it wasn't theirs.

Donna saw an animated Barbara Harlin before she saw Luke. Barbara was all over him, making a show of her affection in front of the gathering crowd. Donna thought it unseemly but said nothing, deciding not to be snippy. She scanned the thickets of seniors in their green-and-white robes until she found Jen, happy among friends. Mark was easy to spot standing next to his father who stood taller than all but one other. Near them lingered Kathy Harlin, quieter, more demure and nicer than her sister. If she had to gather one of the twins into the family she preferred it be Kathy.

The sound system squealed as Principal Curry tapped the microphone before urging all to their seats. In time the room settled, giving way to long-winded speeches and homilies that filled the air, which was getting hotter by the minute. Finally it was time for diplomas. Harry loosened his tie, working his way through the alphabet, waiting until he could stand and take his granddaughter's picture. He was proud of her and wondered if she would bristle at the sound of her full name being called over the loudspeaker. Then it was time.

"Jennifer Anne Miller." He rose and took pictures while Arney and the boys stood and whooped in appreciation and Jen's friends cheered.

Her joy was palpable. She beamed with pride and justifiably so. Most of the people in the valley knew something of her struggle to take care of her younger brothers and, to some degree, her father.

Arney wrapped her in his arms, whispering in her ear, "I'm so proud of you. You may be the strongest of us, a great good heart you are, and you have all of mine. Congratulations. Oh and when we get home, I have a little surprise for you."

"What is it Daddy?" she asked, being his little girl for one more moment.

"You'll see."

When they got home, she saw the banner and the cake and the cards from friends, and knew her father had extended himself in a way she'd never seen before. It filled her with new affection. After ice cream and cake she opened her cards, some filled with congratulations and some with money from other relatives. One from her father simply said, 'Look Up.'

"What do you mean look up, Dad?"

"I guess you'll have to use your bright mind and figure that out," he said with an ever-widening smile.

She knew it was a game and decided to take his instruction literally and looked up. Nothing, nothing obvious anyway. She scanned the kitchen ceiling. It looked the way it always did, white with a hint of smoke.

This won't be easy, she thought to herself. *I wonder what he means?* "I guess I have to hunt." It didn't take long. Once she focused her attention, she found the key tucked in with the ribbon that held up the 'Congratulations Jenny' banner. She had walked right under it without noticing. Now it held immense promise. "Oh Dad, if this what I think it is you've solved one of my biggest problems. But I didn't see anything when we drove up. Where is it?"

"Out behind the barn." He grinned and gestured towards the door.

Everyone except Donna followed Jen down the steps and headed for Arney's barn. "Yahoo! Oh, thank you, Daddy! Thank you, this is wonderful." It didn't matter that the jeep wasn't new. It was her first car of her very own. She loved it. She took the key she had teased down from its perch and started the motor. Then with the motor still running she got back out, hugged her father and said "Thanks Dad, this is best gift ever. I love you so."

9

The Top

Sunday morning Harry was back in the barn making discs when Arney showed up.

"Mornin' Pop, you good?"

"Doin' great, fed and rested. How bout you?"

"All good here. You want me to start cutting more blanks?"

"If you don't mind."

"Alright, it's gonna get noisy."

Harry was already drifting away, lost in a whole other process. Testing the metals made the most sense. *These should be relatively easy*, he thought, without knowing why he thought that.

He spent most of the morning stacking and restacking discs on various axles with different lubricants and spacers, until he hit upon a different approach. *If I spin them internally, they could run closer to each other—the way I see them in my dream.* It stopped him. He had to relax and think about it for a moment. And then he decided he needed more than a moment and took a walk down to the garden to calm his thoughts and let the elements of his quandary simmer. It would come.

He was caught by onions. *Inside, it all starts from the inside*, he thought, and then stopped and turned. It would be hard to make.

With each footstep back to the barn he was designing in his head—a center post, then a tube outside that, then another tube outside them both. He could see how motors drove the spinner from below. The center post would be on the bottom. The shorter middle tube would be driven from the middle platform, and the shortest outer tube would be driven from the uppermost and hold the heaviest disk. Bearings set in each platform would stabilize the spin.

As he stepped through the barn door, a flash of inspiration solved the rest of the puzzle. He had it! A borosilicate glass rod, strong as steel, would spin inside glass tubes that had washers of glass fire-joined at the ends to support the metal disks and steadied by nylon bearings under the flanges. It struck him that his design must be like the last few translucent layers deep inside a fresh spring onion. He set about refining his design until hunger called.

He couldn't remember saying goodbye to Arney. *It must have been well after two. I'll call him*, he thought, as the screen door announced his arrival in the kitchen. "Donna? Where are you, baby? Honey?" he called up the stairs.

"Lying down."

"You okay?" he asked when he found her on their bed.

"I'm fine. Yesterday took it out of me, too many people is all."

"How about we go down to the little Italian place in Springdale and grab a bite. No more work for you."

"This is unusual. Sure. I'd like relax. But you're fit to bust trying to tell me something, aren't you?"

"Yeah, truth be told. I have an idea that has promise."

"I see. Well, I appreciate the dinner offer, but I know you. You'll fidget 'til you get back here. Why don't you save this until we have more time to enjoy it. I'll take a rain check. Now, how about going down to the garden and picking some nice tomatoes. I'll make us spaghetti instead."

It was one more reason why he loved her. She saw the truth of a thing and gave the gift that was appropriate, always helping where she could.

Not long after, the smell of onions frying meant something tasty was coming. He offered to help but she liked her space in the kitchen. There was this line. You couldn't see it, but you sure knew when you crossed it. So he sat on a stool and watched as she diced the tomatoes and chopped parsley.

"Don't watch. It's like you're drumming your fingers trying to hurry me."

He raised both hands in surrender and headed to the den. He wasn't offended, and she knew it. After a while she declared the meal ready and served the sauce over homemade noodles to his profound delight. They ate quietly until she asked the pregnant question. "You gonna tell me about it?"

Harry was designing in his head again. "I've figured out how to move 'em."

"Move what?"

"The discs I'm making. Up 'til now I couldn't see the center, but now I think I understand. I can make out it of glass. It feels right. I've gotta go to Bloomington tomorrow and get some stuff. Probably take half the day but it will be faster than having things shipped. In fact I'm going to swing by the college chem lab and see if Wilky won't cut and join the glass washers and tubes for me. A hundred bucks oughta' do it. You want to come?"

"I don't think so. But say hi to the Doc for me," she said picking up the ringing phone. "Oh hello, Arney."

"Hi Mom, is Pop there?"

"He is, just a sec."

"Hi Arn, I meant to call you earlier and apologize. I don't remember saying goodbye."

"Don't worry about it, Pop. You were talking, just not to me. It's no big deal."

One thing the family knew about Harry was that when he was

in his creative zone, you never knew who you were going to get when he came back to conversation. Harry once counted seven different threads of thought running through his mind at the same time, until he realized that he had forgotten to include the thread doing the counting. It was a family joke. How long would he take to answer your question when he was in his zone, if he ever did. Fifteen seconds was average.

"You wanna go to Bloomington tomorrow? I've got to get some things."

"No thanks Pop. If you don't need me I have stuff to do."

"Right, well thanks for your help today and the other good things you do. I'll call you when I get back."

Harry returned, successful, around three the next day. It had turned out better than he planned. With help from Dr. Wilkes at the Richardson Agricultural College they managed to build two different sizes of tubes and rods, despite his old friend's skepticism.

"What are you going to do with these, Harry?" The question shot through him like a bolt.

"I'm going to use them to separate liquids in a fractional distiller." He left out the details, hoping professorial musings would fill in the blanks.

"Interesting idea Harry, but we've known each other too long. You don't expect me to buy that BS, do you? Fractional distiller, my ass. Really, what are you going to use these for?"

"I'm gonna spin some metal discs with 'em."

"Oh Harry, it's okay if you don't want to tell me. I see how it is. Just let me know if it works." Then, without delving further, Dr. Austin Wilkes, Ph.D., Doctor A. to his students, Wilky to his friends, set about helping. They had known each other since grade school, a friendship of mutual respect, easy and without pretense. This time Harry deferred to the good doctor's sense of process.

He insisted on making the first set out of test tubes to save glass. What he learned making the small set he would apply to the larger. Lamp work was his art and Harry marveled at his skill with the torch. Hot blue flame turned the glass orange where the flanges were joined to the top of the hollow tubes. When he finished, two nested sets of hollow glass pillars stood straight and true, glass flanges ringing the tops.

"What do you think Harry? Is this what you had in mind?"

"They're great, Wilky, thanks so much."

He was going to ask how much weight they might support, then realized that would just lead to more questions. After hugging his friend briefly, he closed the door behind him.

The design and assembly of the drive mechanism required most of the next day, but when he was done he could stack and adjust and spin 3 separate disks independently

The first time he spun up one of the empty tubes on its own and heard it sing, it spoke of balance and precision. He knew he was on the right track. His first test with the tin disk on top produced a note so pure and piercing, Harry promised himself never again without earplugs. That was all balanced by the huge grin on his face. "This is working. Come on baby, talk to me."

The way Harry felt about his connection to the elements made talking to a machine seem natural, just different gatherings of the same life force that made up everything as far as he could tell. He talked to every machine he'd ever interacted with. Everybody did it but Harry thought of the connection as another thread of life, and that set him apart.

He learned to keep it to himself, but he knew. There were whisperings to cars, aspirations to crest the hill and make it home, some help with the journey. Of course they were connected. Everything was connected. The question 'How?' might be answered. The question 'Why?' never would. Harry didn't play with the riddle of life, he just accepted that he belonged, intrinsic and necessary in his quest.

Thank God for adjustable bearings, he thought. *This baby's hummin'.* He knew the bearings understood.

Harry took his time fashioning the frame. It had to be capable of adjusting the disks relative to each other so they would spin as close as possible. When each tier of the mechanism hummed, it was time to test three disks together. He ran wiring to the switches and balanced each disk again until there was no wobble, and everything was level. By sundown the spinner and test disks sat ready near the center of the barn floor.

"Tomorrow, I'll light it up tomorrow," he mused with a grin.

When Arney joined his father in the barn the next morning, Harry was already clamping dial indicators into place to measure any movement.

"How many tests are we doin'?"

"The first round has 2,184 possible permutations."

"You've got to be kidding me Pop. We can't test that many."

Harry turned away, not sure of how to proceed. "I could limit this to notes I can tune. Better to be on the safe side."

"Hey Pop, You're talkin to yourself again. You want to let me in on it?"

"Jeez Arney, I'm sorry. But you grew up with this condition."

"Pop, Pop. Easy. I'm just yanking your chain, having a laugh as I bring you back."

"Sorry, I was right in the middle of an answer."

"You get that look."

"What look?"

"That glazed over, not-quite-here look. I know that's when you're doin' your best work. But when you start to mumble I figure you've bubbled back up and you're fair game."

"Fair enough."

"So what do you want me to do?"

"I want you to help me standardize our tests. We need to put our heads together."

"Oh Pop, we've been banging our heads together for years."

"Very funny."

"I see you're using your guitar tuner. You gonna hunt for notes like before?"

"That's the idea, tune up the low disk to the first pure note and then move to the next. When they're all running smooth by themselves, I'll turn 'em all on at once and see what they do. Maybe it's dissonant and maybe it's wonderful. We're gonna find out. Whaddya think?"

"It's a stroke Pop. I kinda thought you were going to try music."

"Thanks. So here's my plan. I want to tune each disk for the naturally resonant note with the most volume. When that's dialed in, we spin them up together. If there's no movement, we let 'em spin down and try another combination of notes. If we get anything at all, we'll test that chord thoroughly. One of us loads, the other logs. It won't be so bad."

"So you say."

"Ready? I'm starting the aluminum at 1 rpm to keep it from slipping."

It took five minutes before the old digital tuner registered anything at all. The mic was close to the disk's edge but the LED's that hopped back and forth were a long way from settling. Until one was steady green, the note wasn't pure. Harry slowed his increase of current until the led remained frozen and bright green. The disk was humming a low C at 981 rpm.

"She's moving too fast. I'm going to cut all the speeds in half so she don't fly apart."

"Won't that make the sounds harder to hear?"

"Don't matter if we hear 'em, we need to see something move."

They settled on speeds fast enough to feel the forces in the machine but not fast enough to break anything. After testing several combinations of disks with no result Arney asked, "Why don't we go back to the first combination and spin the middle disk in the opposite direction?"

"Because that's when the first spinner broke and I'd rather keep testing for the time being. But you're right, I'm going to have to give it a try. Tell you what, turn off the middle disk and when it stops, start it up the other way." As the middle disk began to spin in the opposite direction, there was an unmistakable sound of wood under strain. Not a groan or a crack, just a soft eeking sound that spoke of force.

"Pop, did you hear that?"

"Hear what?"

"Oh Pop really? You didn't hear that?"

"No, I was watching the dials. Nothing moved. What did you hear?"

"A little creaking sound, like the supports were stressing some."

"Probably just settling under the weight and the motion." Harry saw nothing on his dials that suggested anything else.

Aboard the Xelanar, perimeter Anti-Grav Sensor array 631—the problematic, intermittent one—chirped and flashed briefly. It was enough to catch Shereen's eye. She tapped the now dark indicator and thought to leave a message for Kothry Gradel. He and Ella were the ship's anti-gravity specialists. Jasca would need to know as well.

When Shereen told the captain, he immediately ordered a complete review of the data from the four remote arrays. "I want Kothry and Ella to go over the data as soon as they can. Tell them to check it around the same time you saw the flash."

"Right away sir," she answered. "Would you like me to extend my watch and supervise?"

"That won't be necessary. Please ask Mr. Gradel to check the status of the remote sensors."

"Yes sir." Shereen left the captain sitting at the galley counter and returned to the bridge. He was not usually so formal. She hadn't seen such stiffness since the Carei left for home. Whatever prompted his reaction, a broken sensor did not seem that important. She decided to probe his mind gently when he was asleep.

When Kothry arrived for his watch, Shereen greeted her friend, passed him the input tablet, pointed to the offending sensor and wished him good luck.

"Thanks, I'll need it. How many times have I looked at this anyway?" The checklist included a note to read the log and the captain's instructions. He decided to run a loop test on the sensor and the indicator, just to be sure it wasn't a faulty connection. Testing the path to the sensor could be done from the bridge but swapping it out would require working in a tight space near the hull's outer rim.

He started the self-diagnostic program, then began to scan the outboard data. A touch on the viewscreen brought up the four streams from the anti-grav sensors aboard the bots. After synchronizing them, it wasn't easy to find anomalies.

"What do you see?" the captain asked as he walked in and looked over Kothry's shoulder.

"Not much sir. They collected this stuff because we set a low threshold, but after they were triggered all we got was hash. Think of it as a low hum that rises and drops, a very small wave. Kind of reminds me of a flare or shielding bounce-back."

"Do we have a fix on the source?"

"Not really, same as before, somewhere in the middle of America. It's too diffuse to be certain."

"Alright, do me a favor and increase their sensitivity. I want every whisper."

"Yes sir." Kothry answered the captain quickly, having gotten the word from Shereen that he was having one of those days.

"Where are the remote sensors now?"

"Safely out of reach sir. We're covering the widest area we can."

"Please move them closer. Concentrate around the last known signal. A hundred twenty miles above the surface should do. No atmospheric disturbance though. Hide them in the orbital debris. We don't want to stir up the natives. And Kothry, you won't like this but I need you to replace the outer 631 array with a spare. If it's too cramped, program a bot. Let's eliminate as many variables as we can. I don't need to be dealing with a faulty sensor."

"Right away sir."

10

Marathon

For the next three days, Harry and Arney tested combinations of metal discs, a boredom interrupted by switches turned on, then off, disks spun up, then down. The repetition weighed on their humor and after a while, they emptied what was left of a case of Coors. Then they bought another. The next day it was hard to tell how much attention they were paying. Occasionally the spinner would creak and they thought enough of it to note the combination and spin direction, but since the dial indicators didn't budge it seemed less relevant.

On the third day Donna was the only one who ate breakfast. The two men were sleeping it off, Harry in his bed and Arney on the couch, never having made it up to the spare bedroom which used to be his. Two days of overindulgence had its price. Arney was up by eleven, back aching and in a "What was I thinking?" frame of mind. Harry didn't get up until noon. When they saw each other in the kitchen, Arney spoke to the obvious. "You look terrible Pop."

"So do you, just younger. Is there any beer left? A little hair of the dog would be good."

"We drank it all last night. Don't you remember?" watching closely to see if his father was serious.

"No matter, some brandy in my coffee'll fix me up."

Donna kept the Hennessy in the antique mahogany breakfront. He returned from the dining room with his prize, and the two men began to analyze the previous day. "Sometimes I thought I could feel a little push in the supports when they groaned but that was it. I checked the dial indicators. They never budged. Did you feel anything?"

"Besides drunk? Not really. You know Pop, except for the wood creaking I thought it was all unremarkable. Finish your coffee. We'll go out, look at our notes and see what we can figure."

Empty Coors cans flashed their silver and blue beacons through gaps in the baffles. Harry decided not to disassemble them even though they seemed useless in the absence of results and set about cleaning up. They filled half a trash can with empties. It had been fun even if they were still paying the price.

Harry listed all the times they had heard a creak—seven for sure and two maybes—while Arney gave the machinery the once over. "You know Pop, this is really smooth running." He looked at the topside of the spinner, thinking ever more highly of his father's craftsmanship. He knelt down to check the underside of the drive mechanism. "Hey Pop, come take a look at this. See this dowel that's popped up a little? You didn't leave it this way on purpose, did you?"

"Come on A, you know me better than that. Every joint was glued and pinned. I wouldn't leave a dowel popped up. Where is it?"

"Right here where my finger is. In fact, I think I see another one. Hand me that flashlight, will you? Look at this. There are at least six I can see that have popped a little. I think we've found our squeak."

"Not so fast. What made them do that? Vibration? This thing's running like a top. I'm not sure vibration could do all that."

"Sure it could, sympathetic waves in the right material."

"I suppose it's possible but whatever it was, I can't bang those dowels back down without screwing up the balance. It's running smoother than ever. What I can do is retest the combinations that squeaked and see if they make more noise. And I'm going to reduce the space between disks, get 'em as close as I can and see if that helps."

"Knowin' you it probably will, but since you won't need me for—"

"Say no more. I appreciate your help these last few days and I haven't had that much fun gettin' sauced in a long time. But you're right, there's no need for you to stay. Go rescue Jen from her burdens and blame me."

"What? And admit you run my life, I don't think so." They hugged, and Arney left through the back door to get his bike from the garage. When the motor finally smoothed out from days of sitting, Arney pulled up near the side door and yelled, "Bye Pop, I'll call you tomorrow." Then the motor growled and he was gone.

Harry wished he hadn't sold his softtail Harley. The memory of tarmac rolling beneath his feet put him back out on the road, in freedom. *Ah well.* He spent the rest of the day taming his indigestion and lowering the tubes until the disks they supported barely had air for bearings, just a sliver of light in the gap between them. When he was satisfied, he loaded nickel, copper and zinc next. He spun them and noted the creaking sound once again, but louder than before. He wrote down his results and pondered their meaning until a late afternoon nap claimed the rest of the day. By dinner he had regained his appetite.

"Think we could finish up the rest of the pizza so that I can get the boxes out of the fridge?" Donna asked trying to solve her own problems.

"I don't think my stomach can handle a re-pizza."

"Harry that's terrible."

"I thought it was funny."

She made him chicken soup with crackers and a salad on the side in deference to his impairment. "Feeling better now?" Donna inquired with a knowing voice.

"I'm alright, but I think I'm hittin' the sack early. Maybe watch a little TV in bed, smoke some grass, have a little party and nod. Whadaya say, want to join me?"

"Does a bear—? Never mind. Let me finish washing up. Get out the good stuff, will you?"

With dishes drying, Donna followed Harry up the stairs to their bedroom, looking forward to getting high. "Did you bring whatever it was we smoked last time? What did you call it?"

"It was either Eddy Kickass or Chem Dog."

"Whatever it was, I just remember I couldn't move. It's just what I need tonight."

Harry sat on the bed and started pulling apart a fat bud of Kickass that stuck to his fingers, prepping the bits of flower and sugar leaf and dropping them carefully onto a cigarette paper. Then he rolled, licked the glue, sealed the edge and finished the ends with a twist and handed his prize to Donna.

"Here you go honey, you have the first hit."

"No, you made it. You go first."

Harry lit it with his old Zippo and took a hit, held it and then let out a cloud of sweet blue smoke. "Damn, that's good." They passed it back and forth the way they had ever since high school, coughing and laughing at what good shit it was. Half an hour after the roach clip hit the ashtray the flower children were asleep and snoring softly.

At breakfast the two silver heads smiled at each other in the knowing way couples do when they've been together a long time. They shared something special. "Are you at it again all day?" Donna asked inquisitively.

"Yes honey. Forgive me, my brain won't stop. I'll see you

around lunch unless you need me to do something. Just come get me. You know I'm yours when you need me."

He rose from the table and headed to the barn. Nothing about the previous day's results was definitive. Maybe the creaking meant something, maybe it didn't. Harry aimed to find out.

He walked through the barn door and was bowled over by the obvious. *I just assumed it was sideways. That's what the toolbox...* He stopped in mid thought. "Vertical, I forgot the third axis. Dumb. I hate wasting my own time. Dumb, dumb dumb."

Harry saw his mistake, but it wasn't what bothered him. It was the rest of the puzzle he might have overlooked. "Assumptions, the perennial killer. I think it, therefore it must be so. Crap, all bullshit. Like I whispered it in my own ear and fell for it once again. Bad enough everyone else is trying to brainwash me, when I do it to myself."

If logic required an outlet Harry would do better than most, though not as good as some. He hated chess but loved to innovate. New, different, something he had never seen before, those were the doors to his mind. There wasn't just one vision, there were lots of them. Harry just knew stuff. He could sense an answer without having to put the logic into words. But this time flightiness had gotten in the way of the rational. He set up his last dial indicator so that it would measure a vertical rise.

I wonder if it flies? he thought.

Loading discs into the spinner required finesse now that the spacing was tighter. Harry decided to retest the first combination of disks that creaked. When the tin disk was almost at speed, the whole upper section of the spinner groaned and creaked, then the power shut off.

Harry looked around. The lights were out. "Damn, I've blown a breaker." He pulled the power cable from the spinner and reset the breaker for the bench circuit, then realized the barn's main breaker had also tripped. *That's not right*, he thought. But when he reset the main breaker and the overhead lights came back on, he let it go. That is until he saw the pointer on the vertical dial gauge showed the stack had moved up by 1/64th of an inch.

"Well hello. There you are."

At nine Arney's motor quieted to a sputter and stopped just beyond the side door. "Mornin' Pop, how ya doin?"

"I'm real good. Come look at this." He pointed to the needle that showed how much it had moved.

"Are you telling me you got vertical deflection?"

"As a matter of fact. Look at this. The whole mechanism has loosened. I didn't think to test for vertical, but that's what we've got."

"We've been starin' down the wrong rabbit hole. Sure explains those squeaks."

"Might have been sooner if I had thought to test for a rise. I'm going to have to scrounge some nylon collars off some of those old rods and see if I can't keep these disks from separating. I'll be back in a minute." Harry returned minutes later with a handful of stop collars in various sizes. "A couple of these should do."

The two men set about unloading the spinner, setting stop collars on the shafts and tightening the undercarriage. Then they reloaded. The spacing between the discs had changed.

"Will it work like this?" Arney watched his father's face for any sign of doubt.

"Don't know son. I think so. The collars will keep the tubes from rising and the rubber cement will keep the disks on long enough to find out. This machine's been talkin' to us all along. One thing I see is it keeps wanting to straighten itself out, runnin' smoother when it shouldn't, like it's gathering itself. If it wants to rise like this, let's at least see if we can keep it together when it does. Besides, what do we have to lose now that we're gettin' some action? I think it's just a matter of time.

How 'bout it, you ready?"

"Ready as I'll ever be. Think we should stand back?"

"Yeah maybe. I'm going to hit all three switches at once, instead of one after another. We haven't tried that."

The sound was short and high-pitched. The three disks hopped a foot off the spinner and rolled away in different directions.

"What happened?" Arney asked as the last of the disks came spinning down to rest on the floor.

Harry just said, "Hot damn! That's what I've been waitin' for."

11

Fresh Eyes

Kothry wriggled and shifted his thin frame until he had extricated himself from the ship's rim. The robot sent to repair the 631 detector array got stuck, forcing him to wedge his body into the small space in spite of his best efforts to avoid it. As soon as he had completed the repair and retrieved the robot, he unwound himself, stretched and spoke to Jasca. "It's hooked up sir. We shouldn't have any more problems. Light her up and let me know."

"It's testing green; range is good. Nice job."

When Kothry reappeared, Ella joined them. "Oh good Ella, thanks for helping. Look, onboard arrays have been down almost four hours now. I want you to recalibrate the detectors and download anything the remotes gathered while we were blind. Is that clear?"

"Yes sir," they answered almost in unison."

"Got a preference?" Kothry asked Ella. "If you don't, I'll download and analyze while you recalibrate."

"Sounds good to me. Means I can watch the spaghetti sauce."

When Kothry finished downloading the files, he found more noise than data. The increase in sensitivity resulted in lots of small pulses that quickly died. He messaged the captain in his quarters.

Ducar appeared in a bathrobe and slippers. "Show me," he said.

"It's here, captain. See how we get the same diffuse signal as before, except there are a lot more of these little rises. I think it's because we lowered the input threshold. Now they are picking up every little wave. The only exception is this last blip here. It's a little bigger than any of the rest, but it still has that diffuse signature."

"Where are they coming from?"

"Same place as before, middle of the continent somewhere."

"We need to get closer. Kothry, bring out four more anti-grav sensor arrays and strip them of their shielding. I want them charged and calibrated. Then you and Jasca are going to hide them on the surface. There's no need to waste power on propellant."

Anti-gravity detectors by their nature were hard to power. Most everything of appreciable size had a small shielded anti-gravity stack motor as a power source, but the detectors couldn't use them. Even with shielding, they emitted enough residuals to give the detectors fits, so fuel cells, batteries and solar panels were preferred.

It was a chore traipsing around an alien planet in the dark but they wouldn't be submerged, so both men looked forward to it. "I need the other two arrays and a block of Syngel please. I don't want to run out of food."

"How many blocks did you say?" Kothry asked.

"Better make it two, will you? If we're going to be stuck out all night, we might as well enjoy ourselves."

"Amen to that. Anything else?"

"Yeah, more power cells for the night vision? We don't want to light up the landscape."

Getting off the lake bottom was a relief. For the moment Kothry didn't mind being the grunt. He had danced this dance before. After all, rank had privilege and Jasca helped load, but Kothry was usually the heavy lifter.

When their checklist was complete they dimmed the lights and slipped through the field interface that separated air from water, into the depths. The ascent to the surface was easy as the two Aleri transformed into men. They would limit their appearance and their senses to that of their surroundings. For all intents and purposes they were people of Earth, except that they were not. Better to be completely assimilated if discovered. No one would be the wiser. Two government pilots who would not talk about their craft. The scout could be written off as an experimental aircraft. It was standard protocol.

"Where is our first drop point sir?

"Lose the sir, please. We've been doing this too long."

"In deference to our first away mission this tour, that's all. For old time's sake," Kothry said, settling into the copilot's seat.

"On your viewscreen south of those lakes in America, all points are in sequence. We should be done in about 4 hours, in the dark the whole way."

"I'm for that, like the captain says. We don't want to stir up the natives."

"Exactly. Alright, night vision in the main viewports please. Egress is green. Let's take it slow and easy." An increase in buoyancy and the impulse engine saw the two-man scout safely to the twenty-meter mark. It cloaked and broke the surface unseen in a slight fizz.

"I'm glad to see the sky. Thanks for getting me off the ship tonight. Down that deep, there's nothing to see."

"I know, you can only watch those forest and garden sequences so many times. But hey we'll be back in moonshadow before you know it, just as soon as the captain gets over his obsession with a few little anti-gravity waves." He turned off night vision and the viewport cleared. They flew cloaked across the lake and then across farms and fields.

"Jasca, this is a gift. Not many lights out here, mostly farmland and peaceful people, I would think."

"They're well intended, about where we were at this stage of development. They're utterly afraid of those who don't look just like them. If they don't kill each other off, they might be okay. It's just a matter of how long their social development takes."

"Grow up or fry, right?"

"Same for all of us, but they need to step up the pace. If the captain is right, their science is way out in front of their social skills, and we all know where that leads."

"A lot of worlds just go boom."

"Yeah they do, and it isn't pretty. Don't get me wrong, I like this place. I hope they make it, but we're going to do what we have to, regardless. Here we go, touching in five, four, three."

The scout came quietly to rest in middle of a small, dark valley. Night vision showed an escarpment that looked promising. It would only take a few moments to dislodge the odd bird's nest and conceal the sensor where no one could find it. As the cargo door hissed softly open a pale purple shimmer marked the edge between the cloaked exterior and the shifting reality of Kothry's movement. He pulled a small sensor array from its restraint and closed the door.

The escarpment was a minute away when Jasca's thoughts intruded. "There are two natives, two teenage boys looking at you right now. Hold your position and don't open the cargo door again until I give the all clear."

"Thanks for the heads up. I'll just sit here and enjoy the scenery." Kothry's uniform generated a 3D Holographic image that rendered all but his eyes and mouth invisible. If he didn't move, he was the hill he sat on.

"They've started the engine on their vehicle. It looks like they're going down the far side of the hill. I'll let you know when it's clear."

Kothry resumed his short climb. He was sure he would

disrupt a bird family as he removed the nest but to his relief when he reached in, it was empty. With a little pressure the sensor found a new home for a while. "It's on, want to test it?"

"All good, come on back."

Kothry skittered and slid down the gravel slope leaving a trail of small stones tumbling after him. Then the cargo door opened and closed, and they were gone.

"That's one," he said to Jasca as they rose up over the countryside. "Sure is a shame to waste such a beautiful planet on these violent beings."

"I admit their chances aren't good, but what can you do? We're here to help even if the odds are against them. It's not so much that they're mean, they just hang onto their ignorance with a vice-like grip. And they're easily persuaded. Tell them the same lie often enough, they'll swear to it. They don't even bother to find out the truth. They just repeat things like the birds they call parrots. The lack of skepticism is quite remarkable. That's why the Cultural Science report is so pessimistic."

"Well, if they ever give up this planet, I wouldn't mind moving in. It's a beautiful place."

"If they keep going the way they are, you won't have long to wait. They're so busy starving and burning. They see the poor as a disease and they have to reduce consumption, but they would rather murder than share. So we're here to contain."

"Truth be told, I joined up to get away—see the stars and have an adventure, you know? It wasn't noble. It was an escape and I'm glad I reached for it because I love it out here. If I can do some good that's great, but it's not why I came."

"You know Kothry, you might be more of a romantic than I am. We all made the same choice, somewhere deep down. You look up at the sky and think—I want to be out there. Some of us become Shepherds because that's the vehicle that makes it possible."

"It's less noble than I thought in the face of such a grand

vision but what can you do?"

"Your job is to do good. That's your job. So be as good as you can be. Shepherds don't allow pretenders on board an interstellar. I know what you're saying. Puts those beings down there in perspective, doesn't it? We got lucky. We had a head start. So here we are raising children. It's a job. Doing good got you this ride tonight. Here's your sky."

"I'm just pushing for the truth."

"I know."

They spent the next three hours placing sensors to ring the area of Ducar's interest. It didn't matter to Kothry that Jasca thought the whole idea a bit over-reactive. It wasn't his call to make. Set the anti-grav sensors out in a well disguised location and turn them on. Done. It was a nice ride in the clear air but Jasca had become his boss again and he was glad it would soon be over.

12

The Wedge

The boys' world was mostly confined to the distance they were willing to pedal and how far they could see beyond that. There were good retreats in the fields and woods nearby but if they wanted space to dream they went up to the wedge, a limestone outcrop in the middle of a logged-out field that offered an uninterrupted view of the sky.

It was too far for bikes, especially at night, which meant begging their father and borrowing the ATV. Then there was the race to climb to the top of the triangular rock to see who would get to the comfy spot first. No matter who wound up where, there was enough flat space that both boys could lie on their backs without touching each other. During the day the raft of flat rock seemed trapped in the field of stumps, but at night it was a gateway to the stars.

Lying on his back, Luke could see them from the top of his toes around to the tips of his fingers. If he rolled over, he could see the silhouette of the hills behind his head cut out the rest of the sky. He and Mark spent many summer evenings gazing into the heavens, brimming with promise and possibilities. They knew the names of the constellations and the seasons when they could see them.

They knew when and where to look for the low orbiting satellites that turned over in the distant light slowly blinking on and off as they passed overhead. It was a source of friction and of pride as they pushed to see whose prediction would be the most accurate. It mattered that they knew, because it freed them from a life of corn.

Wednesday night, a week before the last Fourth of July of the twentieth century, the boys were on the wedge looking northwest. Each had chosen a point on the far ridge where the satellite would appear at exactly 9:41 p.m. Twigs propped up with pebbles at the far edge of the outcrop marked their predictions. A natural fissure in the stone served as the other end of the sight. The twigs were close, to be sure, but there would be no winner this night. As they crowded close to their gunsight notch to check the top of the twigs, the air in front of the hills shimmered. It wasn't a heat wave, although it had that shape. And it wasn't lightning, although it had an iridescent shimmer. It came from below, more a blend of the two, and all the while they could still see the hills beyond.

"Did you see that? What the hell was that?" asked Mark in a voice well above a whisper.

"I don't know, man, but we missed making the call tonight 'cause the Intel bird's over here now."

"Man, I've never seen anything like that, have you?"

"Maybe somebody's testing something. Can you still see it in your mind?"

"Sort of. Sure was different." Mark slid off the rock and started for the top of the escarpment, which wasn't so much a cliff as the top of a small landslide that had been there forever, or so it seemed to him.

"Hey, where are you going?" Luke used his best big-brother, I'm-in-charge voice to reign his brother in, to no avail. He would have to chase.

"Race ya." Mark yelled back, knowing he already had an

unbeatable lead.

They legged it out, and it was close. Each stopped a little short of the rim so as not to fall over, not that it would be fatal if they did. Shoes full of sand and gravel were the price. They peered into the valley together.

"I don't see a thing down there," Mark whispered.

"Me neither. Let's go home before it gets too late." Luke lingered before he spoke, and Mark knew his brother was thinking about what they'd seen. The ride home was always slower than the ride up. What was easy in daylight was harder at night, an adventure in downhill path slalom and back road.

After finishing the course, they parked the ATV and went into their house, which was smaller than their grandparents' but newer. It wasn't near as drafty, and the kitchen just adequate, although neither boy cared much about that. They did like having a large refrigerator though, more room for ice cream.

Dinner sat cold on the table. Arney was at his father's and Jen had a date, rare as it was. The note pinned to the board said it all. 'Heat it or don't. Eat it or don't. Jen.' She had that dry humor that was half push, half laugh.

"Damn, Dad's gonna be pissed we're late. Oh well, let's stick these in the oven and warm 'em up."

"Works for me."

They ate a lukewarm plate of ham and mashed potatoes that must have been better when it was hot. Jen could cook, but not like Grandma.

Arney came through his kitchen door around 10:15. The boys heard his motor stop and were busting with stories to tell. "Dad, Dad, we saw something up at the wedge," Mark almost shouted in enthusiasm.

"Whoa, slow down. Let me get my boots off and put my dogs in the breeze. I've been standing most of the day. Nothin' you've got to tell me's going to change the world tonight."

"Come on, Dad."

"Luke, do your old man a favor and get me a beer from the fridge. Then you and your brother clean up these dishes. Jenny's doing all the cooking. She shouldn't have to wash, too. And pass me the bottle opener, will you?" Luke handed his father a cold, long-neck Coors and the wooden handled bottle opener. "Thanks. Now help your brother dry those dishes and then we'll talk." It was half past ten when the boys finished, still bustin' to tell their tale. "Alright, what's going on? What do you want to tell me?"

"We saw somethin' up at the wedge." Mark said still a bit breathless with excitement.

"Let me tell him," Luke interrupted.

"Okay boys, one at a time. You'll both get your chance I promise. Mark you start."

"Well, we were on top of our rock watching for satellites, you know the game we have. Anyway, it was almost time and we were sighting our twigs through the notch when the air shimmered."

"What do you mean shimmered? Like a heat wave?"

"No Dad, this was different. It glowed."

"Probably just a fire and some hot smoke. I wouldn't worry about it."

"It wasn't a fire, Dad," Luke interjected. "It was purple, and the wave had a funny shape."

"Hey Buttball, I was talking. Let me tell it."

"Calm down. Luke, let your brother finish."

"Don't call me Buttball!" said Luke, getting his licks in before Mark resumed.

"Boys, please. Go ahead Mark, finish telling me what you saw."

"Well, like I was sayin' the air got wavy and it glowed. Not like smoke, more like water waves except they wiggled back and forth. Oh, and they were colored like Luke said, kind of purpley, but you could still see through 'em."

"Okay Luke, what can you add?"

"They were strange, Dad. Not like any waves I've ever seen. They were bigger at the bottom and they got smaller as they went out and closer together. And they glowed from the bottom up, so it couldn't have been heat lightning or anything like that. When we got to the edge of the rim to see what it was, there was nothing—no cars, no fire, nothing."

"I sure wish I'd been there. Right now, I have no idea except maybe you saw the headlights of a car that was gone by the time you got there. Other than that, your guess is as good as mine."

"I could try to draw a little of it for you," Mark said, "the wave I mean, if you want. It looked kinda like an S, only a lot of 'em strung together and squashed flat. And it was moving. The waves were tradin' places with each other, sometimes slow and then a little faster. And Dad, it didn't feel safe."

"Luke did you see that, too?"

"Yeah, Mark's got it right for once. Hey just kidding. Go ahead, draw it out so Dad can see it. He'll get it if you show him."

"I can see it. Your description was precise just like I taught you, but go ahead. Draw what you saw."

Mark fetched paper and pencil and sat down at the kitchen table in his father's chair. It spoke to the serious tone in his father's voice and the measure of respect conferred. He leaned into his task alternately moving in close and then leaning back to get a wider view, careful to keep his wrist loose and pull the curves from his elbow to keep them smooth. The pencil lines had a grace about them. Sinuous curves captured the feel of the waves more than the look, but they were close enough that Arney could sense something unique.

"We're takin' this up and show your grandfather in the morning."

"Are we telling him everything?"

"Everything. I want you to tell him what you saw. Now do me a favor, finish cleaning up and get yourselves to bed. You did a good job, guys. That's the way to stay sharp. Keep your eyes peeled. It'll keep you safe on the land. Now go on, get to bed the both of ya."

In five minutes, the last of the dishes were in the cupboard and the counter and table wiped clean. From the porch the sound of feet on stairs told him his boys were aligned without rancor, happy to be in his care. It pleased him that he didn't hear more "Aw Dad do we hafta's?"

Jenny drove up in her jeep a half hour later.

"Glad you're back," Arney said. "I was just thinking about you."

"Why, am I late?"

"Nothing like that. I was just sitting here thinking how much I owe you for all you've done for us."

"I love my new jeep."

He gathered his daughter in a hug and said, "Jennifer Anne, I stole a piece of your childhood, and for that I will forever be sorry. You have become a strong, loving, generous woman well before your time, in spite of circumstance. What a gift you are."

"It wasn't your doing, Dad. What were you going to do, stop farming? Don't fret so. I didn't pay the price you think. I love who I've become."

"I love you too, couldn't be prouder. Now run along to bed. It's late."

Arney was a better parent than he knew. His children trusted his heart and mind and they could talk to him. They were friends, so rare in teenagers. They felt no need to rebel and worked toward a common purpose. He smiled slow and deep as he gathered them in his thoughts. "*Sweet dreams,*" that's what Louise would say.

The next morning Luke came busting through his grandfather's barn door. "Grampa, you out here? Oh, hi! I didn't mean to disturb you."

"What time is it?"

"Quarter to ten maybe. Dad said we should come over and tell you what we saw last night."

"That sounds important. Why didn't you just call?"

"It was late. Dad sent us to bed."

"Well alright, boys, sit down over here." He pointed to an old church pew he had shortened to fit the space. "Either of you want a soda?"

"Yeah that'd be great," piped up Mark. "Got any Dr. Pepper?"

"Maybe. Here's a nickel. See what you can find." Sodas hadn't been a nickel since 1959, but tucked next to the side door was the oldest Coke machine they had ever known. They loved it.

When they were back on the bench, Harry asked. "So?"

Luke didn't hesitate. "So, we were up on the wedge last night checking out satellites and we saw something strange."

"Strange how?"

"It was a wave. Actually lots of waves, in the air. They were purple and wiggled."

"Well lotsa' stuff wiggles."

"Not like this Grampa. These were wide at the bottom and skinny on top. They were squished together in the upper parts and looked like they were always trying to trade places. Oh, and it was purpley and blue coming up from the valley. But by the time we got to the edge there was nothing."

"I don't suppose you took a camera?"

"No, but Mark drew it. Show him Mark."

Mark reached into the back pocket of his jeans and pulled out the carefully folded drawing. "Check this out Grampa," he said, unfolding his prize. "Whaddya think it is?"

Harry sat down. He could feel the small hairs on his arm standing at attention as he slowed his breath. "Where did you say you saw this?"

"At the wedge." Mark seemed anxious for another chance to contribute. "And I ran as fast as I could to get a look, but there was nothing to see. So when we got home, Luke said I should draw it. So I did, as much as I can remember anyway."

"You boys did a fine job. There's just one thing I want you to do."

"What's that?" asked Luke

"Keep this to yourselves."

"That's funny, we were kinda thinkin' you'd say that."

"Listen, is your father home?"

"Yeah. You want me to go in and call him?"

"Naw, you boys run along home. I'd like to keep this drawing, if it's okay. I'll give it back when I'm done."

"Don't worry. We thought you might want it Grampa," Luke said, taking a little more than his share of the credit.

Harry wasn't fooled. "Nice job, Mark. You're getting better, aren't you?"

"A little." He grinned.

Two hours later, Arney came, muddy boots and all, through the side door and sat down in the same pew the boys had vacated. "I sent the boys on ahead. Hope you didn't mind. Figured it was better if they told their own story. Hey Pop, do you ever keep beer in there?" gesturing toward the coke machine.

"No. You wouldn't want the boys buying beer for a nickel, would you? Just soda, beer's in the fridge."

"You sit. I'll get us some coffee. What did you think of the drawing?"

"Tell ya when you get back. And wipe your feet."

After Arney returned and regained his seat Harry stood straight up. "Look at this." He pushed his clearest picture of mercury splash so close to Arney's nose that he had to lean back to grab it.

"Good Lord Pop, what's this a picture of?"

"A splash of mercury in the toolbox. I noticed it when I was taking stuff out, but didn't pay it no mind then. But now— son, there's something spooky here. Whatever made this made that too, same shape and everything." He held up the picture and the drawing, side by side.

Arney already had the feeling they had pushed too far into something they shouldn't be fooling with. He wasn't one to run but he stood wary in the moment, wondering. "What do you think it means? You ever seen anything like this before?"

"I don't know yet, and yes."

"What do you mean yes? Yes, like you have seen this before?"

"These might be the shapes I saw in a dream, two dreams actually. Well, maybe more. They do look like these traces of mercury. And as to your first question I think the mercury's got somethin' to do with the movement we've been seein'."

"Can't be Pop. We weren't near any mercury during those earlier runs."

"We'll see. Let's think this out. Hand me that copper disc, will you?" Arney placed it in his father's outstretched hand. "And the eye loupe in the top drawer too. I want to get a closer look." He pushed a lock of silver hair aside and peered through the lens at the copper surface, moving himself and the disc and loupe until he had the light just right. "Clean as a whistle."

"Told ya'."

"Not so fast. I'm not done." After carefully scanning both sides, he shifted his weight. "Don't make sense. It's got to be here somewhere." He bent toward the lens again. Then he tilted it slightly to get a better look at the inside edge of the center hole and grinned.

"What does?" Arney asked.

"Check this out. Look at the inside edge of the center hole. Whadda ya see?"

"Dirt, a little oil maybe."

"That's not oil. It's amalgam, mercury joined to the copper surface in a thin film. Question is, how'd it get here?"

"Did you wear those gloves over on the lathe when you were cleaning out the toolbox?"

"Jeez Arney, you're absolutely right. I put one finger over

every one of those holes when I was pickin' them up." Harry paused. Arney could tell he was off somewhere else. "Reversing the copper wasn't the cause of them hoppin' off just now."

"Didn't you think reversing was part of your answer?"

"I'm not so sure now. Look at the corrosion on this aluminum disc. Mercury ate the inside of the hole. I think they wobbled off when they became out of balance."

"What about all the other ones that creaked? Is it the mercury, or you reversing a layer?"

"I don't know yet, but I'll bet we find a little mercury on all the combinations that creaked. We need to check." It took less than ten minutes to confirm Harry's hypothesis. Traces of mercury were on all of them. "Can you hang around this afternoon? I want to try something."

"Alright, but let me call Jen and give her a heads up. I've been leanin' on her lately, so I owe her a break. I'll let 'em eat out tonight. She can drive. Besides, she likes showin' off her new ride."

While Arney was on the phone, Harry retrieved the bottle of mercury from the cabinet and Q-tips from their box on the shelf. In spite of the force required to pop the discs off their supports, they left the spinner going straight up, which meant the glass tubes were still intact. Harry loaded the copper disc onto the middle support and set it spinning slowly.

A little bit is all I need, he thought, opening the jar and dipping the cotton into the liquid metal. *Half an inch wide maybe.* The Q-tip brought up little silver beads that he blended together until he had a thin band of mercury shimmering from the center outward. Spinning it made it easier to get a uniform coating, now dulling slightly as it bound itself to the copper.

"Did you get her?" he asked as Arney appeared again.

"Yeah, she's got it covered and thanked me for the break. It's pizza and a movie in town later. What's that?" He pointed to the mercury on the copper disc.

"I gave it a little go juice and swapped zinc for the aluminum. Let's stack 'em up the way we last had 'em and see what happens. Same deal, a little contact cement, then spin 'em up slow, but all together like we did before. 'Cept this time the middle layer's in reverse."

"You sure about reverse, Pop? You remember last time."

"Goin' with my gut here, boy. Just got a feelin'. Another cup of coffee went down while they waited for the contact cement to get tacky. Then, it was time. "Okay let's do this. You ready?"

"As soon as I find some cover."

The two men crouched behind the baffles as Harry slowly turned up the current.

"Crack!" Splinters of wood fell through the dusty air, illuminated by a shaft of afternoon sunlight that shone through the new hole in the roof.

"What the hell!" Harry was already heading for the door.

"It's gone Pop. Went straight up, all of it. I don't see those discs anywhere."

"Come on outside."

The contrail of water vapor was plainly visible, except that it had no end. As high as the eye could see, the thin sunlit plume was being pulled into streamers of waves that changed places.

"Lucky there's some clouds today or that woulda' stuck out like a sore thumb. Where do ya' think it went?" Arney asked head bent back.

"Don't know. It's out of sight. Straight up. Didn't curve like a rocket, but it worked boy, it fuckin' worked! We're going to have to make more discs."

"What worked Pop? How ya' gonna contain that? You don't even know why it moves."

"It flies son, it flies. But you're right. I'm gonna have to sleep on it tonight."

13

Here We Go

The night before, Kothry was happy to see the level of lake water rise in the scout's viewport. "I'll be glad to see my bunk. Too much work crawling over unfamiliar terrain in a new body."

Then Jasca chimed in, "And racing to beat the sun doesn't make it easier."

That was the straw that did it. "Nothing makes it easier ," he said, restraining his urge to think *Bullshit!* Kothry was pissed. Whatever was making Jasca angry had begun to spill all over him. Jasca had pushed him out the cargo bay door at every stop, sensor array in hand. He had climbed trees and hills and rappelled down a rock face to find secure hiding places for the sensors. He couldn't wait to be done. Another effort to be nice had been met with friendly noises and way too much work. He concealed his irritation. Only thirty seconds and the airlock would clear.

Jasca didn't wait for the hiss of the door seal before pushing Kothry one more time. "Tell Ella to test the input streams on all the arrays before you hit your bunk. Make sure we don't miss anything."

"Yes sir." Kothry let formality speak to his mood. It was a

choice to be civil. Getting in Jasca's face could wait. The sound of gas stopped, and green indicators glowed over the airlock doors. He left to find Ella.

She was in the galley humming softly as she tended what would be dinner. "You start early, don't you?"

"You have to if you want good marinara. Roast them slow, Mama used to say."

"Jasca wants you to test the outboard sensor arrays as soon as you can."

"Alright, I"ll turn this down and do it right away. Anything I should know?"

"No, Just the standard sweep. My brain wants shuteye. Call me if you need me."

"You get your rest. I'll be fine." She smiled and sent a thought that spoke to what she knew of Jasca's nature.

Thanks, Ella, he thought and headed down the back corridor to his quarters. Aleri interstellars, even the smaller bells, were known for their well-designed accommodations, carefully placed amenities, a comfortable mattress and viewports that could display vistas that made them feel bigger than they were. Kothry turned them off.

Ella found Shereen reading in the captain's chair on the bridge. "Hi, Sher. Kothry asked me to check the sensor links and put them online. I won't bother you, will I?"

"Not a bit. We got a flicker last night but nothing since. If you ask me, I think the captain's being too cautious. This world's not ready for the stars—too many wars, no generous leaders and they haven't begun to think to each other. Three hundred years, four hundred maybe, I could see it. But not now, not yet. What do you think?"

"I think it doesn't make any difference what I think. If the captain wants to park us on some lake bottom while he chases a hunch, it doesn't change my life much. You all need to eat, and I like to cook. A little extra anti-grav work won't kill me." Ella chose a console that gave her a view of the sensor indicators and began to test the input streams. Except for the usual scatter and background noise, they were normal and quiet. "Everything's fine, I'm going back to my sauce. They'll flash if anything happens."

Across the shank of the day it was the usual routine until all the viewports in Kothry's quarters came on at once, flashing the same message. The four outboard sensor indicators were flashing, and the Xelanar's onboard anti-gravity sensors were howling as well. The klaxon was a mean alarm clock.

"Kothry Gradel, to the bridge. Kothry, get up here, now." Ducar was hot.

Kothry was still buckling his belt when he stepped into the bridge compartment. The noise echoed all over the ship. "Yes sir."

"Turn that damned thing off. How is anyone supposed to think with all that racket?"

Kothry killed the klaxon and left the indicators to blink in silence. "They'll start to go out as their data is correlated," he said to the gathering crowd.

"Let me know what you've got as soon as you can. I want strength and location and I want to know what made this. Is that clear?"

"Yes, sir, as soon as I have anything at all I'll let you know." The event was brief but strong enough for the sensor data to list a small stack motor as one of the possibilities for the pulse. According to the simulator, it left earth orbit moments before. "Captain, I think we've got trouble. According to this simulation it's possible an unshielded motor got loose. It's not one of ours and it's not a Carei signature. In fact, it has no signature. Very crude, if it exists at all."

"What makes you think this is a rogue and not a false positive? We don't get runners this far off the trade routes."

"Well, I'll admit the evidence isn't strong. It shows zinc,

but almost no mercury. No one with half a brain would make one like this. But, see these little side waves that trail the main pulse?" Kothry put his finger just under the wave. "It is spinning, at least according to the simulation."

"Probabilities?"

"About a seven-percent chance it's real."

"Any hope of catching it?"

"Yeah, if we surface now the Xelanar might have it back in five, maybe six hours. The scouts would take longer. And that's if we can keep it targeted. It's not much of a signal."

"What's the chance it's quantum?"

"About double that."

"Well, let's hope this is just a fluctuation that passed the planet. If it's indigenous, we've got trouble. Any chance of a back-trace? Can we pinpoint where this came from?"

"It came from so near the first sensor we put out, I can't be sure it's not another defect."

"For the love of God, doesn't anything work around here anymore?"

14

Ladder Me Not

If Arney feared anything, it was heights. Harry had taken him on a tour of the Statue of Liberty and insisted they walk all the way up the winding metal staircase to photograph the view from her crown. There were railings meant for adults, but small children had a very different view. Arney remembered being sure some grownup would push him under the railing to meet his doom in the tangle of metal stairs below. He could still feel his grip being loosened more than once in the push and shove. That was years ago, but it could have been yesterday.

A twenty-four foot ladder is hard for an average man to raise by himself. Arney managed it easily but he had to prop one of its legs against a rock before he pulled. "Hey Luke, wannna' give me a hand? Put your foot up against that other leg." Once they had it extended, the rest was easy. The ladder banged against the edge of the barn's roof. "As soon as I get this straightened, I want you boys to help steady it. One of you get on one side, one on the other. And once I'm up there, tie that toolbag to this rope so I can haul it up."

"Why are you going up this way Dad?" Mark asked, trying to sound a little more grown up than he was.

"'Cause I don't trust the shed roof and I gotta fix a hole your grandfather made."

"How'd he do that?"

"Never you mind. Just tie on that toolbag when the time comes."

"Be careful Dad."

"I'll be fine."

The boys got another lesson in courage. They knew their father hated this kind of work but always managed to patch whatever leaks there were and get down safely, even if he had too many beers afterwards.

"Tie that bag on will you?"

"I've got it Dad," Luke answered. "Want some help?"

"Not necessary. Just don't go too far." It took Arney half an hour to patch the roof. When he looked down Luke was nowhere to be seen.

"Luke where were you? Come steady the ladder please."

"Right here, I've got it."

Breathing easier as he neared the ground, Arney pressed again. "Where did you say you were?"

"Checkin' out Grampa's stuff." Mark gripped the side of the ladder as his father climbed down.

"You know your grandfather doesn't want you playing in there right now."

"But why Dad? There's nothing but a bunch of metal discs and that contraption he likes to put 'em on. We won't get hurt, we promise," pleaded Mark.

"Do me a favor for right now. Just honor your grandfather's wishes, will you?"

"Okay, if you'll tell me just one thing." Luke was in his best bargaining mode.

"What's that?" Arney answered as he stepped off.

"Well, we could see you fixin' the hole from inside where his spinner thing is. It looked like you were right above us almost straight up. Did it explode or something?"

"Sort of. It won't happen again. You guys go home and tend to your chores while I talk to your grandfather. Run along now and thanks for your help. And listen if anybody asks, it was just fireworks."

"Whatever." It wasn't Luke's way to contradict his father even if he couldn't fit the story to the facts.

Luke and Mark hopped on their bikes and headed into the corn taking the shortcut between the fields as Arney walked into his parents' kitchen and sat down. "Mom, mind if I grab a beer?"

"Help yourself. Your father's takin' a nap. He was up late thinking. Did you fix the roof?"

"Yep, all done, good as I'm gonna do anyway." He felt responsible. If he had put his foot down earlier there would be no hole, no waves and maybe a lot less obsession. Now it was out of control. He could hear his father stirring at the sound of conversation. Soon he appeared in the doorway rubbing his eyes.

"Hi Pop, how are you feeling? Did you get some rest?"

"I'm good, just couldn't get to sleep last night with so much on my mind. I think I know what's happening now, even if I don't know why. It came to me early in the morning, it's anti-gravity. The force I've been lookin' for ain't a pull at all, it's a push."

"And you know this how?"

"'Cause the disks went straight up. They're repelled by earth's gravity. Those waves, they must be anti-gravity waves. I'm sure of it. I'm going to make another test tomorrow. Maybe use a little more mercury just to make sure."

"Whoa Poppa! Stop right there. You need to slow down and think about this. Where do you think the last one landed?"

"Where?"

"Coulda' been on someone's head. You have no idea what you're playing around with and you want to make it stronger? Please! What the hell are you thinkin'?"

"To be honest, I don't think the last one landed. I think it's still goin' out there. Where, I don't know. If I'm right it's gettin' pushed by all the celestial masses, according to how much gravity they have. It could be anywhere by now."

"Oh please. And what makes you think letting another one of these get loose is a useful contribution to the universe?"

"We're gonna bolt it down. I'm gonna use the smaller set of tubes. I can use three pairs of nylon bearings to steady them. I got it all figured out. I'm gonna cut smaller discs. It shouldn't take too long."

A knock at the kitchen's screen door and a flash of badge took them all by surprise.

"Hello Dave. I didn't hear you drive up. Come on in. What brings you out this far anyway?"

"I got a complaint yesterday, something about loud sounds of metal banging and this trail of purple vapor some of your neighbors saw coming up outta your barn."

"Which neighbors?"

"Come on now Harry. My job's to keep the peace, not end it. So what is it? Got any smoke up your sleeve?"

Harry sighed. There was no getting around giving some kind of explanation to the sheriff. "Musta' seen Mark settin' off one of his Fourth of July rockets. They don't remember what a smoke trail looks like during the day. Want a beer? No? How 'bout some coffee?"

"No thanks, I'm fine. Just keep an eye on those grandchildren. We don't want them starting a fire out here. Nice to see you Mrs. Miller, Arney." The sheriff nodded and left the way he came, down the steps.

Harry watched from the door. Dave Bright had parked his cruiser nearer the far end of the barn than might have been normal. He couldn't be sure if he saw the roof patch or not. At least if he did, he gave no sign.

Harry set about turning smaller metal discs. They were

thinner, less than two thirds the size of his earlier samples. There wasn't a lot of raw stock left but there was enough to make a smaller version of the first one that flew.

Perfect, he thought. *I'll get more later.*

The smaller spinner was harder to construct than the first two. Thin white oak circles supported by little model airplane wheels held the smaller glass tubes with their nested flanges in place, one inside the other. He emptied his box of electric motors scrounged out of broken toys and old aquarium pumps. There were enough to power it without having to tear the bigger spinner apart.

There was an urgency to Harry's movements as if he could smell and almost touch his prize. He delved into the problem of containment as he fashioned his smaller machine. It was the way he worked best, solving several problems at once. By noon the next day he'd sorted through the obvious impediments and the work was done. It was less well built and less well balanced than its big brother, but it didn't matter. Harry knew as soon as it spun up it would gather the discs together into a stack that became a thing unto itself.

He put the spinner on the floor with sawhorses on either side. *When Arney gets here we'll put baffles over the top. That should be plenty.*

Arney arrived with two cups of coffee from the house, and wasted no time catching up on how far his father had come with his project. "You about ready to test this thing?"

"As soon as we put a lid on this. Give me a hand, will you?" Harry motioned to a corn husk baffle. "I want to lay these across the sawhorses with some plywood between 'em." They stacked four. "That's about 200 pounds. That oughta' do it."

"You watch the baffles. I'll keep an eye on the discs. All the switches are on. Plug it in when you're ready. Just give me a count."

"Okay, here we go. Three, two, one, Crack! Holy shit Pop!

You okay?" The sound of wood splitting above their heads and the slow descent of bits of corn husk spoke to the force of the lift. Another hole in the roof streamed sunlight. Arney stared up through the opening. "Pop, I thought you said we could contain this."

"Guess I was wrong."

'Onk, onk, onk, onk.' The klaxon and four flashing a-g indicators lit up the bridge.

Ella turned down the sound and paged the captain. "Sorry sir, the anti-grav alarms are howling again. I think we've got real trouble this time."

"What set them off?"

"It's got the signature of a small anti-grav stack motor, naked as a newborn child."

"Did the sensors get a fix?"

"They're tracking it."

"How fast?"

"Nominal for an unshielded."

"Scramble the two-man. We're getting that thing back."

Kothry and PJ arrived at the airlock within thirty seconds. They quickly found their seats, strapped in and activated the controls.

"Seal the doors and open the hull. We don't have time to equalize the pressure," Kothry commanded. The two-man scout broke the surface in under a minute and passed the moon in ten.

"How close are you?" demanded the captain.

"We're tracking it. We should catch it in ninety-three minutes. PJ will man the disruptor."

"Okay, tell him to keep it suspended until we can set up containment for it in the cargo bay. We'll rendezvous with you in moonshadow and make the transfer. I want to get a look at that thing."

PJ had to finesse the capture. He had never tried to grab something that moved away every time he got closer. The smaller disruptor on the two-man scout made it harder still.

"Snagged it yet?"

"I'm workin' on it. This thing's a bitch. First real unshielded I've ever seen. Looks like a child's toy, but it's got some real push." PJ leaned toward his viewport and tickled the joystick until his prize disappeared in the disruptor field. "Okay, got it. Let's go show the captain."

Moonshadow was a specific point fifty miles above the moon's surface on the far side, out of sight of earth's telescopes and telemetry. The two-man scout got there first. It took the bell time to get underway, and care was taken not to repeat the splash caused by the rapid egress of the scout when it broke the surface. Despite the risk of leaving the lake bottom, no one aboard the Xelanar missed the murky darkness. But before they could make the trip to the moon, they had to transit through the atmosphere fully cloaked. That gave them some time to appreciate where they were.

The trouble was—cloaking was not 100% effective at high speed through dense gas. A proximity detector began flashing on Shereen's commport. "Captain, we've got company. Two petroleum-fueled aircraft are closing in. They have scanned us with radio waves. What was your expression? The natives are restless? Well, the natives are definitely restless."

"Are they arming weapons?"

"No, sir. They are trying to figure out what kind of craft we are."

"Then let's give them something they'll have a hard time explaining. Execute a sharp ninety-degree turn and lose them." The Xelanar flipped on its edge in a tight turn and was gone. The long arc up through the thinning air took less than a minute. The moon took nine more.

"We're at rendezvous Captain. Are we using standard transfer protocols?"

"How big is it?"

"About an inch and a half tall and three wide, not very big at all," PJ said.

"Alright when we're alongside, we'll open the main cargo bay. Put your field inside the container, then we'll turn ours on and you can turn yours off."

"Works for me," PJ answered.

The transfer went smoothly. After sealing the airlock against the emptiness, Ducar wasted no time inspecting the slow spinning top. "It's utterly crude. I can't remember anything like this coming from a culture so primitive. Remarkable really. You can see the tool marks." Harry's treasure became the object of considerable interest among the crew.

"This rogue stack is cause for termination, according to article three. You have physical proof of a violation. They should be cleansed. It's your duty to turn them to dust."

"Don't quote the regs to me, Jasca. This is containable. This thing's handmade. One guy in his lab, not a whole society. He may not even know what he's got. Let's give him a chance and find out what this is all about first. " Ducar turned. "You and I are going to check the origin point for traces and do a complete mental scan of everyone nearby. I want to know who, how and why. We'll leave as soon as you ready the two-man."

"Yes sir"

15

Who Dunnit

L uke and Mark saw the vapor trail from the side yard of their house before they heard the sound. "What the hell is that?" asked Mark, squinting and pointing to the slowly diffusing threads of mist that vanished over their heads.

"I don't know, but that trail's comin' straight up out of Grampa's barn. And did you see the purple? It was like the waves we saw the other night. We're goin' over there, now."

Bikes and the shortcut had them skidding up to the barn door in under a minute and a half. The barn door was open, and dust was still settling. "What happened over here? What was that we saw comin' out of the roof?" asked Luke.

"I think we better tell 'em Pop. Can't keep this a secret any longer."

"Alright," Harry said. "Sit down boys. I've got something to tell you but I need you to keep it a secret. Can ya' do that?"

Luke nodded. "You bet, we won't tell."

"It's important you don't. Now listen. A couple of months ago I started having some dreams about moving shapes. They were more colorful than my normal dreams and I can still see 'em in my mind's eye, clear as a bell. Different shapes were spinning, with light purple waves coming off 'em. I got a message, too." He waited for the questions.

"What? Who from?" Luke watched his grandfather's brow, looking for some sign of truth.

"That's the real question. I don't know Luke. But I believe the message was clearly meant for me. You know how I reach out with my mind and try to make connections, same thing I teach you to do? Well, this time I got an answer. Not so much in words as a push to make these machines I see in my head. I'm supposed to make them. And that's what I'm doin'."

"I get all that, Grampa. I want to know what made this hole and that vapor trail we saw."

"My spinner and some flat metal discs," answered Harry, pointing to what wasn't covered in corn husks and chicken wire. "Down there on the floor. For now all you need to know is that this won't happen again. If somebody asks I want you to tell them that you set off another rocket. Now, I need you to scramble onto the roof and put one big patch over both holes. And remember, don't tell anyone. If they ask, tell 'em a joke. Make 'em laugh. It eases the mind. Now go on. You can use the silo stairs but be careful. And thanks."

The silo stairs weren't really stairs at all, just loops of rebar set in cement on the outside, wide enough for feet and hands, an easy climb to the roof's edge when you're young. Arney didn't use them because they hurt his hands even through his work gloves. Luke and Mark had no problem.

"Ain't you a might free with the boy's safety Pop?" Arney asked after the boys had left.

"My son, my son, where have you been? Those boys have been goin' up on this roof for years. They're safer up there than you or I ever were."

"Wish you'd said somethin'."

The boys were as good as their grandfather's promise, easy with heights and graceful in their task. Luke was just about to spread tar on the edges of the patch to finish the job when a coy

"Whatcha doin'?" floated up with promise. He handed the putty knife to his brother and moved toward the edge.

"Hi, Barb, where's your sister? You always travel in a pack."

"She's coming. But before she gets here will you please tell me what's going on over here?"

"What? You mean my rocket?"

"In your pocket maybe. That was no rocket, no bang at the end. The bang came first."

"Well, I heard a bang before I lit it but that was because one of my grandfather's tools broke."

She looked as though she didn't buy it. He wondered what was really on her mind.

"Come on down, I want to talk in private."

"Hey Mark, can you finish up?"

"I heard, go kiss your girlfriend, but you owe me."

Luke and Barbara were in full embrace behind the barn when the sheriff's car broke the mood, coming to a gravel stop just out of sight.

"You go first," Barbara said as she straightened her blouse.

"Come on, we'll go together. What's he gonna see, he doesn't know already?"

The sheriff watched them walk up. "Hello Luke. Is your grandfather about? I'd like to talk with him for a moment if he don't mind."

"Sure sheriff, I'll get him."

"Afternoon ma'am." The sheriff tipped his hat to Barbara with slight grin. "You sure look pretty today."

Harry heard the car and the conversation and told himself to slow down and ease up to it as he came down through the barn door. "Hi, Dave. Back again? What can I do you for?"

"Harry, can we talk inside?"

"Sure, how 'bout some lemonade?"

"Now that'd be nice."

Harry steered his old friend right past the barn door, up the

103

porch steps and into the kitchen, deciding on a big glass as a sign of welcome. "Here you go."

The sheriff took a long drink. "Thanks. Tastes real good. Now listen Harry," he paused to take another sip, "there've been some complaints. Something about another rocket, except people have reported hearing something that sounds like wood breakin' too. I know you like to tinker, and I know you don't like to share and that's fine. But Harry you're scarin' these folks. And when they get scared they call me and my phone's been ringin' for the last half hour. So whatever it is you're up to this time, I need it to stop. Let's not let this get out of hand. Is that fair? Otherwise I'm gonna have to lock you up for disturbing the peace."

"Dave I promise, it won't happen again."

"See that it don't. Now how's Donna? You two okay?"

Small talk wasn't one of Harry's strengths. *Please let this end*, he thought. "We're fine, just fightin' off the aches. You know how it is."

"Where is Donna anyway?"

"In the basement doin' laundry."

"Well, give her my best."

By the time the sheriff left, Mark was off the roof and Harry was glad to hear the crunch of gravel under the cruiser's tires. *That was too close for comfort*, he thought to himself as he waved goodbye in an effort to seem relaxed. And he was mostly relaxed, until the squeaky steps announced Donna's return.

"Harry, we need to talk." Donna had her hands on her hips, never a good sign. "What the hell are you doing out there? And why's the sheriff been here twice? And how come there are two holes in the barn roof? And don't you dare try to hand me the rocket story. I know that's crap."

"It works. My spinner and the metal discs work. Not like I thought, but it works."

"No it doesn't Harry. It goes straight up out of sight. What good is that? Start talkin' to me for real, old man. What's going on?"

"Alright honey. First of all you should know, I'm not makin' any more discs. There'll be no more holes. I'm shuttin' down. Whatever's happenin' is beyond me. I thought if I made them smaller, they'd have less force. Then I could trap the stack in the baffles and study it. But you saw what happened, just like the first one. At least the hole's smaller. I'm not stupid honey. Since I can't contain it I can't play with it. It's fire."

"So what did the sheriff say?"

"He told me to stop whatever I was doin'. He didn't pry. More like he didn't want to. I told him I would."

<hr/>

The two-man scout settled in at 1500 feet fully cloaked above the escarpment where the first sensor was hidden. "Ping it. I want to know if it's still with us." Ducar dimmed the console lights and turned down the volume on the commport.

"It's fully functioning and still reports the initial pulse was within three miles. Do you want me to reset it?"

"No! Please don't adjust anything, no agitation, no change. If the sensor's okay our rogue maker is close. I want to reach out and find the creator of that pulse. This motor wasn't built by some backwoods rube. I want to scan for a scientific mind, someone of considerable intelligence. And we need to find the laboratory. Whoever made this didn't do it in some barn by the side of the road." The two men leaned back in their seats, dimmed the lights and prepared to reach out, sending tendrils of thought into every corner before moving on. "Let's divide this in two. Any preference for which side you scan?"

"If it's all the same to you sir, I'll take the side I'm sitting on."

"Starboard it is then. I like to get a look at where I'm probing too."

Cutting the problem in half made it easier. Neither Ducar

nor Jasca was particularly proficient at mental scanning. That was left to empaths like Shereen who would have laughed at the idea of a dimmed room and silence. Proximity was their main advantage. Over a couple of miles they were as good as most empaths, and Shereen could work through them if necessary. And so they began.

"Ready?"

"Aye sir." He leaned back and began sweeping.

It wasn't long before Jasca turned up a possibility. "Sir, I sense something. There's a farmer about three miles from here who has images of flat discs in his mind. They could be the components but there's no lab and no scientific frame of reference. He has no knowledge whatsoever of anti-gravity theory that I can read from here."

"Move us closer then."

"Aye sir." Jasca moved the scout to a point above the field on the far side of Harry's barn. It was close enough that they could probe deep into the minds of those below and still remain undetected.

"See the patch on that barn roof? I'll bet that's where our rogue came from," Jasca said pointing.

"I see it, but it doesn't make sense. Tell Shereen to scan my mind as I probe these farmers. She's much better at feelings. I want a complete profile on all of them." He leaned his seat back and closed his eyes. He could feel Shereen's presence. The 250,000 miles between the two vessels was nothing to her. After all, if civilizations could communicate between the stars, this was a short hop.

"Ready when you are sir," Shereen said.

Ducar had half heard her voice as he opened his mind to those below, a jumble at first until a clear idea emerged. *It is the old man*, he thought. Images and snippets of ideas coalesced around Harry's inventive mind.

Shereen got a great deal more. Her thoughts intruded into

Ducar's own, suggesting he focus on the son. *"It's not just the old man. His son's in it too, not just as a helper. I'm archiving everything."* Without a word, Ducar began focusing on Arney's reaction to the mess in the barn.

"Oh my," Shereen said out loud. There was something different about Arney. She felt it move through her, filling a hole, healing a wound long left behind. "He can feel me. He knows I'm here." She could not let it go even after Ducar's attention had moved on.

"Where are you?" the captain inquired aloud.

"Sorry sir. Please send your thoughts to Jasca and let him record you locally. I want to focus on the son from here."

"Isn't that a little far?"

"No problem sir. I can do it my sleep."

"Then what do you need me for?"

"I don't sir. It's more of a courtesy."

She leaned back and began to probe deeper. There was no doubt the old man had produced the rogue stack. He had the temperament and the mind for it, but his telepathic capabilities did not intrigue her. Arney's did. Every time she focused on him, she felt herself relax. She began to let him wash over her, oil poured on the waters of her discontent.

"You okay?" interrupted Ella. You've been that way for a while now."

"Oh I'm fine," she said, bringing her seat back up. "What time is it?"

"Well Jasca and the captain are on their way back. I'd say you've been like that for half an hour."

A hiss announced the airlock, Jasca first, followed by the captain. Ducar touched a commport. "All hands to the common area, we need to confer. Five minutes please."

"What's this about sir? We need to send a notice to terminate. They've discovered anti-gravity and they can barely think. Our protocols dictate Command should be informed," Jasca said, pushing the regulations again.

"Shepherd Command can wait. Come with me." They entered the common area where most of the crew was gathered. "Who's missing? Oh good, Ella. Thank you. Alright we have a problem. There's an old man down there who's discovered how to make an unshielded anti-grav motor, far earlier than was predicted." He held it up, now safely locked within a crystal. "He can't contain it and he doesn't know how to harness its energy. We've caught his little time disruptor but that leaves us with a choice. We can take away his toys and hope that there's been no strong signal that brings more scrutiny, or we can let the powers that be raze this world. Seems a shame to me that everyone should perish because of one old man's curiosity. And yes, I know this is against standing orders but I'd like to try and save them. What do you think?"

The room was quiet and then noisy as chairs and feet shifted. "Anyone?"

Jasca was first. "I think we should follow standard procedure and eliminate them. We all remember the destruction the Krell caused when we failed to be thorough."

"Jasca what if we initiate contact and try to persuade him to stop for his own safety. Would you agree to that?" Shereen suggested.

"Why would we do that? It's another violation. No watch ever interferes this early. Not to save savages like this anyway. We're talking career here."

"Jasca you want to turn a whole world to dust. It's the lives of all these beings for one man's mistake." Shereen's tone was persuasive. When Jasca read the rest of their minds, he knew he had lost.

"Alright, alright. I agree but under protest. The bigger this gets, the messier it becomes. You must keep this contained. How do you propose to make contact?"

"Shereen, what do your profiles show?" Ducar asked.

"He likes old cars. He's got two under the barn. The scan shows a Corvair Monza and an old Model A Ford. I'd go with the Ford. We could synthesize one and drive past his house. It's sure to get his attention."

"That's a good suggestion. Do any of the rest of you have anything to add? If not, do we agree?" The harmony said yes. "That's all then, except thank you. I think we made the right decision. Let's execute it. Jasca and Shereen, you two will accompany me. Jasca, you pilot. Shereen, you and I will pose as father and daughter looking for a small farm to lease. If he asks about the car tell him it's family."

"I'd like to come. I could be your son."

"No, you're too old and Shereen's a better empath. Besides, I need you piloting the six-man. This will be a messy egress."

Jasca masked his disappointment. First Contact was a privilege few would enjoy.

PJ met Ducar in the corridor. "Want me to synthesize the car?"

"Yes. And do it inside the hold of the six-man so we don't have to move it around. If the synthesizers squawk about the size, assemble it from parts and it needs to be accurate."

"Yes sir, right away." PJ left to find Shereen who was using the ship's scanners to produce a model for the synthesizers to replicate. Details had to be modified so that Harry would not encounter an exact duplicate of his own car. That was Kothry's contribution, different dents and move the rust around. When the synthesizers were finished, a fine old 1930 Model A Ford Coupe sat nested in the hold of the six-man scout.

Ducar left the bridge without making an entry in the ship's log about the rogue motor, the meeting or First Contact. *Just a little sight-seeing cruise*, he thought to himself. He had never deceived his superiors before.

16

Pickup Lines

E veryone has a list of things they want to do when school lets out. Luke's was short. Stake out the valley from the wedge and spend time with Barbara, not necessarily in that order.

They had a date with the night sky, but he had more than stargazing on his mind. He was sure Barb felt the same. They piled on to the ATV, anxious to begin their adventure. But first he needed to borrow his grandfather's camera. It was that task that found him knocking at the barn's side door.

"Grampa, you in there?"

"Come on in Luke." The door brushed open to reveal a grin. "Well, don't you look happy. What can I do for ya'?"

"I want to borrow your Handycam."

"Whatcha want it for?"

"I want to start filming the valley at night and see if I can record that wave Mark and I saw. I need to know I wasn't seeing things."

"Top section of my cabinet. You can borrow it. Just be careful. You takin' Barb?"

"Yes sir?"

"Well see you be nice to that girl."

An evening with Barb was worth the wait. Under the stars

arm in arm felt like a great plan. Yeah, she was a little brassy and flirtatious but she was nice to him. She never made fun of his low-key ways. And he loved how she spoke her mind, unafraid. The first time she whispered, "I love you," he knew she meant it. And in that moment he floated up, light, happy beyond measure into a place he had never been before. He said it back to her, and they were one.

The ATV was not her favorite conveyance, but persuading her to come had been easy.

"Am I goin' too fast?" he asked with a caring tone.

"I'm fine. Why do you like coming up here anyway? It's just a clear cut with stumps and rocks."

"That's why I come at night. You don't notice 'em. There's this rock me and Mark lie on and watch the stars 'cause no one's around. It's our private place, kind of our door to the sky. I'll show you." He drove as close as he could and took the blanket and the snacks then grabbed his grandfather's camera bag and clambered up the rock. "Come on Barb, just give me your hand. It's nice up here."

She put her foot where he pointed and let him lift her into his arms. She took it as a sign and entwined herself further. "You smell nice," she cooed.

"Not yet, I want to set up this camera."

"You'll do no such thing."

"No, no Barb. I didn't mean it like that. I'm taking a picture of that far ridge and the valley between. It'll be pointin' the other way."

"Is it going to have sound?"

"No sound, just pictures."

"Oh, okay." If it ever occurred to Barb to ask what for, she never did. She was too busy making the most of an opportunity that might not come twice. She spread out the blanket in anticipation. She wanted whatever her kiss might start, the glue of it deep between her thighs, and began to undo the top buttons

111

of her blouse. "Can anyone see us?"

"No, no one can see us."

"Then come here." It wasn't hard. She enveloped him slowly, whispering in his ear a warm breathy, "I want you."

That was yes plain as day and Luke fell in, pulled by the primal. They kissed until all resistance was gone. Buttons were in the way. "Here, let me." Luke carefully unbuttoned the rest.

"Undo me," she said taking off her blouse and turning her back to make it easier. When he managed to unhook her bra, she took that off too, then turned her attention to his belt. "Now it's your turn."

Luke kneeled on the blanket looking down at her while she undid his belt and pulled his pants and his underwear down before he could stop her.

"Oh my," she whispered. "Take those pants off and the shirt." They undressed and when they were finally side by side, skin to skin she found his tongue with hers and in her joy she whispered a soft, "Touch me there," and pulled his hand into the warmth. She wanted what the first time discovers and whimpered in anticipation until she could stand it no more. "Please, I want you in me. Fill me deep down. I've been waiting for you."

Luke found the bottom of her and pure joy in the same moment. A love not born of passion but sailing on it, bound him to her. Long strokes probed deeper each time until...

"Oh please, now, fill me up." Satisfaction gave way to moans of joy, "Yes, yes." When his back finally arched in release, the hook was set. He was hers.

They dwelled in that place that first lovers know when they have shared all they are, the touch that makes one being out of two as they embrace. Until she asked, "What's that?" She pushed him off, pulling part of the blanket up to cover her naked body.

"What's what?"

"That wave in the air behind you, where your camera's pointed."

Luke hopped, naked as a jay bird, over to the camera as the shimmer began to fade. "Damn, I hope we're getting this. I've been waitin' for this."

"That was spooky looking. What was that Luke?"

"I'm not supposed to say. I'll tell you when Grampa says it's okay." Then the wave was gone and Luke stopped recording. "Let's pack up now. We've got to get back."

"What's your hurry? It'll keep 'til tomorrow. Come here, mister. I'm not done, and neither are you."

He could feel his testicles rolling in his groin, adding to the next load that he would leave deep in her safe darkness, but for now he was intent on what her moans said about rhythm and her needs. Sighs of pleasure told him what she liked, a little deeper and a little faster, only to pull almost all the way out, then plunge ever deeper toward the bottom in one long thrust. He could feel her ease away from the power of his need only to yield to her own. And when he felt her release, he exploded in waves of pleasure again, sending seed from loin to loin.

She loved him utterly. They stayed wrapped in each other until the odd contact with their bed of stone became too much. "Come on Barb. It's late. We've got to go." They cleaned themselves, dressed, packed up and drove back down the hill. She would not let go of him. His head was in the waves.

<hr />

Jasca landed the six-man scout just off the road near the escarpment. "Did you see those kids on that rock as we were coming in?"

"I saw them. They were too busy to notice much of anything, don't you think?"

"You wouldn't catch me on a bed like that," Shereen interjected.

Jasca wasn't so sure. It was a thought he wished he had held on to. Shereen surely read it, so he decided to be nice. "The cargo door will open next to the road. You two need any help pushing the car out?"

"No" said the captain, "I think we've got this."

The purple shimmer around the open cargo bay door lasted less than a minute. As soon as the bay was sealed Jasca lifted silently into the night sky, leaving the Model A and a father and daughter by the side of the road. They looked like most rural folk from Iowa or Indiana. That was their cover, poor around the margins, more Scot than Irish, looking for a farm to lease.

Ducar brought up the start sequence instructions in his mind. Spark up, throttle down half, open the gas, give the choke a full turn, keep your thumb out of the way. It went on, but when he finished the 1930 Model A Ford Coupe started right up, like a toy he played with as a child. The memory left him smiling, as he tried not to reveal his truths. Secrets were best kept, until he could not help himself and grinned a childish grin that comes when expectations are exceeded.

"She runs great. This should be fun. Got your story straight?"

"Good as I'll get it. Come on, show me what she's got."

It took a couple of tries to get a feel for the clutch but the pilot in Ducar made it a study. By the top of the rise, he was cruising along as if he'd owned the Ford all his life. That was the rest of his cover, old car aficionado.

When they were in sight of Harry's farm he pulled out the choke and let the engine cough to a halt. Then they got out, lifted the engine cowl and waited, but not for long. The sound of an ATV coming up the road behind them meant their timing had been accidentally good. Ducar planned to be more direct but the need to knock on Harry's front door had vanished.

"You folks in trouble? I see where you've got the hood up. You know my Grampa's got one of these down in his garage 'cept his is under a tarp. I could go get him if you like. He lives right over there," the young man offered, sounding friendly.

"That's nice of you son. I'm Jack Danny and this is my daughter Leslie. We're headin' for Graston tonight," trying out his best local accent for the first time. "Not sure what's wrong. Is your grandfather a mechanic?"

"Nah, just handy with stuff. I'll go get him."

"That's most obliging of you. What's your name?"

"Oh sorry, name's Luke. This here's Barb. We'll be back in a minute." Luke drove up the road, heading for the barn.

"This is going to work out better than we planned," Ducar said to Shereen, "but we'll have to disable this so he has something to fix." He popped off the distributor cap, pulled the rotor off the shaft and broke off the metal contact, then put the rotor back on and left the contact loose beside it and replaced the cap. "We've just disabled our transport. You did find this part in his barn when you scanned it, didn't you?"

"Yes sir, and I cross-scanned it with their terrestrial libraries. They are new old stock. They've never been touched. In a lower right-hand drawer on the second level, I seem to remember." She pushed her superior memory at him to punish him for ever doubting that she had covered every detail before he had even thought through the problem.

"You could have a ship of your own, you know. You're the brightest of all of us," he said knowing he had disparaged her. "I'm sorry. I'm the one with the issues." There it was again, another truth leaked out. He resolved to stop his mind from betraying him.

"I sense your apprehension sir, but we're not here to eliminate them. We're here to help."

Ducar nodded acceptance and confessed no more. The sound of a tractor starting up and the appearance of headlights from the ATV seemed to happen at the same time. He was glad for the diversion.

Luke arrived in a cloud of dust and spoke enthusiastically through the swirl. "My Grampa's coming. He's bringin' the tractor and some tools." Luke said, hopping off the ATV and watching as the '59 John Deere came up the road and stopped. "That's my Grampa."

"Harry Miller," the farmer said extending his hand. "I see you've had some trouble. What happened?"

"Jack Danny," replied Ducar, shaking Harry's hand. "This is my daughter Leslie. We were drivin' along and she just died. Not sure why."

"Did you try startin' her?"

"I did, but she wouldn't catch. She's making a metallic sound I haven't heard before."

"Well it's too dark to be doin' this in the middle of the road. Why don't you let me tow her over to my place. I've got one of these in my garage under the barn, a '30' too, and she still runs. We'll get yours under some light and see if we can't sort her out." Harry towed the Model A under the light on the side of the barn and climbed off the tractor as Donna came down the porch steps to greet the strangers Luke told her might be coming.

"Mr. Danny is it? I'm Donna Miller and you've met my grandson Luke, and you must be Leslie? Do I have that right?"

"Yes ma'am, Leslie."

"Can I fetch you both something to drink?"

"Thank you Mrs. Miller. You're very kind. I wonder if I might use your bathroom?" Shereen inquired.

"Of course dear, come on inside."

Shereen had read her well. She used an easy speech pattern and the right choice of words to slip without presumption into Donna's life as if they were old friends. It was a casual conversation that quickly went to truth. Donna appeared to brighten up and smiled at her. It was a gift of empaths like Shereen that made them essential to assimilation, becoming whoever someone needed them to be.

Ducar had few if any of Shereen's empathic talents. He could read minds but most of the time he trusted his wits. They had agreed Shereen should win Donna over first, which left the good captain to engage Harry, who was now aiming his flashlight at the obvious trouble spots, calling out his diagnosis as he went.

"It's not the fuel line and your battery seems okay. I'm going to pull a plug wire and see if you've got any spark." Harry saw nothing to indicate the spark plug was getting any juice at all. "I think it might be your distributor." Harry released the clips that held the cap in place and smiled. "Gotcha! You've broken a rotor." He held up the pieces in triumph. I might just have one of these lyin' around. Same year, should fit. I'll be right back."

"Can I help you find it?"

"No thanks, this place is kinda cluttered right now." Harry knew it was a lame excuse, but he could sense intrusion. "Give me a minute." He tried to fathom why they should be driving up his road. It seemed a strange coincidence as he closed the door behind him. He went up the stairs in the barn and found two old rotors and brought them back outside. "One of these ought to do it," and one did. In the gratitude that followed Harry forgot about his suspicions and let them go.

Ducar missed his chance to reconnoiter. Still, better to be absolutely casual. It wasn't just the old man's paranoia. He could feel a sensitivity. Harry's mind was making connections.

The Model A started up and ran but not quite as smoothly as before. It needed a tune-up that wasn't happening in the dark.

After thank you's and goodbye's Harry and Donna watched the ATV go one way and the Model A the other. "Nice folks. Not from around here," Harry observed.

Donna was more pointed. "I thought Leslie was nice but there's something odd about her. Maybe it's 'cause she's too pretty not to be married at her age. Otherwise I can't put my finger on it. But I liked her a lot. She has a charming way about her that isn't pushy. She knows just what to say. Maybe we should invite them over, get to know them better. They're stayin' in Graston while they look for a farm."

"Why would we do that?"

"Just to be neighborly Harry. Same reason you helped them. Don't be such an old curmudgeon. You can talk cars."

"Alright, if you see 'em, invite 'em."

"Oh, thank you your majesty. If I see them, I will."

The old Ford carrying Ducar and Shereen chunked up the gravel road toward the Starlite Motel on Route 54, outside of Graston. When they got onto the tarmac road, carloads of teenagers on summer vacation waved at them and their old ride. Shereen waved back. It hadn't occurred to them they would attract so much attention and Ducar was not pleased.

They had a reservation. It was just a matter of getting there. When they saw the sign, they were happy the way weary travelers are when rest is in sight, even if the quality was questionable. "Which bed do you want sir?"

"I'll take the one near the door. You take the one near the loo, excuse me, the powder room."

"Thank you sir, I'll be happy with the one nearest the lavatory. The usual discretionary protocols?"

"If you had other interests I would decline. Although I confess that when you first came aboard the Xelanar..."

"I know sir."

"How did you know?"

"I can read you and you don't know when I do it."

"That's not fair. It gives you a huge advantage."

"Yes it does. Goodnight sir. I'll see you in the morning." They disconnected from each other's thought processes and masked the incoming to get a better night's sleep.

17

Bugs

The Starlite Motel was right across the road from the Walmart, Donna's favorite emporium. It was a tidbit Shereen had gleaned the first time she scanned Donna's mind. That the motel turned out to be so near was no coincidence. Her good planning meant she could wait for Donna's approach. She left a tendril of thought wrapped around Donna's whereabouts and intentions. When she sensed Donna was coming, she stood watch and waited. As soon as Donna's pickup pulled into the lot she walked across the road, followed her into the store and waited until she could be accidental.

"Oh, hello Leslie. What are you doing here?"

"Good morning Donna, I was just getting some lunch and another toothbrush for my dad. He lost his."

"My Harry's like that. Misplaces something and then goes and buys another. He's got more screwdrivers than one man will ever use. Listen, I'm glad I ran into you. Seein' as how my Harry and your father have the same old cars in common, I hoped you might come to dinner. Harry loves to talk old cars, and he's the only one left around here with a Model A. It'll be good for them both, don't you think? Where are you staying anyway?"

"Right across the road. See our car just around the side of the

119

motel? It's just to the left of the gas station."

"Is it running okay? It sounded a little sketchy when you were driving away last night."

"It's alright, it got us here."

"That sound's iffy. Why don't you and your father come to dinner tonight, say around five. That'll leave plenty of light for the boys to work on the car, and you and I can get to know each other better."

"That sounds very nice, Mrs. Miller."

"Donna, call me Donna. Five then?"

"We'd be honored Donna."

Shereen knew how to guide behavior with her movements and facial expressions. It made her a spot-on empath. She could get into a person and tell them things about themselves they didn't know were there. And she could make someone think they needed to invite someone over, just to be neighborly.

When Donna got home she found two bikes leaning against the house. "Boys? Luke, Mark? Come help me with these groceries."

Luke appeared. "Hi Gramma, I've got 'em. You go on inside and get cool." The boy seemed to grow a little taller.

"What'd you boys come over for?"

"To show Grampa some pictures we took from the wedge last night, me and Barb."

"Luke, you mind your manners with that girl. You're still too young for children. They take all your strength."

"Yes ma'am, I'll be careful." It seemed a reasonable, almost amicable admonition. He knew she was right. She knew he wasn't stopping. Barbara Harlin however was not on Luke's mind at the moment; the video was. He wanted to see the wave, but before he could do that he needed his grandfather to transfer the videotape into his computer so that he could inspect each frame closely.

Harry called his grandsons into the den after the transfer had finished. There wasn't much to see, except an old car coming up the road. There was no shimmer at all. Luke could not hide his disappointment. "I don't get it. I know this thing was rolling when I stopped recording and that was after the shimmer ended. It has to be here." He scrolled back and forth through the recording, scowling. "I know what I saw."

"Maybe it's something that can't be recorded," offered Mark as the phone rang. Harry answered.

"Hello Barbara, you want Luke don't you."

"Yes please, Mr. Miller."

Harry handed Luke the phone.

"Hi baby, what's up?"

"I'm sorry. I know I shouldn't have said anything, but I told my dad about what we saw up on the wedge last night and he's furious."

"What's he got to be furious about?"

"He and Mom think your grandfather's playing around with black magic with the hole in the roof and the things he saw go up into the sky. So when I told him about the waves I saw, he just flipped."

"How'd he find out about the hole in the roof?"

"I guess I told him. It just slipped out. I'm really sorry. I thought it was just a hole and you didn't tell me it was supposed to be a secret."

"We'll figure something out. Don't worry."

"He's real pissed off about us too. So is Mom. They know. Mom says she could smell you on me. They're not stupid."

"Okay, so we won't see each other for a while until they calm down. It'll be fine. Just relax and be nice to them. And please don't say any more about the barn. Tell your dad we set off some fireworks."

"I don't know, my dad's fit to be tied. I can't tell if it's you or your grandfather he's angrier at. Just thought you'd want to know. Sorry. I've got to go, bye."

Luke pondered whether telling his grandfather about Barb was the right thing to do. No one would take black magic seriously. He decided against it since company was coming. "Grampa, can I keep borrowing the video camera for a while?"

"Sure, just be careful with it."

The boys could tell by the amount of noise coming from the kitchen, it was time to go. They rode away as Luke pondered his choices. "If I tell him about Barb's dad, he's pissed and if I don't tell him and this blows up, he's even more pissed, swell."

Ducar could sense his favorite word being spoken. He sought the origin and then asked Shereen to help find the mind that formed the word.

"It's the oldest grandson Luke. He's trying to decide whether to tell his grandfather that his neighbor thinks he is playing with dark magic. Apparently they saw the unshielded rogue as it left."

"Come on Shereen, I think it's time we dressed for dinner." The Ford coughed to life with minor protest and then began to reassure. "She's running alright don't you think?"

"Respectfully sir, she's right on the edge and you know it. I will turn my mind toward the motor. We'll make it."

"You look nice, you know."

"So do you sir. You're easy to read.

"Really? I always thought I was hard to read."

"That's what makes you so easy." A little smile began to curl across her mouth as she watched her captain gather in the import of her words. Tarmac turned to gravel and Ducar slowed to cut the dust and the noise.

"It's not far now. Do you know how you're going to approach her?"

"I think so, she's not as straight forward as Harry. I'm going to play some of it by ear. Speaking of ears, what's that sound?"

"That's not good is what that is. I don't think this old girl's gonna make it. Maybe we can get as far as that house over there."

"I'll settle for close." Shereen could no longer add to the

motor's life. She pulled her mind away and it died abruptly."

"Close enough. I'm going to walk down there and see if those good folks won't let me borrow their phone. Want to come with me or stay here?"

"I'm coming with you. They'll be more inclined to say yes to me than you, even if I never open my mouth."

The front door had a grace about it, just enough ornament to say there's more here than meets the eye. Ducar was lifting the brass knocker when the door opened. "Can I help you?"

"Yes sir, I hope you can. My name's Jack Danny and this here's my daughter Leslie. We broke down a little way up that rise and I'm hoping we can use your phone."

Arney didn't answer. He couldn't take his eyes off Shereen. Aw shucks took over. He tried not to look, which just made it worse. Something deep tugged at him. He knew he had seen her before.

"We're going to dinner at the Miller's. They live close I think." Shereen spoke to his mind as much as his ears. It flowed in like honey, down deep.

"Come on in. I'm a Miller. Name's Arney. You must mean my dad. He's the next farm up the road. By all means, use the phone. He's gonna laugh." He couldn't stop looking at her every chance he got and seemed embarrassed. "I'm sorry I'm staring."

No, you're not, she thought to him and smiled, waiting to see how long it took him to realize her lips hadn't moved.

Ducar's thoughts jumped in. *Shereen if you must, save that for later. You'll tip our hand before we've had a chance to persuade his father.*

Sorry sir, she thought back. It was hard because Arney wasn't just a distant read anymore. He was next to her, sending his spirit into her.

Ducar feared affection more than conflict. *Be careful*, he thought. *Your feelings will lead to forbidden contact.*

I will sir, I promise.

"Phone's right over here. I'll dial it for you." Arney handed the receiver to Ducar after it started to ring.

"Hello Harry, this is Jack Danny. We had more trouble with our car."

"You're still coming for dinner, aren't you?"

"Yes, we are. We're stuck on the road just up from your son's place."

"Well, don't worry. I'll start the tractor and be there in a jiffy."

Harry had the car in tow and halfway home before he shouted back from the tractor's seat. "How long have you had her?"

"Since my dad died," Ducar shouted back. It wasn't long before the old A was parked once again underneath the barn's outside light.

"Had mine since '62. My dad didn't want to fix it anymore. I see you met my boy."

"Fine man. I'm lookin' forward to gettin' to know him."

"He's the best of us, never let you down. Here's Donna. Let's go inside. After you, young lady."

Donna smiled at her guests. "Come right on in. Sorry you had more trouble. I'm sure Harry can fix it." She showed them to the parlor, which was her favorite room, filled with family pictures and embellishments that wove her preferences into a proper middle-class decor. Shereen liked it. Ducar looked for escape.

"Where's Harry?" he asked.

"I think he's going to work on your car. Why don't you get a beer from the fridge and go join him."

"Thanks, I think I will. Please excuse me."

Donna heard the screen door bang. Newcomers needed a reminder to close it slowly. "Tea dear?" Shereen nodded.

Harry was bent over the fender, popping off the distributor cap. "You didn't last long," he said pulling off the rotor.

"Can it be fixed?" Ducar asked coming down the steps.

"Sure. I think you might benefit from a new condenser. I've got a used one. It'll see you up the road 'til you can find a replacement."

"Mighty kind of you, Harry. Can I watch? I might learn something."

"Well, come on to the barn then. Let's see what we can do." Harry hadn't changed his mind about Jack's being in the barn. Too soon to trust him, but there was less to see now. "I'm going up to my auto parts storage. Be right back."

The moment he was inside, Ducar had his answer. Although Harry had cleaned up recently, there was evidence of discovery everywhere. When Harry came back he asked, "What are you making?"

"Nothin' now, just tidyin' up after some experiments that didn't work. Turned out be a waste of time."

"How so?" Ducar wasn't sure about pressing, but the dam burst anyway.

"I was looking for energy, somethin' I saw in my head. Listen, I'm sorry. I shouldn't be sharin'. I hardly know you."

"You know me better than you think."

"What do ya mean by that?"

Ducar picked up a short piece of 2x4. "Do you feel any connection with this wood?"

"Not particularly, why? You gonna hit me with it?"

"What if I told you that you are joined to this wood in spirit and in fact?"

"I'd say you were crazy."

"Well, what if told you everything is alive? Would you feel joined then?"

"Don't think so. That lumber's dead and ain't comin' back. How can it be alive?"

"Okay, I'll put it another way. You know those little bacteria inside your stomach that help you digest your food? Well, they're alive inside you, and without them you'd die. And they've got smaller living things inside them that they need, little bits of life so they can exist. And it doesn't just work as things get smaller. It works the other way, too."

"Whaddya mean the other way?"

"You have to allow the possibility that you are a part of some larger lifeform, so big you might not see the edge of it. And if that's true, then everything inside it could be alive as well."

"Rocks ain't alive and never have been."

"Really? Don't be so sure. What are you made of?"

"What do you mean?"

"What elements are you made from?"

"I don't know—carbon, oxygen, calcium, hydrogen."

"That's enough. Where did they come from, the elements I mean?"

"From the stars, I think, when they exploded."

"Close enough, so how were the stars made?"

"From gas and dust they swept up."

"Right. And where did the dust come from?"

"It's star ash, I guess."

"A lot of it, yes. So, allow me to pull this together. New stars form from the ashes of old ones. They burst forth and shine, and eventually explode or collapse and are gathered up by the forces of the cosmos to do it all over again. Birth, death, rebirth, death, like here on earth—all part of the same process. All part of the same being, just much larger. We wouldn't be alive without the death of stars and the elements they produce. We're a part of each other, the same way the bacteria within us are bound to our fate and we to theirs. Don't you see, Harry? It's all alive, the universe I mean, one vast living thing. And we, we are a small but necessary part."

"Bugs?"

"If you want to look at it that way."

"What kind of religion are you preachin'?"

"It's not religion Harry. It's science."

"What's your science mean to me and mine?"

"It means we're all connected to each other. It means because we are part of the same lifeform we have the power to communicate with each other, mentally. Does the living microbe in your gut understand the totality of where it is? Of course not. We are a living part of an infinitely larger living thing that is aware, even if we, like the microbes, may not be. It is the same problem for all of us, learning to understand the totality. It is part of caring and compassion, just taken further. And it's why I said you know me better than you think. You do Harry, and I know what your dreams are made of."

"What?"

"Something bigger, something better, something inventive and unique."

"I don't know about that." Harry's alarm bells were going off again. Surely no one outside the immediate family had the slightest inkling of his passions, much less some broken-down, preachy passerby. He pushed away the man's theories, as much as he could. "Let's go in for dinner."

Donna had set the table in the dining room. Usually it held piles of paperwork on the way to somewhere else, but tonight it was clean and decorated with flowers from the garden. Shereen could tell that she had extended herself. "This is nice Donna. You shouldn't have gone to the trouble."

"It's no trouble dear. We never have much company besides family. Please, sit down." When everyone had stopped shuffling after grace and were as quiet as they were going to be Donna asked, "So Leslie, what do you do with yourself?"

"Oh, I mostly help my dad." It wasn't much information, but Donna didn't press. By dinner's end the conversation had wound toward family, and they were easy with each other. Donna and Leslie chatted in the kitchen, while Harry and Jack hung out on the porch.

Harry picked up where they had left off. "You make it sound

like everything's chewin' on somethin' else, like we're all eatin' each other."

"You could look at it like that, but I prefer to think of it as something growing and evolving. When we decay, we nourish other parts of life in a continuous flow. Your atoms become part of something else. Do you think there's life out there?" He gestured to the night sky.

"Don't know. I suppose it's possible."

"I saw that telescope in your barn. Do you ever look through it?"

"Sometimes."

"What do you see?"

"It looks pretty much the same everywhere. The stars don't seem any bigger, but I see the moon real good."

"What about the galaxies?"

"Can't see 'em clearly but I've seen pictures. They're swirls, full of stars and dust."

"Are they alive?"

"Can't see how."

"What if I told you they were just cells in a larger living thing, flowing in veins we don't see until we get real far away from them."

"I'd say you're batshit crazy. Somebody's been fillin' your head with nonsense."

"Well, I'm not going to argue with you. I just thought you might be interested in a different point of view, seeing as how you're interested in science. All I ask is that you consider the possibility."

"Possibility of what?"

"That it might be all alive as one living thing." His hand traced a curve across the sky as if to animate it. "The enormity of it, the fact that you can see its form and then ponder its meaning. Why, it's staggering. I come back here to be amazed."

"Back here?"

"Just a figure of speech. I mean philosophically, mentally, not physically."

It turned on an inflection. The smallest shift in tone of voice that told Harry it wasn't true. "You sure? Not tryin' to pry. You don't look like you're from around here."

"No Harry, I'm not from around here." And there it hung on a long pause. He pointed to the sky. "I'm from out there."

"Oh please, spare me. Out there my ass, out there?" He shook his head. "Not by me you ain't."

"Harry, I knew this moment wasn't gonna be easy, so I brought you proof. This is yours I believe." He held up Harry's tiny anti-grav motor locked in its crystal prison.

Harry didn't move a muscle. It wasn't fear that froze him. It was the staggering amount of information he was processing with so many implications. "Where did you find that?"

"Harry, we have a lot to talk about."

18

The Hookup

Arney rode his Harley right up to the steps of the porch where Jack and Harry were seated. "Hi again Mr. Danny. I see you found my dad alright. You guys talkin' cars?"

"Cars and other stuff," Harry offered. "Did you bring the timing light?"

"Got it right here. You want me to do it?"

"Nah, I'll get it. You go say hi to your Ma." Harry and his new friend left for things automotive. Arney was glad he didn't have to be the mechanic this night. He was looking forward to a special smile.

"Hi Arney, I didn't think I would see you again so soon." Leslie's voice flowed through him again. She knew exactly how the woman of his dreams should sound.

"Didn't think I would see you either, but I'm glad for the chance. Hi Mom. I didn't mean to disrespect by not greetin' you first."

"I know. I'm not dead. You two run along while I finish up."

Arney and Leslie took over the seats that the two men had left. "This sure is a beautiful place," she offered.

"Yeah I grew up in the bedroom right over our heads, that is until Dad helped me buy my own farm."

"Can I see it? Your place I mean."

"You've seen some already. It's just a farm, nothin' special."

"Take me for a ride on your motorcycle. I want to see your farm."

Arney could barely contain himself, the obvious not lost on his libido. It just never occurred to him with her father so close.

"You don't really want to see my place, do you? My kids are home. It'll be chaos."

"I want to get to know you. You're generous and kind and a little sad down deep, too busy raising kids to have much time for yourself I expect."

"How do you know that? You don't know anything about me."

"I know nice when I see it." She moved her hand closer to his. "And pain, too."

In that moment something in Arney came loose. He had resisted affection to protect a memory for too long, keeping love at bay with heartache. He touched her to see if she was real and a current flowed. What was Aleri in her began to work its way through his nervous system, unstoppable and binding. The neurons of two very different species began to knit, not to be undone.

Leslie turned and slipped her hand through his hair and melted him. Louise used to do that too. He'd forgotten how much he missed it. He wasn't used to being led, but he let himself have the pleasure of it for a moment, and then pulled back.

"You're gonna call me old fashioned, but I'd like to get to know you better first. I've been single since Louise died."

"Don't you date?"

"Nah, too busy with the kids. There's women around here, all nice enough and smart enough, some of them pretty. But none of them catch my fancy. Something's missing. You're different and that makes you special. I don't want to screw this up. So if that sounds like I'm pushin' back, well yes ma'am, I am. Start by talkin' to me. Explain to me why I feel connected to you—and I know you know it."

"How can you be so sure I know anything?"

"Because you have been in my mind, and I think I have been in yours. It happened a few days ago. I saw your face, only you were different and far away. I don't know how or why you're in my head, I just can't stop thinking about you."

"Maybe that's something else."

"I know what you're implying, but it's not so much romantic as it is knowing without speaking. Does that make sense?"

"It makes perfect sense. We connect. We can think to each other. We do think to each other."

"Well I'd sure like to know why it's happening with you, now. I was just cruisin' along, until all of a sudden there you were outta' nowhere, kinda smilin' at me in my head."

"Do you think people can send thoughts to each other?"

"Yeah maybe. My dad and I do it sometimes, but I don't know how. I'm still trying to figure it out. It's been happening to me since I was a kid. A thought pops into my head, an answer, a bit of conversation. Sometimes I think it's just coincidence. Could I have guessed it, or hoped for it, or thought it was a possible conclusion? Sure. But there it is all the same, a bit of knowledge that just comes to me."

"Why are you so sure it's from another person and not just something you make up?"

"Because sometimes I think 'go left' when I see someone, and they do it. Sometimes I think a silent question and get an answer back, as if I had asked it out loud. I was in this bar once that had a dart board. I couldn't see it from where I sat, but I could see this guy throwin'. So when he finishes, I think to myself 'what's the score?' And I get this answer right back in my head '191'. Came in so clear I had to walk over and see for myself. Sure enough, he's writin' 191 on the scoreboard. Where's that comin' from? I know I get messages and sometimes send them, but I can't control it. So tell me why I can read your mind but can't make sense of what I find."

"I think we're trying to read each other's mind, don't you?"

"Yeah, sometimes I get that, but you're different."

"Not so different. I acquired this knowledge the same way you did. Your mind knows a new fact or hears a voice answer and you don't think much about it. And then that kind of spontaneous knowing starts happening more often, slow at first, but you begin to think 'I'm not imagining this, I can do this' and then you start to test it. And that's when it gets interesting because there are all sorts of possibilities that might explain it. But after you go through all the reasons you can think of that it can't be possible, there's the chance that it is... possible."

"What exactly?"

"Mental contact, mind to mind, telepathy. That's where you are now, Arney. Telepathy is real, at least for you. So allow the possibility that when you get a message out of thin air that turns out to be true, it might be because you have communicated with someone else. You allowed another person's mind to make a connection." She saw his eyes widen ever so slightly.

"Familiarity is key. Trust is the gatekeeper. All this happens more frequently among family members for obvious reasons, but not always. There's stranger-to-stranger contact, too. Times when, out of the blue, you ask a question in your mind and get an answer right back, as if you'd had the conversation out loud, but not a word was spoken."

"Like with the darts."

"Yes, like with the darts. Then there are times when you change your mind without knowing quite why, but the reason becomes apparent later. Maybe you avoided a calamity because you took another route. But you write it off as coincidence. The idea that you knew what to do in advance is too far fetched. What kind of connection would that have to be, you ask yourself."

"I thought it was just person to person. You sayin' there's more?"

"A lot more. You're beginning to experience the collective. Human beings are thinking to each other all the time. Most just don't realize it because the idea seems so mind-boggling, so impossible. But is it? What is the next logical step in the evolution of the species if it isn't that minds should join together for the benefit of all. Nothing else makes sense."

"So the fact that I can do this is a good thing? Sometimes I'm not so sure."

"Oh Arney it's a wonderful thing. You have a gift."

"Why me? Why you, now?

"Happy accident? Maybe, but you don't think so and neither do I. It's because we share something. I know you know it, too. Please give me your arm and close your eyes. I'm going to touch you, and I want you to tell me what you feel." She laid her hand gently across his bare arm.

"That feels good."

"Why does it feel good? It's just my hand. What else do you feel?"

"Like something's flowing into me, threads of something good. It's like you're in me but you're not."

"Now, will you kiss me?"

The sound of the old Ford coming back to life split them apart like a bolt from the blue. Arney was in mid-spin floating back down from a place he hadn't been in a long time. He could see through her eyes, unwinding his hand from her hair so as to cause no pain. "I don't know if I can do this again."

"Why? Because of how you feel about Louise?"

"Because I never thought I would—"

The sound of a stretching spring interrupted him.

Donna came through the screen door at the first chug of the motor starting and began to applaud her husband's gift until he noticed. "Nice job honey." He bowed.

Ducar echoed the sentiment. "It is a nice job Harry. She sounds better than she has in years. Thanks, and think about what I said tonight, about what it means that I have this device you made. How did I get it Harry? I didn't just find it in some field. I'll come over in the morning and we'll talk more."

"Can I have it back?"

"No."

Ducar could see Shereen and Arney had joined Donna on the side porch to listen to the old A run. "Thanks for dinner Donna. It was a fine meal."

"I'm glad you enjoyed it."

"Are you ready Leslie? It's time to go." Ducar climbed into the driver's seat and stared at her until she could feel the pull.

"I gotta go. See you tomorrow."

"Goodnight Leslie."

Arney watched the old Ford pull out onto the gravel and begin working its way up the hill behind the house and out of sight. "Hey Pop, did you watch them leave just now?"

"No, why?"

"'Cause I thought I saw some kind of purpley shimmer underneath the car when it went over the rise. Must have been moonlight on the gravel."

The old Ford had barely left the grass when Ducar thought. *Don't do that anymore, Shereen. It's not safe and it's not fair to him.*

I know the rules, she thought back. *This just feels right somehow. Why isn't it safe? Do you have a history here?* The pause was telling. *Did something happen to you here? Is that why you keep coming back? Did you make contact with someone here? Who was she, Captain?* She probed and found a shield of privacy around the answer that would not yield, even to her.

135

19

Copper

Arney's observation about a purple wave underneath the Dannys' car had Harry up pacing way past his bedtime. Jack Danny he could dismiss. But his son and grandchildren were all in agreement. Something about the waves moved stuff and it damn sure didn't belong under an old Ford.

"Where are these waves coming from? Who are these people anyway?"

"Harry? You comin' to bed?"

"Not right now, I've got a few things to sort." He lit up his computer and found the video Luke had made. "That car must have been comin' up the road about the same time they saw the wave. Got to be here somewhere." He scrolled near the end of the video. "No wave in the sky, but there's dust here, so there oughta' be dust farther back. Wait a minute," he said out loud. "That's not right."

"What did you say Harry?"

"Nothin' dear, have a nice dream." He checked it again. There was no dust to the left of the escarpment, only on the right. "That car started up behind the rocks. So how the hell did it get there?" That question set him thinkin' about Jack again, if that was his name.

He scanned the video again, searching the dark sky for any anomaly. The signs were not in the sky but in the dust as it rose. He could just make out traces of the waves in the billows of debris.

"They know about my experiments. That's why they're here checkin' me out. I must have discovered somethin' top secret. They're feds, FBI maybe. That's why those two don't feel right. Jack and Leslie, my ass."

Weaving the possibilities together kept Harry up until almost 3:00 trying reconcile their stories with what he thought was fact. The waves appeared when his stacks took off. Even the neighbors had seen them. Both boys and Barbara saw them at the wedge.

"It must be the Feds 'cause whoever made those other waves were already here. They had to be. They didn't just drop out of the sky." Harry's mind eased. "They're just cops. No such thing as aliens."

The knock on the front door woke Harry up in the easy chair where he had spent the night. "Dammit, it's five-thirty in the mornin'. Who the hell is that? I haven't even had my coffee yet, ain't fair." He kept his voice quiet in deference to Donna's slumber and opened the door.

"Hello Jack. It's kinda early. You need help again?"

"Yes, but not the way you think. I told you I was coming back. Can I come in?"

"Alright. Your daughter with you?"

"I left her sleeping. We need to talk alone."

"You want some coffee? I'm gonna start the pot."

"That'd be nice. You look a little ragged. Are you okay?"

"I didn't get much sleep last night. Listen, Jack. Why don't we cut to the chase. Tell me who you work for, and I'll tell you what you want to know. Who are you? FBI? CIA? 'Cause this alien crap ain't flyin' with me. You're in my face at the crack of dawn. Why don't you just arrest me now and get it over with?"

"That's not what this is Harry. I don't work for the government, not yours anyway. I came to talk about this." He held the small stack up again.

"You found that in a field somewhere. Good for you. I'll admit, I made it. What's that prove?"

"It proves you're a smart SOB, too smart for your own good. No Harry, I didn't pick this up by the side of the road. One of my crew chased it down 532,271.3 miles above where we are right now, and it wasn't easy."

"I didn't think we had rockets that could do that."

"You don't. No government on this planet does. Remember, I said we're not from around here and that's what I meant, not from this planet, not from this solar system. That's not my home star coming up over that hill. Mine's forty-one light-years away."

"Oh please, I'm takin' my coffee outside. This is gonna be good." Harry held the screen door, taking care not to let it slam. When they had settled, he began again. "Well, at this point all I have is your story. Might make a good book, but so far it's bupkis. Show me your ID. Don't you people have to produce identification when a law abidin' citizen asks?"

"Look at me, Harry. Look closely at my eyes. Come on. I won't bite. Look at them."

Harry fixed his gaze on Jack's eyes. They began to change color from brown to green and the whites to pale blue. The skin around them went from farmer's tan to shimmering copper. Then Jack's brown hair turned gold. "Who the hell, no, what the hell are you?" As the transformation progressed Harry had to admit it fit nothing he knew. "Okay, let's say I believe you just for the sake of argument, even though I suspect this is a parlor trick, a good one I'll grant you but a trick nonetheless. I think you hypnotized me."

"Really?" Jack's appearance snapped back instantly.

Hairs stood on end. Everything guarding the walls of Harry's doubt came crashing down and he was afraid, without refuge.

"If you're not Jack Danny, then who the hell are you?"

"Like I said, we have a lot to talk about. I want you to listen for a while and I will try to answer all your questions in turn. My name is Andin Ducar. I am captain of the U.A.S. Xelanar."

"Don't you mean U.S.S.?" Harry interrupted.

"It stands for United Aleri Ship. I'm Aleri. I come from Aleria, a planet forty-one light-years out that way." A copper-skinned hand appeared in mid gesture and was gone. "My crew and I are part of the Shepherds Watch. We volunteer our time to help emerging worlds like yours, to keep you from blowing yourselves up or starving yourselves to death before you mature as a species."

"Are you the only ones watching? I mean you Alerians."

"It's Aleri, and no, we're not the only ones. There are four other worlds nearby. We rotate the watch."

"Why would you bother?"

"Sometimes we ask ourselves that very question. I guess the best answer for you is self preservation. Evolution has lots of traps. Think about it. Survival of the fittest works to select the best genes going forward. But after the choice is made aggression gets in the way, especially when the need for combat is over. It festers as an instinct that proves disastrous. The key to survival is cooperation. If you don't learn to share, you either kill each other off or you overpopulate and use up your resources."

"Sounds to me like you've been listenin' to the tree-huggin' nut jobs. Are you tellin' me the way we are now won't work? I know we've got problems, but there's nice folks around here, wouldn't hurt a fly. They go to church every Sunday."

"But do they help, Harry? Are they giving, or are they getting? Are they bringing people together or pushing them apart? Sometimes it's money. Sometimes it's color. Sometimes it's politics or religion. Sometimes it's which side of the river you live on. It doesn't matter what separates you, it matters that it does. And you have to be smart enough to see that for what it is, because your world cannot survive divided."

"Excuse me if this is a stupid question, but I still don't see what's in this for you. Why bother if there's no hope for us?"

"Because water planets like this are rare, and one as beautiful as this is rarer still. If your species doesn't make it here, perhaps another will." He waved his hand across the sky as he had a moment before, flashing copper skin for emphasis. "Remember this is all alive and wants to know itself. And it needs eyes to see. That's our job. The rest well... Only the sum total of it all can know itself. All we can do is live out our part in this process the best way we can, and then die as we must."

"It's the dyin' part I'd like to put off a little if I can."

"You don't vanish when you do. You are gathered up by the rest of life. Everything living dies, including all this." Again, he gestured up. This time his arm transformed along with hand and fingers. "Everything changes and gets rearranged and reborn. So what does all this mean? If everything is over in the end, what's the purpose of our lives? I would suggest it is thought. That's what we leave behind, our thoughts. But I digress."

"What difference does that make? It's not how I was raised. Just a lot of bunk as far as I can see. You sure are a preachy SOB."

"Your problem Harry is you can't believe anyone would bother to travel from star to star to help this world, so I can't be real. Let's go back to bugs. If the bacteria in your gut are good for you, you prosper. If they're not, you don't. Because you need them, you want the best bacteria you can get. We're just trying to help that idea along on a bigger scale by helping whole worlds."

"Let's say I buy the do-gooder part. Where's your spaceship? How'd you get here in the first place, that is if you're from anywhere other than up the road. I mean seriously, this has been interesting. Don't get me wrong, I love the story. That trick with your skin is great. I just ain't buyin' it. I don't believe you. I know you can sell a boat load of shit when you have to, just not to me is all, not to me. What about time? These distances you're talking about are so great you should be dead by now. How long do you live anyway?"

"About 350 hundred of your years. It's not forever. We get tired of dealing with the discomfort of old age. I'm sure it's the same way here."

"Just because you have a long life doesn't give you time to get here. As fast as you can go can't be near fast enough even if you do have a couple of hundred years on me."

"When you learn to control gravity you can control the effects of time and space. We bend it, space I mean. How I love the phrasing of your language. We fold it so that two points in space lie close together. Then we slip the gap."

"No way in hell do you fold space."

"Actually Harry, we do. We use a more refined version of this motor you built to do just that. It's what makes this device so dangerous to the rest of the galaxy. You can really screw things up with an unshielded anti-gravity motor like this. I'm here to prevent you from hurting yourself and everyone else on this planet. Why do you doubt this? Wake up Harry, I'm trying to help you here."

"Show me your true self, the way you look to your own people, not just a little peek."

"Alright, if that's what it takes. I suppose you're entitled."

The transformation was complete in less than a second. It happened all over, all at once. Before Harry sat a copper skinned, gold haired alien with two light green eyes and whites turned robin's egg blue. His ears lay flat against his head until they bent forward to catch the sound. His nose was thinner and flatter than a human nose; his lips thin, closing over light green teeth, more like him than not.

"Holy shit, how'd you do that? That's a great illusion or you're a shape-shifter."

"Maybe you ought to walk around and catch your breath."

"I don't get it, you're not that different from me. How come?"

"Because equally viable planets give rise to similar looking beings. It's just a matter of time. Atoms bang into each other and things change. Eventually the laws of physics win out. What is inefficient is lost, what works goes on." Ducar swept the sky. "Almost all of us have two eyes and two ears and one mouth and one nose, because that is what's efficient. We are not so different." He changed back to his human form. "It's just that we got started much earlier and have learned more."

"I thought you were supposed to be green or gray and short."

"That would be the Tulars and the Carei. They are part of this watch. We just relieved the Carei. They look very much like us except that they're a little shorter, and their skin color is gray. Their interstellars are cigar shaped."

"I know lots of people say they've seen something in the sky. Different shapes and sizes of lights that go real fast and then turn on a dime and vanish."

"An anti-gravity field is a bubble of force that removes the effects of mass. So, inside the bubble you effectively have no mass. You can change direction at will."

"That's cool. Never could figure how that might work. So you're telling me all these aliens people see with different saucers and different skin are really the Shepherds you're talking about?"

"They're all here to help. We watch over you while you mature."

"I'm mature. Hell, I'm old. How much more mature do I need to be?"

"It's not you personally. It's the whole human race. You have to grow up and join together. It takes a long time. Learn to share and you have a chance. Look Harry, I know you're having a hard time with this, but ask yourself how long have you been hearing about UFO's?"

"All my life."

"And you think it's all bullshit, well it's not. We've been here continuously since the first atom bomb tests. The moment you are capable of destroying yourselves we try to make sure that you don't. We see it over and over again. It's one of the main reasons we Shepherds exist."

"Unbelievably noble if you ask me."

"Like I said, it's self-interest. We're not saving you so much as this planet."

"What are some other reasons?"

"Well, there's a situation like yours. Your discovery here is a problem. Scientific knowledge is always meant to expand, just not so fast Harry. We know what you must learn, but there's an order to it."

"How so?"

"It's evolutionary. You can't safely control the science of anti-gravity until you develop the mental discipline. First, you learn to communicate with each other telepathically. That leads to a world-mind. Then you discover the anti-gravity motor and then you master the stardrive."

The screen door squeaked open. "You boys are up early. What's this about a drive? Are you two going somewhere?"

20

Little Green Men

Donna didn't seem surprised that Jack had shown up so early. She did what was normal and gathered him in. "You guys want something to eat? Jack, you will stay for breakfast, won't you?"

"Thanks, that would be nice."

"Scrambled or fried?"

"Scrambled, thanks." Ducar could hear the sounds of breakfast cooking not long after the screen door closed.

"That was close Harry," he said. "Don't tell Donna about this until we've had a chance to finish talking. I know you have doubts. It's a huge leap. A lot to take in, because if I am who I say I am, I've come a long damn way to have this conversation."

"Donna's not ready for any of this."

"Let's talk in the barn after breakfast? I've violated enough protocols already. None of this is to be shared, for your own safety and mine."

"It's ready. You boys go and wash up now," Donna called out from the kitchen.

It was a big meal, eggs fried and scrambled, bacon, sausage, hash browns and fresh coffee. "This looks wonderful Donna. I haven't seen a meal like this in a long time. You shouldn't have gone to the trouble."

"It's no trouble cookin' for one more. I do this for Harry." She paused, then held his eye and asked, "Jack, what were you and Harry talking about? What's with the whispers? Is it about what I heard at the market? Kids talkin' about what they saw at the wedge?"

"I don't know what the wedge is."

"It's a place, a clear-cut that overlooks a valley over there." She pointed west. They saw waves of light out there at night, purpley and not like heat waves." She could feel Harry glaring at her.

"I'm sorry Harry. This has gone far enough. People aren't just talking about the wedge, they're talkin' about right here, right out there in your barn Harry. And here you are, the two of you, up at the crack of dawn whispering. Which is it? Little green men or black magic? They can't seem to make their minds up in town. So you two put your heads together and figure out how to tell me what the hell is going on."

It was not the Donna he was used to, and the rest of the meal was awkward.

After the dishes were cleared, Ducar tried for peace. "You know Donna, that was one of best breakfasts I've had. You are a fine cook."

"I'm glad you enjoyed it. Now why don't you and Harry grab some coffee and retreat to his sanctuary. And boys I'm serious about gettin' an answer I can count on."

When Harry and his new partner in crime had retreated to the safety of the barn, Ducar spoke first. "We've got a problem here Harry. This is the danger of First Contact. It can go very badly if panic sets in. You need to listen to me. Don't put up a mental block, just listen. First, ask yourself why would I be willing to risk exposure? It must be important to me, my mission, and the crew I command. And it's of critical importance to you. You see these devices you've been working on, the stacks that fly from the spinners as you call them, they're very dangerous. You don't know what you're playing with."

"Well, I have some idea. Since they keep pushing up, they must be some kind of anti-gravity machine."

"They are more than that. These are unshielded time disruptors, crude anti-gravity motors with no way to control them. If they get away, the future is forever altered. They leave eddies in the currents of dark matter. Nudge a planet into different orbit and down through time something happens that wouldn't have but for the kick of one of these."

"That makes for a nice story but the more I hear, the more I'm thinking great makeup, the illusions in your costume are first rate. You're a fine actor, and sometimes I get sucked right in except I can't afford to be. Jack, I think you found my stack of discs by the side of the road, although I don't understand how you got them inside that crystal. What do you hope to gain from this charade? This ain't Area 51."

"It was going straight up Harry." Ducar held up Harry's escapee once again. "But as it's out of balance and unshielded, as soon as other gravitational forces started acting on it, its path became hard to predict. I know you have thought about this Harry. This isn't a new idea is it?"

"No, it ain't."

"Alright then. Let yourself have the rest of the puzzle, because you have a big problem and you need my help. The reason we're talking in the first place is all about this little terror of yours. My crew and I are here to make sure this discovery happens when your world is ready for it, not before. Our scientists estimate that will occur no sooner than about 250 years from now. So this doesn't belong here and neither do you. Except that here you are. Are you beginning to see the problem?"

"I was just tryin' to discover a new force."

"Well that's the issue— isn't it Harry? If you hadn't of been so damned smart, we wouldn't be facing this."

146

"Facing what? "

"Sanctions."

"Sanctions, on what? What are you talking about?"

"Shepherd Council protocols require the destruction of anyone or anything related to anti-gravity science breakthroughs before a species has achieved a world-mind. All this has to go, the farm, any neighbors who know."

"Me?"

"Sorry Harry."

"My family, too?"

"Probably. There cannot be a trace left of your idea. Most of the time an entire species is turned to dust just to prevent infection."

"You can't be serious. I am not a disease!"

"Your discovery is. This is a motor, but it's also a stardrive and a time machine. It doesn't just take an advanced mind to produce it; it takes an advanced frame of mind to regulate its power responsibly."

"You want to blow me up because of what I've discovered. A government coverup if I ever saw one."

"Government yes. But not yours. I don't make the rules. The local systems decide on the protocols. The faster you gather this in, the better your chances are."

"Chances of what?"

"Surviving. This planet is still at war. We cannot allow your species to become interstellar before you find peace. You must learn to think to each other before the peace I speak of is possible."

"I hear unspoken thoughts. Sometimes they're in my head without words, and sometimes I hear them like we're speakin' now."

"Yes, you do Harry. You and your boy both do. You are quite sensitive."

"How do you know about Arney?"

"Let's not get bogged down. We've got a lot to cover."

"No wait. How do you know about Arney's gift? We don't share that with anyone but family."

"I read his mind. Well, I didn't read it. One of my crew members did. Harry, I want to focus. We'll deal with Arney in a moment. This is what matters." He waved his hand over the spinner and the debris on the barn floor. "All this has to stop."

Harry opened his mouth as if to ask 'why?'

Ducar sensed the thought and cut him off. "I told you why. We use these to power our worlds and to travel between them. But everything has to be balanced for that to work. These unshielded devices disrupt navigation. When that occurs nearby anti-gravity devices go into a fail-safe mode and cease to function. You can't imagine the chaos that envelops a world when critical motors come to a complete stop. So it's time for you to show me exactly what you've been up to out here."

"I've been making discs of various materials and seeing what they do when they get spun up together. I'll stop for sure if it saves my family. What else do you want me to do? This technology can't be that important if I can figure it out."

"You have a piece of the puzzle Harry, just not all of it. This needs shielding to work properly. Once you have both sides of the equation, you are on your way. It isn't easy. Still, those who do manage to constrain one make their species' greatest discovery... unlimited energy, the key to the stars."

"The more you talk, the less I'm buyin' it. Are you tryin' to tell me someone or something's gonna keep tabs on us until we grow up, however long that takes? How did you get here anyway?"

"Anti-gravity Harry. The big ships use black holes like gas stations. Remember, we fold space. Then we slip the gap. That's how we got here."

"And when you say we, that means your daughter too? She's got copper skin, like you?"

"Yes Harry, she's Aleri."

"So what the hell am I supposed to tell Donna?"

"I'd go for little green men."

Harry dreaded the whole idea of trying to explain to Donna that she might have just cooked breakfast for an alien from a planet light-years away. That would be shock enough. He decided to keep the danger to himself.

"Donna where are you honey?"

"Up here making the beds."

Harry climbed the stairs searching for something that wouldn't tip her over the edge. In the end he settled for, "Jack says he's not human. Says he's an alien from a planet outside our solar system. And his name's not Jack."

"Have you lost your mind Harry? Are you really going for little green men? Really?"

"I had a choice—make somethin' up or tell you the truth. We've always said we wouldn't lie to each other and I'm not startin' now."

"You're serious. Really? How do you know you're not getting your chain yanked Harry? Don't be such an old fool."

"Jack showed me what he looks like, not how he appears to us. He's copper and gold and green sometimes, different but more like us than not."

"How come he speaks perfect English like he was born right over the next hill? And he's got Levis older than yours. Where'd he get those from? And the old Ford? Harry I know you mean well, but you're going to have to prove it to me and I've still got beds to make."

"Come out to the barn when you're done then. He can show you, too. I still don't know if I believe him or not, so I want you to tell me what you see."

The next time Harry heard her voice, she was calling both men from the top of the porch steps. "I want to talk to both of you. Can you come into the kitchen please?"

Even Ducar felt a little sheepish in the face of such an imperative. "Take a seat. Thanks. Now Jack, what's this Harry tells me about you being from outer space? Because I don't think this is funny and I've got no time for foolishness."

"Donna, Harry is telling you the truth and I would love to explain, but I don't have time. Harry can fill you in. What I will do is show you a little of how I appear to my people. But before I do, let me say that I learned to speak like I was born over the next hill using the language library on board my ship."

"How do you know I said that?"

"I can read your mind."

"Are you saying you can get inside my head?"

"I am. We'll talk about all this later. Right now, I need you to watch." Ducar revealed an eye and cheek and some hair. "Enough or do you need more?"

"The whole enchilada. Peel mister. So far you're just a skilled makeup artist. I want to see it all."

Ducar decided to abandon modesty in favor of leaving no doubt. It took a second to transform from older man to middle-aged Aleri. Donna promptly fainted into Harry's arms.

"Why don't you put her to bed Harry. She'll wake up when she's comfortable with the idea."

21

Whatcha Got

Once Donna was resting, Harry began pulling the covers off his experiments. All the tarps and carefully stacked boxes of concealment were moved back to reveal his treasures. Ducar could see he had been resourceful. "You made a lot of these, didn't you? How long before you found a combination that worked?"

"Nothing worked until my toolbox moved. After that it was easier, because the possibilities got narrowed down."

"What happened with your toolbox?"

"It moved by itself, when I was throwing some old parts into it, parts from my earliest experiments. Broke right through that wall. Well, not right away. It slid into the wall and cracked some planking first. It only went through the wall when I tried to pull it back."

"How long ago was that?"

"I don't know, three weeks maybe."

Ducar thought to Shereen, *Ask Kothry to check the sensor logs around the time we first started having trouble with them and send me back what he finds. I want to know when they happened and how much time elapsed between the first two readings.*

Yes sir, I'll project it now. Ducar used Shereen's greater mental range to his advantage. She could reach the ship's crew without effort. *He says about 90 minutes.*

Which one was stronger?

The second one, maybe twice the force of the first, still just above background levels.

"Dammit!"

"What did you say that for?" Harry asked, since it came out of the blue.

"You've been emitting pulses Harry, waves of anti-gravitational anomalies, looks like starting with your toolbox. We have anti-gravity sensors in place to monitor this, and they've been alerting for weeks. But the levels were so low we thought they were malfunctions or dense body collisions. Now I see they were not."

"Is that bad?"

"Worse than bad Harry. Eventually more distant sensors will pick up these pulses and compute that there is a problem. We just have to hope that the Shepherd Council decides they are quantum anomalies. How many of these stacks of disks actually moved, just the one I caught or were there others?"

"Well a couple of times my spinners creaked and some of the support boards separated. And then there were the two that got away. Damndest thing I ever saw. They both went straight up."

"Two Harry?"

Harry pointed and Ducar saw the holes on the underside of the roof that was only one big patch from above. "

"The other one, was it as big as this?" It was show and tell again.

"I made it first. It was bigger."

"How big?"

"Five inches in diameter."

"Dammit Harry." Ducar cursed again to make his point. "How much mercury?"

"Just a trace. How did you know about that?"

"It's an essential part of an anti-grav motor, mercury in combination with certain metals spun in different directions. It all depends on which metals and how much mercury you use. Can you remember how fast it was going?"

"Well now that you mention it, it was out of sight within five or six seconds."

Ducar did a fast computation. It was beyond catching. *Loose and gone who knows where*, he thought.

"What did you say?"

"I didn't say anything. This little stack is dangerous enough. Unfortunately the other one is much worse, because that's the one that got away. We've got a big problem. The initial pulse from your first stack has probably reached other sensors by now. That means another Shepherd patrol may have picked up the signal."

"I really didn't mean to hurt anyone. I thought it would make things better if I found more energy. Made sense to me anyway. Then the toolbox moved and changed everything. It went from being 'if' to 'I know you're here. I've felt you move.' I had to make it real. It was more than a dream."

"What did you see in your dream?"

"Sets of shapes. There was two of 'em. First one looked like a wire spring wrapped loosely around a rod with a small plate on the end. The other looked like spinning disks stacked on top of each other. I saw them for days until I decided to make them. Then the dreams went away. I figured it was a sign. But the first stuff didn't work out. At least I didn't think so, until the toolbox took off on me. Don't ask me how I got here. I don't know. It just came to me and wouldn't stop, and I could see how to do it. Not the first stuff, but the discs, I mean. I knew I could make these, and I did. And they work. Well, they move anyway. I just can't keep them down yet."

"You won't contain them with baffles full of vegetable matter.

And the big one's not coming down. It's gone. It will find a path between the gravity sources, until it is captured."

"Well, if you don't mind my asking, how come it's so dangerous if all it does is avoid things?"

"You now know anti-gravity motors are repelled by mass. What you don't know is that they are attracted to each other, so they have to be shielded, to help steer and to avoid a spontaneous joining."

"What the hell is that?"

"It's when a naked stack gets close enough that the attraction can't be broken. The layers try to line up by density. It usually rips both motors apart and destroys the bearings and sometimes the frame as well."

"I didn't mean to make trouble, I swear."

"It's alright Harry, unfortunately the game's just changed. First of all, you need to know I will not hurt you or this beautiful world, but there are some coming who will. It's not a matter of if. Second and more important, there are things we can do."

"You gonna let me in on it or do I just have to sit here?"

"You could come with us."

Harry stood straight up. "I could what?"

"Not just you, your whole family too. You could come with us. We'll wipe out the traces of your experiments and plant suggestions in the minds of your neighbors. In the end, they won't remember you. When the Carei show up, there will be nothing to find."

"You mentioned them. How come you know it's them comin'?"

"Because they're closest and I know Tergana. He's a stickler for the rules, but nice enough right up to the point where he has a legitimate reason to dust you. Then well, I just think he likes it. That's not right." Then Ducar rose and said, "You need to meet my crew Harry. Everybody does—your whole family, at one big dinner aboard the Xelanar. Tonight. Make some calls and change some minds. I want everybody in that valley below the wedge by eight o'clock tonight. A door will open. All you have to do is step through it. I promise you smiling faces. These are good people—well, good Aleri—and you're gonna love the cooking. Say what you have to, but get them there."

"Donna isn't going to like this at all."

"Get them there Harry. Your lives depend on it. I've got to go."

Minutes later when Ducar opened the door to #21 at the Starlite Motel the room was empty. Ducar thought, *Where are you, Shereen?*

I'm walking back to the motel. I won't be long, five minutes maybe. I just couldn't stand the bad smells and nothing to eat. I'm bringing coffee and doughnuts.

Ducar was pacing when she opened the door.

"Are you alright sir?"

"Not really. We have a big problem. I need you to message Jasca. Tell him we're going to have company, and tell Ella there will be six more for dinner. Use your subtlest approach. I don't want him to overreact. He won't like this breach of protocol, so soothe him if you can without him becoming aware."

"And when he asks why, what should I tell him?"

"Tell him we are doing a species comparison. We'll wipe their minds when we drop them off, the way we usually do. We'll need a rendezvous at the same place we unloaded the car—eight tonight, the big scout, cloaked."

"He won't buy that. You know visitors aren't allowed outside the lab. That violates our protocols. We can't just let them see us. These people aren't ready. Why are you doing this?"

"Because our farmer friend Harry has solved most of the stack and coil problem."

"I know that, but you caught the rogue."

"We should have caught two. We missed detecting his first

one when we were repairing our array. It's been on its own for days. We won't be catching it, but the Carei might have detected it. So we have to prepare for their return. If Tergana has proof of a violation, he won't warn. He'll just dust this place, probably raze the whole surface to be safe. I don't want that to happen."

"I know you've been here before, several times in fact."

"Three, this my fourth tour."

"Okay three. Even so, whatever affections you have for this place can't be allowed to get in the way of good judgment. We have the proof. So if it has to be, we should be the ones to do the cleansing, not the Carei. Why hesitate? Why do you care at all?"

"Because my wife and son might be here."

Shereen stared at him. "Oh Captain, you can't be serious. Your wife? Was she human? How long ago? Given the time compression between shifts here, she's probably... " Shereen's voice trailed off to silence.

"Gone. Yes, I suppose so. But I can't find an obituary in the records."

"Why didn't you tell me? I would have helped you find her. What's her name?"

"Anne Gillespie, Gilly. She brought me to life."

"You must have loved her, to risk so much."

"If I tell you, you can't—"

"I promise, no one will ever get it from me."

"I suppose I've held this in far too long. I bumped into her in 1964 not far from here. I was there to observe. Her touch sent me spinning. She flowed through every part of me before I had a chance to shield my mind."

"You should have followed protocol and moved away immediately."

"I didn't have a choice. The cross-neural transfer was instantaneous. By the time I pulled back it was too late. She was inside me fizzing through my nervous system. I wanted her so I left, out through the front door and started walking away.

Didn't look back, just kept moving. When I got down around a bend, I took a quick look to see if anyone was following. But they weren't."

"And you didn't think to ask for help?"

"I thought I could shake it off. My body would eliminate it over time. But it just got worse. The more I tried not to think about her, the more I thought about her. She warmed me up swirling through me, calling. Like there was this path between us, threads of thought pulling us closer. I could smell her, a perfume, calling. I had to see her again. I know. That's when I crossed the line. But I didn't have a choice. It was too late. I was already bound. She was beautiful, inside and out. I had to see her again, so I set up a meeting. Before I knew it, we were us. She wasn't an empath, but she knew exactly what to say and where to touch and when to say nothing at all. She was everything I couldn't find at home—a passion for life we seem to have lost in our homogeneity."

"She was the love of your life, wasn't she?"

"And the mother of my child. There was never anyone else after."

"You broke every rule here, didn't you? Now I know what you've been hiding behind your solitude. You don't want this world to fail in spite of its slim chance. You'll save this place at any cost. You have put every member of the crew at risk because your heart is broken. Captain, you are a sworn officer of the Watch. You should know better. You do know better. What the hell were you thinking?"

"If I had been thinking we wouldn't be having this conversation. It isn't about thought. It has no words. I can't really describe it. We became one being in two bodies, and we knew we belonged to each other and together. And that's how we stayed until I had to ship out. When my tour was up, I told her I had another mission that would keep me away at least three years. Then I left. I haven't been the same since. I miss my boy. I miss my wife."

"You got married?"

"Not legally. Things were a little looser back then. We just said we were. Look Shereen, if I had it to do all over again, I would have walked away before anything happened. Instead I left a wife and a little one to fend for themselves, and it wasn't right. I've been living with it ever since."

"What happened when you returned the next time? Did you go back and see her?"

"I couldn't, they had aged. It didn't seem fair to intrude and try to explain why I was still so young. I resolved to keep watch over them."

"I'm sorry I pressed you. I had no idea. Don't worry, I'll keep your secret.

22

A Night Out

Mark lifted the receiver and answered before the second ring had finished, a new personal best. "Dad? Grampa's on the phone. He says it's important." Mark ramped up the volume. "Dad?"

"I'm coming, I'm coming."

"Hi Pop, what's up? You need my help for something?"

"I do, but not the way you think. Come over as soon as you can. I don't want to do this over the phone."

"Alright, give me fifteen." Arney hung up the phone and smelled his armpits. "Oh well, the old man'll have to take me as I am,." He put on his boots. "What the hell. If I don't shave I'll be there in two," and started the Harley. It took less.

"Well that was quick. Thanks for gettin' on it."

"You seem kinda agitated this morning. You alright? What's going on?"

"It's the waves. There's people attached to em', well not people exactly, but they look like us."

"What are you talking about?"

"Those waves we've been seeing, and the motor I made, these people say it's too soon. I shouldn't have made it yet. We're not

159

ready."

"Slow down Pop. Who's not ready for what? And who are these people you're talking about?"

"Jack and Leslie, only his name's not Jack, it's captain something, Ducar. He says his planet's forty-one light-years away. Calls it Aleria."

"I think you need some sleep Pop. Did you stay up late or something?"

"Fell asleep in my easy chair, must have been three."

"So when did you have time to talk to Jack? Was this something he said last night?"

"Partly. But most of it was early this morning. He showed up at dawn, said it couldn't wait."

"What's so important then?"

"They're gonna blow us up. Ducar says the gray ones we hear about are coming from their world to wipe us out, turn us to dust he says."

"And just why would they want to do that?"

"'Cause of me. 'Cause of what I built, what we built. It's an anti-gravity motor, 'cept it has no shielding. That's why they took off. He caught it."

"You tellin' me Jack found your stack of discs?"

"He didn't find it. He chased it and caught it, and his name's not Jack."

"Well Pop, I gotta say. You have quite an imagination, but I still think what you need is a lot more sleep."

"He showed me something Arney. He showed me what he really looks like. Skin's copper and his eyes... well you just gotta see em' that's all. They've been comin' here a long time, them and these other guys. They change shifts every couple of years. Been checkin' up on us for a long time, but since we've been atomic they don't leave. There's always one group or another lookin' after us steady now. He says they're waitin' for us to grow up, make sure we don't hurt anyone else 'til we do."

"Grow up?"

"That's what he said. Says the motor we made is the key to the stars but because we've still got wars and poverty and stuff, we're not supposed to have it yet."

"I don't know if I buy this but let's just say if I did, how come they don't just fix this for us?"

"They can't. It's ours to solve. They can nudge a little but that's all. He says we have to learn to think to each other and take care of each other, kinda like the way you and I do. If we don't learn to do it, we're toast."

"What's he talking about think to each other, you mean telepathy?"

"That's what I mean. Come to think of it, there were times last night and this mornin' when I wasn't sure his lips were movin', but I could hear him plain as day. He was doin' it with me Arney. Thinkin' a conversation instead of talkin'. We gotta' learn to do it with each other."

"Does he mean everyone, all of us?"

"All of us who can, all over the world. He had a name for it but I forgot. But that's not important. We can ask him tonight."

"What's happening tonight?"

"We're gonna have a picnic on board his ship."

"That's it Pop. You're flat out of your mind. On board his ship, my ass. You've been up too long old man. It's time you had a long nap."

"Please son, if you've ever trusted what I have to say, trust me now. Look me in the eye. What do you see?"

"Bloodshot eyes."

"Please, what do you see?"

"Conviction, I guess."

"Damn straight you do skippy. I'm tellin' you, I know what I saw and I know what I heard. I'm not imaginin' this. You'll have your proof tonight. I just need you and the kids to be off the valley road near the escarpment at eight o'clock. No girlfriends, no

161

boyfriend, just family. I don't care what you have to tell them. Blame this on me if you have to, but get 'em there."

The sky was not quite dark when Harry and Donna neared the escarpment with minutes to spare. "Park over there next to Arney." Donna said in her best backseat driving voice.

It hadn't been easy getting her to agree to anything that involved a picnic in the middle of nowhere, especially with strangers she had never met who could change at a moment's notice into God only knew what. She didn't want to think about it. It took Harry over an hour to convince her that Jack and Leslie, or whoever they were, would be coming too. She let the memory of their familiar faces persuade her.

"Where are they?"

"They're comin', I promise. It's almost time."

"Are they bringing the tables? I don't want to eat in the car."

"I think they have tables on board."

"On board what?"

"You'll see. Jack said a door would open and we should just walk in."

"I don't think so Harry. This don't seem right."

"Honey, I promise it will be alright. Come on."

They gathered by the side of the road and waited.

"Look at that. What's that?" Luke saw it first. The outline of a rounded rectangular opening fizzed into view surrounded by streaming purple filaments. Then Jack and Leslie stepped out.

"Evening Harry, Donna, nice to see you. Arney, glad you and your kids could join us. We're going to go for a little ride. Don't be afraid. Just because you can't see her doesn't mean she isn't here. Go on, touch along the sides if you don't believe me," Jack said, urging the boys to help convince Donna she wasn't seeing things, which she wasn't.

"Hey Mark, check this out." Luke tapped away from the door opening and sure enough, even if he couldn't see it, he sure could touch it. "Time to go boys. We've been here too long as it is." Jack was insistent enough to propel Donna across the threshold and into the six-man scout which could hold more with the jump seats down.

"This is so cool," said Mark, grinning as he gathered in the interior of the scout. Any ride in something different was an adventure. "How fast does she go?" he asked the pilot who wasn't sure how to answer.

"Fast enough to singe the hair right off you if you're not careful. It'll fold a parsec if you gun her."

"Can I watch you drive it?"

"Sure, sit right here. The captain won't mind."

"Who's the captain?"

"Right there, Jack."

It was Jack's turn. "Welcome aboard. I know you have a lot of questions, and I promise by the end of the evening you will be right back here with most of them answered. For now, I need you to find a seat. Donna, I don't want you to worry. This is a short trip up to the Xelanar, like a ride in a commuter plane except you won't feel the takeoff or the landing. We are going to have a picnic, and I promise you'll like the food."

"It's not a picnic if it's not outside. Are we going to be outside?" Donna was feeling a little better, since everyone else seemed to be acting normal.

"Sorry, that won't be possible. What do you call an inside picnic?"

"Lunch or dinner, or you could call it a party."

"Alright, young lady, a party it shall be." Ducar knew when to flatter, and it eased Donna to a grin and filled the time it took to get to moonshadow.

"The airlock is sealed. We'll be equalized in thirty, sir."

"Thanks, Kothry. That was an easy ride. I see you had help." Mark beamed. "Alright folks, this is it."

The interior of the Xelanar filled them with wonder. What was sparse on the scout was sumptuous inside the main part of the bell. It was soft and quiet, a feel of luxury without show. It hummed quietly and there was music."

"This is nice," Donna said, being polite in spite of her fear. "I like the music. Who is that?"

"Janja," Shereen answered. "They were popular when we left. Come in and welcome to the Xelanar. This is our home away from home. Can I get you something to drink?" Donna was glad for something to hold on to. The more strangers filtered in to have a look at them, the more nervous she became.

"Leslie, who are these people?"

"The rest of the crew. You already met Kothry. He was our pilot. And that's Jasca and Mrs. Bartole. She does the cooking."

"Are they married?"

"No. He's single and she's married to David Bartole. Don't worry you'll meet them all in time."

"Why is that Jasca fellow frowning?" she whispered to Shereen. "He doesn't look too pleased."

"He just hasn't made peace with this yet. He'll come around. Donna there's something else I should tell you. My name's not Leslie. It's Shereen. And that man you think is my father, he's not my father. That's the captain, Captain Ducar."

"He's not Jack?"

"No, he's not Jack. His first name's Andin, but we just call him sir or captain, or if you know him real well, you can call him Ducar."

Donna decided she would call him Andin since he held no sway over her. What he did hold for her was a bottle of wine, two in fact.

"White or red?"

"White please. Thank you Andin, this is very nice."

Now a good party always hits a point when the volume of collective voices and the pace of conversation increases. A savvy host knows the crescendo marks its success. Make sure nobody gets too drunk and keep any potential combatants apart. Don't talk politics, which they always do, and it has a chance. Despite differences, Shereen could tell the two groups were enjoying each other. After all, they had a lot to talk about.

"How much water do you give your tomatoes?" Ella asked Donna.

It was going to be okay. Inhibitions began to fall. They were not so different after all. Some sharing could begin. Heads leaned closer to catch the nuances that revealed truth.

Arney needed his own. "Leslie, or whatever your name is, I want to talk. Is there somewhere we can go?"

"Sure Arney, down this way. Come on." The walls were smooth with handholds for people of all sizes, family friendly and safe. "These are my quarters. Please come in. But before you say anything, before all the questions, please know I care about you. My affection is real."

"Show me what you really look like. I don't even know your name. Who are you? What are you?"

"My name is Shereen Delare. I am Aleri, not human. Our transformation is for your sake. It's just easier and safer if we get to know each other without fear. First Contact is hard. So many possibilities open all at once. It takes time. Imagine how your mother would react if she saw us as we appear on our own world. I know I owe you an explanation so let's start with what I look like. There are parts of me I wish to keep private but here is the rest of me."

From the slightly edgy redheaded country beauty emerged an elegant woman, forthright and self-possessed, copper skinned with reddish bronze and gold hair and green eyes, utterly alien and beautiful.

"I need a moment to gather this in. How can you look like us but be this?" He fell silent and stared.

"Do you want me to change back?"

"Be who you want to be."

"That's what I want for you, too. Since you can't change your form, I'm going back to being who you know. It's easy for me. Please come here and sit down." She was country by the time he sat. "I think about you. I have for some time. When we were searching for your father, I scanned you. I'm sorry. I didn't mean to intrude but I'm glad I did. I got to know something about you. You don't say much but you send powerful thoughts. You are a compassionate man of strength and skill and I respect you, so ask what you will."

"Tell me why, when I think of you, I feel like whatever happens it's going to be fine. And the sensation when I touch you, what is that?"

"It's our minds knitting our nerves together because we want to. We're trying to become one if you'll let us. Can't you feel the pull?"

"All the time and it scares the hell out of me. I've been here before. I know what this can be. But it doesn't matter. This isn't right."

"It is right. Take my hand and close your eyes." It was like before, pleasantly invasive, but this time he let it in. The tingle of her neural connections entwined him. Then he felt himself joining hers as well. His mind was on both sides at once, and his body followed, tongue deep in her mouth, her head gentle in his hands. He would not give her up now. She opened her bed with one hand and leaned back as he leaned in, all panther and hungry and sure. He knew if he could have his way she would roar and so would he and set out to stir her wet places to life with small temptations. Each new connection increased the desire for more. It fed upon itself, pushing reason down the well of passion. And then she was his and he, hers. They were becoming one being.

He matched bone for bone, pushing ever deeper with each thrust crying out for release red and tender and ready. Then there was no more resistance. Deep within her she throbbed a "please," a pulse of now, a whisper, "Yes, oh God, oh God. Yes!" And she let go. He arched his back and released an arrow of love which she took with little waves of pleasure until she was sure he was empty. It was like nothing she had ever known. "What did you do to me? No, don't go. Stay in me. Don't move. I want to kiss you from inside."

"What are you doing?"

"Taking all of you into me. Hold me and kiss me and... tell me that's not the call to dinner. Arney, we've got get dressed. They'll be wondering where we've been." Arney wasn't sure he knew where he had been. She was as human as any woman he had ever known. As he watched her dress there was no hint of difference lurking. She was a bright-minded, redheaded beauty with a warm heart smiling right at him. "I don't know what to say. I know we crossed a line here. Don't get me wrong, I wouldn't change a thing. That was wonderful."

"It was inevitable. I've been waiting for you. I didn't realize it until now, but we are meant to be. So worry not my love, we are among friends." They walked into the party together.

"Hi Dad, where've ya been? Get lost?" Luke was sure he knew the answer.

"Shereen was showing me around the ship."

"Shereen? I thought your name was Leslie." He had no trouble calling it like he saw it.

"Let's do this again. Hello Luke, my name is Shereen. Glad to meet you. Have you met my sister Niriar?"

"She's your sister?"

"She is."

"She's been looking at me."

Shereen smiled. "Of course she has. You're a good-looking young man. Have you spoken to her yet?"

"Why? We don't belong together. Besides I've already got a girlfriend."

"Aren't you even a little curious?"

"She makes me nervous."

"Oh Luke don't be afraid. She won't bite. Go talk to her."

It was hard for Luke to be casual as he made his way toward her. He caught himself looking at her feet and lifted his head. "Hi, my name's Luke." He knew it had started badly.

She was way ahead. "I'm Niriar. Don't worry, this is always hard, I hear."

"I don't know what to say. You look just like the girls in my school, only prettier."

"I've never met someone 'different' either. You're my first. Do you want to sit together at dinner? We could talk."

"That'd be nice. You've got a younger sister, right?"

"Filaire."

"Where's she?"

"I don't know, and I don't see your brother Mark either. Excuse me. I need to check something."

Niriar could walk the corridors of the ship blindfolded. Filaire's quarters were close to her own. She could barely hear their laughter from the corridor, but it was plain that things had gone too far. She pressed the commport.

"Filaire, it's almost time for dinner. Mark, are you in there, too?" She knew he was but being polite gave them time. There was a shuffle to find shoes and buckle belts. "Hurry up then. It's almost time."

Dinner began with an announcement from Ducar. "Gather around please. Before we take our places there are a few things I would like to say. My name is not Jack Danny. I am Andin Ducar, captain of the Xelanar. As you have no doubt surmised, we're not from around here but we've been your neighbors for a long time, kind of looking out for you while you grow."

"Are you going to do experiments on us?" Mark asked.

"No Mark, the reason we are meeting like this has to do with your grandfather's recent discovery. What he has found is the same source of energy that drives this ship. Usually this discovery takes place after a society becomes telepathic. But your world will not reach that point for centuries to come. So the purpose of this dinner is to get to know each other because we have choices to make. I'll explain what those are after our meal. Let us commune. For our guests, this is like saying grace. If you hear a note you like, feel free to join in."

The harmony began in unison, one note that split apart a tone at a time until the room was filled with five parts of harmony and peace. The guitar player in Arney found it easy to join. The chord made sense. Even Donna felt an urge to contribute what she could, humming a note she could carry. "That was lovely. Do you do that very night?" she asked no one in particular.

"We do it before every meal," responded Jasca, seated beside her. "It helps bind us together. Do you sing in a church, Mrs. Miller? You did that very well." It was hard for him to accept she could join in at all.

"I used to but not so much anymore. What do you do here, dear?"

"I'm second in command."

"Oh, that's very nice. I'm honored then."

Ducar was counting on the wine more than the food to soften resistance. As for the kids, a sense of adventure would have to do. When the last of the frozen dessert melted into empty bowls and the table was cleared, he began. "I hope you all enjoyed your dinner and have had a chance to get to know each other. What I am about to say may frighten many of you, so I want you to know these ideas are not absolutes. I am open to any suggestions."

He waited until he had all eyes. "The members of my crew are volunteers in a collective known as the Shepherds. Water worlds are rare, so the sentient societies that emerge need to be nourished and protected. It is our duty to steer them in productive directions without obvious interference. We want you to join us when you are ready. But before that can happen, there are benchmarks to be met, phases of development that cannot be skipped. And therein lies our problem. Harry's discovery skips over some necessary steps in your evolution." He waited to see if the import of his words had registered. It hadn't. "Let me put this another way. Unless you meet these criteria before the discovery of anti-gravity propulsion," he held up Harry's motor, "well, there are consequences."

"What consequences? Why should there be consequences?" Arney's interruption stirred his group.

"We know Harry means no harm, but this technology is dangerous. It's so dangerous in fact that unless a world is mature enough to develop it sensibly and peacefully, they are considered much like your cancers. So they are cut out."

"Cut out how?" Arney pressed.

"The world is recycled. It all depends on how many people know of the technology. In most cases, a large group makes the discovery over time. If their society is not ready for it, they are all eliminated. The process is not cruel or painful. They just cease to be. They are turned to dust and returned to the ground.

"Usually an entire planet is dusted so that no one is left in anguish. Such an infection cannot be allowed to spread into the galaxy. We fought the wars that resulted when worlds took to the stars intent on conquest. That is why we Shepherds exist, to make sure that never happens again." The room was dead quiet. The message hit home.

"Are we going to die tonight? Is that what this is? You make nice and then what? You just grind us up and spit us out?" It was Arney's voice above the others, speaking for the family.

"Harry, I want to go home." Donna was wiping her eyes.

"Donna, Harry and the rest of you, please. Listen. It would fall to me to perform the excisement, but I will not. Only you gathered here and a few others know anything about this, so there are other possibilities."

"What are they?" Arney demanded.

"You could come with us."

"No, they can't!" Jasca was on his feet in protest. "That violates all our protocols. You can't do this, captain."

"Sit down number two! That will be enough." Shereen immediately started sending thoughts to ease and quiet without being asked. "Please," continued the captain, "calm down, everyone. It is not the only option. We might be able to use this ship to go back in time. It would put us out of reach."

"How far back would we have to go?" Harry asked, gathering in the implications. "How much time would we lose?"

"A few months just to be safe, enough to put the Carei off our trail. But don't think of it as a loss. You'd come back to the present in the end." Ducar waited to see if his suggestion was palatable especially among his own crew, because it was they who would have to keep the secret.

"Is that it?" asked Harry. "Our choices I mean. Are those our options? Go with you or go back?"

"Unless you can think of something else, yes. You don't have to make up your minds tonight. I want you to choose among yourselves, quietly. Do not share any of this. Have a family meeting and let me know what you decide. I know this is a lot to take in, and the choice will be difficult. So while we have each other it is my sincere hope that you will ask as many questions as you can. Then I will take you home."

"I need to feed my animals." Jennifer had been quiet up until now. "And I don't like any of these choices. I'm going to college in the fall. Why should I suffer for a stupid experiment that didn't hurt anybody? It's not fair. I want to go home."

"No, you want to feel safe and nothing about what you've just heard is that, is it? No, it's unbelievable all of it. A choice so bizarre that you can't let the reality sink in. This can't be real. But this is not a movie set. You are on board the U.A.S. Xelanar, an interstellar spacecraft on station, in the shadow of your moon. Come with me Jennifer. I will show you. Don't be afraid. I'm really here to help." He guided Jen away from the crowd and down the corridor to the bridge. "That's the backside of your moon."

"How do I know it's real?"

"It's real, believe me."

"When you put it like that, I'm not sure I do."

"Look at my eyes. I am going to change to the form I was born with, just around my eyes and just for a moment. Are you ready?

"I guess so." The transformation was quick. "Oh God, that's creepy. Is that how you really look?"

"Yes, but I can become who you need me to be without effort. We adopt your form so as not to frighten you. If we were here to harm you, it would have happened already. Does that make sense?"

"I guess so."

"Good, because I need your help."

"Why me?"

"Because you're the level-headed one."

"I am not," she said protecting her rebellion. "That's my dad."

"If he could help me with this, I'd ask him. I want you to keep an eye on your brothers. Try to keep them away from Niriar and Filaire."

"You're too late. At least as far as Mark's concerned. Didn't you see Filaire? She couldn't take her eyes off him. They must have snuck off before dinner."

"Oh please, no. It's time to end this. Follow me."

"Folks, everybody, sorry to break this up. It's time to go. If you'll just follow Shereen to the shuttle bay, we'll be on our way. I hope we can continue this at your place tomorrow, Donna. We'll bring the food, and there's no need to clean the house. We just need more time to blend."

Luke and Niriar were heading to her quarters when Ducar's message reached her mind. "Luke, I'm sorry. You have to go home now. The captain's calling us to the shuttle bay. Tomorrow maybe. We'll see each other tomorrow."

23

Tergana Slips the Gap

The patch of cosmic dust in a field of endless stars began to shimmer, then blur and fill with the shape of the Carei cruiser as it materialized, another hop complete. Warping and folding space-time to shorten distance required tremendous energy. A vessel could only travel as far as its anti-gravity motor's storage capacity would allow. Then it had to stop and compute a new plot before spinning up to recharge and hop again. It was impossible for patrol vessels to make the journey home in a single hop. Only the biggest ships of the line could do it, and that was discouraged as far too disruptive to the fabric of space and time.

It became necessary to assign empty zones, safe areas where a ship could reappear without colliding and strategically placed sentrybots that monitored every wavelength for information, keeping an eye on the road. They searched for anomalies and they were good at it, but they couldn't hop. They counted on ships of the line to convey their data home. The mail and chit-chat they held was incidental. The anti-gravity data however was critical to safe passage.

"Alright, boys and girls, retrieve the sensor data while we prepare for the next one. I don't want to leave anything useful behind. Have we completed the analysis of the first sets?" Tergana's acerbic tone avoided pleasantries as a sign of weakness. Barking got results, so he stuck with it. He would be glad to get home. "How much time left on the recharge? I'd like to get moving."

"Another fifteen minutes sir." The ship's second was tall and handsome, the way the admiral was not. Commander Evin Torel did not need to shout. He gained allegiance with quiet tones that balanced the admiral's cynicism, and everyone loved him for it. "I do have your preliminaries on the early data."

"Anything of note?"

"Maybe. See these early blips, the ones that look like shield scatter? They're the only ones the computer has any trouble with. The rest seem to be quantum anomalies, microbursts of anti-gravity. They've been triggering the sensors with some frequency. So far we see no irregularities except in these last two peaks. The spikes are narrower and stronger but not by much and they don't last long. We'll know more when we've finished correlating the rest of the data from the remotes."

"Alright Commander. Let me know when we can get under way." Impatience oozed from beneath his tapping fingers, the lack of rhythm leaving turmoil exposed and vacant. *Someday someone will invent a sensor system that can be read from home. That will be nice*, he thought. He understood the necessity and resented the lost time, but then Chief Petty Officer Salter approached.

The chief was swarthy and carried his confidence with a low-key boldness. "Here's the latest from the remote sensors, Admiral. Looks like we've got a runner."

"Not possible, not out here. Let me see that."

"It's been moving for days, hard to tell where it came from. Near as I can tell it's unshielded. Naked as your first love. See here, this peak. It's coming fast. And look at this vortex. It's a really small one."

174

"How long before you can get a track?"

"If I tap these local sensors in realtime, maybe five minutes 'til the first hop. Then we'll have to keep jumping on the fly."

"Do it. We're nearest."

The admiral sat up, thinking, *I hate runners, what a waste of time.* He was getting too old for it. No matter how they tried to sell it in flight school, chasing a runner was never fun. At least it was rare. Still a meteor could knock some shielding off a motor, and there went your whole day. The partially shielded ones were erratic. This one would be relatively easy.

"Admiral?" Salter tested for humor. "Anytime you're ready."

"All hands, this is Tergana. Strap in. Thirty seconds. We've got a runner."

The best place to be to avoid any inertial effects was right in the middle of the local anti-grav field, so seating around the perimeter of the main stack was plentiful for those who were bothered by the rapid changes in force. Ninety-degree turns on the space of a dime going 1,000 klics an hour, no problem if you could be right near the center of the stack. But every bit away from it increased the sensation of rapid change of direction and it took its toll.

Three hours went by before the cruiser could sync up with the rogue and corral it. Both main bank computers were warm to the touch from the effort. "Got it sir. It's in a containment field. We're neutralizing it now." Everyone on the bridge could hear in Salter's tone that he was the man of the hour.

"Good job Chief. You're as quick as anyone out here. Lucky it was coming at us. That could have taken a lot longer. Got any ideas about its origin?"

"Not really, sir. We'll know more when we've neutralized it and it's out of containment. One thing for sure though, it's crude, crude as I've ever seen. It looks homemade."

Tergana did not move for almost a minute before he turned to Torel. "I want you to give the chief whatever he needs to compute the backplot. Get as close to the point of origin as we can. This thing didn't build itself. I'm going down to see it. The helm is yours."

"Aye sir."

The admiral took the back corridor down to the containment area. "Is it inert?"

"Absolutely," said Salter. "Do you want me to lock it?"

"If it's not going to fly off, don't bother."

"Alright. Mind the door sir. There's going to be some blow back." The containment field loosened its grip with a rush of gas that sucked into the vacuum.

"Get it out. I want to see it."

"Jeez, this thing is crude sir. Look at these tooling marks. It's handmade, no shielding at all. One person must have been testing a theory because this doesn't look like the work of a collective mind. I think whoever it was hit the right ratios by accident and it just took off. See the scratches on the edges? It went through something. That wouldn't have happened if they knew what they were doing."

"Thanks Chief. I'm going to take it with me? I want to connect with it if I can."

"Sure sir. Let me box it."

Tergana found his way to the bridge, prize in hand. All the early anti-gravity stacks he had seen in science museums were the products of advanced robotics. None of them were handmade that he could recall.

"Is that it?" Commander Torel asked in fascination?

"This is it. I've never seen anything like this. It can barely keep itself together now that it's stopped spinning."

"Admiral, do you think this has anything to do with those sensor blips we registered a few days ago?"

"I very much doubt it. Those were well within the range of quantum anomalies. The maincomp's rated it at 95% certainty. It's rarely wrong."

"Maybe we could test the spinup of this and see what kind of signature it has. What if it fell in the range of a flare or a quantum burst?"

A scowl crossed Tergana's face. It was an ugly possibility he hadn't thought of. "We will have to test this." He held up the clear box turning it slowly in his hands. "Take this back to the chief and ask him if he can do the experiment in a containment field. I don't think my body can handle another round of race and chase today."

"It will take time for him to make a custom spinner. Do we delay our next hop until he's had a chance to test this?"

"Hold this position. If he can't do this in a containment field and this gets away, we'll need room to chase it. Better out here than closer to home. Let me know when he's ready. I want to be there."

CPO Salter loved a challenge, especially when the problem was unique. But he could not give the admiral everything. "Sir, I can build the spinner, but I can't test it in a containment field. There's no way to get a reading. We're going to have to push it out and get some distance, then switch it on. It'll be safer anyway."

"Alright do what you have to."

It took the better part of six hours for the chief to be certain of his setup. He couldn't test the full function in advance. It was all or nothing. "Your stack's loaded in the spinner sir. We can push it out of the airlock anytime."

"Vent when you're ready and let me know when we're clear."

An electromagnet that moved the shuttles pushed the pallet with the spinner out the main cargo door. "She's away sir, about twenty-five feet off the right deflector and two degrees down."

"Helm, ease us back a hundred yards and align the main detector array. I want as much information as we can get."

"Sir, this is Salter. Better make that a thousand and put up shields. I can't promise the force net will contain it."

"Come on Chief, this thing's crude."

"Admiral, take my word for it. Strap yourself in."

God dammit, he thought. *I hate runners.* Then he gave his command. "All hands, this is Tergana. We have taken up station one thousand yards from the rogue stack. We don't know what to expect because we cannot be sure we have all of it. Right now it's naked. If it gets away, we'll have to chase so stay close to your seats." He leaned closer to the monitor and stared at the stack loaded in the spinner.

"You ready Chief?"

"Anytime sir."

Tergana spoke into the intercom. "Alright crew, find a seat. We are about to test our little friend." Even the old hands could not remember anyone bothering to relight a runner. The point was to render them inert. Grumbling could be heard in the corridors as they secured themselves and waited.

"Okay Chief, hit it." The spinup was uneventful until the first glimmer of purple wave, then... "What happened? It's gone."

"Are you plotting the run Chief?"

"She's not running sir. She blew up, copper went right past us."

"Three trajectories?"

"That's what I see. It did give us a little sensor blip before it went its separate ways."

"Very funny. How would you read it?"

"Well within normal fluctuations. We would have missed it every time."

"I was afraid of that. Are those loose discs going to cause trouble?"

"I don't think so sir. Motor's apart, they'll be easy to spot, shouldn't be a problem."

Tergana thanked the chief and turned his attention to his

choices. Instinct said retrieve the runaways and tie up loose ends, but logistics said no. He'd been out three years and twenty-seven days and he was running out of supplies. Torel was waiting for the order he knew had to come. "Plot for home Commander. We need provisions."

"Yes sir"

"Got any ideas?"

"You mean about the runner, why it blew? Not really. My guess, different gravity on spinup, the wrong speed? Hard to say."

"No, I mean where it came from. Some clown built this on his own, without theory from the looks of it. Some of our children have been naughty and we're going to have to find them and—"

Salter cut him off. "We can trace the sensor's data back and see whether it's a relay or it picked up this signal itself. If it's the original receiver, then the cone gets wide fast. Hard to tell."

The chief wasn't interested in being more specific. He and Tergana had served together during a previous need-to-eliminate mission. He never wanted to be a part of one again. He wasn't so sure about the admiral. At least for now, speculation would wait. It was time to go.

Tergana felt the force as though something had emptied him, then put him back together. *I'm too old for this*, he thought, *but I'm coming back to find the dickhead that made that thing. That's for damned sure.*

For those whose constitutions could handle more of a wrenching, watching a starfield fold over itself and then snap back through an outer viewport was the experience of a lifetime. It was dizzying and exhilarating at the same time, a roller coaster that snapped them home, one fold at a time. Tergana found no peace in it and was glad when the hops finally ended. He caught a glimpse of his own city. Argantha was just slipping into night as Cartere spun beneath him. He was glad to be back.

Good humor eased the ride down to the surface, but there were debriefs and mission transfer protocols that kept home at bay. Tergana resented the personal intrusion that was part of every debriefing session, the insinuations that flowed as undercurrent. He sat trapped by circumstance answering their questions. It was pro forma up until the mention of the rogue's disintegration.

OIC Admiral Rell pounced. "Did you retrieve any of the parts for further study?"

Tergana hated traps. "No sir. We determined they wouldn't be a danger and let them fly."

"Gratto, you know I like you, but in retrospect don't you think that was a little short sighted?" Rell couldn't resist the knife twist, but then he pulled it out. "I'm going to give you a chance to rectify your error. Stand down the minimum resupply time, and then get out there and find those parts. Find whoever made that rogue stack and do what you have to now." And stuck it in again.

It wasn't much better at home. Time realignment taxed the body, but the kids looked good and his wife Tirga was still quite pretty when she smiled, so he settled down to wait. He waited for the questions to fall away and the din to die, and then he turned to her. "I've only got two days, then I have to go back."

"I knew something was wrong. I'm sorry."

"Don't be sorry for me. I did this to myself, stuck a fork right in my career. Now I'm going to have to fix this or retire. I don't want to leave with a blemish like this on my record. I've got to find him, no matter what it takes."

"Find whom?"

"Whoever made the runner we found. Somebody out there invented the crudest early stack we've ever seen, all handmade.

They have centuries of science to learn before they can hope to control it. It's my fault. I wasn't thinking. But we didn't find out much when it was inert. So we spun it up and it disintegrated. We had all the digital diagnostics, a complete profile, so we let the parts go. It would have taken days to get them back. Now it's going to take a lot longer. I'm sorry Tirga, I am."

"We'll manage."

They had barely cleared the upper atmosphere of Cartere when the grumbling resumed. Two days off was two off for everybody, and nobody was happy. Cold beer, a quick lay and real fresh fruits and vegetables were not enough to suck exhaustion from their frames. "If you don't mind my asking sir, are you sick?" Commander Torel asked without rancor.

"Like you I suspect, not enough rest. I'll be fine. Plot the first hop when we've cleared home. I want to get this over with. I'll be in my quarters."

"Very good sir. I'll inform you when we're ready."

A hum and then Torel's voice woke Gratto from his daydream. "We're ready sir. The chief says he's computed a plot that will put us in front of the copper plate. If this works, we should be able to catch it as it goes by. But we'll be going lickety-split in the wrong direction when we do. Getting back to the others will take time."

"You'll have what you need. Give me five minutes to find my seat and then initiate. Let's get this over with." The lurch hit him the way it had lately, deep in his gut and hard to contain. And then it was over, for the moment.

The chief had an eye for skeet shooting, which helped him lead a target. Given the variables he came even closer than he had hoped. The plot was far enough in front to make it easy. "Damn I'm good."

"What did you say Chief?"

"Nothing sir, just talking to myself. We're coming along

side. Permission to open the bay?"

"Granted."

Salter was a fisherman too, when he could get the time off. This was one of those moments when some skill with a net was required. The disruptor made a useful scoop. "Come here, you little dickens, just a little... more. Come to Poppa. Gotcha!"

"Chief?"

"I'm pulling it in now sir. Should be secure in two. As soon as it's buttoned down, I'll start on the next plot."

It took thirty-six hours to see the discs back in their box. Finding their maker would not be so simple. Plotting backwards into the cone of uncertainty was mathematically complex. Salter gave it voice. "There are a lot of possibilities. Even the probables will take time. Do you want me to build a grid so we can start narrowing this down?"

"We don't need to narrow it down. We're only watching seven planets in this sector, so overlay those with the most likely origins for this thing. Plot our last mission location and our route in and out and overlay that too. I want to see if there's anything close to our last station. We got those readings we thought were flares, but now I'm not so sure."

"The route vectors are in two shades of green and the targets are purple. Looks like it's right on top of our last station sir. Nice call. What made you think of it?"

"I think we might be dealing with a conspiracy."

"Regarding what sir?"

"Well ask yourself why we have no report from the Xelanar. If these pulses are man-made then Ducar knows about them. He's sitting right on top of whatever this is, so there's a reason he's keeping his mouth shut. Who's our best long distance life-form reader? I want his mind probed."

"That would be Ensign Tillen Haster sir. She's our best empath for the living."

"Tell her to go in lightly. He can't find out. Never mind. Where is she? I'll tell her myself."

"C deck, corridor five, number four. I'll tell her you're on your way."

Tergana met Ensign Haster in the corridor outside her quarters. "I need your help, Ensign. I want you to locate and probe Andin Ducar, captain of the vessel that relieved us. Find out what he's hiding."

"It's too far."

"You haven't tried yet."

"Five hops, it's too far."

"You're sure."

"Sorry."

Tergana resigned himself to another round of lurch as he spoke to Torel. "Okay, I want a hop that puts us as close as possible to our last station. Otherwise, we'll be here forever." His snarl wasn't lost on the crew.

Once more into the twist, he ditched his pride and took a seat next to the main stack, caring less what they thought, then clicked the restraints and nodded.

Once they were close enough, Ensign Haster started fishing for one mind among many. She kept the small probing tendril at a safe distance, waiting for enthusiasm or truth to leak out. Strong egos were easier to find; that made Ducar difficult. He preferred reason to force. She had to widen her net and let go, trusting more than training.

"I think I've got him sir."

"Anything about anti-gravity stacks and coils.?

"From this distance, I get mostly heartbreak, a deep longing over time."

"Can you be more specific?"

"I see a face. She's beautiful, but she's not Aleri, she's human."

"Nothing else?"

"Sorry sir. It's the best I can do from here."

"Thank you ensign, you may have answered my question after all."

◆

Light-years apart, things were not quiet aboard the Xelanar either. "Sorry to interrupt your coffee Captain. We've detected another runner with a crude signature." Kothry's tone was telling.

"What do we know?"

"It's the same signature as this spike here, the one that got away, right where my finger is."

"How much like it?"

"The same, except this one is shorter and stops abruptly instead of trailing off. It's like it disintegrated. But it's the same signature Captain. I'm sure of it."

"It can't have turned around can it? That makes no sense. Do what you can to refine your analysis and let me know."

24

Lunch

Harry got up full of confusion about the future. Outlandish choices would not resolve themselves without more information, and that wouldn't happen without Ducar. "What time are they comin' over anyway, or rather down should I say?"

"It's lunch, twelvish I think. Too bad we can't just call them up and ask," Donna said.

"I think Arney can. He's got a connection to Les, I mean Shereen. They can get inside each other's mind, sort of like we do sometimes, just stronger."

About 12:15 the shuttle door fizzed into view behind the barn, out of sight of the neighbors. Harry heard his dog before he saw Ducar and the rest of the crew but when they appeared, Bogie was wagging his tail.

"Good morning Harry. Where should Ella and Warehan set up?"

"Who's Warehan?"

"He's her son. Good lad, you met him last night, helps out in the kitchen and with logistics. Just a little older than your granddaughter, I think."

"He's a good lookin' young man."

"Probably just becoming who she wants, if he's set his eye on her. It won't mean much to us, but she'll get it if she's interested."

"God help him."

"What's that supposed to mean?"

"It means that young lady knows what she wants. And God help the person who stands in her way."

"He won't get in her way. Where should he set up?"

"In the barn. I set up sawhorses with plywood on top and pulled the benches out from the wall. There's more room and the kitchen's not far."

Warehan caught glimpses of Jennifer a few times as he was prepping their last meal, not long enough to really sort her out. He wanted another look and was waiting for her. And then there she was, brothers in tow, Levis and light blue work shirt, coming through the side door smiling. Something washed through him and over him, and he turned back to his work lest whatever it was should reveal its secret. He chopped faster with nervous enthusiasm.

The pull was stronger for her. He had morphed into the man of her dreams, a fantasy fulfilled. "Hi, my name's Jennifer. I didn't see you much last night. Where were you hiding?"

"In the galley. My name's Warehan, Warehan Bartole. I'm—"

"Ella's son."

"That's right."

"Well I have that much straight. Glad to know you, I guess. What do you like to do out there?" She motioned to the barn roof but he understood.

"I like to explore and learn."

"Me too."

It was easy to see what was coming. One touch set the weaving in motion. Once feelings took over, the future was out of their control. The young Aleri lacked resistance to the emotions that came with unfamiliar neural entanglements, so Warehan was overtaken before Jenny. But poor Jen fell like a stone, with a deep, hard, out-of-control need. "Please don't look at me like that."

"This is all set up. Want to take a walk with me?"

"Where?" Jen asked.

"I don't know. It's your place not mine. Anywhere out of here for few minutes. Once lunch starts I'll be busy."

"Come with me."

"Where?"

"You'll see, someplace quiet." Now how fast a relationship sparks to life depends on many factors. The obvious ones like looks and brains and a kind disposition get the reward that comes with patience, a predictable upwelling of passion that ends with three words spoken. This attraction was different, a need born on the wings of a single touch that pushed connection into every fiber. They wanted each other without being sure of who or what it was they wanted. He looked like the boy of her dreams but coming from so far away, she couldn't get her mind around the difference between them.

"Up here." Warehan followed Jenny up the steps to the hayloft she knew so well as a child. "Stop. Don't come any closer. I need to see you, not the face you choose to show me. You."

"What if you don't like it?"

"Then no, maybe I don't want to dance. Show me what you look like to your family. Who do they see?"

Warehan's transformation from pale-skinned with dark hair to a copper-skinned, fair-haired Aleri did not frighten her. Quite the contrary. He took off his clothes so that she could see all of him.

"Aren't you embarrassed?"

"You mean ashamed, don't you? No. This who I am. I made peace with my shape long ago. I had no part in the choosing."

"What happens if I touch you, the way you are now?"

"I'm not sure. I know that you and I are already thinking to each other without speaking. Find out. Touch me."

She walked up until she was close enough to challenge her

resolve, then took his hand. The race for connection that sped up her arm to her brain and then through her whole body was the same sensation he was having as she coursed through every fiber of his being. She could hear the first notes of the music that would be their binding. Just a touch. Hold my hand. School? Indiana? It all vanished in the face of the fork in the road.

"Touch me too."

She only asked him once. He seemed to know where to touch her and what she liked. He had an unfair advantage.

"Show me what you want. You know me better than I know you."

"I will change back. Then we will be equal."

The Warehan she knew swept her up and kissed her as if she were a movie star. There would be more, much more. They knew what they wanted and wrapped around each other, warming and tempting the inevitable with tender touch. He pushed into her warm dark cave with a gentle thrust that made her shiver. Then a slow tease to the bottom and a thrust to prove it, pressure on right spots. Then he moved a little faster and deeper and would not let go until he could feel her pulse with satisfaction. She yielded to reception and love and held him tight.

"Don't move, stay right where you are. I can still feel you. It's like we're one being."

"We are and will be."

Once again it was glue like no other, a destiny they could not avoid. Nature got what the collective wanted while they lay on piles of straw that littered the loft, soft enough with a blanket on top but less comfortable as they became aware.

"We've got to get back."

"I know. My mom will be pissed. Can we meet up after?"

"Please." Jenny smiled, a whirlwind in her head. She could feel him in her mind as they walked back, and in warmer spots as well. She tried not to admit she cared, but she did. She loved all of it, every delicious bit—how he smelled, how he sounded, the way he carried his confidence.

Ducar could sense it as the two walked through the door. He asked Shereen to probe.

"Like rabbits as far as I can tell, out in the hayloft. She loves him."

"Swell." Ducar knew the bond could be teased apart. It just wouldn't be easy, and it would have to wait. "Ella, could you begin to serve? I need to start this conversation."

The benches scraped the barn floor, until everyone was seated. Then they were silent until a note and then the harmonies began to rise in the air as if in a church without religion.

When the music ended, Ducar began. "I hope you all got some rest. I know it's a lot to digest and the implications are staggering. Still, you must choose. Those of you who think coming with us is a good idea should make use of the ship's libraries. Those of you who want to skip back in time should consider what you may lose. There is no guarantee things will unfold the same way twice. Sometimes when you try to push the ripple forward again, you miss the spot. You come back close but not the same. And there's something else." He paused, searching for a phrase. "Members of this crew will not be going back in time. The Xelanar stays here." He counted the anguished looks. *It's all of them. They're all paired up, already. No wonder I can't shake her. I should never have left.* They stared at him. He wasn't sure whether he had spoken or simply thought the words. "Sorry I was just... Any questions?"

"How come you can't stay here with us in the past?" Arney asked trying to keep loss at bay. All the youngsters, faces crestfallen, needed their answer too.

"Because if we break our covenant not to interfere, we can never go home. We would be choosing this world over our own."

"What about us? If we go back, do we have a chance to evolve to this mind thing you speak of?"

"There's always a chance. Learn to think to each other, like you were talking to each other. Then ask yourself, how you would want someone to think about you and behave in the way that gets you that. It isn't hard. Or you can program your minds with drivel, and fail to heed the truth. Do that and you will be dust. The Carei, us, the sun, take your pick."

"What can we do to help make this mind thing happen?"

"It's coming. In a few years your world will develop worldwide communications. Everyone will be able to speak with and write to everyone else. If all goes well, the sharing of ideas will result in a common purpose. World-mind evolves from there."

"You make it sound like that's a long way off."

"It all depends on changing your view of wealth. If you just want to accumulate you become a pariah. You prevent your world from evolving and ultimately kill it. The top predator yields to the roach and the mouse. It's hard to fix."

"How do we do this mind thing then?"

"We call ours Unomeri, Arney. We think to each other, telepathically. Maybe think in each other is a better way to put it. You have to let go and trust the things that come in to your mind, that you shouldn't have a way of knowing but you do. The more touch points you find that cannot be explained away by coincidence, the more you realize you can hear words before someone else speaks them. Or you know who's on the phone before you pick it up. What is that? That's the connection your world must share, the next step in your evolution. Call it whatever you want."

"Me and Dad can do it sometimes—that thing where you just know the other one's okay when you think about them."

"That's part of it. You and Shereen can do it."

"Real good actually."

"So what do you think it's going to take to spread this all over the world?"

"A shitload of you guys, probably."

"Arney! You watch your mouth." Donna was mom again.

190

"Sorry Mom, but it ain't like they never heard it before. And since I have your attention, there's somethin' else. Shereen well, we like each other." She moved closer to Arney, then looked at the captain.

It was going to be tougher than he'd thought, prying romance apart. Shereen had made her position clear. "Are there any more questions? If not, Shereen may I have a moment?"

"Yes sir?"

"Let's go outside." They walked out in the sun beyond the barn's shadow before he spoke. "Tell me. What's going on with you and Arney? Why are you to making this mistake?"

"I love him sir. He's a fine man, tough as nails with a good heart. Something resonated the first time I scanned him. We're supposed to be together."

"Well that's one vote for come with us."

Kothry walked briskly across the grass toward them. "Sorry to interrupt sir. There's something you should know."

"What is it?"

"It's about the signature, sir. The sentrybot it came through wasn't one of ours. It was Carei."

"Please tell Ella to start packing; it's time we returned to the ship."

Ducar entered the barn and spoke quietly to Warehan, who left to pack when Harry walked up.

"Got a minute?"

"What is it Harry? I have to go."

"Well that's it, I guess. Donna doesn't want to."

"Want to what?"

"Go. She doesn't want to leave the farm. If she ain't going, neither am I."

"I see." Ducar couldn't handle it while he was square in the middle of a bigger problem. "Sorry Harry, I have to get back to my ship. We'll talk about this in the morning, just the two of us."

191

The scout departed before dusk, lessening the fizz between door and sky. Ducar was glad he could pull the tempted couples apart for the moment. Their attachment to each other made a hard choice harder. But it was Harry and Donna who troubled him most.

When airlock equalization was complete Jasca met him. "Did you have a nice lunch, sir? he asked in a clear tone of disapproval.

"It achieved its purpose."

"And what was that sir? To interfere by disregarding protocol?"

He did not have time but noted the commencement of enemy fire. Jasca could wait.

"Mr. Gradel, with me to the bridge now." Kothry picked up his pace.

"What's with Jasca Captain?" Kothry asked as they took their seats.

"He'd rather dust them than save them. I can't let that happen."

Shereen appeared in the doorway. "Captain, someone's been probing you. It was subtle and distant, not much of a trace at all. But one thing's for sure, they were looking for you."

◆

The morning found Harry sitting on a tall work stool, coffee in hand, surveying his workbench and wondering how he had managed to screw up so much.

"If Ducar's coming he'll know where I am. He'll read my damned mind. In the meantime, I guess I need to start gettin' rid of this stuff." By the time Ducar knocked, Harry had stacked his remaining discs in logical combinations and cleared the obfuscation that covered the main spinner, no point in trying to hide it now. "I was just cleaning up. Want some coffee?"

"No thanks, I'm good. You sure made a lot of stacks. How

many flew?"

"Just two."

"What about these?"

"They made the spinner groan."

"Did they lift up?"

"Yeah, some, I think. They loosened dowels."

"Well you don't have the theory but you do have vision. You're lucky Harry. Most of these stacks could have flown if you had the right spinup frequencies."

"It don't feel lucky from where I'm standing. You've been nothin' but bad news since you got here, even if you are the nice guy you seem to be. How much joy did you bring me today?"

"None. I thought we had some time to figure this out, a few days, a week maybe if we caught a break, but it's gone. The Carei know what we're doing here. They aren't stupid. They could show up anytime. We have to leave right now Harry. You don't want to be here when they dust this place."

"That means I have to leave my farm and spend the rest of my days on your world, right?"

"That's right. You'll be welcomed."

"Well if it's such a great deal, how come you want to spend all of your time here with us? What's so special about this place? You wanna tell me that?"

"Alright Harry, I guess you should know. Years ago I met someone here. It was an accident. We were researching some of your foods. I went into a small convenience store about ten miles from here to buy chips and cookies and candies."

"Hold it. Ten miles from here. I thought when you said here, you meant our planet. You mean here, this county. That's crazy."

"I know, I'm asking myself a lot of questions. Seems too close to be coincidence although I was never over this far in your direction. She was paying for gas and brushed by me. I had no idea what her touch would mean. When I got back to the shuttle, she was all I could think about. I had to see her again, so I asked the best empath on board to find her. Then I went to the bar she liked and waited. Now I know what a mistake it was but it doesn't change my feelings. She was, is, the love of my life. But I don't feel her anymore."

"I thought you just said you love her."

"I do, with all my heart. I just can't find her with my mind."

"So why care about this place if the attachment's over?"

"It's not...over, I mean. My boy Don might be here somewhere."

"Ducar you must be out of your mind. I'm not part of your world or your crew but even I know that can't be right. I thought you were supposed to be hands off, no interference and especially no hanky-panky. What did your people do when they found out?"

"They didn't. I lived two lives, one on and one off the ship. I told my commander that my research required me to blend into the population and observe. Then I got a place near her. Then we married, had a child and then I left. My three-year tour was over in a blink. By the time I returned they had aged but I was still young. I couldn't find them because they had closed their minds to the possibility I might still be alive. It didn't seem fair to light it all up again, so I content myself with watching over this world to keep them safe."

"How could you have a child with us? You're a different species from a different world."

"When we learned genetic manipulation we chose the path of the chameleon. We can change more than our appearance Harry. We become your species so that we can totally assimilate if we have to."

"Then you do have a dog in this fight after all. I thought there was somethin' you weren't tellin' me."

25

Deep Shit City

Harry was putting the pieces together. He knew he was in more trouble than he bargained for but so was Ducar. "Can you fix this? Are those Carei people gonna blow us up today? What if we just get rid of all this stuff and disappear, like you did?"

"They weren't looking for me Harry. They were my people. They knew where I was. They didn't know about Gilly because I blocked it out in my mind. We get to be private when we need to be. They can't read everything except for empaths like Shereen. She gets most of what there is to get."

"So why not start blocking now? How much time do we need to evolve? You could speed it up, right?"

"I wish I could Harry. We're up against a big stinking pile of trouble. Everybody here thinks they need to be better than the next guy, all trying to get to the top. Money, education, none of it's fair unless it's shared for the benefit of all. Until your world learns to do that, it's adios amigo. "You don't see that sort of cooperation happening soon, do you?"

"We need more time."

"Yes, we do. I'm going to have Shereen ferried down in another shuttle. In the meantime I want you to get Arney and

195

your grandchildren over here as soon as you can. We need to fix this on your end Harry. My crew can't help. It isn't fair to involve them. After all they have families, too."

"I'll go call Arney."

"Wait Harry. Before you do, think to him. Send the message that you are about to call, that you need him over here. Then go inside and call."

Harry could hear the phone ringing as he came through the screen door into the kitchen. "Hello?"

"Hi Pop, did you just call me? I was outside. I thought I heard the phone. I don't know why I thought you were calling."

"I was about to. Ducar told me to think about calling you before I actually did. You must have gotten the message."

"What were you calling me about?"

"Ducar wants you and the kids to come over as soon as you can. Shereen's coming down from the Xelanar to help. Seems we don't have a lot of time to figure out what we're gonna do."

"I thought we were going to vote or something, leave with them or go back in time. That's the way we left it."

"Your mother doesn't want to go anywhere in any time. I can't say I blame her."

"But Pop, that's suicide."

"Tell that to her. I'll appreciate all the help I can get."

"We'll be right over."

The boys made seats out of two hay bales in the pickup's bed, leaning back against the cab. Jennifer got to ride up front with her father. "What's Grampa want to see us about?"

"It's not him. It's Ducar. He wants to talk to us about choices."

"Um Dad, I've got something to tell you."

"Can it wait? We're here."

"Sure."

The shimmering outline of the cargo door on the six-man scout fizzed into view around the back of the barn. Arney had been waiting for Shereen from the moment Ducar told him where she would be. An easy smile grew on her face as she saw him.

"It's nice to see you again. How's your dad?"

"He's alright but Mom's having trouble with all of this."

"Don't worry, I'm here to help. We'll figure this out. Where's the captain?"

"Everybody's in the kitchen."

The heat made it sensible to be where tea and ice cubes were an arm's length away. Donna was still in her nightgown.

"You'll have to forgive me, it's too hot to dress up. Besides I've seen you so much in the last few days you're almost like family. Do you want some coffee dear, or would tea do?"

"The iced tea looks good. Thanks, Donna."

Shereen and the captain left for the porch. "Do they know?"

"Harry does. I just told him. He says Donna won't leave and neither will he."

"Sir with your permission, I'd like to try something. It's a long shot but I think a children's mind-training session might work. If they could get some of the basics down it might persuade the Carei that they are more evolved than they appear."

"I'm out of options, go for it."

"There's something else. Jasca's having a hard time with the amount of contact we have already had here. I probed his mind. He's in turmoil."

"I'll deal with him when I get back. In the meantime let's see just how good you really are."

Empaths were not teachers by nature, more like mental spies. Shereen had never conducted a world-mind training session, much less one aimed at beginners who weren't sure of their telepathic abilities. She had no idea if it would work. One thing she did know was that she could share with Arney, and she was sure he was the key to opening doors.

"Can everyone find a seat? The captain has asked me to see if we can't put our minds together literally and find a solution."

"You gonna read our thoughts?" Harry was sure she could read him like a book.

"Not exactly. We're going to try and share. I want you to remember what you heard at our dinner aboard the Xelanar. Remember the harmonies before we ate? We're going to try to do that here. Don't worry about which note, just find what feels comfortable. If you feel something try to let it in. Don't fight it. Let it expand in your mind. How many of you have ever sung in a group before?"

Donna raised her hand and answered. She was back in school again. "I used to sing in the church choir, soprano, sometimes alto if the altos were short."

"That's good Donna, you can help me then. Anyone else? No? Alright then. Donna, I know you sang lullabies to Arney when he was a boy, so I want you to remember his favorite and sing it to him, just the first phrase over and over again. Can you remember it?"

Donna paused for a moment and then began to coo to her boy a long-lost melody that reached in deep and soothed him. She was soft and measured, but Shereen could feel Arney ease toward an ancient peace. *Send it back to her, Arney,* she thought. *Give her back what she is giving you. Sing with her in your mind.*

What tugged at Arney tugged at them all. Mothers all sing the same song. It's not the notes that matter. It's the mind's intent, the thoughts of calm and peace that matter.

Shereen probed each of them as they began to relax and planted the same suggestion. "Use your thoughts, sing with her. Give it back. And when you are sure everyone is ready, sing softly out loud until you feel each other's good intent." And then she waited.

The music arose out of an undiscovered well. Even Shereen was surprised at the synchrony. They had joined in with one voice as if an unseen conductor's baton compelled them to begin as one, repeating the same phrase over and over until as one it fell away to silence.

"That was excellent. Do you know what you have just done? That was your first gathering. It's just a simple thought, one of the easiest to do. But it's a sharing nonetheless."

"Damdest thing I ever heard," said Harry.

Arney had more. "I could feel you, all of you, including you Pop. And you were in me, Ma. When my mind said 'now' you all started to sing out loud. I could feel us all together as a family but more than that. We were one."

"In a family setting it's easier because you trust each other. Could each of you feel the moment when you realized you had joined? Can you remember the difference?" Shereen asked.

"I think I can," Jennifer offered. "It's the same feeling I had with Warehan."

"Who's Warehan?" Arney's paternal antenna went full alert at the mention.

"I was going to tell you before we got here. He's Ella's son. We—"

"You what? What did you do?"

"I'm sorry Dad. I couldn't help it. It just happened."

"Arney, please calm down. It's not her fault." Ducar tried to regain control. "It seems that each member of your family has paired with someone in my crew. The attraction is far more compelling than would be normal for either of our worlds alone. There is something about the interaction between us that amplifies desire and bonding. Your sense of individual purpose and adventure is addictive to those of us who have lived in the middle for so long. I confess, I too loved someone here. So Arney, please try and understand it was inevitable. It's not just Jennifer. It's all of us. It's you too, isn't it, Arney? You love Shereen."

"Yes. I love her. I'm sorry boys, you too Jen. I'm not trying to take anything from your mother. Louise was in my heart all these years. I wasn't looking for this. It just happened."

"How many of you are missing someone on my crew?" asked the captain.

The boys' hands went up.

"My God, it's worse than the sixties," Donna said, but Harry had to smile. "Wipe that grin off your face old man. I know you."

Ducar had lost control, minds were elsewhere.

"Captain if I may, could we step outside?"

"Did you sense something?"

"A possibility. What if we could train everyone, the whole planet? If we can teach Unomeri to the skeptics in that living room, there might be a way to save them all."

"It's never been done to my knowledge. Is your mind that strong?"

"It's not just me Andin. It's me and Arney together." It was the first time she had acknowledged her feelings for him, even if it was just his first name. "When Arney and I pair he amplifies my abilities. He's very powerful."

"You will free this world if you can do this. No one will interfere once they have crossed over. I will help all I can, whatever you need?"

"Time, I need time."

26

Back to Class

Shereen became the teacher the moment the screen door closed. "Please settle down everyone. The captain and I have an idea. We think it just may be possible to gather a world-mind together using the approach we just tried but it will require your help. And we need to start right away."

"Will we survive if we do this? I thought trouble was close, a day or two maybe."

"You're correct Mr. Miller. The Carei are not far off, so it's important we begin."

"Please, call me Harry. How long's this gonna take?"

"I don't know. It's never been done before. Try not to be negative. Find a seat and let's see how far we get."

The last of the tea splashed over the last of the ice, then chairs caught keisters and her students settled down. "Alright Arney, I want you to pick a note and hum it softly. Donna, if you can do a harmony that would help. Everyone else, pick one note or the other and let's see what happens. If you feel a resonance inside your mind go with it. Reach for it. Let it carry you toward the next mind singing. We are looking for the feeling more than the sound. Are you ready Arney?"

Arney tried not to let stage fright make his voice crack and began in earnest.

"That's good Arney. Perhaps a little softer. Now Donna, can you find the harmony? Wonderful, just keep that going."

Once they were comfortable, Shereen added her own voice high above, floating on the top of it all. She probed for reactions and made a list of what worked. Some notes seemed to resonate with everyone, some with just a few. The same combinations of notes did not work among all worlds, each harmony was unique. It proved to be true among her charges.

"Harry, can you change seats with Jennifer? I want her and Donna to sit closer together. Let's try again."

The rest of the afternoon was spent refining their technique. They got closer to each other and could feel it even if they didn't have the words for it. "I can almost see through your eyes, it's spooky," Jennifer said to Mark.

"Cannot."

"Can so."

Shereen took it as a good sign but there was a long way to go. When she gave the captain her assessment, it landed like old fish. "I need a week, maybe less, but not much. They can only be pushed so far."

"Is there any way to speed this up?"

"Not unless you can help me find what resonates. You've got a tin ear and you can't probe deeply. I'll let you know when I'm close. In the meantime I need as much breathing room as you can give me."

"I'll see what I can do. What time tomorrow?"

"As early as we can. Captain, may I bring Arney?"

"He bunks with you."

"Thanks."

Jenny kissed her father goodbye. Mark had insisted on watching the cargo door fizz closed before he left. "Are you mad at Dad sis?"

"Oh, just irritated. I'd like to go too."

"What about us?"

"We're all supposed to get as much rest as we can."

"That's not fair."

"Life's not fair." She drove her brothers home and cooked dinner yet again, the lot of an older sister. "Go to bed, please. Don't make me tell Dad."

◆

When the main airlock on the Xelanar opened, Jasca was surprised to see Arney step out and even more surprised to see Shereen take his arm. It was hard to pretend it meant nothing. Jasca felt his hope fade. Soon a forbidden burst of rage moved through him and he locked his mind so as not to be discovered.

When dinner began Arney assimilated easily into the group, which irritated Jasca even more. Ducar could sense the anger.

Keep an eye on him Captain, Shereen's mind floated into his.

I am, he thought back, and felt better that Shereen was probing. *What's he so angry about?*

He's blocking, but it's jealousy. It's Arney and me. He doesn't know how to cope, perhaps a lapse in his education. Who knows. It's too late to try and fix it now. Just be aware sir.

Dinner concluded with more than the usual pleasantries. Kothry and PJ liked Arney. So did Ella. As the warm connections grew around him, Jasca began to boil. Shereen could sense his temper rising and gently pried Arney from his admirers and away down the back corridor toward her quarters. A flash of frown and wrinkled brow betrayed the extent of anguish behind her.

I'll fix... Jasca thought as he clamped down tighter against an unfamiliar emotion, careful not to let it escape. He went to his commport and began to type a message, better a keyboard than mental transmissions. It read. 'Attn. Adm. Gratto Tergana, be advised first stack creator and appropriate tooling discovered on S3alpha, per your last mission. Your assistance is requested to complete a cleansing. Please advise. Lt. Cmdr. Jasca Sitor U.A.S. Xelanar.' He encrypted it and locked it in his personal folder, a bullet in the chamber to be fired.

The moment the door to Shereen's quarters had sealed itself Arney asked, "What was going on back there?"

"Jasca's having a hard time with you being here."

"You mean he's jealous."

"He's not supposed to be. He wants me for himself." She slowly pushed her fingers into his hair. "But it's not what I want." Her pelvis began to speak without words slowly moving as she kissed him. It wasn't fair, not even a contest. He couldn't help but yield. Clothes were the least of the barriers that fell away.

He could feel what drove all life forward calling to him, whispering need from the deep recesses. He pushed a finger into the soup of life and drew the moisture to the surface to wet and tempt and torment, then went back again for more. The same unavoidable attraction overwhelmed them both, the hungry wrestle of it aching for release. More pressure and sounds that said more please more. He moved over and through her in deep strokes slowly getting faster and deeper as he plunged over and over again until at the very bottom of the well, passion yielded to release.

Shereen let go in little shudders, a climax that shook her loins with pleasure and as she did, he did.

"That's my love. Here." His back arched and seed flowed down deep in pulses until there was no more to give. They lay quietly in each other's arms. Shereen was bound to him and he to her, a family born, their nervous systems welded in the joining.

"We have knit together. Our neurons are intertwined. You are in every fiber of my being, the other half of me."

"I feel it too. What are we going to do?"

"I love you Arney. We'll work this out. Now I see why the

captain couldn't leave."

"What about the captain?"

"This love we share, this is what happened to the captain. His heart will always be here. This is where he lost it. We have to save this place for all our sakes."

Morning in moonshadow was the province of circuits that raised the light and changed its color from red to daylight blue. "Shereen. Wake up baby, it's time to get going."

"Good morning handsome. Where's my friend? Oh there you are."

"Shereen my love."

"Alright I'll get dressed."

Ducar wasn't quite tapping his feet in impatience when she found him but he was close. "This is your schedule Shereen."

"Sorry sir. It won't happen again."

The shuttle door opened behind the barn without witness. Everybody was in the kitchen eating breakfast, ham, eggs, hash browns, the tastes of fine country cooking. "Good morning all," Shereen said as she opened the door, "that smells wonderful."

"Well come on in honey, and have some. You too Andin." Donna decided to let Shereen get closer. She could tell her boy had made a choice and as strange as it felt, she would honor it. When the dishes were dry and the silverware put away and the surfaces wiped clean, she joined her family in the dining room.

"Sit here Mom." Arney was holding her chair for her.

Shereen noted the pleasure Donna got from the gesture. "Good morning again. I hope everyone is well rested. We've got a long—" She had barely begun when Arney interrupted her.

"I've got an idea! I know how to stop them. I know how to stop the Carei. I'm sorry Shereen. I've got to go Pop. You and the captain, we've got to go out to the barn, now."

"Easy Arney, we can talk. Give us a minute will you Shereen?" Ducar asked.

The threesome jammed the barn door trying to get the first word out. "What's so important, son? You got a burr or somethin'?"

"No Pop. I've got an idea. What if we build more spinners and launch every stack that will fly. Give 'em something to chase. Launch 'em at the same time. They'd be a bitch to track. They'd have to chase them, wouldn't they Captain? They'd have to catch them and turn them off."

"Yes. However, the unshielded ones don't tumble so they'll be relatively easy to catch. Still, it's a good idea."

"Well what makes them hard? I mean if these are so easy?"

"Partial shielding makes them tumble. If there are two or three holes you can fry a maincomp trying to compute a plot. They bounce, depending on what part of the stack is exposed. You can imagine the difficulty, especially if they're moving fast."

"What's it made of, the shielding I mean?" Arney pressed.

"Did you notice the rods around the main stack on the Xelanar? Each rod has a plate attached and a coil surrounding the rod. You and Harry made some small ones."

"You mean like this?" Harry held one up from the toolbox.

"There you go, just like that. When did you make those?"

"I made these first. Saw 'em along with the stacks of discs, but the stacks weren't so clear, so I started with these. Tried all sorts of combinations. They didn't work though, 'cept when the toolbox moved. I guess they might've had somethin' to do with that. It's over here."

Ducar walked over to inspect the contents on the bench. "Anything else?"

"A bunch of leftover small parts that didn't amount to much and I had a bottle of mercury but it broke."

"When did it break, Harry? You see the reason I'm asking

is the stacks require liquid mercury to operate. Nothing moves without it."

"I figured that out when I found the amalgam on the inside of the copper disc. Took me a while. The bottle must have broken when I was shaking the box to settle stuff. That's when it took off on me, busted into those boards over there. When I tried to work it loose, it took off again, got buried in the side yard. Arney helped me dig it out."

"Kothry was right. It was back scatter. I'll be damned."

"What did you say Captain?"

"Nothing important Harry. Mr. Gradel noted two early sensor readings and labeled them as shielding back scatter. It seemed odd to me at the time, but things are falling into place. Every reading we detected came right out of this barn. You old dog. You sure are a smart SOB Harry. Do me a favor. Get all the rods and springs and plates that you made and put them out where I can sort them. Our answers are staring us in the face. School's out for today."

27

Mind is Faster Than Light

When Admiral Tergana took command of his Zirin class interstellar he made it clear that junior officers were not to freelance their decisions. Everything of any importance on the Morowa came to him personally, no matter what the hour. It was one of those hours. Torel was in his commmport.

"Sorry to wake you sir. One of the sentrybots at the edge of our last hop indicates it's holding a priority-one message for you. Do I have your permission to retrieve it?"

"How far away is it?"

"Our empath might get it, otherwise we'll have to go back."

"Call Haster and let me know." He could remember his lessons about the limits of the speed of light and how much science changed after the force of mind was discovered to be instantaneous. It became possible to fold space and leap across great distances, but light and radio waves were trapped within their limits. Skilled empaths became the key to retrieving information otherwise locked by light.

"Ensign Haster to the quiet room. Empath to the quiet room asap.

Torel was already in the corridor when she arrived. "I need you to retrieve a priority-one message from this sentrybot. It's beyond our current time frame at the far edge of our last hop."

"Pardon my language, but that's a long damn way."

"You're as close as I can get you. Do your best."

Tilly, as she was known only to her closest friends, leaned the recliner back, dimmed the lights, cleared the room with her eyes and closed the door. Then after she had eased and calmed herself, she reached out in the bot's direction. High-priority messages were not just stored in circuitry, they were also held in an organic gel that could be read by trained minds. Tilly was good, so good they had given her a commission just to recruit her, good enough to reach all the way across.

"Commander I've got something. It's not clear but I've identified the sender, a Lt. Commander Sitor, Jasca Sitor. He's Aleri. Do you know him?"

Torel was about to answer just when Tergana appeared at his side. He had heard the question and cut Torel off. "I've got this Commander. Please return to the bridge." Then he opened the commport and spoke.

"Haster, this is the admiral. I know him. What else can you get?"

"It's something about the rogue stack we chased sir. He's found the builder."

"Let me guess. Somewhere back near our last station?"

"I can't pinpoint it exactly but yes sir. I'd say that's right. If we go back, I could read it all."

"That won't be necessary. Thank you. You have been most helpful." Tergana grew up knowing that the propagation of thought was instantaneous, but to watch a skilled empath reach out and read a memory gel across light-years as if time stood still was proof of the theorem. He stifled his awe and headed for the bridge.

"Success?" Torel could see Tergana's brow had eased and some worry lines had smoothed.

"This is going to go much faster than we thought. Our empath is really good. She read a file all the way at the far edge of our last hop. She didn't get it all but she got enough. We're going back, back to our last station, now."

As good as Ensign Haster was, Shereen was better. She could reach farther and read more clearly. Machines were no problem. She thought to her motors and they thought back, as two parts of the same living thing. In school they nicknamed her 'Circuit' because she could get into computers. Some said she was as good as they came, maybe better. *They know. They're a long way out but they know*, she thought to herself and went to find the captain. They met at the screen door. "I was just coming to find you. They know. I can feel it."

"The Carei? Is it Tergana?"

"Definitely the Carei, someone on his ship, not sure about Tergana."

"Same thing isn't it? How far out?"

"Two days, less maybe." What had been conjecture turned to fact.

"Rocks and hard places."

"What sir?"

"Nothing, an old expression, between a rock and a hard place?"

"Never heard it before sir, but I get your meaning."

"Shereen, please send to Kothry. Tell him I need him down here asap and bring a toothbrush. He'll understand."

Ducar grabbed the last cup of cold coffee left in the pot and headed back to the barn. He had acquired a taste for the brew and was looking at a long night. "Harry, Kothry Gradel's coming down to help."

"What with?"

"He's going to help us make more spinners."

"How's he gonna do that? I'm the one who invented 'em."

"Harry please don't take it personally. I need him to isolate the synthesizers on the two scouts, so they can't talk to each other. Those glass tubes you made to spin your disks, I don't think it's ever been done that way before. It might not even be prohibited by the replicator function."

"Why would something be prohibited?"

"Synthesizers are not allowed to produce spinner parts or discs or any other anti-grav motor components for that matter. You can't have every Tom, Dick and Harry making homemade motors. It would be chaos. But yours Harry, yours might fool them. If we feed your design through the chemistry parts library it could pass as labware but we can't let them talk to each other or they'll figure it out for themselves."

Kothry knocked before he opened the barn door. "Captain my captain, what can I do you for?"

"Well, you've been studying the language, haven't you?" He paused to make sure Kothry was listening carefully. "I need your help my friend."

"Whatever you need."

"Don't be too quick. I need you to break some rules. It could cost us."

"What do you have in mind?"

"First you have to tell me if this idea has a chance in hell. Can we reprogram the food synthesizers to make metallic or ceramic parts? Because if we can, then maybe we could make more of these." He pulled back the tarp covering Harry's spinner and pointed to the glass core.

"Ingenious. Did you make this?" Kothry asked of Harry on his stool. "Nice work, never seen anything like it."

"What do you think Kothry, can they be swapped over or not?"

"Maybe for metals but certainly for drinking glasses and baking dishes and plates. If we wipe out the kitchen protocols and convince it that it's in a lab it might work. But then it might figure it out and shut down before it made more than one. We'll see."

"Are you going to isolate them?"

"Figured that out already, did you? Because you're right, they can't be allowed to communicate." Kothry liked Ducar, liked the way his mind worked, always keeping the extent of his intelligence in reserve until he needed it. "You set me up sir."

"Not at all. This is your show. Let me know if you can make it work."

"It's a good idea Captain. I can make it work."

"You and Harry work on the glass parts then. Arney and I are going to make more of these wooden bases, exactly like this one here just to be safe. I'm going to get him." Ducar's trip to the kitchen was as much an excuse to see if he could beg coffee from the empty pot.

"I can make some more if you'd like. It is coffee you want, isn't it Captain?" Donna inquired somewhat cheerfully.

"Yes fine lady, we can use more of your good coffee."

Arney stepped in upon hearing Ducar's voice. "Captain, Shereen and I—"

"Not tonight Arney. It's all hands on deck. I need your help. We're going to be carpenters."

"I've driven a spike or two."

"I'm counting on it. How much plywood do you think there is between your two barns?"

"How much do you need?"

"Enough to make at least five more spinners, six would be better."

"Not enough to make all those, not by a long shot and it's too late to buy more tonight."

"Then we'll just have to return to the Xelanar and let her make some and anything else like those nylon bearings that we need."

Back in the barn, Harry supplied the short list of missing parts he needed to make six more spinners. Ducar added nylon strapping, which prompted Harry to ask, "Why the cargo straps?"

"When we're finished, we're going to use the big sentrybots to ferry the new spinners away from here, the farther the better. If we spread them out before we start them up, they'll be much harder to catch."

"Set 'em off all at once, that'll do it."

"Not all of them Harry. I thought to hold two back. While the Carei are busy chasing the first five we'll have time to get the last two around to the far side of the planet. They'll be long gone in the other direction by the time Tergana realizes what's happened. That should keep them busy for a while."

"Brilliant. You're a smart SOB yourself Ducar."

"Takes one to know one."

"You know what I'm thinking, don't you? I mean when you want to, you just float in and have a look. You've known everything all along."

"Not everything. All living things have a sanctuary. I don't intrude unless it might put a life in danger. Mind sharing does not mean everyone gets to peel you like a grape, and I'm not interested in prying. You don't get that feeling, do you?"

"No, you're one of the good guys, even if you're not from around here."

"I've got to get plywood Harry, so I'm stealing your boy for a while. We'll be back as soon as we can."

Jasca could barely contain his disdain when Arney reappeared. The mutual dislike simmered, permissible in Arney, forbidden to Jasca. Ducar stepped deftly between them and ushered Arney aft.

The synthesizer in the bay that functioned as the machine shop was programmed for industrial parts and supplies. Feed it with Syngel, and it could crank out plywood all day long, nylon bearings, electric motors and cargo straps too.

Jasca showed more than usual interest in the growing stack of small plywood sheets. "What are you going to make with those?"

Here was the moment Ducar feared. "We're going to create a diversion."

Jasca was about to speak when Ella showed up with refreshments. "I thought you gentlemen could use some coffee or tea to see you through your labors."

"Thanks Ella, I'd have a couple of those biscuits too if it's not too much trouble." Ducar watched Jasca take a sip of the tea out of the corner of his eye and relaxed. It wouldn't take long. The ruse was simple. Jasca didn't like coffee, so Ella spiked the tea. They caught him before he hit the floor. "Help me get him sequestered and pull his code. I want him out of the way until this is over. How long Ella?"

"You've got about ten minutes."

"Thanks again."

"Arney, let's get him to his quarters. I want him buttoned up when he wakes."

It didn't take long for the tranquilizer to wear off. Ducar watched Jasca drag himself up off of his bunk and look around as if he didn't know how he got there. When his cabin door wouldn't open, he complained, "What's going on? Why am I locked in?"

Ducar was waiting near the commport to answer. "You can't be a part of this. I'm sequestering you for your own good. I've got to save these people and you're in the way."

"You're too late. I messaged Tergana. They know what you're doing. You've broken your oath to the Shepherds. You'll pay the price and so will your friends."

"Why do you think you're locked up? I know about your message. Sit down and shut up, you're not going anywhere."

The two-man returned jammed with the necessities. "Forty minutes, not bad. What took you so long?" Harry couldn't resist. "Nice plywood."

"Let's get this stuff into the barn and get to work. We haven't got much time." Fortunately no one was there to witness stacks of plywood appearing out of thin air.

When they were done Kothry approached with what could only be described as a shit-eating grin. "Welcome back Captain. Will these do?" He held up his latest attempt to replicate the glass tubing with flanges in place.

"What did Harry say?"

"He said they're perfect."

"Then that's what they are. Do you have five more?"

"I will by the time you're done. What else can I do?"

"You can help me cobble together shielding from Harry's pile of parts over there."

Kothry walked to the bench and began to turn the possibilities over in his hand noting their lack of uniformity. "These are so crude, I don't know how he got a reaction."

"Bottom line, can you make any of them work?"

"I can make all of them work. I just need a bending jig and some time. Give me an hour." Kothry used the rods and springs and plates to wire up shielding that flapped and dangled so that each stack would randomly change direction from moment to moment.

"We don't have much time. I want the first five in place before dawn."

It was hard to keep the noise down but by 3:00 a.m. six new spinners and Harry's original stood lined up at the far edge of the floor. "It's time to load them up Harry. Can we open the doors on this end of the barn?"

"Sure, if I move some stuff out of the way. What are you

going to do?"

"I'm going to fly the Sentrybots in here, attach the spinners and send them as far away as I can. Do me a favor and turn out the lights for a moment while we bring them in." The two larger bots had no trouble but the smaller ones failed a test lift. "We won't get them all placed tonight, not if we're stuck with just the big bots for transport. I suppose we could use the scouts but for your sake and Donna's, I'd rather not."

After running cargo straps under a spinner and securing it to a large sentrybot, Kothry tested the loading. "She has no trouble with the lift but there's not enough power remaining to extend the cloaking to the spinner. We can get away with it in the dark but not in daylight. They'll be visible for sure." He didn't like having to give the captain bad news, but he didn't have to. The captain's expression said it all. "What do you want to do, sir?"

"Hook up the first two and get them out of here now. Make sure they're dropped before first light. I don't want any trouble. Even if two is all we can do, any insurance is better than none."

"Right away sir."

"Harry, can you kill the lights again? I don't want your neighbors to know any more than they already do."

Simultaneously the large sentrybots rose, cargo in tow, and slipped silently away in darkness picking up speed as they went. "I can still see the plywood in the moonlight. We should have painted them black. We'll be lucky if nobody sees them."

"Well Kothry old friend, let's hope we don't get caught. We'll paint these black later. There's not much more we can do now that the sun's about to rise."

"Actually there might be. I've been thinking about making a much smaller stack using a silver, gold and platinum combo. It would be quick and powerful and really hard to control, no way to shield it at all. Could go right through a hull if we were close."

"What about synth restrictions? Can you make everything you need yourself?"

"Everything but the precious metals."

When Arney finally arrived home, he found Shereen sleeping softly in his bed and slipped in beside her. He could hear the boys already stirring. If Jen slept in, they would have to feed themselves. Right now he just needed sleep.

When the phone rang around ten it was Harry. "Sorry to wake you. What time are you comin' over?"

"When I can. I've got to take care of my own this morning. Do me a favor, tell the captain that Shereen's going to be here for a while. We need to reassure the kids about what's coming. Just not right now, I've had a long night."

"I'll just bet you have."

"Now Pop, don't be cruel."

"That's a Presley tune, ain't it?"

"Stop Poppa, please. I'll see you later."

Arney needed family time, and the kids deserved an explanation. Things had been going hot and heavy, and they were mixed up in every part of it. The commotion had awakened the rest of the house. Jen was up and so was Shereen. The smell of coffee brewing and eggs frying meant he owed yet another debt to the ladies in his life.

Breakfast proceeded apace, and when seconds and thirds had emptied the skillets Arney gathered his herd.

"Find some place to be comfortable and get whatever you want from the fridge but come back and sit. We need to talk."

"What about Dad?" Jen could feel some of it in the air.

"About love."

"What about it?"

"What it is and what it isn't, about what's happening to us, all of us."

A quiet settled over them in anticipation. Even Shereen wasn't sure what was coming.

"I want to apologize to all of you, first to you kids. I've been away from relationships for so long I just figured this was the way my life would be after your mom died, but things have changed. I made a new friend from farther away than I could have imagined, and something wonderful happened. I know it seems fast and even crazy but I am bound to her heart, mind and body all interwoven. I'm better when I'm near her." He looked at the other half of him shining back from where she stood.

"Perhaps I can help." Shereen moved closer. "I know all this seems sudden, but it's not. From the first time I scanned your father he touched something in me. I kept hearing the words 'heart of the matter'. He was always looking for the best."

"Dad's always saying that."

"Do you know how different that is? Men like your father are rare. So are the relationships you boys have with my sisters. It's the same with you Jennifer. It feels like you and Warehan have known each other all your lives, doesn't it?"

"I'll have no one else."

"It's the neural entangling, a deep and abiding love is inevitable. How could you not be totally attached to someone who fits perfectly into your life? This doesn't happen with either of our species alone but when we combine, we excite what is missing in the other. So you see it's not so strange to feel the way we do. I know the sex is wonderful but as your father says it's the heart of the matter that counts."

Jen jumped at it. "I don't understand. Are you saying this is okay? Dad is that what you're saying too?"

"Let Shereen finish and then we'll talk."

"Jennifer, may I call you Jen? I think what we have established is that we could not prevent this if we tried. So right and wrong don't enter in. We have to manage the situation as it is. Right now, I would caution all of us to be prudent. That means no pregnancies and no public displays of affection. I don't want you to be afraid, but I need you to be alert. Don't talk to anyone outside the family. Let's not make this any worse than it is. We can always leave if we have to but we owe everyone a resolution. The rest of the world did not ask for this."

"What can I do?" Mark was first.

"Yeah Dad, what can we do?"

"Do what Shereen is asking Jenny. Learn to think to each other."

Harry hung up the phone and found Ducar and Kothry in the barn checking their progress. "Shereen's over at Arney's."

"And exactly when did my junior officer intend to inform me of her continued absence?"

"Sorry, she said to tell you she knew you'd understand." It was a small lie but Harry liked Shereen. She was clearly good for his boy.

"Well they're not far off if we need them. It's fine." Ducar knew Harry had covered for her and didn't blame him. He liked her too. Besides she had a lot of work in front of her. Any break she got would help.

Kothry took advantage of a lull in the conversation as he inspected Harry's lathe." Listen Harry, do you have any gold or platinum?"

"Not lying around loose, why? How much do you need?"

"About an ounce of each, it's part of the formula."

"Ducar mentioned you were going to make a little stack, but I thought you were supplying the precious goods."

"Sorry, it's not something we carry."

"You can make some right? Synthesize it?"

"It's a prohibited commodity. You upset cultural balance if the technology gets loose. Harry this shouldn't be a problem, there's gold right there on your finger. Donna's got one of these too, doesn't she?"

"Hold on Kothry. You're talking about our wedding rings.

Even if I give mine up, you'll never get Donna's. There's got to be another way."

"If you can find one, I'm all ears. Otherwise you need to put all your gold and silver and platinum in one place and make some choices. And I'm going to need some time to smelt it so sooner would be better."

Harry had gone from liking Kothry to not so sure. A lot of family memories and sacrifice clung to the rings and necklaces and broaches that lay hidden in their velvet vaults. Donna would be pissed. He wasn't looking forward to the conversation.

"I'll speak to her if you want me to, save you the pain."

"No, I get it. I see. It's for all of us. I'll talk to her. But I can already hear the explosion that's coming."

28

Mean and Stupid

Tergana sat debating whether to take a seat next to the main stack or tough it out in his command chair. He opted for the stack. It didn't go unnoticed. "Here sir, take a little swallow of this. You'll feel better." He thought his embarrassment complete until he saw the silver flask.

"Single malt phana sir, best I ever synthed. Been working on the recipe for years."

"You know Chief, I have a new appreciation for your skills. Could you leave a little of that in a cup?"

"Sure, a fine medicine, not without its charms."

"It's just what I need. Thanks."

Tergana could feel Torel asking if he was ready for the lurch. He thought back, *Announce away. I'm as ready as I'll ever be.*

"Attention all hands, this is Commander Torel. We will be commencing our next hop in sixty seconds."

Waiting was a bitch. Tergana couldn't decide between wanting to know when and not, but wound up watching the clock like everyone else. Having your hand on the button was always easier than waiting for someone else to push it, and the second gulp of phana now seemed like a mistake.

"Why me?"

"What did you say Admiral?"

"Nothing Chief."

I hate runners, he thought quietly to himself and waited for the empty feeling to subside. Fortunately for everyone afflicted the hops didn't last long, usually under thirty seconds. But this was the big one. *Forty-one...forty-two... Oh, please, oh thank you.* "Finally." He let his mind and then his stomach relax and settle back. *This is my last tour*, he thought. *I can't do this anymore. I'm just too dammed old. Finish the mission and I'm done.*

"Why the sad face sir? Didn't you like the phana?"

"I loved the phana. It didn't love me. I'd like some more when I'm not about to be a rabbit." Tergana got up a little worse for wear. "Let's talk over here." He walked to a viewport that gave a view of the stars. "No, I was just thinking."

"What about?"

"Oh, time, age, what it all means."

"You mean the mission?"

"That too I guess. I was thinking bigger, you know, what it means to be a part of all this, why it matters. Did you ever ask yourself what the universe would be like without you? I mean, what difference could it possibly make to all of this if we had never been born?"

"But you were sir."

"Well you see, there it is. I was born. And I can contemplate what I see and try to fathom it."

"And what have you concluded?"

"That I'm necessary. That I wouldn't be here unless I was needed, but that I don't matter much."

"That's the way I see it."

"I think it's the way most people see it, but that leaves me in a quandary. If I'm necessary, so is Ducar. So are all the people we are about to dust. Does that seem right to you?"

"Sure does. They're savages, endless corruption, endless wars, psychotic children running countries. They watch each other starve. Look at how they treat their women. We can't let them loose among civilized worlds."

"That's the current thinking, I know. But from this distance all I can be sure of is that someone put together a very crude stack and then spun it up. It's inconvenient but they're not jumping off that rock any time soon. Our worlds are not in danger, not yet anyway."

"That's why we have protocols, so we don't have to make these choices."

"And that jams me up against who did the choosing. The worlds that got dusted sure didn't choose. Neither did we. We thought it was the right thing to do, but maybe it wasn't. I know we think because we have achieved a world-mind we're better. That somehow we do no wrong because we think we can do no wrong. But is that true? I'm not so sure. Perhaps we should interfere more. For all the Shepherds' altruism, the protocols, the hands off... maybe we should be more hands on. Why do all these people have to die? Maybe they don't deserve to be judged and executed. They're behind, so what? It could be their leaders are just mean and stupid."

"Here you go Admiral. Have another little sip."

"Why? Do I look like I need it?"

"If I didn't know you better, I'd say you were having some serious second thoughts."

"Maybe it's just the truth in the phana. This stuff is really good. Eighty-seven proof?"

"Ninety."

"I'm just saying, I see things differently the older I get. The more I understand, the bigger things get and the smaller I become. It's an irony I've made peace with, except that my tiny contribution, my speck of time spent darting about trying to help, means very little. And if that's true then piling up a stack of money at someone else's expense shouldn't mean much either. Can I have a little more? Thanks. Maybe we should be going after mean and stupid."

"Can't fault people for being stupid, can you?"

"I guess it depends on how willfully they hold on. Sometimes you can whisper in their ear and it works. And sometimes you can't shout loud enough. If these people had used their heads, they might have a world-mind by now and we wouldn't have to chase these runners in the first place. I'm just saying."

"That sure is kind of stupid, isn't it?"

"God damned right it is."

"You okay Admiral? Want any more?"

"No, but thanks for the drink. I think I've had my share. And Chief, don't wave that flask about, will you? I don't want the rest of the crew getting ideas."

"No sir. We wouldn't want that. No ideas sir."

29

Smelt Me

Donna was putting up a fight. "The hell you say Harry Miller, I'm not giving up my wedding ring."

Harry had found her in the basement doing laundry. It was going about as he expected. "Honey, it's for all of our sakes. I'll get you another ring when this is over."

"It will never be the same."

"I promise, we'll only use it if we absolutely have to. What else do we have?"

"You could melt down your grandfather's gold coins. How 'bout those?"

"I'm sorry, I totally forgot. Keep your ring on honey. The coins should be plenty. Now, do we have any platinum?"

"No, but Arney does. The necklace and earrings he gave to Louise were platinum. I'm sure he still has them. By the way Harry, where's your ring?"

"Don't worry, I'll get it back from Kothry." He headed for the barn, one third of his assignment complete.

"What did you bring me?"

"I got the rest of the gold. Can I have my ring back? These should be more than enough."

"Coins, good. What about the silver and the platinum?"

"Arney's driving over with Louise's jewelry."

"Then I'm going to make a forge. You wouldn't have some modeling clay or plaster of paris, would you?"

"Why would you need that? Doesn't the Xelanar have a machine for this?"

"You mean a robot like the ones that build your cars?"

"Yeah, something that automates the process."

"A thousand years ago, yes. We don't manufacture anything anymore. We synthesize. We replicate. We don't melt. We assemble, particle by particle. The trouble is out here our synthesizers aren't programmed for precious metals. A machine that makes gold is a weapon in the wrong hands."

"I might have some quick setting cement. Would that do?"

"And chicken wire, I need some chicken wire to strengthen the casting."

The sound of tires on gravel interrupted the hunt. Jennifer, Luke and Mark jumped down from the bed of the pickup as Shereen got out of the cab.

"Arney, I'm going to log in on the six-man."

He waved acknowledgment. "I'll give these to Kothry. Sure is a shame though. Louise lit up when she saw 'em, like there never was anything so precious." He stopped in the shade and opened the blue velvet box. A filigree of platinum held the frosting of small diamonds that surrounded the emerald. It wasn't a big stone, but the necklace and earrings had a grace about them. Louise was ecstatic. If crystals and precious metal were ever imbued with affection, the message was loud and clear. *That must have been the night Mark became Mark*, he thought as he stepped across the threshold of the barn's side door, remembering her smile.

"Is that the platinum?"

"These are family. There's got to be some other way."

"They're just as likely to be dust anyway if we can't get this together. Please. Give me the box."

He held up his treasure. "This is an affair of the heart. Use only what you have to."

"I understand. I'll only use the chain. It won't be as powerful as it might have been, but it will be way stronger than those guys." He gestured toward the five remaining spinners and their charges.

Kothry had two big tasks left—cast a concrete forge and machine a smaller spinner mechanism to accelerate the discs of precious metals. He was searching the barn's shelves when Harry showed up.

"You want some help?"

"Absolutely. I need to make a small concrete box with cut outs and a lid. Two inches thick should do. And I have to make crucibles big enough to melt down about two ounces of metal. I'll start with any small cardboard cartons you might have and that quick-setting cement."

"We've got the boxes that came in the other day. Chicken wire's in the corner by the bench."

Arney could see that in spite of his offer, there wasn't much he could contribute and excused himself. "Since you and my dad seem to be making this work, I'm going to find Shereen."

His mood lifted until he discovered that no one in the house had seen her since they arrived.

"She came over with you, right?" Ducar's brow furrowed slightly.

"Yeah, she said she was going to log in."

"Excuse me, I'll be right back."

"Can I come?"

"If you want." The two men walked around behind the barn. Arney feared he would crack his head and started to feel his way with his hands as he got closer to where he was sure he had seen the scout's door open.

"How do you know where it is?"

"Better memory for locations." Ducar started to press the

entry sequence when the door opened.

"Howdy boys," she said with a knowing grin. "Come on in. You're gonna to love this one."

Ducar could tell that by the setup. "Did you probe?"

"Is it okay for me to say with Arney here?"

"We're all in the soup together, aren't we?"

"Yes sir."

"So?"

"It's their admiral Tergana. They made their first big hops, but he got sick. I sense the crew is waiting for him to wake up. I think he's passed out. This isn't like him, is it? I don't remember alcohol in his profile."

"That old dog. I may have to rethink my opinion. So that's the good news. What's the bad?"

"They're here. Not on top of us. They still have another hop, but by late tonight their bots should be on patrol."

"This means the first five fly tonight. I want the next pair moved into position now. Keep them low and out of sight, if you can. We'll take the oldest one and set it off from just outside the door. As soon as the bots get back, reload them. The last two should be on their way by midnight but be sure they're on another comm channel. We're going to hold them for later. Let's help Kothry get this together. His little treasure will have to wait."

30

Pole Position

Tergana hadn't intended to get drunk. It had been a long time and his head reminded him why. He looked at his clock. Five hours had passed. *I won't do that again*, he thought and opened the commport. "Commander Torel, status please."

"Feeling better sir?"

"I feel like...never mind. What's our status?"

"We are holding station, awaiting your orders for the last hop in deference to your condition sir."

"What condition is that?"

"Both of them."

"I see. I'll be on the bridge in five minutes. Start programming, we need to get moving."

Tergana wished it wasn't so. Given his unsettled stomach and the pain in his head, more rack time was what he needed. Another hop was the last. *Still, better to get it over with*, he thought, working his way up to the bridge.

"Evening Admiral. Rough afternoon?" Torel kept his tone as neutral and light as he could while acknowledging that the admiral clearly looked and felt like shit. "We're almost ready. How close do you want to be when we come out of the hop?"

"I want us on station, in the shadow of the fourth planet.

Don't spook them. Hop in between the eighth planet and the ice dwarf so we don't disturb any orbits, and we'll work our way in on local gravity."

"It will take a few moments to plot."

"Do that then and give me a little time to prepare, please." Tergana took a seat near the main stack and buckled in. When the countdown began, he didn't bother to watch the clock. He couldn't possibly feel worse than he already did, or so he thought. His dry heaves betrayed the truth. He remembered his first cruise. Hop sickness got to all the able airmen at first. It took some getting used to and for decades he had adjusted and then shown the customary bravado. Now he was unbuckling next to the women and another man his own age, glad he had not encountered the chief.

On station, sir. Torel's message entered his mind. When Tergana appeared on the bridge no one said anything.

"Status?"

"We're in the shadow of the gas giant. If they have a good empath, they'll know we're close."

"Not close enough. Use a transport and put cloaked sensors in orbit around the third planet, as close as you can get them without being detected. I want to hear and see everything."

"Right away sir." Torel issued the necessary instructions, watched the admiral retreat to his cabin, sedative in hand, and then settled into the command chair. *I could get used to this,* he thought. *Besides, the old man doesn't look like he's long for patrols at this point. He's a desker for sure.*

The sedative's effects on Tergana made the sound of the klaxon seem dreamlike. "Admiral to the bridge. Admiral to the bridge, please," sounded in his ear.

"What the hell people, I'm trying to get some rest. What's so damned important?" He immediately regretted addressing the bridge personnel in such a manner but it was too late.

"You need to get up here sir. We've got runners, five of

them. They came off number three. Might be partially shielded. They're already tumbling."

"That you Chief?"

"It's me sir. We've got big trouble." The chief wasn't trying to understate the problem but the expression on Tergana's face made it clear that he had. A flight lieutenant was vacating the command chair just as Tergana scanned the alarm panel. "Four of 'em went off all at once, then a fifth one. Never seen two at once in my whole life, much less five."

"Neither has anyone else to my knowledge. Is Torel aware?"

"On his way sir."

Torel came through the door. General quarters was deemed unnecessary, but the crew was informed there would be intermittent hops for at least the next five days and maybe more. The admiral sat forward in his chair, head in his hands before he rose to address them both.

"Commander, I need you to hunt these down for me, you and the chief. My body can't take a week of hops. It's nothing we haven't handled before. There are just a lot of them. If you can't catch them all, get me up. I'll make the case for reinforcements. Otherwise it will be better for all of us if we manage this ourselves."

"What about dusting number three? They're clearly in violation. Let's just get it over with before they light up any more."

"Too late Commander, they've won this round. We don't have time to do anything but chase. Whatever they're up to down there will just have to wait. We'll find out soon enough. Remember, this world is not full of rocket scientists. It's one guy, maybe two. Five stacks at once going in different directions is the puzzle. That's a sophisticated diversion, something Ducar would do. At any rate, carry on gentlemen. I'm going to my cabin and take another sedative. Keep me apprised."

The race was on. Wisdom said tackle the most difficult runner first. But the closest one would only take a few hops to retrieve. It was tempting, although not to Torel. "Can't do it Chief. I know it's close but we need to catch this twister first. It looks like it's shedding shielding at every turn. Put the main comp on it and try not to fry her. She got really hot the last time we crunched the numbers on one of these."

"Aye sir, commencing the plot now. Down ten percent from main-comp maximum. That should keep her cool enough."

"Thanks Chief. Let me know when you have a result. I want to move as soon as we can. This is going to be a long week."

The eleven hops that would be required to get in front of the most erratic runner meant the others would have plenty of time to get away. It didn't go unnoticed.

Shereen sensed Tergana was still hungover before any of the stacks had been released. But once they flew, the stream of information immediately increased. "They're going nuts up there Captain, trying to decide which way to go. And I'm not getting much from Tergana. It's mostly the second in command, a Taral maybe."

"Torel?"

"Yeah, Torel. He's leading the charge. A day and a half just to catch the first one, that's what they estimate. From what I'm getting, we've bought ourselves maybe a week's worth of time."

"Then my friend for the next week the show's yours. Do whatever you can to get these people ready to join in a world-mind. Push them. I'll give you whatever you need."

"The first thing we need is rest, all of us. That means you too sir. I can't hope to train sleepy people. I need everyone alert."

"The crew too?"

"Everyone we can spare. There's a chance one of them will make a neural link that I don't find. I want all the help I can get.

Warehan and Niriar and Filair should be here too. Jennifer's head over heels about Warehan, and Niriar loves Luke. He's all she talks about. And Filair's writing a poem for Mark. Those connections will help bring their minds into the fold. They trust each other and that's half the battle."

"Is there anyone here not in bed with an eligible member of our crew?"

"Not as far as I know. The attraction is undeniable. If they touch and then spend any time with each other, they're in love, totally bound up and I don't mean infatuation. I am with Arney, and you are too sir. You've been through this with Gilly, so you know what I'm talking about. We need as many strong attachments as we can muster if we're going to make a world-mind work. And we need them all in one place. Close proximity helps them communicate in the beginning. If they sleep near each other, so much the better."

"Then we'll have to set up down here. Harry's got two spare bedrooms and Arney's got one. Some of us can bunk in the scouts. We should be fine. Meals will be the problem."

"Donna's got a big kitchen. We can manage."

"Ella will help."

"That's going to be interesting. I can't imagine those two women peaceful in the same kitchen together. Can I send Kothry to fetch them all in the six-man? The sooner everyone's here, the better."

Harry was feeling crowded, and Donna was totally put out after having been a reasonably good sport through some of the biggest changes in her life. Shereen needed all her powers. "Donna, I promise it won't mean more work for you. I'll help take care of the house, so will the rest of the crew. It's just for a few nights. You and Harry get some rest. We'll begin again in the morning."

Kothry walked around the back of the barn, opened the door of the six-man, took a seat in the pilot's chair and programmed the trip into the autopilot. For the moment, he was just the family chauffeur picking up the kids. It struck him oddly that he preferred where he was to where he was going. He would be glad to get back to the green of the place. The big scout slipped unseen into the sky. It wouldn't take long. Warehan, Niriar and Filair were already waiting by the airlock door. Rushing gas announced the seal between the extending dock and the scout's hull. When it was quiet, they opened the doors and stepped into their carriage.

"Home, Jeeves," said Warehan, unable to resist.

"Very funny. Strap yourselves in, I'd like to get back."

"Hey Kothry, how fast can this thing go?" Warehan was leaning over the console.

"Faster than your little tummy can handle. Sit down."

"Aw Koth, baby, gun it just once." Kothry saw the green disconnect lamp and flicked a joystick with his finger, making the scout shudder. It knocked Warehan off balance.

"Fast enough for you?"

"Not funny."

"Really? I thought so." Once Warehan had taken his seat, Kothry made good time, adding a few extra turns for perspective. "Alright Warehan, what do you think?"

"Way cool. That was fast."

"Picked up a few expressions from the natives, didn't you? Well the show's over, it's time to get to some sleep."

In the morning, except for the new arrivals who slept in Harry and Donna's guest room where Harry's snoring kept them awake, everyone was as rested as they could be. Three sets of giddy, rutting teenagers did not help to calm things but the greetings were entertaining. Ducar noted that a playing card would not slip between them.

Shereen thought a number of other things might but she had

a big task and time was short. "I know you are glad to see each other but we have a lot to do and we need to get started." The kitchen was a tight fit but it had good acoustics, and Shereen decided to trade room for resonance. "Alright everyone, if I could have your attention. It's a little close but it's easier to hear each other and the food's here. So before we begin, I know some of you are not sure that you are capable of sending and receiving thoughts, even though you do it all the time without realizing it. I'm going to help you get in touch with that sense and then learn to control it."

"Get me some tin foil."

Harry howled. It was the funniest thing he had ever heard Luke say.

"Come on boys, this is serious. For all you doubters I'm going to walk not run. Just a few ideas to think about. Look at Warehan and Jennifer, the colors they chose to wear today are almost alike. You could write it off as coincidence but it's more likely an unspoken communication between them that Jennifer isn't aware of, even if Warehan might be. These unspoken thoughts fill the void. They are everywhere. Most aren't meant for you, and you have developed a filter to keep out the noise. Unfortunately your filter—while keeping you mentally safe as your mind develops—gets in the way of broader social contact. The easiest way to break through this wall is with trust."

"I trust Warehan. I love him."

"I know you do Jen, but how much do you really know about him? One of the reasons family members have telepathic experiences among themselves is that they've had time to develop the trust that breaks down resistance and lets thoughts through. The more time they spend trusting each other the more the walls come down.

"I know a girl who does it. Yvonne and her boyfriend seem to dress in the same colors every time they go out. They don't plan it. They just do it. Is that what you're talking about?"

"Exactly. They are connected mentally without words. Telepathic communication doesn't just manifest itself as a phrase in your head. It may have no words at all. Your friends are proof of that. I imagine they speak of it as a curiosity, just a coincidence in their love life, but it's much more. It's evidence of the deep trust they have for each other's state of mind. They think to each other without words. We all do. The way to make use of this gift is to allow the possibility that it exists and let the walls come down a little at a time."

"Show us. I want to see it work. Do it with me, Shereen. Get into my head."

"Alright Mark. What would you consider proof? How about the day you lost the green and yellow Super Soaker you took to school. You were on the playground during recess. Your teacher was Miss Pierson."

"That's not fair. How do you know all that stuff? I never told anyone about that, not even Luke. It was his."

"I apologize. It was never my intention to give you up, just to make the point. And you're right, it's not fair. I'm better at this than most empaths. I can get in deeper and faster. I was trained as a child to understand that thoughts have force, and I'm going to teach you to expand the same capabilities in your own mind. Let me ask you, did you feel anything while I was probing?"

"Not really, not words anyway. Maybe a sense I was letting you look. I guess I knew you were looking, but it didn't really have a feeling."

"Exactly. Thought transfers can be helped or hindered by emotions. They control whether your walls are up or down, but the thoughts you receive are more ideas than orders. It takes a receptive mind on the other side to reintroduce emotion. Because I wasn't trying to accuse you of anything by telling your story, you felt very little intrusion. Emotion came into it when you realized the consequence I exposed. I am sorry for that."

"Peckerwood. You stole my squirt gun."

"No I didn't Luke. I just borrowed it. You got so angry when you couldn't find it, I just clammed up. I'm sorry I didn't tell you. I couldn't."

"Boys please, I didn't mean to start a fight. I'll synth another squirt gun if you need to have it back. I'm sure I can find the design in your libraries."

"I don't need it back but Mark's gettin' a shoulder noogie."

"Boys, you'll have to settle that later. Right now you need to let it go." Shereen was careful to answer the flood of questions as gently as she could. Donna expressed the most doubt but even she had to admit that Harry sometimes said out loud the very thing she was thinking. When everyone had shared a similar experience, it was time.

"Do you remember our harmonies from yesterday? There was real strength there. I could sense the affection. Well now there is a lot more. Except for our bachelor friend Kothry here, everyone's found someone they hold dear. It is without precedent. I confess I don't yet know how to live with all this passion but we are going to use its energy to our advantage. I want to start with just one note, an A, everyone should be able to sing it."

"I can't sing."

"Sure you can Luke. You can whistle, can't you?"

"Yeah."

"Well if you can whistle you can sing. Just think the note you want to whistle in your head and then hum it. Don't try to speak, just hum the note as steadily as you can. Do it softly until you can hold the pitch. Then when you have it, join in. I'll be glad to have you any way you want to be. So will they."

"Okay but don't laugh."

Shereen had perfect pitch and sang an open A, easy on the ear that drew them in. It wasn't just the note she held, it was the community she gathered, without their knowledge and without intrusion. Her thoughts went out to each of them, saying, *Hold the note and listen for the slow roll, then smooth it into one pure tone. You are so close. Find the pure tone. Keep your eyes closed. Find the pure tone. That's it, good.*

Sometimes in church there are musical notes that transcend the moment and become unique unto themselves as they echo up. This note, this A they held, bound them to each other, mind to mind, a trust that let them share each other in the bosom of the sound. Shereen could tell she had them all and used the moment to awaken them to the conscious reality of what they were doing.

Welcome, all of you. How does it feel in this space? Isn't this wonderful? To be a part of each other is such a joy. You realize we are all still singing our note, but we can stop and still be in this fine mental space, because this state of mind you are experiencing is the beginning of a communal mind. Sense this for a moment and then after we stop singing, see how fast we lose the experience. Ready? Okay stop.

Harry was the first to drop, not that he moved at all, but that's the way it felt to him. "I'll be damned."

Donna was next, to no one's surprise. "Harry, did you feel me? I sure felt you."

"Yes honey, that was quite fine, totally connected. I want to do that again, even if it is a little scary."

"I'm glad you said it first. That's exactly how I feel. And Harry, I don't know how young I can be."

"Don't worry, it's all in your head. We can be just as young as we want to be."

"Did you feel other people inside your mind? Not really looking but there?"

"I don't know, maybe. Shereen was saying something, I thought."

"I never spoke a word Harry, not to you or anyone else but I did think to each of you and all of you at once. Does anyone remember what I thought?"

"You were tellin' me to find a note."

"That's right Luke, you more than anyone, because you said you couldn't sing but you can, can't you?"

"Yeah, I guess so. Nobody laughed but I wouldn't call one note, singing."

"You'll get a chance to expand your range soon. How about the rest of you? Did you hear me in your head? Did you connect with your love?"

Stupid grins spoke to the sheer number of connections that had been made without touch. Luke and Niriar couldn't take their eyes off each other. But it was Mark who summed it up.

"I didn't know you could do that."

Filaire blushed, turned away and then turned back grinning. Mark decided more mind training would be good, very good, maybe even wonderful.

Yeah that's it, wonderful, he thought, then laughed out loud.

"What's so funny?" asked Luke.

"Nothin', you'll find out."

"Maybe I already have and don't feel like embarrassing myself."

"Is this a mine's-bigger-than-yours contest?"

"Boys, that will be enough now." Arney had to reign them in. "Shereen, let's take a break so the kids can cool down."

Everyone was glad to get some fresh air and put butts in the breeze. There comes a time when your ass just says, "Get off me."

Arney was about to hit the porch when Shereen hooked his arm and whispered, "Come with me, mister. I want to talk to you. Let's take a little walk."

"Okay, what's on your mind?"

"Arney, what did you feel? What did you hear in your head? You haven't said a word about it."

"I didn't think it would be smart, someone might get hurt. I saw or rather heard everything you were thinking—what the boys were up to, what you want to be, everything. Mom and Pop had a good time. I don't know how I feel about it right now. I'm still sortin'."

"That's what I want to talk to you about. I know you understand how to do this already, and I need your help. I can't do this by myself. We need to turn everyone here into a teacher capable of gathering in millions of minds. I want you to help me push them, not with force but with encouragement. Let's try a quick experiment. When I think to you, I want you to think the same thing back to me. Ready?"

Turn, turn turn, to everything there is a season, turn, turn, turn, and a time to every purpose. He heard the song in both their minds but asked out loud. "What about the harmonies? Can I do what I hear in my head?"

"That's what I want you to do, Arney. I want you to do the harmonies. I know the melody, that's my part. I want you to fly Arney, gather your people in. You will speak to their minds in the gathering stage far better than I will."

"What's the gathering stage?"

"We have to find a message that will touch all people everywhere around the world in the ways they will understand. It will tell them as gently as possible not to be afraid and that friendly voices and friendly minds will ask them to join in song. Once they start hearing it and humming, you will gather as many minds as your harmonies can reach and I will knit them and encourage a world-mind to become self-aware."

"That's a tall order. Everyone?"

"As many as can, yes. When we get back, just follow my lead. When you feel like flying, do it. Sing over the top the best way you can. Let harmony lead you where it will."

The rest of the day, and into the evening, the sessions went on—three-part and then four-part harmonies rose like a church choir, only there were no words. They were getting better at trusting and opening up to the incoming flow. Letting the filters down was selective and discretionary, like making new friends, talking about everything in the end. When she sensed she could push no further, Shereen cut them loose, hungry and restless.

"Grandma, are you going to cook dinner?" Luke's stomach got ahead of his manners.

"I should think not. I cooked breakfast and lunch. I'm tired. All this thinkin' makes me sleepy."

"Don't worry, Donna. If it's alright with Arney, Ella and I can make dinner over there. How about Italian at Arney's tonight? Say around six?"

31

Dinner at Arney's

They started up the steps to Arney's front porch at 5:45. The walk over was easy and motives transparent.

"Hungry, eh?" Arney swept the screen door open and held it with one hand. It was going to be tight but it felt more like a party than dinner. Everyone was tired but closer to each other. Conversations rang with the laughter of old friends, work done for the day. "Glad to see you all. Spread out to wherever you're comfortable. I've got beer, wine, tea and lemonade."

"You wouldn't have any whiskey, would you?"

"I sure as hell do Captain. But I was savin' it for after dinner."

"Fair enough. I'll have a beer."

The smell of onions frying filled the air, sweet and fat as if they were a meal in themselves. Then green peppers and tomatoes and sauce and more olive oil made the pan sizzle and steam. Ella meant it as a message.

"Some of you are going to have to find another place to be," she suggested, "The kitchen's getting crowded."

"Come on folks, let's sit on the porch. I know how Ella gets." Ducar and his beer led the way to the screened-in part that kept airborne intruders at bay. It was an easy view of corn and soy and a short piece of the road that wound around the back of Harry's farmhouse and barn farther up the rise. Ducar was finishing his beer and about to get another when he noticed a familiar looking vehicle pulling up at Harry's.

"Hey Harry, I think we've got trouble. I just saw the sheriff pull up over at your place."

"What the hell does he want?"

"Come on Harry, reach out. You know what he wants."

"He's put two and two together."

"Damned straight he has. It won't be long before he's down here looking for you. It will be better if you're not here."

"I can't leave now. He'll see me."

"In the basement Harry, you and Arney. I'll get Jennifer to answer the door and say you're out walking in the fields and she's making dinner. In the meantime it's everyone out of sight 'cause he's going to get tired of knocking up there. Everyone inside. It's time to be quiet. He's getting back in his car." Ducar watched the dust rise and heard gravel snap under the tires as the sheriff's big Crown Victoria came to a stop. "Alright Jennifer, you know what to say."

She took the lead at the front door. "Hi sheriff, what brings you out here?"

"I'm lookin' for your father and your grandfather. Are they here?"

"They're out inspecting corn. They walked off that way about twenty minutes ago. What's this all about?"

"Never you mind missy. It don't concern you. Just tell them when you see them, I want to talk to them both in my office, before noon tomorrow." Sheriff Bright turned to go. "Sure smells good in there. You always were a good cook. Noon. Remember?"

"I'll tell them."

"See that you do."

By the time the cruiser was out of sight what had been crowded was cramped. Legs and arms were unwound and stretched as the denizens emerged from hiding. It wasn't long before more drinks had rendered the sheriff's visit an amusing tale among those allowed to indulge.

"You know we're going to have to go down there in the morning."

"I know Dad. But in the meantime I'm hungry. I love Italian and this smells great."

The *mm's* and *ah's* and thanks to Ella spoke of just how good the spaghetti with sausage meatballs really was. And when it was over there were plenty of volunteers to help wash and dry, an encouragement that such cuisine might continue. That left Arney and Harry and Ducar time to sip some whiskey and plan.

"How many do they have left to catch?" asked Harry.

"Two maybe, if we're lucky. Shereen's going to probe after the dishes are done."

"What are you going to do after they catch them all?" Arney asked. "I mean how will we know? Are they going to show up and just start scorching the place? Don't seem right. One minute we're here and then poof."

"When Shereen senses that Tergana's chasing down the last one, we'll set off the two stacks parked on the far side. That should buy us an extra day, maybe two. And if Kothry can finish his little powerhouse we may get more time. Pass that bottle over here, will you Arney? I'd like to take the edge off. It sure is smooth goin' down. Why do they call it Wild Turkey? Nothing smooth about that bird."

"Beats me. Listen. I've been meaning to ask—"

"Will it hurt? That's what you want to know, isn't it? Will it hurt to get dusted?"

"How did you? Never mind I forgot who I was talking to for a moment. Yeah, will it hurt?"

"No, it happens fast. You might see it coming, but I doubt you'd feel much. It's supposed to be as benign as possible."

"That's not very comforting. Benign mass extinction? How

can you Shepherds justify this? And don't hand me the it's-for-the-good-of-the-galaxy crap."

"Arney, you've got to understand, this isn't my first rodeo. I've been there when worlds failed. It's not pretty. I fought the Krell. Things do go wrong. Science gets ahead of maturity, and worlds get savaged." Ducar went on at length, telling him what had evolved over time. "It's the same thing you are doing to your world right now. From where I'm sitting, just for the sake of argument mind you, you don't look so good."

"It ain't fair lookin' at it like that. This world's been gettin' better. Slow, I grant you, but better."

"Fair, that's the word. Treat women as equals. Feed the hungry. Help the poor. Start distributing your wealth equitably. Like I said before, nobody gets to choose where or how they begin their lives. Some get a break, most don't. Should the rich get to punish the poor because of a difference in circumstance that none have a choice about?"

"I guess not."

"Of course not. Look at you Arney. You're sitting on a farm that can feed a hundred. By most standards, you're a rich man. But you don't see that do you?"

"Not really."

"That's the problem. You were born into your own normality. You hold high ground you don't see yourself standing on. At least you're not mean about it. You think everyone has the same chance and sees the world the way you do, but they don't. They can't. That's why a world-mind is so important. It can bridge the gap by allowing individuals to gather in the billions and make collective decisions that help. Not because it is the moral thing to do but because it is the only way to survive. Your species will all live, or you will all die. There is no in between. It's all dust in the end anyway, if you think about it, so you might as well learn to cooperate."

"What do you mean, it's all dust?"

245

"Entropy Arney. The random decay of everything. This will all be dust in the end, tiny particles equidistant and still. You and I, we're just a blink and then we're gone, turned to dust. What do we mean to the totality of it all, whatever that turns out to be? Stars live and die. Galaxies live and die. We are so small. But before we join the dust, we get to contribute."

"What am I supposed to contribute besides what I already do? I'm a good man. I help."

"You do and you don't. If I told you the truth, we would no longer be friends. And we need to be friends right now."

"Whoa, buddy. What do you mean tell me the truth? Go ahead, piss away. Tell me your truth."

"Arney, I'm not trying to be mean, just widen your vision some. Got any black friends? How about Hispanics? How about anyone who doesn't look like you. Anyone at all? No? See, you've got your blinders on. How about poor people? Do you reach out to those souls living under the plywood and tar paper roofs out on the main road? No, you don't, not really. You leave that to the church-going folks and the government. I'm not saying you don't help your family and friends. I'm saying you have to expand and give back to something bigger."

"Maybe I have been a little self-centered but it doesn't make any difference now does it?"

"It makes all the difference now. Being ignorant of a problem is almost as bad as being the cause. It is the difference. Your dad might be set in his ways but you know the world has changed. You have to find a way to lose your fear of others. Shereen says you have the potential to connect with large groups. You don't want to scare them away just when you're trying to gather them together, do you? Remember everyone has the same problems. They want the best for themselves and their offspring just like you do. How different can they be?"

"They don't wish me well."

"That's because they're afraid Arney, just like you. Did you ever play your guitar in front of a group where you didn't know anybody? Sure you did. Solo, too. And what were you trying to do, get famous or give them something?"

"I was trying to connect and give them something."

"Bingo. And how did that feel?"

"There was this one time I was playin' at a club called the Cellar Door, and I remember there wasn't a sound besides me and my guitar. No movement, not a glass or fork, not even a whisper, just me and the music I was makin'. I knew I had 'em all. And when I finished, for a moment it was dead still. Then the whole place erupted in applause and whistles and hoots. They were all celebrating that connection, that moment in time when they were in the same place, feeling the same and behaving the same. I get what you're sayin'. Dammit Captain. You've been rootin' around in my head, haven't you?"

"A little."

"I feel it sometimes, the connection, like thoughts without words, just knowing without knowing why I do. I feel like it ought to have words."

"Let yourself have whatever story makes you happy. In the end the connection is a direct one and the need for anything in between falls away. Relax, it will come. Reach out with your mind. Find out what you can from the sea of thought. I promise you will not be disappointed. What you seek to gather in seeks to gather you in. You have but to allow the possibility and let go."

"What's it feel like?"

"It feels like you're floating, that it's safe and you have help, which of course you do. Countless minds like your own, searching for solutions."

"Sounds like religion."

"More like democracy. Everybody has a vote, all the time about everything. In the end those choices usually work best for the vast majority. Once you see the oneness of it, you become aware of much more. The collected mind of your species will become one of many and join with them."

"That's a lot to think about, and me and Pop have to see the sheriff in the morning."

"Don't worry, your dad's a smart cookie. You'll be fine."

Harry awoke to his own alarm in his own bed, not looking forward to the conversation he had rehearsed. He wasn't going to be able to fool Dave. They could tell when the other was lying. Dave Bright and Harry were friends in school but he was the sheriff now and that was to be respected. He decided not to wear his overalls and after his second cup of coffee and other necessities, Harry felt sufficiently fortified to call Arney and get the show on the road.

"You ready to go?"

"Oh, hi Pop. Yeah, I'm ready, been ready. What do you want me to say today?"

"Fireworks. Stick to the story. Must be a bunch of people bought the same ones. Don't say more than that. The more you try to explain yourself, the more it smells like bullshit. Give Dave enough to set him thinkin', that's all."

"Gotcha. I'm almost ready. I'll pick you up in a few minutes."

The sheriff's office was over in Callenville, far enough to discourage Dave from just dropping by but close enough to respond to trouble. Dave saw them pull up and decided on low-key. He had won the round, no need to push.

"Glad to see you boys could make it, Harry."

"Hi Dave. What'd ya want to see us about anyway?"

"You know those disturbances out your way, the fireworks that ain't quite that. Well we've had reports of other people seeing something just like what your neighbors saw. You know, they say it went straight up and out of sight and never came down. Doesn't sound like any fireworks I know of. Does it to you, Harry?"

"I guess it just depends on where you're standing, don't it?"

"What do you mean?"

"Well if you're close to it when it goes off it could look like it was goin' straight up."

"But they say it vanished."

"Any clouds?"

"I don't know, maybe. Look Harry, I take your point. But you and I both know there's something more going on. Whatever it is, it has to stop. I do not want another disturbance like that last one in my jurisdiction. Understood?"

"Understood."

"The pickup had barely left the parking lot when Arney spoke. "I gotta say Pop, that was a master class."

"Thank you. See how you can lead 'em to it? You just have to be quick on your feet. Don't step in it. Keep askin' questions and smile, but not too much."

Arney nodded.

They put in five miles of dusty silence on two-lane blacktop before Arney spoke again, "It ain't over is it Pop?"

"Don't worry about Dave. If he wanted to stick a foot in it, he'd have done it already. He's just puttin' up some fence-posts and we're just buyin' time. Ain't we, just buyin' time? Sooner or later somebody's gonna find our spinners. Then they'll know whatever went up wasn't made in China. Then we could see Dave again. But what's he gonna do? The barn's empty. Our real problem's crowd control. People are bumpin' into each other and Donna's fried."

"What about some early warning for the sheriff? He could roll up on us and catch us scurrying around like rats."

"Excellent thought. I don't know how to do it but Kothry might."

"I like him. He doesn't talk much but you can see how his mind works by the way his hands move. And he's easy access when we're training."

What do you mean?"

"I don't sense resistance from him during the mind-training sessions. He lets me discover him. He's Shereen's friend too, and that helps me understand what those telepathic connections feel like. What are you gettin' outta these sessions for yourself?"

"Me and Donna are closer."

Arney knew that was the truth without being able to share how he knew. One thing for sure, his relatively cool, relatively loose father would have been appalled at just how deep he was able to probe. He would never tell him.

As they came around the curve that put Harry's front porch in view, Arney could see Shereen sitting on the steps watching them approach. She stood up with an easy grace and smiled with sure eyes. She was in his mind, and a part of him flew out to bring her closer as she gathered him in. She got in Arney a good heart and a strong smart mind, a powerful natural empath as gifted as herself, just untrained and reckless. Arney knew it too. He knew all about what Shereen thought of him because she let him in.

"I've missed you. Have you been waiting long?"

Her knowing half smile broadened a little before she answered. "I know where you are. You're no surprise to me Arney Miller. I know how you are too, but I'll always ask because I know you like it." She took his hand as they walked up the porch steps, which caused Harry to stop walking and watch. He could not separate alien from daughter-in-law, and the thought warmed him and chilled him at the same time. They belonged together plain as day, like they'd always been that way.

"If I didn't know better, I'd say you grew up nearby and been together since high school like me and Donna."

She turned and smiled and thought to him. *That's the plan, Harry. That's the plan.* Then with a turn any dancer would envy, she slipped behind Arney and opened the screen door for him with a flourish and a bow. Harry felt a bolt of affection go right through him and wash back over him for the fine, funny lady who was now spinning around his son.

She'll do, he thought, *nicely at that.*

Why thank you, Harry. I like you, too. There she was in his head again, smiling.

At one in the afternoon mind training began again. Perhaps mind blending would have been more accurate, but for the newcomers acquiring the skill was a test of resolve. They were better than they knew, closer than they thought. That was Shereen's constant message as the afternoon wore on.

By four that day they had seven-part harmonies to sail upon, chords that opened their minds to each other and to something far greater. The awareness of the unity of everything crept in to rest, in the back, in the corner by itself, whispering the possibility of one mind.

"It's time to rest." Shereen's suggestion allowed the hard work to end. Keeping the connection open required effort because it was unfamiliar, a new muscle to be trained.

As the group began to speak instead of think, a party atmosphere arose with the usual need for food. "I just want you all to know that you came close to Unomeri today. Everyone was in. Tomorrow we will begin to reach out to others and see what works and what doesn't."

"Are we going to be able gather everybody in to this?" Luke asked.

"That depends. Getting a small family group going is one thing. Expanding that to a point where it's self-sustaining and capable of gathering other minds into the group on its own, well that's another matter. We'll try again in the morning. For now Ella and Warehan and I will make dinner. Have some wine, open a beer, you've done well today."

"Can I have a beer?" Mark asked, as if it was about time he should.

"No, you may not," answered Shereen, who then looked at Arney. "Oh never mind. Go ahead. Your father thinks it's alright."

Then Arney thought directly to Mark. *Go ahead, son, enjoy it. You've earned it.* Mark turned to see his father smiling, outside and inside his mind. They met in the middle.

"Hey Dad," Mark said out loud, but only thought the rest. *Thanks.*

32

It's Catching

Tergana's crew was exhausted from the strain of too many hops. Still, they bore it better than the admiral, who was in his quarters under sedation. It was the most charitable approach Torel could muster, definitely better than hearing the jokes that circulated about his distress.

Four runners had been captured and rendered inert. Catching number five was proving tricky because of loose shielding. Another hop was imminent and Torel's approach to the chief was bristly at best. "I'm tired of this," he muttered under his breath. "Five days is enough. Have you plotted the next hop yet chief? The maincomp's getting warm." In the moment it was civil enough.

"Just about there sir. A minute or two more and we'll have it. I can't guarantee its accuracy. The core's dropping bits due to the heat, and traces are getting skipped."

"Doctor Mack to the admiral's quarters, Doctor Mack to the admiral's quarters." An encrypted message flashed on the commband on Torel's wrist but it might as well have been announced all over the ship.

"The old man's up or something bad has happened. This won't be good."

"What did you say sir?"

"Nothing Chief. Cancel the hop and inform the crew. I'm going down to see how he's doing." Torel didn't wait for an acknowledgment, traversing the portals and corridors in hurried strides. If Tergana was in trouble, so was he. It was easier to speak for the admiral than be the admiral. A mission loaded with political trouble was an unwelcome command.

He knocked and opened the door to the cabin. The doc was in the chair taking Tergana's blood pressure.

"How's he doing Doc?" He never got answer. Tergana cut him off.

"I'm fine. No, I'm not. I suck if you must know. You couldn't have invented a worse scenario for my gut. The Doc wants to up my sedative dose. But if he does, you'll have to assume full command. So the ship's yours Commander. How's the hunt going, anyway?"

"We've got four. Just one to go but this last one's got more loose shielding. It's harder to catch than the first. Something's happened to it since we scanned it. It's bouncing all over the place."

"When you catch it, I want my sedatives pulled. And under no circumstances are you to dust anything without my authorization. Ducar may be bending rules left and right but I sense he's containing something. Why would anyone send us all over creation chasing after rogue runners if not to buy time? They were set off simultaneously in different directions with incomplete, loosely attached shielding. You couldn't have made a bigger mess. I want to know why. So wake me. That's an order."

"As soon as we're in range. When the cargo doors are closing, you'll be watching. In the meantime get some rest sir."

Torel waited in the corridor for the doctor to finish. "How is he really?" he whispered.

"No need to whisper, he's out cold. But to answer your

question, I'd say he's got one of the worst cases of hop sickness I've ever seen. Not a happy puppy. I shouldn't joke. He's okay, not great. Some guys his age are fine with all this. He's not one of them. Is it affecting his judgment? Maybe. But whatever dance he and Captain Ducar are doing makes me think it's personal. He's pushing himself."

"Thanks Doc. That helps." However the responsibility that began to weigh did not. Whatever was next was Torel's to do or not. And the feeling of satisfaction upon assuming command washed away under the weight. When he reappeared on the bridge the chief was waiting.

"Everything alright with the admiral? We heard Doc went to see him again."

"He's under sedation. I have assumed command. To that end, please resume plotting the next hop. I want to finish this as soon as possible."

The chief's best efforts got them closer. If things didn't change, one maybe two more hops would do it. The whole crew joined the chorus of grumbling. Some even envied the admiral his sleep. They all felt the shifts in force. They didn't get sick but they did get tired. It took energy to compensate and they were running out of patience.

"Hey Chief, I'll give you half my share of the pool if you can nail it on this next hop," a junior engineer offered.

"Is everybody betting on this?"

"Are you kidding? Of course. Beats watching stars curl around each other. Besides, there's almost a thousand creds in the pot now."

"I've been missing out. I guess you couldn't have me fixing the result. But why tell me now? Are you trying to bribe me Benejy?"

"Nah Chief. It's not that. Everybody knows you're doin' your best. We just want it to be over is all. Stop all this bouncing around."

"I'll see what I can do." The next hop got them closer but not close enough. It would take one more, which proved to be the end of the chase at least for the moment.

"Doc, wake the admiral, will you? I promised him a show." Torel had insisted the doctor remain close at hand to facilitate the admiral's return to duty. It took the doc several minutes to revive Tergana who looked none the worse for wear except that he was groggy.

"Good morning Doc. How long have I been out?" Tergana slurred slightly.

"It's evening, about eighteen hours. How do you feel?"

"Like a truck hit me. Are we close to the last runner?"

"It's in the disruptor beam. They're just waiting on you." Tergana thought about getting dressed, decided against it and pressed his commport.

"Commander, tell the chief to bring her aboard. I don't need to be there. I'll be on the bridge as soon as my head clears."

The relief expressed by the Carei crew was strong enough that Shereen read it several hops away. They were done and glad to be. She left the kitchen and found Ducar in the barn with Kothry. Before she could speak, he did.

"I know Shereen. I can't read them directly but I can read you. They caught up with our last stack, didn't they?"

"Yes sir, just a moment ago. I also think Tergana might be sick. I get a sense of empathy coming from the crew and exhaustion. They're tired of the chase."

"That's good work. Spin up the last two stacks. I don't want to give them time to breathe."

Ducar's quiet order sent her out of the barn and through side door of the six-man scout. Her fingers found the touch-points with grace and speed, a facility born of habit and dedication.

When the screen acknowledged the launch and initial track of the last of Harry's experiments Shereen felt a loss she hadn't anticipated. *What do I feel about this? I shouldn't care. They are not mine to lose. Oh, I see. I envy the pioneer his genius.*

Harry sank when he knew his creations had slipped away so Shereen reached into his mind. She found his favorite lullaby and sang it back to him in his mother's voice deep in the back recesses, quiet and calming. It was enough. She felt him ease, then shut down her console and departed.

The walk uphill to the house held magic when the light was right. There was charm in such existence, connection too. *He might be my father in law and Donna my mom. What a kick, such nice people*, she thought, and immediately cast about for Arney's location, sending a swirl of thought that let him know she was thinking about him.

I'm glad you like Mom and Dad, he thought back.

You got that? All of it?

All of it, Mom and Dad, why you sang him his lullaby, all of it.

That's a deep read. You're getting better at this.

How far apart are we? Can you see me? It's like you're standing right next to me having a conversation.

I'm walking toward the porch steps heading for the kitchen and you are just flushing the toilet, sorry to intrude.

You can see everything can't you? Everything you want I mean.

Everything that is important to progress, there's no need to intrude into what's personal and private. I dig in only for safety's sake. I promise we will delve into this but right now we need to focus. We don't have much time. Finish and meet me on the porch.

When they saw each other, they slipped into a warm, easy embrace that lasted almost a minute. The first time Mark saw them do it, he thought of his grandparents. He told Luke they looked like slow smoke. Mostly they thought about all the ways Shereen was not their mother. An idea not lost on her.

When she could feel Mark watching she thought to her other half *Mark's...*

Mark's watching, I know.

So, ease him. Think to him, reach in and tell him it's going to be okay. You are going to be a more effective parent than you ever thought possible. Invite him to come out here and see what happens.

It was as if Arney had asked the question out loud. Mark smiled, turned and appeared in the doorway.

"You two having fun?"

"As a matter of fact, we are. How's your training going?"

"Shereen knows. Okay, I guess."

"Don't let it bother you son. You'll get it."

"Sometimes it feels like I never will. What's the point anyway? We're running out of time. What's a dusting look like? Does it roll across the land, green in front leaving dust behind? Or does everything vanish at once?"

Shereen reached into Mark's mind to calm his fears. "*Don't worry my friend. I will not let that happen. We will all be gone before that.*"

"I can hear you in my head."

"You can speak to me in mine. Go ahead, try it. Don't talk, think it." Shereen kept the conversation going as she led Mark out of his shyness. Simple questions with easy answers kept his brain engaged and answering. He did not realize that he had become a conversational telepath until Shereen pointed it out.

"Well, what do you think?" she asked out loud. The difference startled Mark. A slow ever-increasing grin began to rise at the corners of his mouth.

"See? You can do it. What's more you are good at it. So there."

"Thanks Shereen."

"You're welcome Mark. Very welcome."

"You guys want some iced tea? I'm gettin' some."

Shereen nodded. "That would be nice." She relaxed and eased away from Arney. Pillows in the wicker chair were calling.

"We need to talk, my love. You just saw what might be possible, one on one, if we put our minds to it. But we'll never make this group strong enough in the time we have left. It's up to us, or more accurately it's up to you. But I think you already know that, don't you?"

"You want me to gather, so that you can organize the minds I bring into the fold using the comfort of the collective. That much I understand. But how do I make all the harmonies we need to call to them? I can't sing all those parts by myself."

"Think them Arney. You're stronger than I am here. This is your species. You swim in this. You were born in this. You can connect with your own kind in a way I never will. You only need to bring them together. I'll point the way. Once they are self-aware, they will lead themselves."

"I don't see how, not this rabble."

"Your pessimism's in the way. You don't think it's possible, but you must."

"Help me then. What do they want?"

"They want a whisper of hope, something to hold on to. Something that lets them know, it's going to be alright, no matter what comes. We will give them more. We will offer unity and peace."

"What about the evil in the world?"

"There is great power in the collective mind. Imagine the pressure that can be brought to bear when the collective senses an undesirable trait. It persuades individuals to stop harmful behavior, ridding the body of disease. In other words, things are going to get better. You have a chance to save your people and give them a great gift in the bargain. You can do this."

"I'm still not so sure. Why me alone?"

"Because you are a pure voice by yourself. You will reach

farther if you aren't burdened by the confusion of half-trained minds. I should have seen it sooner. I've been expecting too much. It takes generations to develop this skill. If you hadn't become so singularly powerful, we would have no other options. But you are strong enough to stand the strain and we don't have much time. Between the two of us, we possess more power than anything I have sensed from our larger group. From now on, it's just you and me."

"Thanks for the pressure."

"Find a place to relax and reach out with various melodies and chords. See what resonates. Don't try to get their attention yet. Just find what works to activate receptive awareness. They'll light up and tell you without ever knowing they are doing it. When you get at least a quarter of them to respond at the same time, we can begin. But first I've got to contact the captain."

Ducar read Shereen's thoughts and noted her progress, then turned his attention to Kothry. "How long before the small one flies?"

"You mean *if*, don't you Captain?" replied Kothry bent over Harry's lathe. "It's a tight fit at this small scale. I wish we had more time."

"You are the more time we have. Do what you can and let me know immediately if you need help."

"Then send Harry."

Kothry seemed thirty years younger than his new friend but their tinkering natures spanned the difference. "Hey Harry, glad to see you. I think you can help me if you can figure out a way to secure this silver disk in the jaws of this chuck."

"What's the finished size?"

"Twenty millimeters with a five-millimeter hole."

"And the thickness?"

"Three millimeters."

"Turn the disc first, then center it and drill it."

The two men worked their problem for the rest of the afternoon until Ducar walked in to check on their progress. "Well gentlemen, where are we?"

Kothry was proud to report that the small stack was finished but it couldn't be spun internally because of its small size. "We are going to try little rubber wheels to spin them up from the outside. Harry calls them faucet washers. They should work fine once we have this axle figured out. We're working on it."

"As soon as you can, please. I want to know I have the option."

33

Pissed Off

The first anti-grav sensor to detect the two new rogues now corkscrewing away from Earth immediately broadcast its warning. An hour later Ensign Haster read the message in its memory gel during a routine scan and reported her findings to Tergana.

"You've got to be kidding. Two more? Where?"

"If my read is correct the nearest one is now three hops out and moving away fast on the far side of the planet."

"How long? Never mind. We're going the wrong damned way." Tergana pressed his commband. "Salter to the bridge." He repeated his command and mulled over the thought of more sedative. "Chief, get up here."

"Coming up behind you sir."

"There you are. Have you had a chance to review Ensign Haster's sensor reading?"

"The two new runners? Yeah, she thought to me in the corridor just now. You want me to start plotting?"

"How long? For both of them, how long?"

"Just a guess. Nine hops maybe, over two days. Unless we get lucky. More, if we don't."

"Get lucky, will you? Because as soon as we've caught them,

I'm putting one across Ducar's bow. Enough of this."

Even among a big crew, rumors run like rabbits. Inside a half hour everyone knew Tergana had changed his mind.

"I hear the old man's getting doped up again. I've seen it before. You get too old, can't handle it and then boom. It's your last rodeo. Must be why he feels he can play this fast and loose. He should have just dusted them in the first place. Ain't that right Chief?"

"That's an unwise speculation. Don't get eager for this Benejy. If your dislike evolves into cruelty, you'll get yourself sequestered. It's clear to me Captain Ducar is buying time. The question is for what? And that's for Admiral Tergana to decide, not you. Understand?"

"Loud and clear, Chief. I'll zip it."

"Do more than that. Get it out of your mind. You're an E5. How about giving the old man the benefit of the doubt?"

"I don't know. Did you see him when he was riding out a hop in one of the stack hugger seats? His brains were between his knees followed by the rest of him. He's not well. I don't care what you say. Torel needs to keep taking his temperature and make sure his head's on straight. I'm just sayin'. He's not the same guy anymore."

Benejy was right. That was the doc's opinion as well. He'd been sitting beside the admiral waiting.

"You don't look so good Dratto."

"About the way I feel, I imagine."

"You've got a bad case of hop sickness and you're becoming addicted to all the sedatives you've been taking. Dial it back some, if you can. When you're ready put on the IV cuff. I'll see you after it's over."

Tergana waited until he was alone. The cuff pricked him slightly and he was gone. Direct-inject euphoria set him sailing straight out of sight, floating and lost. He liked the ride.

It was left to the third shift to plan and execute the retrieval of the two new runners. The only one working a double shift was Salter, and he was pissed. "Someone else is going to have to learn to plot these hops. I need a break. As soon as we get back, I'm putting in for leave. This back-to-back shit has got to stop."

The hi-temp alarm on the maincomp began to flash a warning that it was slowing computation to maintain a cooler temperature.

"I swear if it isn't one thing, it's another." He folded his arms and waited with as much patience as he could muster. When Torel appeared at the maincomp's input console to check on why the first hop had not yet happened, he could feel the chief's frustration.

"Problems?"

"She's throttled down again Commander. This is more math than she likes to do. I want to devote more resources to cooling, with your permission of course."

"Do it. I'll instruct the crew to conserve. How much time do you need?"

"If I could get maximum cooling, each plot might take five or six minutes. Right now, the way these runners are shifting, it's closer to thirty."

"Make it so Chief. We need this."

The additional refrigeration saved hours but meant there was less time between hops for the crew to readjust. When the first stack had been retrieved after five separate hops, Torel pushed for a break. He could not remember hearing about anything like this, and when he scanned the archives, indeed no ship from any of the five local planets had chased more than one runner at a time, much less seven.

If more started flying, he resolved to dust the Earth himself, without Tergana's permission. He sent a message to Ensign Haster. *When you can find seclusion, I want you to probe every Aleri that you can sense near the third planet. I want to know what they are thinking and what they are doing, as much as you can get, as fast as you can get it.*

Ensign Haster silently acknowledged the order, found seclusion in an isolation chamber and began reaching out. It proved fruitful but confusing. "Commander, I've got something, several things in fact. To your primary concern I don't read any more rogue stacks, at least nothing like what we have been chasing. I believe they have sent the last one up, but there's more that's not so clear."

"Like what?"

"When I reached out for Aleri minds I got some cross readings, hybrids maybe. Anyway, some of them aren't pure Aleri. They have joined minds with the ones they are watching, and one of the earthlings has been profoundly changed by it."

"Good or bad?"

"I can feel him, and he knows I'm probing. He's untrained so he has no idea how powerful he is, but he is learning. He calls himself Ahnay. He's angry with us."

"What's his potential, if he figures out how to push minds?"

"Good as they get. It all depends on what path he chooses."

"Could he bring us down?"

"He's close now, just not so inclined, in spite of how he feels. I just wouldn't press it. He's rapidly figuring out he's not alone and he's coming to terms with why he's not alone."

"Thanks for the good read Tilley."

Torel decided to lighten his load and went to wake the admiral. As much as he wanted to lead, sometimes it was good to be number two. He removed the cuff but the question caught him before Tergana's eye's were fully open.

"Did we get them?"

"Not exactly sir. We got one."

"And what, pray tell, about the other one?"

"It's still running but we had a maincomp overheat and something's come up."

"I can't wait."

"Haster reads a powerful mind that just arose on the planet we were watching. He's a hybrid, mostly human but part Aleri, too. She says it was most likely a sexual encounter. There are four pairings but the strongest individual is Ahnay, followed by his mate. They've broken every rule sir, every admonition about contact. I didn't want to wake you sir, but you see how it is."

Tergana rolled over and sat up. "Get Haster in here, now."

"Yes sir, right away sir."

Torel hustled out of sight, grateful to have been relieved of his burden at such a bargain price. He passed the ensign in the corridor below the bridge. "Tergana wants to see you about what you read."

"I'll go up now. Am I in trouble?"

"I ordered you, remember?"

"Right. But I also know the admiral's picky about where and when we go probing, so you'll forgive me for being cautious."

"It's wise. I would give it a minute for the air to clear if I were you."

When Ensign Haster arrived at Tergana's quarters the door was already open. "Are you alright sir?"

"Come in. I need your help. I need to know everything you've read so far, as much as you can give me."

"The Aleri mated with earthlings, sir. Not just that, some of them have joined for life like pairs of birds, one being in two bodies. They are utterly synergistic, their minds are much more powerful together than alone. There is one in particular, Ahnay. When he becomes fully aware, he could bring us down."

"I want you to read his intent right now."

"From here?"

"Here, now, whatever you have to do. I'll be quiet."

Haster leaned back against the bulkhead and closed her eyes. They began to flicker under her lids. "He's unpredictable but quiet for now. I think we are okay in the short term. He's focused on getting stronger but not for himself, yet."

"Thank you Ensign."

"Are you going to dust them all or try to be surgical?"

"When I decide I'll let you know. In the meantime I'm going to catch a runner. You are dismissed."

"Yes sir."

Tergana swung to his commport. "Chief, this is Tergana. Start plotting the last hops. I want this over and done."

"Nighty night sir."

"Just do it."

34

No Time

Arney sat quietly, trying to fathom his thoughts, if they even were his thoughts. He wasn't sure. Other faces flashed in his head. Faces he'd never seen before, dreamlike and hard to remember clearly.

Not from around here, he thought. *Concerned with this place, concerned with me. But why?* The sensation of intrusion in his head subsided, as if asking the question was enough to scare the interlopers away, when Shereen spoke.

"They've found you."

"What Sher?"

"They've found you. The Carei or rather the empath aboard Tergana's ship has found you. She senses your mind is powerful, and so do others. They are wary, maybe even afraid and that makes them dangerous. We must try to gather as many minds as we can right now. The best place for you is in your easy chair. I'll tell the children to go over to your father's. Make yourself comfortable, this is going to be a long night."

"What do you want me to do?"

"Float on those tunes in your head like they're water. Let ideas go in boats that find their own way. You don't need words. Those who are inclined to join will hear their own language."

"But if it had words."

"Right now, it can't. It has to be a pure vision of what you want to happen. It's an offer, a suggestion that everyone can join a larger mentality without risk to who they are. But first, they have to believe they can make that connection. That's your job. The music you send will echo in the minds of many. Some may even ask your name. Just close your eyes and drift. As you gather, I will knit."

He began with simple melodies, a tune hummed in the back of his mind, a tendril-thin thread of connection that wrapped around its branch. Then he sent harmonies to build a chord. One by one he could feel minds switch on, drawn by easy syncopation in music they could not hear, but hummed in their heads nonetheless. As he let go of apprehension more minds gathered. The more they did, the stronger they became. People began to look at each other, knowing that they were in the same place, together without words, eased by inclusion. Every now and then someone in a crowd would hum a note out loud that resonated and reinforced the same note in others nearby. Minds gathered so quickly it was hard to know their number.

Arney, my name's Arney, he thought and moved on until his name became a slow rolling sound. *Ah-nay, Ah-nay.*

"Arney honey. You can stop now. Arney. Stop, please. Quiet your mind. Easy now, let them go. They will rejoin without reservation when you call them again."

When Arney opened his eyes. Almost an hour had passed. "How long have I been asleep?"

"You've been awake the whole time. You become detached as you gather. It can feel rather dreamlike when you float."

"How many did I get?"

"About two-fifths."

"Of the country?"

"Of the planet. You got almost two-fifths of people all across the globe to hear you and join in. They will only remember a melody but it's a good start. It's just that you're not powerful enough by yourself. I'm going to see the captain and let him know where we stand."

Ducar watched Shereen come walking up as he sat on Harry's front porch, listening to the rise and fall of cricket legs singing in the summer heat. "I felt you bring him back. It didn't work did it?"

"Not entirely sir. I need a way to expand his reach."

"Please let it go for a moment. I need you to get a read on that Carei empath again."

Shereen decided to dig in to her counterpart's mind from a wicker chair on Harry's porch. She excused herself, leaned back and sent out her tendrils of thought until she found Ensign Haster probing in her direction. Haster was good but lacked the finesse to tiptoe in, quiet on cat's feet. She left breadcrumbs that gave Shereen her answer. Haster was probing every sentrybot she could read, combing the banks of memory gel for scraps of disruption, anything that might reveal a pattern and leave behind a trail of intent.

When her eyes stopped flickering Ducar figured it was okay.

"Do we know what their plan is?"

"I'm not sure. Tergana's angry. I think he might be getting ready to dust us."

"Torel or Tergana?"

"Tergana. He's up and embarrassed, something about not handling the hops well. His whole crew knows. I got it from his empath. Her name's Haster. She's reading the memory gel in all the sentrybots she can reach. She's probing for patterns, trying to tie individuals together and she's given me an idea about how to push Arney's message out. But I'm going to need four bots and memory packs for each of them."

"What's your plan, why do you need bots and gel packs? Are you trying to confuse Haster?"

"No. This is for us, or rather Arney. My thought is to space the bots around the planet and have Arney think to the gel pack in the six-man and ask it to propagate to the packs on the bots. They should be close enough to help him reach all the citizens of this lovely planet if they are in a high orbit. What do you think?"

"I think you have a sharp mind is what I think. Earned your pay today, you did. Since we don't have enough spare memory packs, perhaps Kothry can be persuaded to synth us some."

"Right away sir. I'll think to him now."

"Belay that. He knows already, doesn't he?"

"Yes sir, he does."

Kothry loved a challenge, even if the memory gels pushed his smallest stack aside for the moment. Ducar was adamant. "I know it's a pain but we need the gel packs first. If we can't get these people thinking to each other soon, we may not get another chance. As soon as you've made them you can go back to working on our little friend."

"Captain, you're going to need to enter a code for this, and the synthesizer will make you one replacement, it won't make four."

"Then work your magic Mr. Gradel. Now's when I need you."

Mr. Gradel, he thought. *Deep doo doo right up over my feet. Thanks Cap, I'll get my boots on.* They were friends and in truth he was drawn to the challenge. The problem had a certain intrigue, no straight answers. He would have to cheat.

He started the way he always did when a solution wasn't clear, stretching his arms over his head and loosening his shoulders. Then he rolled his head slowly back and forth in lazy loops, dancing toward an answer. Sometimes they came quickly. This one wasn't easy. It took its time before clicking in clear all at once.

"Short the fuse, force the reset." Kothry stopped dancing. "If I do it just before it completes, it will think it never finished, And when it finds nothing in the chamber to add on to, it will start to make another one. Hah, gotcha sucker." He reached up over his head, grabbed a handful of air and pulled it to his chest as if to say "mine." Then he thought to the captain. *I think I have an answer sir but I'll need to rig up an auxiliary power source completely detached from the scout. Otherwise it will shut down when it finds no reason for the short.*

What short are you talking about? the captain thought back at him.

The short circuit I'm going to use to fool the synthesizer.

You mean the magic don't you? Good on ya' son.

With Harry's help, Kothry rigged up a power supply. He used an old laptop to feed a copy of the scout's electrical supply protocols into one of the synthesizers, which fooled it into thinking it was still on board the six-man.

"Not bad, not bad at all."

"Brilliant I'd say."

"Aw Harry, you're just being kind."

"Just makin' a comparison. How's this supposed to work anyway? I thought it could only replace a broken part."

"So we'll break one. I'm going to short out the memory gel in the two-man and capture the repair message as it's generated. Then we'll let the synthesizer make the replacement and time how long it takes."

"How does that help?"

"I'm going to feed the repair order into the synthesizer connected to the laptop but trip the breaker before it finishes making a new memory gel. I'll pull out the partial, top off the syngel, then resend the signal. As long as it never finishes, we should have gelpacks that are only missing their protective shells."

Making the four gel packs wasn't quite as easy as all the backslapping pretended. It was the exact timing that proved most difficult. Cut the power too soon and the gel wouldn't propagate. Cut it too late... Well, there was no too late. If one more was allowed to complete, that would be the end of it.

Kothry, sharp as he was, made three more, contained in one-quart jars, then informed Ducar they were ready to fly. It was just a matter of which size bot to use.

Ducar was clear. "The small ones, please. We don't need cloaking. They're either going to work, or they won't. Just park them in an orbit so that each one is in sight of two others. They'll be easier for Arney to light up. Do they need special care or can we ship them naked?"

"They're in glass jars, so they'll need some padding. But if you mean a bio-environment—no, nothing special. They won't last forever but we don't need them to, do we?"

"Hook 'em up and let 'em fly then."

"You're sounding more like Harry all the time."

"Rubs off on ya, don't he?"

35

Message of the Gathering

Tergana opted to lead the chase for the last rogue stack himself. The chief's 'nighty-night' comment nagged at him. He used to handle hop sickness without thinking. Now it was his mountain to climb.

Insolent prick. When I don't need him anymore, I'm going to read him the riot act. Should've kept his stupid mind shut? Now everyone's snickering. His thoughts spilled out to the receptive minds among the crew.

"The admiral's doing this one himself. Can you believe it? Bad as he feels, he's going for it. I'm proud of the old bugger for stepping up."

The chief heard Torel and interjected, "I thought I was doing this one."

"You plot the hop. When you've got it, the admiral will give the order. You should have kept that last thought to yourself Salter. Tergana's not a happy man."

The chief turned back to his console, sought refuge in silence and let his fingers do his talking. When he was finished he nodded to Torel. "It's plotted. You can commence any time."

Torel's thought to Tergana was met with an almost instantaneous lurch that left the weakest stomachs among the crew grabbing for support. The grumbling was ship-wide. *A little notice would have been nice*, thought Benejy, who wasn't one of the worst afflicted. *He's getting a little pissy but I don't blame him. This shit needs to stop.*

Four hops later it did. With Tergana breathing over his shoulder, the chief closed the door on the containment chamber and the last rogue was secure.

"You ever ridicule me again, and I'll bust you down two stripes. For now, you've lost one. Anyone who calls you chief from now on is going to hear it from me. You're an E-6 now. Spread the word." It was all in a whisper, dripping with anger.

"But sir, I didn't mean—"

"Listen up, you stupid twit. You want to command a vessel, put in for OCS. Otherwise, you will do as you are told without further comment. Is that understood?"

Everyone in the crew got that message. Those who were in earshot knew Salter wasn't going to be a part of Tergana's next crew if there was a next crew. The rest either got the mental message or by rumor in conversation. What remained of Tergana's charity had vanished. By the time he reached the bridge the mood had shifted. Crew members snapped to attention.

"What are your orders sir?" Torel led the new posture by example.

"Find Ducar. I want to know exactly where he is, how far the infection has spread and what it's going to take to wipe it out. If it's half the planet, fine. If it's the whole place, fine. If he was trying to be surgical, that's not what's happening now. This amount of diversion screams of guilt. I've never seen so many rogues. Every time we think we've caught them all, he sends up another one or five. I want to run up on him at maximum speed, take a quick read on the most likely targets and dust them. Plot it now. I want to land in their laps. Set the disruptor for a half kilometer swath, but don't hit any Aleri vessels. I don't want to be cruel."

At that moment, Torel knew Tergana had walked right to the ethical edge and off it. The mention of cruelty opened the possibility it was exactly that.

"What about the humans? Do we start the eradication?"

"We don't use that word anymore, do we? This is a cleansing, a necessary step. Begin with the fields. Dust them in stripes and leave the terrain contours and vegetation, just take the humans who know and the cross-linked ones, especially this Ah-nay. This is a shot across Ducar's bow, nothing more for the moment."

◆

That was the message Shereen got loud and clear as she and Arney and the kids were driving over to Harry's. When the pickup stopped, she went to find Ducar, who already knew most of her thoughts. When she appeared at the barn door he guided her back out and toward some privacy. "How bad is it?"

"They caught the last stack and they think we're out of diversions. So now that we've lost our cover what happens if we can't pull this off? Are we just going to sit still and let ourselves be dusted? We've got families."

"I know Shereen. I know. How far out are they? How much time do we really have?"

"If they do nothing but fold and bounce, four hours maximum. But I don't think Tergana's up to that. The last read I got he was still sick but trying to tough it out. That hasn't changed so your guess is as good as mine."

"Then we have to start now. Go back, find Arney and make yourselves comfortable. I'm going to check on Kothry. If the gel packs are in position, we can begin."

"What about the little stack? Do we know if it will fly?"

"We're trying not to think about it. The less we do, the less the Carei have to read."

Shreen grasped the implication and nodded, turning back up the hill toward the porch and Donna's kitchen door. She felt responsible for her love and her friends and the possibility the farms and perhaps a great deal more might vanish in a few hours. She wondered if the Carei would take everyone or just a select few. It could not be allowed to happen. She resolved to rescue her friends in the two scouts and hope the dusting would not be excessive. It was selfish, she knew, even if the emotion was unfamiliar.

Then it all hit like a hammer, the passion and want swirling in confusion. The Aleri did not cling to each other. There was no need. They were already joined. But here, where the beings were not sure of one another's feelings, passion and love were the glue. She wanted its intensity, and the memory of the night before made her long to abandon control of her body again and let herself be consumed in waves of pleasure. But such speculation would have to wait. She cast her mind for Arney's whereabouts and saw him coming through the kitchen door and down the porch steps.

"It's good to know I still have some charm left," he said with a grin.

"You're going to need every bit you have to get out of this."

He couldn't help it. "Six foot four and a little bit more gets you every time."

Please stop. We have work to do. Shreen's voice filled his mind. She began to impart method and attitude, how the music should be used to gather minds and what might touch all people everywhere. But to gather them was not to bind them. They would have to do that for themselves, enough of them anyway.

"Not everyone can or will join, but for those who allow the possibility, a door opens among like-minded friends and gathers them in."

"I felt the gathering but I can't keep that up forever."

"You won't have to. When the collective becomes self-aware

it becomes an entity unto itself, inclined to grow. Unified, it is knowledgeable and benignly intended, because it is more efficient to be that than not. You will be connected to it more than most. It is your nature. But before we can do that, you have to use this gift you have been given and call them. I will help you knit them together but I should not become a part of it. This for your species. It should be a pure record of who you are. There is only so much I can do, my love. The rest is up to you."

"You make it sound ominous. If there's more I should know, I'll take any hints you have."

"You will have to push back the darkness even as you call to them. It won't be easy but this is not a test of your physical being. It's a test of your mind's ability to communicate with other minds. This comes naturally to you and that strength will make you a leader. What kind of leader will you be? The good man I know, I hope. You will, by your nature, impart a flavor shall we say, an initial personality from which the new communal mind evolves."

"That can't work."

"You're a good man Arney Miller, and you are the reason I have hope. But everything you fear will push upon you and beg to be incorporated. You cannot let that happen. Begin in hope that you might end in joy."

"What's the rest of it?"

"There's no guarantee that a collective will merge just because we begin. We may not have the strength. I am counting on you to find the heart of the matter, to see the thing for what it is and help it become the best it can be."

Shereen reached out to the captain to check on the preparations. The four naked sentrybots carrying the memory gel did not go unnoticed. But they were deemed trivial and slipped between the cracks to find an orbit among the debris, glass jars winking in the sun.

"We are ready. The captain says it's time. Lean back, relax.

278

Let your mind drift into this. Try not to push. What's your expression—more flies with honey?"

Arney leaned back against the headrest and closed his eyes. The music began, one note upon another swirling away. The memory gel attached to the protocol circuits on the six-man scout began to propagate to its orbiting cousins, which amplified Arney's thoughts.

Millions of minds waited to join something more than culture and legality. He felt them call for choice and recognition. Threads of thought arose everywhere, curling out, searching for connection. He did not have to ask or encourage.

He let go and the music in his mind eased into syncopation, an echo of ancient drums beating as the harmonies began to build, one upon the other. Once again the minds of living beings began to join in harmony and threads of thought.

Across the globe, clusters of people became aware that they were experiencing the same thing at the same time. As Arney kept up the harmony, people started to compare notes. The music was in each mind but there was no sound, and that was what they spoke about, how it was all in their heads.

Shereen knew it was time to weave. *"I speak on behalf of the music that you hear and invite you to rest and find a place to relax, that you might call to others. Relax. Be peaceful and find the heart of the mind that unites you. This is the next step in your evolution, the awareness of a greater being incorporating your minds, uniting you. It is your gift to yourselves."*

Ducar tried to break into Shereen's mental flow. *Protocol circuits*, he thought and pressed until she responded.

"What is it?"

"You have to stop immediately. The six-man is about to catch fire. Shereen, get to him. Make him stop before he strands us."

Arney, Arney honey? You have to stop. The scout's frying under the load. We need the Xelanar. Arney. Arney, STOP!

Arney came crashing down, mentally exhausted. "What's wrong? Did we make it?"

"Not quite. We were close but we are burning up the protocol circuits on the six-man. We need to get the Xelanar down here so that you can use the maincomp's bigger memory gels. The captain's agreed, so he's going up in the two-man to get her. We don't have much time. We've interrupted normal thought patterns and people all over the world are asking what happened. They know something is very different. They're just not sure what. But phones are ringing in police stations everywhere."

Five minutes later, the two-man scout was approaching the midpoint of the journey between the back of Harry's barn and the dark side of the moon. With Jasca sequestered and everyone capable otherwise engaged there was a pilot shortage. The net result was the captain would now pilot the Xelanar to the hover point. Then PJ would maintain the correct position, which was the most difficult part of the mission until the captain could fetch Kothry to relieve him.

"You had pilot's training. What's the problem?"

"I've never piloted one of these before Captain, except to fix something. I could screw this up bigtime."

"Don't. Stop programming yourself to fail. You can be smooth, and you will be. Tell yourself that. She might creak during a tight hop but she's been reliable and predictable. You'll get the feel of her in no time." Ducar punched Jasca's quarters into his commport, watched him sleep for a moment and switched to the heads-up pilot view. "Are you ready?"

PJ was more resolute. "Ready as I'll ever be."

Young pilots were deft and quick but the old man had a grace about him. It came through his hands, the training and habit born of countless hours in command of small and then larger craft of various shapes and purpose. PJ could tell the difference when Ducar was at the helm. There was smoothness in his maneuvers that took his passengers' comfort into account.

"How am I going to keep from running her aground in some field?" PJ asked as he noted the easy takeoff. "You've been doing this for years."

"Yes, I have PJ. But these vessels are built more for guys like you than me. You'll have a hard time bumping into anything as long as you keep the shields soft." Ducar settled in at 50,000 feet, engaged the autos and stood up. "We want reach that point on the left side of your screen and hover at 35,000 feet fully cloaked on a silent approach. Program it and then execute it. I've got my fingers on the overrides."

"Now?"

"Yes, now. Take the joystick in your right hand and push gently in the direction you want to go. A little goes a long way."

"This is very cool sir. I thought it would jerk more."

PJ managed not to make anyone sick and soon got the feel of the controls and his sense of where he was. The feedback from the displays began to feel natural. He was admonished only once. "Slow down a little PJ, and make the shields softer still. Easy. Hold it right there. Let the autos take over. There you go. Nice job."

"Thanks sir. That was easier than I thought it would be."

Ducar walked down to the main airlock and loaded three cases of Syngel into the two-man scout. Putting PJ in command was a gamble, a risk he would have to take. He returned to the bridge and put his hand on PJ's shoulder. "Be good to her. I'll send Kothry as soon I can."

"I will sir. It looks like Jasca's up. What do you want me to do if he gets animated?"

"Flood his quarters with endorphins and calm him down. I don't want the rest of the crew distracted."

"Yes sir. Good luck sir."

The two-man scout returned to its parking space behind the

barn a half hour after it left. Shereen had come over but Kothry saw the captain first. "Who's piloting the Xelanar?"

"PJ's got the helm. How's our little friend coming along?"

"Fine, taking a nap. Ready to wake up any time."

"Stay close then. If we have to light it up, we'll need to be quick about it."

Kothry rechecked the little spinner's wiring just to reassure himself he had not forgotten anything, and found some comfort in Harry's easy chair.

The captain refocused on Shereen. "Is Arney ready?"

"I think so. He could be looser and more relaxed. The less anxious he is the better."

"Did you give him anything last time?"

"Nothing."

"How about some grass? I know he used to smoke and Harry's got some great dope."

"Excuse me sir, but how the hell do you know that?"

"That first night when we came over here, when you were talking with Donna, Harry lit up. A big spliff sent me spinning until I got control. Harry just seemed to keep on cruising. And remember, I've been here before. Gilly and I, we used to smoke grass in the sixties."

"You old dog. You sure are full of surprises."

"Make Arney comfortable. Supplies are on the way."

Ducar found Donna, who referred the whole project to Harry. Before long he appeared with three fat joints of his finest. Here you go honey, the best herb we ever hid in the corn, right here. A couple of hits and you'll be floating."

"It's not for me. They're for Arney."

Shereen wasn't sure what to expect when she walked into Arney's kitchen but her fears were allayed the moment she saw him. He looked more confident and his mood was lighter. "I brought you something."

"I know."

"I can't get anything past you these days, can I?"

"Well, you might be able to get some of Dad's good weed past me. It's always helped the music. Have you ever tried it?"

"No, I like your grapes. A little wine, I'm fine."

"Give me that fat one. I'm going out on the porch and get loaded. If they're gonna get me, they're gonna get me grinning."

Arney sat down in his favorite porch chair and disappeared into a blue cloud. After four hits Shereen saw him visibly relax even more and decided to give his medicine a try.

"You sure you want to do this?"

"I think it will help me to understand you better. So yes, I want to try."

She saw him grinning as her eyes turned red and she started to laugh. And then he was gone, spun out and away by a soup of mind and chemicals that she joined without notice. He scanned a sea of minds looking for easy entry and began to hum in syncopation.

"How am I going to know when I've got 'em?"

"When you see crowds dancing to music you know they cannot hear."

"Right now there is a new melody in my mind I've never heard before."

"Begin there then. Let it flow out the way it flows in, any pipe to make a sound. Be the conduit. I love you honey."

Arney heard her sweet affirmation along with millions of others who felt the need to say I love you, too. He found himself swept away in the chorus and began to hum his unfamiliar but compelling tune. Some got it the first time they heard it. Others needed repetition. As more swept in, a magnetism drew more voices across cultures and traditions. It was an infectious melody that once remembered was never lost. And still more voices swirled in. Where Arney had pushed before, he now floated easy among many.

What is your name? Who calls us? a mind inquired. Without

thinking what a response would mean he thought his name and heard it reverberate, a whisper in a cavern.

Ah Nay, Ah Nay. It rolled away like a soft rumble of thunder. When more harmonies began, they were not his own. Other minds tried to shape the song and the mood, until the mood was broken.

Shereen slipped away from the gathering and spoke aloud. "Arney? Arney, where are you? Hear me for a moment. I have to leave but I will be back. Stay here and do not stop gathering. No matter what you hear do not stop."

"Where are you going?" he answered half in and half out.

"I have to help the captain, now!"

Time had run out. Shereen almost screamed into the captain's head. *They're here. They are already dusting near the escarpment. They came in without a fixed target just wiping out a swathe of ground.*

Her mind heard the captain bark an order to Kothry. "*Aim low to the southwest and fire now. The barn be damned.*"

Kothry tipped the small spinner as far over as he could without disrupting its balance, aimed for the southwest and flipped the switch. He did not see the stack move. One moment it was there. The next it was gone. Through the side of the barn, straight through the Carei's outer shielding, through the main hull, through the tanks of liquid and crates of solids, through crew quarters and engineering and finally the main drive stack as it forced its way between layers aligned by atomic weight.

———◆———

The Morowa stopped. Power flowed only from storage.

"What the hell was that?" Tergana's face blanched, then flushed with blood.

"The main stack's had a catastrophic failure. Main hull too sir. A small rogue tried to go right through us. Well, not through us exactly. It behaved like it was a magnet. It burrowed between the main bearings and joined itself to the rotors. It's stuck there, and we're stuck here until maintenance can repair it."

"Are we visible?"

"No sir. Not yet anyway."

"Can I still use the disruptor?"

"We can try."

"Then keep dusting stripes. That son of a bitch crippled my ship. Toast his ass!"

Another quarter section of cornfield vanished in a cloud of dust before the disruptor shut down to save what was left of the power. Tergana was beside himself. "How long Chief? How long is it going to take you to fix this?"

"I don't know sir. We'll have to drain the rest of the mercury and rebuild the main stack a layer at a time. If we can free whatever that incoming device turns out to be without cutting, we'll be okay. Otherwise it all depends on how much damage we do trying to get it off."

"I want all the spare power rerouted to the disruptor, now."

36

Ohmera

Shereen slipped back into Arney's mind, following his chase of melodies. When dissonance occurred, he eased the melody toward simplicity. Many more danced to the music in their heads, which leaked away in gestures that linked strangers in rhythm. They were dancing in silence to the same music, they knew it and became aware.

Shereen sensed it was time. "Arney, push toward self-awareness. Imagine the heart of it, the unity, the peace it brings, the struggles that end. Encourage its awareness. Think of the gift it is, and they will bind themselves to it. You only have to open the door. They will follow."

The second stream of Arney's thoughts spoke of what was to come, the safety and comfort of the future. The collective would need a name, a focal point for their energies. Those who had joined in earlier labors remembered "Ah Nay" and raised that thought as a possibility. It arose in more minds than any other and became the mantra, quietly and slowly at first.

"That's my name. Arney."

The collective answered in thought. *Yes, Ah Nay, the name given at the moment of awareness. We honor the one who called but you did not make us. We bind ourselves. Yours was the gift of knowing sight, a path from mind to mind, but our name shall belong to all.*

What will you call yourself? Arney thought to the collective.

We are named for the world of our birth. We choose Ohmera, the sound of the chant that covers earth. Be gathered in, it is time to proclaim.

Across a thousand light-years, world-minds became aware of a sibling born with the name Ohmera, a water-eye of peace, common sense and good heart. It was premature and would need nursing, but it was a beloved child nonetheless. A blanket of protection was placed around the infant mind—that it should mature without interference during its transformation.

There were dictators to topple. The people would reclaim their power. Once wars were seen for the wasteful diseases they were, arms and ammunition would become irrelevant and conflicts would end.

Things were instantly better, though not all things and not all at once. It took time to agree on the most benign and painless way to eliminate social infections. Despots were to be focused on with as much mental energy as was necessary to bend their will. If they refused, stress stopped their hearts. It became easy to find the evil in the minds of the unkind. As Ohmera rid itself of disease it would become acknowledged as the one mind of the Terrans as they wished to be known.

"Arney, honey wake up. You did it. You made them see themselves for what they might become. Ohmera knows itself."

"What happens now?"

"Well, what do you sense?"

"That the Carei have stopped recharging their disruptor. They're not after us anymore. This Admiral Tergana is not happy but apparently he's being sedated again. And we are not to be isolated. We are to be given the tools to educate ourselves about the totality of which we are a part."

"That's what I sense. Anything else?"

"Jasca, the one who's locked in his quarters aboard your ship, he's angry. He didn't want this to work. He's been relaying information about this to Shepherd Command. What does that mean?"

"That we can't go home, at least not those of us who have mated with you. We are no longer pure and won't be welcomed back because of what we've done. I don't know what the Shepherds will do. We broke the covenants and what's worse, we interfered."

"Stay here then."

"Does that seem likely?"

"When I reach out you are all I see. Do you have to leave?"

"I don't know. It depends on what the Shepherds decide to do with your father and his knowledge, and with yours for that matter. There are centuries of social growth and scientific discoveries that need to be assimilated before you can handle anti-gravity motors, much less the rest of our technology. Your father cannot be allowed to steer science toward inquiries that Earth is not ready for. They will want to sequester you as well, and the kids. We are half-breeds. We won't be allowed to mingle."

"Can you live cut off from your world?"

"Arney, you have become my world. The people who are close to me will be here. My sisters are not going to leave Luke and Mark, and Warehan's not leaving Jennifer. So we're going to have to make room because the family just got bigger."

"What about the captain, Kothry, and Ella and PJ. What happens to them?"

"I don't know about Kothry and PJ. Ella's got family. She'll go home. Kothry, too, I expect. I don't know about PJ. The captain's stuck. They'll come for him. He's ultimately responsible. Neither the Aleri nor the Shepherd Council will let him just walk away. The Carei want to transport him once they've repaired their cruiser but I'm not sure that's such a good idea. It will be better if Kothry takes him home on the Xelanar.

37

The Trip Back

PJ had practiced enough to get a feel for Xelanar's handling but he was glad he wouldn't be in charge much longer. Even though he wondered why the captain came alone, he didn't ask.

"Welcome back aboard sir."

"Thanks PJ."

"Nice job down there. You saved them."

"I didn't have much to do with it. Arney and Shereen saved them for all the good it will do them. The Council will come after Harry and Donna and the kids. They'll all be reeducated and not for the better."

"What about you sir?"

"Well, that's what I've come up here to talk about. I need your help. From now on, do your best to keep your thoughts to yourself."

"Sure Cap, whatever you need."

The captain's first question took him by surprise. "Could the disruptor be reprogrammed to go back years instead of milliseconds?"

"Maybe. How many?"

"Thirty."

"Thirty years?"

"Thirty-two, actually."

"Damn Captain, I don't know. Maybe. I see no scientific reason why not. I'll have to figure how to feed it new data."

"You should know... we're not moving rocks."

"What are we shifting?"

"Us."

"You've got to be kidding. Me, too?"

"If you want. Think about it. Wouldn't we be better off if we were out of the way when Shepherd Command comes looking? Why risk reeducation? This is a beautiful world. Make a life here. If we go back thirty years and program the disruptor to reset itself, they'll never know where we went in time. You don't have to go if you don't want."

"Don't get ahead of yourself Captain. I don't know if I can do it yet. But if I can, I might be coming with you. I'm not interested in having your location squeezed out of me."

One thing Andin Ducar had going for him was an uncanny talent for picking talent. Everybody on his crew was sharp and fast about the things that held their interest and PJ had made a thorough study of his pet machine. He was already working out how to adjust the beam's dynamics to account for soft tissue. Timing was the easy problem.

"Captain I'm going to need to test this on something living."

"How about one of the noisy cats?"

"Not funny. No, I need something smaller, like an insect. It won't take long. I just need some sugar water and a quick trip in the two-man." PJ returned with two flies he had sucked into a small vacuum jar.

"How do you want to do this, PJ?"

"I want to float this jar out one of the waste ports, get the beam on it and see what happens. If it works, the flies and the jar will be gone."

"Could you get them back if you had to?"

"We're about to find that out, aren't we sir? But first we've got to see if we can push them."

"Okay, let's see if you can give them a ride."

PJ put the jar in a small clear survival bag and ejected it through the port nearest the disruptor's main beam. Tracking picked it up immediately. He turned off all the automation and intrusion controls and switched to manual control. Nothing was recorded. There would be no data to analyze. He could see the jar inside the bag on his monitor. It was time.

"I've got the beam right on them sir. Are you watching?"

"I can see them. Give me a count."

"Three, two, one..."

"Poof, vanished. How far back did you send them?"

"Forty years. I don't have an endless supply of flies. I figured what the hell, go for it."

"Well, get them back, son. Bring them home. Give them a round trip ticket."

"Here we go then. Damn."

"Damn nothin' PJ. That's a nice job. I see them buzzing in that jar like they were never gone."

"I wouldn't want to guarantee anyone's safety just 'cause the flies made it."

"We don't have a choice, my friend. You're what rescue looks like. I want to know what kind of range this has. Could we push people and cargo from a mile or two up?"

"I don't think so sir. The closer we are to our target the less disruption there will be. Five hundred feet's more like it."

"We'll have to do this at night, and quickly, because we're going to be right on top of somebody no matter how good our cloaking is. And the disruptor gives off waves when it contacts matter, so somebody's bound to see us."

"So what if they do? They see a UFO and then see people disappearing out of a field. What are they going to think? I'll tell you what they're gonna think. They're gonna think we've been abducted. It's perfect. We just give them what they expect."

"Can you program this so that everyone goes back to the time they want?"

"No can do, sir. There's not enough time."

"Then can we set it for September 6th, 1967?"

"Was that a good year?"

"The best. The year I got to know Anne. Listen, I've got a question. Can you make me younger?"

"I suppose so. How old do you want to be?"

"Thirty. And can you could do this for Harry and Donna? Make them younger, I mean?"

"Yeah, I can do that."

"Alright then, that's the gift you're going to give them, as persuasion."

The year everyone agreed on was 1967. The year before everything went crazy. Six weeks to see the coast or go wherever they liked, as long as they were back near the escarpment at the appointed time. Just enough time to put the Shepherds off the scent, enough time to explore or relive and then go home. Everyone who chose to escape picked an age that suited their dream and met near the escarpment. Then one by one, with a satchel full of clothing and cash, they stepped into the disruptor beam. As soon as the land shifted in time they walked away, careful not to start out on the same path as the person who preceded them.

The Carei watched them go, lifeforms winking out. They had their suspicions. But without a timestamp, a search was pointless and they were not inclined to interfere now that Ohmera was born. When Tergana watched Ducar disappear he knew he had made the choice to stay and envied him his beautiful world.

Eleven sets of footprints already radiated away in a fan as

Ducar stepped from the origin rock. No one else would follow. He had stayed behind to free Jasca and help him heal his heart, a talk that brought perspective.

At least now he understands, he thought, opening his satchel. PJ had been thorough. On another voyage in another time he could have been a rich forger. The documents were ironclad, PJ's money, flawless. Then the Xelanar resumed its watch over S3alpha in moonshadow, informing the council that the responsible parties were no longer aboard.

The Farmington Gazette reported the story the next afternoon. 'Tom and Laura Snowden saw purple lights in the sky while driving near the quarry last night about 1:30 in the morning. Mr. Snowden said the sky shimmered slightly over a large area. The sheriff was notified.

By the time the sheriff woke up, put on some clothes and drove his cruiser out to the flat under the escarpment, there wasn't much to see. Dust was blowing from Ozzie Ferrell's farm where a cropduster appeared to have dumped its tanks. At least that was the story. Another late summer prank was all he needed.

"Airplane goes over and they think they've seen a flying saucer." He muttered to himself as he turned his spotlight on and twisted its handle to sweep the beam from side to side. There below the escarpment was a fan of footprints that began from behind the various bushes and ended their march at the exact same flat rock. None went back in the opposite direction. He told the reporter it was the damndest thing he had ever seen. The rest of the sheriff's comments could not be printed.

In '67 you could hitch a ride almost anywhere. People were just more trusting. Even in the country long hair had hit the high schools, and the young were inclined to give a ride to their own. But this was an older man, so Diana and Betty Jo Justice had a talk about it.

"He looks okay, but it's really late."

"He ain't hitchin'. Maybe he's out for a walk, " said Betty Jo.

"Come on B, not with that satchel. He'll do this with or without us. Let's pick him up."

"If I get a bad vibe, I'm gonna give him some justice."

"Be nice B, be nice." Diana slowed as she neared him on the darkened gravel road, making his way under the stars, bag in hand. "Need a lift Mister? We're going as far as Springdale."

"That would be a help. Thanks."

"Mind if I ask you what you're doing out here this time of night? 'Cause if you're hitchin' this sure is the wrong road for it," Betty Jo said.

"You picked me up. Couldn't have been that wrong."

"That's funny. He's alright D."

"Actually, I'm lost. I thought my friend's farm was on this road but I can't find the mailbox that marks the top of her drive. It's the right road. At least it's the right name of the road."

"You know this picks up again on the other side of town. Maybe you got turned around in the dark or started off on the wrong way to begin with. How long have you been gone, if you don't mind me asking?"

"A few weeks by the look of the ground, maybe more."

"You alright, mister?"

"Ducar. Call me Andy. Yeah, I'm alright, just tired."

"I'm Diana and this here's Betty Jo. We're the Justice sisters. How come you're walking? Don't you own a car?"

"I used to... an old Ford. But it kept breaking down so I sold it."

"Say, you didn't happen to see any lights in the sky out here tonight, did you? Kinda purpley and flickering?"

It was the gift he needed. "Do you believe in UFO's?"

"You mean little green men and flying saucers, stuff like that?"

"Yeah, stuff like that."

"Why you—hey, wait a minute. You know something about those lights in the sky, don't you. Did you see 'em?"

"Sort of. A beam like that picked me up outta' our garden, maybe six weeks ago. Then all of a sudden, I was out here by the side of the road. I don't remember much, lights and probing, some pain. They aren't like us."

"There's your answer, mister. You were abducted, taken away for some sort of experiments. That's why you're so disoriented. What did they look like? What color were they—green or gray or copper? Did they have slanty eyes?"

Ducar knew it had been just enough bait on just enough line. Hooked! Diana anyway, with sympathy to boot. "Gray and a little shorter than us. Say you wouldn't know about a farm on this road that got sold a couple months back, would you?"

"Only one I know about is the little truck farm Anne Gillespie bought a couple of miles on the other side of town. Why? You know her? She ain't your girlfriend, is she? Everyone has that beauty figured for a spinster. Shame too, 'cause she's nice, just too particular for folks 'round here."

"Think you could give me a ride over to her place or at least drop me close? Never mind, I know it's late. Where are you two going anyway?"

"We were going home until we saw the lights. UFO's have been coming here for years. We like to watch for 'em when they do. Sheriff says we should call him if we see anything."

"You gonna tell him about me?"

"No. The sheriff don't believe in aliens. He says we just make this stuff up."

"Do you?"

"Hell no! They're as real as we are. We've seen 'em, ain't we B?"

"The saucers or the aliens?"

"Both. Tell him B."

"It's the copper-skinned ones this time. We saw some of the grays last year. Their light's bluer. It's purple now and the ships are smaller, so the coppers are back. I want to get abducted by one of them."

"Why?"

"I want to know what it feels... nevermind."

That was pretty much the end of the conversation. Whatever imaginations were turning over as possibilities didn't need description, so Diana steered the discourse. "We'll swing around by Guernsey's farm and drop you off on the other side of town. The sheriff ain't up yet anyway. You don't mind walking a couple of miles, do you?"

"Put me on the right road and I'll be forever grateful."

Diana loved the adventure of it, having never had the pleasure of meeting a real abductee before. She turned off her headlights and drove around the north side of town in the dark, then stopped. "The farm you want's up that way a couple of miles. Mind the ditch."

"Thank you ladies, for all your help."

October sun tempted the colors red. Flowers were vibrant and greens greener. Morning sunlight peeked under branches to land on fallen leaves that blew across the patio and up against the low garden fence. Anne Gillespie took in the view as she sat, tea in hand, thinking of the winter to come and trying not to let that thought intrude on the beauty.

The coming winter wasn't what haunted her, it was the loneliness. There were two kinds, she decided. The kind that comes when friends and family are far off, and the kind that tears you apart when the love of your life has been away too long. She remembered saying goodbye and watching him walk up the drive until he turned, put his hand on his heart and held it out in offering...and was gone. She lasted less than a week before admitting there was a profound hole in her being and steeled herself for the long wait yet to come.

She had grown up in a small town, waiting her whole life to meet someone like him, and could not have imagined it better. It was his ease that drew her. He moved without pretense, a bright, friendly mind. It caught her off guard. She was the beauty of the county who had barricaded herself away from an army of suitors full of snappy come-ons that all sounded the same, no matter what words were spoken. He was different.

As soon as she had turned to look at him a second time, he walked up close enough that he could whisper in her ear as he passed, "You are enchanting. I want to get to know you better."

It wasn't the come-on you might expect in a country bar. His words went right through her, instantly electric, lighting up emotions she had long ago promised to resist. When she turned to confront him, she found no pretense. If there was a mask, it was her own. He stood a few feet away, watching with a smile that allowed her in. She knew they were already communicating without words, testing veracity and heart. When a question arose there were no warning bells of doubt, nothing that gave pause.

She beckoned him closer. "You are a pushy SOB. Do you approach all women like that?"

"As a rule, I don't say anything at all. At least not right away. But something in you touched me all the way across the room."

"How could you possibly know anything about me?"

"We crossed paths the other day"

"This isn't fair."

"I'm sorry, I don't mean to upset you. My name's Andin, Andin Ducar. Please, sit. I just want to talk."

"Well Andin...Andy, whatever your name is, I don't appreciate the presumption, or the hustle. What are you doing here anyway? I've never seen you before."

"Looking for a small farm, somewhere I can retire to."

"A bar is an odd place for dealing in real estate, don't you think?"

"Not at all. These are the people most likely to know what's for sale. I've been asking a few of them."

"Why don't you ask me?"

The message flew like an arrow. Ducar had been reading a sense of charity when her curiosity took over. He felt her probe the nature of his character. It was a good sign. The more she looked him up and down, the better he liked the way she did it. Testing strength and soothing weakness. When her inner beauty burst through the smiling face, he couldn't pry his eyes from— Thunk. The missile hit its mark.

Ducar fell in love without so much as a whimper. The command persona abandoned in the face of an empty heart filling up with hope. She could read his mind and knew who he was, and where he wasn't. She didn't shift or betray the discovery in any way. Without a word, she thought her question. *Who are you really, Andin Ducar? I know you are much more than you appear, but you want me to see you as you are now. That's right, isn't it? Yes or no will do.* She looked up slightly, eye to eye, waiting.

"Yes."

"Well now, that's refreshing."

A smile crept over the good captain's face as he thought, *You see me in a form I choose but this is not a dance to be done here. If you understand what I'm thinking get up, tell me it's been nice to meet me and leave. Drive a mile down the road to the right. I'll find you. Then we can find some place to talk.*

She rose and pulled her faded Levi jacket from the back of her chair, picked up her purse and executed his instructions as if she were one of his crew. "Well, goodnight, Mr. Ducar. I hope you find a farm."

"Goodnight Ms.?"

"Gillespie."

"Ms. Gillespie. Be well then." He watched her easy grace that didn't push or fetch. He could tell the rest of the bachelors in the bar had tried and failed long ago. Now they were more curious than angry. He waited through the rest of his long-necked Bud, left a tip in the jar near the register and was about to go through the door when he heard.

"She ain't for you mister. She ain't for anybody."

The laughter followed him out the door and into the night, fading only when his '52 Ford pickup was well down the road. He found her without effort, parked on a side road with her lights out. "You didn't have to send me your location. I knew where you would be."

"Show me and then tell me."

"Tell you what?"

"Don't be coy with me. I've been running from what I find in other people's heads all my life. I have had to get away from the noise just to keep my wits about me. But you're different. You're like me. You can see and be inside other minds even better than I can. So, I want to know who you are and why you can do this."

They talked in the front seat of her Chevy Biscayne until she had heard enough. "Show me. If you come from where you say you do, show me. I promise I won't scream."

"Then I promise I'll not try to frighten you. If you close your eyes you won't see the more difficult parts of the transformation. I'll let you know when it's over."

"Not a chance. Just do it or this has all been a waste and you're not who you say you are."

He held up his hand to end the conversation and began to concentrate on his form. The morphing shape went through an infantile stage before maturing and coming to a rest. "This is the body I was born into, not so very different from your own. My skin color is a reaction to our sun's light and the minerals in our soil. You're smiling. Do you find me funny?"

"I find it funny that you think I might. You have a wonderful face, handsome on your world too, I expect. Why did you choose the form I first saw?"

"It's how I feel about myself among your people." He reverted to the shape she knew. There was nothing more to prove.

Little by little, questions broke down barriers. Gilly, as she liked to be called, fell in love with him as a night turned into days of walks and touch. She found a fierce friend and with a warm breath in his ear, chipped away at his reticence to break the covenant against contact. The walls fell on a summer night when she ran her fingers through his hair and his last deep resistance melted.

"There is no one but you, no forward path without you in it. I want to spend the rest of my life with you, have kids if you think I'm not too old." She could remember it like it was yesterday, she just knew it was right.

She bought the farm eight days after she met him. Twenty acres of truck garden, outbuildings and a small house. She loved it when she first saw it, and still did. It lacked only the man she hoped would return to fill the hole he'd made by leaving. Too important not to honor, she was trapped by circumstance, the wife left behind to take care of everything.

They had most of three good years together but when his posting was over, she knew she would wait another three before she saw him again and resigned herself to the task. It took everything she had. A month and a half already seemed like forever and the seasons were turning, blowing leaves across the long gravel drive. Then she saw him. She was sure it was him. But it couldn't be, not until she heard his voice in her head. *It's me, Gil. I wanted to surprise you.*

She started to walk and then ran toward him, crashing against his body to entwine and be entwined. "I'm so glad. I missed you so." She sought comfort against his chest. "I thought you would be gone for years. What changed?"

"A lot has changed, more than you know. I knew if I ever saw you again, I would never leave. I had to prepare. What you mean to me has kept me coming back here every chance I got."

"What do you mean, every chance you got? I thought your tours were three years long. You've only been gone six weeks. You told me you weren't coming back for at least three years. What happened?"

"It's a long story—about an old farmer. A smart old geezer, too smart for his own good. I'll tell you when we have more time."

"That depends on what you think the future looks like. Are you going to leave again next week?"

He put one hand on her cheek and the other around her waist and slowly gathered her in. "Where would I go Anne? When I spent all this time trying to find you? I've made my choice. My flying days are over." Then he found her lips slightly parted and kissed her with waves of affection that bound them back again. It was supposed to be. "Where's my boy? Where's Don?"

"Sleeping. Something kept him up last night. Me too. I had a dream about you."

"A good one, I hope."

"You were older, but it was right here."

"Gilly, I treasure you and will happily grow old with you, right here on this ground. In twenty years we're going to have one of the nicest organic farms in the country. The kids are going to love it."

"Well come on, let's go inside. I've missed you mister."

38

The Past

Those who preceded Ducar chose varied paths. Shereen marked the origin spot by scratching the rock with another rock. In six weeks all except Ducar would return, stand on it again and wait to be shifted forward in time. But now it was time to scatter.

The boys stayed with Arney, the girls with Shereen. Getting a ride, four at a time, would be hard enough. Shereen and the girls walked up to the state road and started hitchhiking, hopeful thumbs wagging in the breeze. Arney would follow. They would meet up again at a commune in Butler, PA, and work on a truck farm as a family.

Communes that rely on truck farming always need help because the hard work weeds out the less dedicated. The kids didn't like it much, even though the 60's had a certain mystique. They would be alright. They had each other. For Arney, it was stoop labor and he regretted his choice.

Shereen whispered in his ear, "Remember Ah-Nay, you saved the world to come."

"Doesn't leave much room for an encore, does it?"

"Not much," she admitted.

The last time anyone saw Harry and Donna, Harry had long

brown hair and a guitar. Donna was easy in her beauty, shell beads and turquoise earrings and a cotton blouse from India She was determined not to watch the sixties go by on another farm's front porch. She knew what was coming and they were going to the coast.

"Good vibrations. I want more good vibrations and less get ahead and get on top. I vote San Francisco." Harry wanted some place farther north. "How about Sonoma?"

"There's nothing but small towns and grapes, and we've only got six weeks. I want some city life Harry."

Out of their doors in the summer of love, lured by an adventure to somewhere sunny and free they hit the road, hitching like in the dust bowl days. There was joy in the air, in the music, a hope one could escape the madness, break convention and prosper. At intersections where main roads crossed, couples with infants and teenagers and young adults of every persuasion waited to catch a ride, angling for a brass ring into the unknown.. Then it was Harry and Donna's turn, westbound Interstate 70 out of Terre Haute, heading for St. Louis.

"Are you alright with this baby?"

"Harry my love, I wouldn't miss this for the world."

"I didn't mean to put us in danger." He couldn't help feeling he owed her an explanation. "I was just tryin' to help."

"Shh, I know Harry. We don't speak of this remember? If you want a conversation, think it." She said no more but continued thinking. *Who would have thought we were being watched? All those UFO's people were seeing. If you had told me my boy would fall in love with an alien, an alien Harry, with different colored skin and eyes, who grew up forty-one light-years away... well, I'd a said you were out of your mind. But here we are, and everything's different. So we alter as little as possible, leave a small footprint and spend six weeks being gracious and kind.*

California was working on taking it easy when Harry and Donna had their belongings searched for fruits and vegetables crossing the state line at Truckee. They eased their way south on the coast highway down to the bay area and then into the Haight, counterculture central. The parade went on all day and night, newcomers with dream-filled sleeping bags and no money. Long hair, bell bottoms, grass and acid, music everywhere, people were trying to live a better path. Harry and Donna fit right in.

For a while Fog City as Donna called it, lured her away from the farm. But she missed her kitchen and her views and the sound of Harry tinkering in the barn. And then she said it out loud, "I want to go home Harry. I miss my house and my garden and the trees and the green of it."

Sometimes things just work out. Jasca honored Ohmera's birth which made his return with the Xelanar possible. Ducar had done more than ease his heart. He left a message that insured the broken rules might have beneficial results. What had been done could be undone.

By the middle of the sixth week, the return migration was well underway. Nobody wanted to be left behind. The 60's had been fun but it wasn't home. As they neared the origin rock they traveled by night, disguised against discovery until they met.

"Pop, is that you?"

"Shsh, keep your voice down. Is everybody here?"

"All here. Are you and Mom good?"

"We had a nice time. How 'bout you?"

"Turned out to be a lot more fun and a lot more work than I expected. Too bad we won't be able to talk about it."

"Not if you care about your family. What are we waiting for?"

"Shereen says to watch for a purpley shimmer near the rock.

When we see it we just walk in."

Jasca had retrieved the message with Ducar's time coordinates and ordered PJ to reprogram the disruptor. PJ aimed at the rock and turned it on, then watched the indicator flicker. One by one, the time travelers reappeared as they walked into the beam. They had gone back thirty-two years and returned six weeks after they departed. Everyone went home and fit in with the time they'd left, a little older but quickly gathered back by friends and neighbors, due to the profound change in attitude Ohmera had brought to the world.

39

The Future

Sheriff Dave was at a loss to explain the disappearance of the two families. Doors were unlocked and clothes still hung in the closets as if they might reappear at any moment. But as time wore on no one returned, the fields showed a lack of attention and structures deteriorated. It was assumed by the locals that the Millers had been abducted, just one more link in a long chain of stories about mysterious craft in the sky and missing relatives who would show up weeks or months later, unable to explain exactly how they got there or where they had been.

To the locals it didn't seem strange. After all, Harry had an unusual reputation. Of course, *they* would come for him and whatever he was making in his barn. Rumors had time to percolate and it became the buzz in the local bars until it went on too long and nobody much cared any more. Someone would see something strange in the sky and it wound up on page four of the paper, barely worth the headline 'UFO' until the day Harry and Donna returned.

The Herberts, Harry's nearest neighbors, reported hearing tinkering noises from the garage under the barn. Then they heard Harry's old Ford turn over, cough and catch, not smooth mind you, until she evened out. The news hit town, lighting up the minds of the ladies who used to chatter all day on the phone but now sent thoughts about how young Donna looked and how strong Harry was. A parade of well-wishers drove up well into the night.

The sheriff showed up in the morning as Donna was cleaning her kitchen windows. She steeled herself for the test.

"Nice to see you looking well Donna. Folks 'round here been worried about you. Where you been all this time, if you don't mind me asking?"

"We got taken."

"Taken, taken by what?"

"By a beam of light. It took us up and then they drugged us. It got scary. There were needles and tubes coming out of me and then I don't remember much." Donna's voice trailed off and she slowly hung her head, careful not to overplay the part. Once was enough.

"You got any idea how long you've been missing?"

"Somebody told Harry it's late October."

"October twenty-second, six weeks and a day, if memory serves. And speaking of Harry... where is he?"

"If he isn't in the barn he's probably down in the garage."

Dave started with the barn. It looked the same as the last time he'd checked. He could hear Harry beneath him and walked to the top of the steps. "Harry, it's me Dave. I'm coming down."

"Come on down then and mind your head on that beam." Harry looked up across the hood of his old ride, waiting for the inevitable. There would be endless questions.

"You disappeared right after you came to my office. I don't remember seeing you after that. What happened Harry? Where did you go?"

"I don't know where they took us, I'm just glad to be back."

"Well, I hope you're okay, because you missed some better times. There's no real crime to speak of any more, seems like folks just feel better about themselves after that night you disappeared. They can think to each other now and converse. Not all the time, but they're getting better at it. And people are out at night just staring at the stars, being in them and with them, the eyes of one living thing, so they say. Did you have something to do with all this, Harry?"

"Not me so much. But do you remember the things I let fly away? It was an accident but I think they might have had something to do with the changes."

"Well, whatever it was, folks 'round here are real pleased. A bunch of greedy, selfish old men are dying off and giving their money to the poor. And politicians aren't lying anymore. People are thinking to each other about what's needed and doin' something about it. Took a while to get used to. But now, well I sure wouldn't go back. I can't remember when I felt this good. Seems like everybody's got some hope." Dave waited to see what Harry was going to do with such a notion, but he got no reply.

Harry and Donna and the rest of the time travelers missed the first signs of transformation that followed Ohmera's birth. They could only imagine the change. The promise of hope unfurled gently, never compelling, an open hand waiting for minds to alight, egos eased in the healing union. The results amazed Harry.

The Aleri and the Carei resolved their differences and shared caretaking duties, monitoring the cultural changes in the headlines. The reporting spoke to the events as they occurred. Politicians were no longer divided. Women were accorded equal rights in all cultures, but not all at once. It took two weeks for the last jurisdiction to abandon the past and acknowledge women had always carried the heavier burden. Giving became commonplace. Farmers started donating part of their crops to the poor. Children were being educated by the best. A five-billion-dollar prize was offered to the first person or group to develop practical carbon sequestration. People got raises and houses and help. Skin color and culture began to vanish as divisions. When there was enough for everyone differences seemed not to matter. As equity reigned, anger diminished. The great skew of wealth was offered up to the less fortunate and people stopped yelling and fighting and fearing. The unity that arose in the hearts of men was manifest in the street. Voices were measured and kind, and hands were offered to ease each circumstance that had led to the great division.

The individuals who joined the collective lost their sense of being active participants. That was the nature of the gathering. It worked because the problems of ego were swept away by the need for something greater. As the rhetoric cooled, a long breath was let out when peace became the norm.

Harry was still getting used to the change. Traveling back to the past meant he had no time to adjust. The unity of Ohmera had been quickly snatched away. He had always tried to be kind, but the great peace surprised him, how generous each exchange had become. He relaxed into the awareness and saw Dave in a different light.

"Whatever happened to that other fella with the Model A Harry? Was he one of them, one of those people we saw after the purple lights in the sky?"

"He was a friend. He helped make this happen. Coulda been your neighbor for all the difference there was between us. Besides what does it matter now that they're gone? We're all part of the same life force. He just wanted to make sure we were okay. It's sentimental, I know, but we liked to talk old cars."

"Whatever you say Harry. I'm inclined to buy it, seeing as how it's you but I want to hear the story, all of it. Folks are talking about how your boy's got a pretty new redheaded wife and three more kids. How did that happen?"

"We all got snatched about the same time. They got paired up by them alien fellas, had a ceremony and everything. Love at first sight, they were locked together right from the start. We thought it might be something in their atmosphere. Don't worry

Dave, the kids are wed surer than most around here. They'll be fine."

"They got papers?"

"They've got papers."

"Not from any church around here."

"Bigger Dave, you've got to think bigger."

"What about his wife? Where'd she come from?"

"Shereen and her sisters are from Virginia. She's got a good heart Dave. I don't think Arney mourns the loss of Louise anymore now that she's in his life. When we were let go, I knew they meant for all of us to remain together."

"You keep saying *they* and *them*. Who are they Harry? There's something you're leaving off the plate. You want to put the gravy on this for me?"

"They call themselves the Aleri. They look like us and talk like us, so they can blend in and help. Aleria, that's their planet, is forty-one light-years away."

Dave's eyes went for the ceiling. Then his head came back slow. "You know Harry, I hope you can draw, because this is going to make a great comic book." And then the sheriff thought, *Have a nice day.*

Harry just smiled and thought, *You're welcome.*

That evening Harry and Donna were rocking together on their front porch, talking about Arney and Shereen and how well the kids were doing when the sound of a Model A coming over the hill caught Harry by surprise

"I sense Ducar's mind but I don't see a dent anywhere. And there ain't no purple underneath. And who the hell's that old black fella driving? I ain't never seen either of 'em before and they're pullin' in." Harry was off the porch in a shot, quick to defend against the strangers. "Can I help you?"

"You sure can Harry."

"Do I know you?"

"Better than you think. I know you've seen a car like this before, haven't you?"

"Looks like a friend of mine's, but his had dents and it glowed. It used to belong to... you old dog. You've got a new body, don't you? Andin Ducar, how the hell are you? Is this Anne?"

"Meet Anne Ducar, Gilly to you. We've been running our little truck farm all these years, waiting for you to return. Didn't dare show up until now."

"How come you're black?"

"I needed a disguise and what do you think I would look like if this had happened in Africa? I sure as hell wouldn't look like you, now would I? I am independent of form, so I can become any shape or color I choose." Ducar morphed into his true form, shimmering copper and green. "How many times do I have to do this? Color can't make a difference. Can it Harry? This is all surface, mind is what counts. The heart of a thing is what counts."

Ducar returned to the form Harry knew and put his arm around Anne. They had grown to look somewhat alike, the way old couples sometimes do.

"As glad as I am to see you, you didn't come by just to say hi."

"I came to apologize. I think I set all this in motion. I'm to blame for your dreams. My need was too great. I had to get back to Gilly. You can see that can't you?" He pulled her closer, letting Harry know they were one.

"A hell of a ride you put us through, but why tell me now?"

"I need to make this right. I am being called back to Aleria. I sense I may be repurposed soon, and I didn't want to go without saying goodbye."

"Are you going to be alright?"

"I'll be fine. The Shepherds may not like the method, but it's hard to argue with the results. Besides, they knew where I was. If my actions were an issue, they would have done something about it. No, I think this is something else. The scout's coming for me. It will be behind the barn in a few minutes. This car's going too. It doesn't belong here. And I've got a favor to ask you both. Can you take Anne home and look in from time to time?"

"Sure we will. Don't give it a thought."

"I'll miss you and Donna."

Donna smiled. "Thank you Andin. I like you, too."

"Donna, capable women like you hold civilization together. I can't thank you enough. Without you, Harry wouldn't be Harry.

"And Harry, I just want to say, a mind like yours doesn't come along every day. Put it to good use. Share what you can, your thoughts are your gift."

"Thoughts don't last. They're here today, gone tomorrow."

"Thought's the only thing that does last. That's what you're joining." Ducar looked at the starry sky. "I was telling Arney how everything's going to be a fog of dust in the end."

"Wait. This is all going to be dust?" This time it was Harry's arm that gestured up.

"It's not everything Harry. Thoughts remain, mind remains. Someday, our collected minds will unite and at the very center, the need for form will rise again. Two particles pulled by thought will gravitate towards each other, drawing everything else to them, only to be born again in a burst of light. What will we be then if not a little better for hearing its heart beat?"

"Are you sayin' the big bang's just a heartbeat?"

"Just one beat from the heart of a living thing. Remember the bugs in your gut, Harry? You're their whole world, everything they know. And they belong in you, like you belong here inside this." His arm and hand shimmered copper in a grand sweep of the starry sky. "When you're looking up, does it make any difference that you won't ever know how big it is, or what part you play? You're a bug Harry. We all are. Isn't it wonderful to be part of something so grand?"

"We are so different."

"No, we are part of the same totality. You and I made this

world better. Ohmera's mind will be included now, gathered in by the others and helped to grow. This was not an accident. Our paths were meant to cross. Fate, the stars, call it what you will..." A faint purple glow shimmered behind the barn. "They're here. Help me load this into the scout will you?"

"Sure, just for old times' sake. Listen, before you go, I've got one more question. What does Aleria mean?"

"All the sentient worlds are named the same. It means earth."

"I should have known. Of course they are. Good luck Andin. May you go on forever."

"See you next time Harry."

The purple shimmer around the scout's door faded and a slight breeze swirled the dust and bits of husk that sang their familiar song. Harry turned and looked back up the hill. Donna had already risen to the needs of the moment.

"It's Anne right?"

"Gilly, Call me Gilly."

"Then Gilly let's go into the parlor and sit down and think a while. Get to know each other better."

That would be wonderful Donna.

Tea dear?

ABOUT THE AUTHOR

Born in Boston, Toby Mason has lived most of his life in the greater Washington DC area where he raised his two sons. He lives with his wife Chris, the high school sweetheart with whom he reunited thirty years later.

Toby is an inveterate storyteller who has found a voice in widely varied callings. A singer and songwriter since his early teens, he has performed on both coasts and abroad. His distinctive mosaics of stone and colored mirror hang in offices and gracious homes. Notable work in three decades of broadcast journalism brought him an array of awards including Emmys for photography and sound.

Now the novelist presents his current offering, rich in his signature openness to new perspectives and the commonality of all life.

Made in the USA
Middletown, DE
01 September 2019